ALSO BY NANCY BARONE

THE HUSBAND DIET TRILOGY
The Husband Diet
My Big Fat Italian Break-up
Storm in a D Cup

OTHERS
Snow Falls Over Starry Cove
Starting Over at the Little Cornish Beach House
Dreams of a Little Cornish Cottage
No Room at the Little Cornish Inn
New Hope for the Little Cornish Farmhouse

STARTING OVER AT THE LITTLE CORNISH BEACH HOUSE

Nancy Barone

An Aria Book

First published in the UK in 2022 by Head of Zeus Ltd,
part of Bloomsbury Publishing Plc

9 7 5 3 1 2 4 6 8

A catalogue record for this book is available from the British Library.

ISBN (PB): 9781803284361
ISBN (E): 9781803284354

Cover design: Nina Elstad

Typeset by Siliconchips Services Ltd UK

Printed and bound in Great Britain by
CPI Group (UK) Ltd, Croydon CR0 4YY

Head of Zeus Ltd
First Floor East
5–8 Hardwick Street
London EC1R 4RG

www.headofzeus.com

To Lidia, the strongest woman I know and love.

Prologue

July

'Gabe?' I called, shoving the front door closed with my hip as the heavy grocery bags slid to the floor from my now purpling fingers.

'Faith, you're back...' Gabe leaned over the glass railing overlooking the two-storey living room, his hair still wild from our marathon last night.

'You bet your Gibson guitar, I am, baby!' I chimed as he rushed down the stairs to help and I leaned in to kiss his luscious mouth while chucking off my sandals that were full of sand and grass.

'Please don't tell me you climbed all the way up the path again,' he said. 'Why don't you drive?'

'Because the views are worth the effort.' Especially on a gloriously sunny day like this, the south-west coastal path was like paradise, especially in this part in south Cornwall.

'I stopped by Cornish Born and Bread to get you your favourite blueberry muffins. Let me just put the kettle on and I'll be with you in a jiffy.'

'Wait, Faith...' he said, tugging gently on my hand. 'Come and sit down a minute, will you?'

I obeyed instantly, my knees turning to rubber. I knew that look. That was his *bad news* look.

'Oh God, is someone ill? My sister? One of the kids? I left my mobile here—' They were all I had now, besides him.

'Your family's fine,' he reassured me, his hands on my elbows almost as if to keep me from jumping to my feet.

'Then what is it?'

He ran a hand through his blond hair, taking a deep breath. 'I don't know how to tell you this, Faith, but... I've met someone else. Please don't hate me.'

Any second he was going to laugh and say, 'Fooled you, you silly sausage!' But he didn't. Instead, he looked at me while he joined his hands as if in prayer, exactly the same way he did at the end of his concerts when he played 'Impossibly You', the most beautiful song he'd ever written for me. I sat still, my mind numb and my lungs frozen in a sudden permafrost.

'But... but... up until last night...'

And just like that, even if I hadn't even been born yet, I saw my father on the night he left my mother. I saw her bawling, begging him, and him pushing her away, telling her he was already married. How betrayed and abandoned she must have felt! I didn't want to bawl like she had. But all the same, tears fell hot on my cheeks as I struggled to understand. And I'd thought that buying this house would have been, in a sense, a way of vindicating my poor mum.

Because Gabe and I weren't *like* my parents. We were happy even with each other's faults. Where Gabe had tendencies to live the life of a rock star to its fullest by being scatterbrained and a spendthrift, I kept him on the straight and narrow. Where I was insecure, he reminded me about my qualities, assuring me I would never have to doubt myself – or his love for me. Until a moment ago, we had been 'Indelible', just like another one of the songs he'd written for me. So how had this happened all of a sudden? How could he go from loving me one minute, to leaving me the very next?

This was my own mother's trauma all over again, and, by a strange twist of fate, in the very same house.

'S-someone else?' I repeated.

'Yes.'

'B-but how? Why?'

He sighed as if to say *Where do I begin?* Which was insane. I was the one who put up with a lot of nonsense from him – not vice versa. And then he shrugged. 'You've done nothing wrong, Faith. I just... Jesus, this is so hard – I just need someone less staid, less sentimental. Someone less dependent on me, is all.'

'Less dependent?' I knew it. I knew that pouring out my heart to him about my childhood was more than he could take. But then, if I didn't tell him, my fiancé, who was I ever going to tell?

'I mean emotionally independent. Someone more proactive.'

'More proactive?' I dashed a hand across my eyes. 'I started my own design company at twenty-four. Despite my childhood. I have six people working for me. I don't take a penny of your money. Who is she? Someone you've met on tour?'

His eyes shot to mine, and then down to his hands. 'It's Vanessa...'

'Vanessa?' Which meant nothing to me, because I only

knew one Vanessa who was a cross between Courtney Love and Paris Hilton. And then I saw it on his face. 'You *do* mean Vanessa… *Chatsbury*, my professional nemesis…'

'Yes…'

The one who has made it her life's goal to steal all my clients and who took a picture of me at the design awards ceremony when my skirt split open. She'd even posted it on Instagram with the caption *Half-arsed creativity*, to boot.

'But… you know all that she's done to me…'

Gabe sighed. 'She's driven. That doesn't make her a bad person.'

'No, it makes her a regular Florence Nightingale,' I blubbered, covering my face with both my hands. When had all this happened?

'Come on, Faith. You must have felt something between us wasn't right anymore?'

'You mean like last night?' I bawled through my fingers.

How was I supposed to have felt it, when he said he couldn't get enough of me? It was all my fault for loving him too much. Just like my mum had loved my dad. And where had that got her, if not into clinical depression and alcoholism, leading to her death? But that wasn't going to happen to me. I was not my mother, despite my own teenage struggles with alcoholism, which I'd overcome. I would never go down again.

I shot to my feet and dragged the shopping to the counter, fumbling for the muffins, which I shoved into my handbag.

'Faith, please don't hate me…' he whispered, coming to stand behind me.

'These,' I bawled, 'are coming with me.' There. Let him buy his own blasted blueberry muffins. 'If you want some, go and face Karen and the rest of Perrancombe and tell them what an absolute heartless arse you are, because I'm out of here!'

He hung his head, stuffing his hands into his pockets. 'Are you going to Truro? To your sister's?'

'Where else do you want me to go?'

He followed me up the glass staircase into our master bedroom where I began to pull open drawers and cram some of my stuff into a wheelie suitcase.

I loved every inch of this house and every moment of our life together. If I had managed to be happy here, then my life would have served a meaningful purpose. But not anymore.

I tucked my mum's diary among my clothes, nestled and protected from the ugliness of the moment, all too similar to her own break-up. I wish I could take this entire home with me, for her as well. But I could only take my memories and my broken heart, just like she had. A diary and a picture of the house, with the breakwater in the background. I'd had so many dreams for our future. And a proper family, something I'd never had. I couldn't believe he didn't love me anymore and that he was doing this to me. I couldn't understand why he hadn't told me before going straight to dumping me. Who *did* that?

I shoved the last of my things into the suitcase and rushed down the stairs, my luggage bumping against each step.

He followed me, rubbing the back of his neck, obviously upset, but not as much as I was. I took one last glance around before throwing myself out of the only happy home I'd ever known, the very house where I had been conceived. The very house where we could have started the family I pined for.

I

Hello (It's Me)

Six months later

'Hello, Faith. Long time no hear...' comes Gabe's gravelly voice over the phone, making my heartbeat shift to a rumba dance. I'm so shocked at his phone call that I've dropped my mobile and am scrambling to retrieve it, his contact photo still filling my screen to assure me I haven't lost the connection.

Long time indeed. Six months of singledom is an entire lifetime when, after three years of love, your boyfriend dumps you for your professional nemesis.

'Er... hello, Gabe...'

Everyone, from my sister, Hope, to my girlfriends to my design crew had all supported me through it, assuring me I was much better off without him, and that being the golden boy of the pop charts didn't give him the right to treat me as he had. And, over endless evenings and tons of chocolate (just to make sure I didn't hit the bottle all over again) I had somewhat reluctantly, though *technically*, agreed with them all.

But I can't help but remember that Gabe and I also had good times. No one would ever understand what Gabe and I had when we did have it. No one had ever loved me the way he'd loved me – while it had lasted. And no one knows about the time he'd stayed up with me all night to help me finish decorating my best clients' new home – or how I'd supported him through a nasty bout of depression when his cousin Charlie died.

Gabe would do simple but kind things for me, like bring me a cup of chamomile and give me a shoulder rub when I was stressed or down or simply exhausted. Whenever he was away on tour, which was very often, he'd call me just minutes before going on stage, just to hear my voice. 'It makes me feel ten feet tall, to know you love me,' he used to say.

And no one, not even my sister Hope, knows how he would hold me in the middle of the night when I woke up sobbing after dreaming about the night my father had abandoned my mother, leaving her a mess. And consequently Hope and myself, daughters of a home that was already broken before we were even born.

But when I met Gabe, it was like the floodgates had opened and years and years of loneliness had simply gushed out of me as I'd poured my heart out to him. And he, in turn, had confessed his own awful childhood to me and his fears about flubbing his career as a rock star. But all it would take was a quick pep talk from me and he'd be back in the saddle, whilst it had always been difficult for me to believe in my own worth. We were twin souls drifting that had finally reached safe ground, finding somebody to love.

We'd been through all the stages: meet, date, fall in love, commit and buy a house. And when we'd viewed this one, my heart had stopped at the realisation that this was the same house my mother and father had vacationed at. I had recognised it from the views from the back to the sea. What were the odds of something like that happening? It was a *sign*.

But after that, the following stages of Us were pretty basic: cry, move out of the beach house – the only place I'd ever felt safe and wanted since I was born – and move out of the picture-perfect Cornish seaside village of Perrancombe to a flat in Truro. End of.

Perhaps, I now acknowledge, I loved him a bit too much, because eventually, even Gabe had tired of my insecurities. I had, in effect, proven to him I was no better than my mother. And that's when *all* my insecurities came flooding back as if they'd never left me, memories of my childhood flushing out my happier ones with Gabe as if they'd never deserted my mind in the first place, filling every inch of good headspace.

Had I actually pushed him into Vanessa's arms without realising it? Had I not been good enough for him? Or perhaps not famous enough, like Vanessa? After all, he is a rock star. Or is it simply because I'm just not lovable enough? Am I more *leaveable* than lovable?

It's surprising how quickly sad thoughts can take over, dominating and domineering despite your best efforts to keep your head above the raging waters of fear. It has taken me the whole of these past six months to understand just how much my insecurities had ruined our relationship.

And now, six months A.G., After Gabe, I take care to

not depend on people emotionally. Nor do I even dream of getting involved with anyone lest I revert back to my previous weakness and fall in love again.

But despite myself, even after all this time, he still has this effect on me. He is the only person I have ever loved – and ever will. What could he possibly want from me, after all that had been said and done, and just as I've finally convinced myself to at least *try* and forget him once and for all?

'Happy New Year, by the way,' he says.

I look around my flat. There is absolutely nothing new or happy about it, if you don't count the Christmas cards stacked on my kitchen counter that I haven't even bothered to open. Festive is not exactly one of my top priorities at the moment.

And then his voice drops an octave to a more caring tone. 'How are you, Faith? I mean really?'

If I didn't know him better I'd swear he's gloating. How am I? Not as good as he sounds, that's for sure. Because while he's having wild sex with Psycho-Vanessa in our beautiful home, I'm barely holding it together here with my new friend, i.e. my goldfish Jawsy. Not even she (he?) is happy with me, staring at me with those huge eyes day in, day out, probably wondering what I'm going to do with the rest of our lives.

'F-fine, thank you. What can I, er, do for you?'

'You always assume I want something.'

'Am I wrong?' *Please tell me I'm wrong.*

'Ah, but this time it's different. This time, I'm giving *you* something. A huge job. I want you to renovate the beach house for me.'

The beach house? My former *home*?

'Faith? Are you there?'

I swallow the knot forming in my throat. 'I'm here.'

'I'm on tour in Thailand at the moment, but I've left you a cheque on my desk in the study. All you have to do is say yes, cash it and get to work.'

I sigh. 'Gabe, just a tip for you: never leave a signed cheque lying around – and never, ever tell an ex-girlfriend where the money is. I could easily take it and run.'

He softly strums his guitar. 'You would never do that, Faith. Besides, this was your home, too.'

He can't be doing this to me! I've just barely managed to pull all the shards of myself together, reorganising my life without him and all the things we used to do, and now this?

'So what do you say?'

I say I'm sooo not ready for this, and I don't think I ever will be. Because merely stepping through the front door and plunging back into a past I'm still trying to get over would kill me. So I straighten my shoulders and take a deep breath.

'I'm sorry, but I just can't do it.'

The now pleading twang of his guitar comes through the ether. He's never far from his guitars, Gabe. 'I understand, Faith. But you must have seen what Vanessa's done to the place? It's an absolute shambles.'

Seen it I have – four full glossy pages in *Arch-Design*, the publication belonging to the gurus of interior design, Lord and Lady Wickford, where my rival in work and love Vanessa boasts about how she has *transformed a traditional Cornish beach house into a rock star's dream home*. And to think that everyone secretly refers to her as 'Hurricane Vanessa', and not in a good way.

'Apart from my recording studio, Vanessa has completely changed the atmosphere,' he complains.

She's also changed you, I want to retort, but my decision to be amicable about the split, and to not go under as my mum had, has compelled me to make an effort to be civilised and not say everything that I think. Which is a feat in its own.

I can just picture him in his usual black skinny jeans and his *Girls Love A Rock Star* T-shirt, with his boyish face and spiky blond hair, strumming away, desperately searching for his next hit. He always got rather panicky when it didn't come to him immediately, and I would encourage him to be patient.

'You have to grow into an idea, Gabe,' I used to tell him. 'Let it come to you, nurture it and see where it takes you.'

And he would knit his brows and nod. 'Yeah, yeah, you're right. I need to be patient.'

I was the only one who knew the real Gabe York once the spotlights were off. He would let only me go anywhere near him when he was having one of his down moments, and trusted only me to set him back on his feet. But that was then. And now he didn't need me anymore. Except for my professional design skills, apparently. Because Vanessa's style was something that you would tire of very quickly, unless you were colour-blind.

'Faith, only you can make it ri-ight,' he suddenly sings with another prolonged strum and I'm grateful that for once his amps are switched off. Like all true musicians, Gabe uses his music to express his emotions. Like when he'd proposed to me on the piano. Literally. We'd just had sex on it and he'd rolled over to play a tune while he asked me if I wanted to marry him. A promise of marriage that died a short while later.

As our careers were just blossoming and everything was so exciting, I had been adamant in maintaining the stability I'd lacked as a child while being bounced around foster homes with my sister. No silly star behaviour for us in our future, but sensible decisions and conduct. That had always been my motto, as I wanted to be strong and level-headed – the opposite of my mother.

So at the end of a gruelling workday for both of us, we would crash on the settee with dinner and dream of a future where we would attain our goals, however far-fetched they seemed at the time. Because, back then, we thought we could rule the world. Not that I wanted to, but it felt good to think we could.

Before Gabe's money started to roll in, it had been only him and me. And we had been happy. Until we weren't any longer. Or at least, until *he* wasn't. I thought we would be together forever, but obviously he'd had other plans.

Gabe strums a new chord. 'I loved it the way you had done it up, Faith. And I loved it, when you and I were together.'

I swallow.

'Please, Faith, say yes?' he begs, still strumming. 'I'll make it up to you.'

How? How on earth can he ever make it up to me? He left me. For Vanessa, to boot. And after that, I had chosen to not hate him and remain civilised, simply for my own sanity. Am I a pushover? Perhaps. But in my relationship with Gabe I often found that I could either be always right, or I could mostly let go of some things and be happy.

Now I'm neither. Vanessa has taken everything from

me – the man I love, our future, the possibility of my very own, normal family, something I'd dreamt of since I was a little girl sleeping in a foster bed. The one thing I craved the most had been a life with loving parents, children, a garden and a dog. And I'd thought that our beloved beach house would have been the start of it, so I'd decorated it with all my heart, spending hours on end in vintage shops and reclamation yards. It has always been my signature style, decorating well without spending the earth.

And now, to add insult to injury, Vanessa is on a mission to steal my prospective clients any way she can.

'I can't believe you'd even feel comfortable asking me this, Gabe,' I say. 'What does *she* think about that? Surely my style is too boring for the likes of her?'

'It doesn't matter anymore,' he says softly.

The hair on the back of my neck stands to attention, just like my nerves. 'Why?'

He hesitates. 'I was going to tell you when I came back to England, but I just knew you'd suss me out first. You know me so well, Faith.'

I huff. 'Gabe, I have absolutely no idea what you're on about, so why don't you just make it easier on both of us and come straight out with it?'

'You deserve to know the truth, after all the hurt I've caused you. Vanessa and I are over.'

I sit up, an electric shock jolting through me. Over? As in, finished? Split up?

'I'm, uhm, sorry to hear that,' I lie. Because, even if Gabe and I are no longer together and he has hurt me more than I can say, I never wanted him to be in the hands of an out-of-control psychopath.

I've known her since my art college days at Falmouth University and only her aristocratic parents have kept her out of prison for her numerous OTT acts – displays of public nudity, drugs, DUI being her minor capers. Her outrageous lifestyle is reflected in her designs that equally outlandish rock stars vie for. You know – solid gold refrigerator doors and all that.

She's the worst thing that could have happened to someone as fragile-egoed as Gabe.

'Don't be sorry, Faith. I ended it. And do you want to know why?'

No, I want to say. *Your life is your business.* But I am literally salivating and swallowing at the same time. 'Uhm… yes…'

'Because I… Jesus, I can't believe I've finally found the guts to tell you this…'

'T-tell me what, Gabe?' My heart is about to explode out of my ribcage.

Silence. Then: 'That I was a right tosser leaving you. I made a huge mistake. I never wanted to hurt you, Faith. I want things to be the way they were between us. I want you *back*. If you'll have me? I swear I'll spend the rest of our lives making it up to you, sweetheart.'

I clutch my mobile as my entire world turns topsy-turvy once again. Is it possible? I haven't misunderstood? Subsumed my desires and woven them into this already surreal conversation?

'You know my heart always belonged to you, no matter what,' he continues. 'We were made for each other. We *belong* together.' Another strum, soft and melancholic and he begins to play his number-one hit: 'Impossibly You'.

Only now his voice is choked and I can feel his genuine pain.

At the realisation of what he is saying, I wipe my suddenly wet eyes.

He wants me back. He is *sorry*.

But taking on Gabe again, so quickly, out of the blue? I still love him, of course, but is it wise to throw myself back into a relationship, heart and soul? How can I know he won't abandon me again? I couldn't deal with that – not twice. Especially when I used to see him as a sort of karmic reward for having survived my crappy childhood. I thought that with him by my side, life would behave itself and finally treat me kindly.

But then, when he broke up with me, I realised it was not so. Life doesn't owe anybody anything.

'Remember how happy we used to be, Faith? You were the only one who ever got me, and I was the one you always turned to after a bad day. We were amazing together, Babes, and I…'

Say it, I pray silently. *Please say it. And please mean it this time.*

'I can't believe I was stupid enough to leave you. And now – now, I don't know how you could ever trust me again.' He lowers his voice. 'I screwed up big time, Babes.'

'Yes, you did…'

'I know, sweetheart. I only wish I could turn back time so I could erase all the times I made you cry.'

'So do I,' I croak. But he still hasn't said it. Is he even going to?

'It will be different, if you'll have me back, Faith. Because I still love you…'

There it is. He still loves me. But it's not enough. Because, as strong as I have become, I doubt I would survive another similar blow, and at the moment I can't risk losing it all again unless I'm absolutely sure that Gabe is for real this time.

It had been six months of hell after he left me, and I had almost slipped back into the horror of my teenage alcoholism years. I'd stared at my mobile a thousand times a day, if not more, in the hope that I'd get a message from him saying that he was sorry, and that he wanted me back, all the while scolding myself for being such a fantasist. Things like that never happen in real life. Because I'd thought that once love is gone, it's gone forever.

It had been pure hell digging myself out of that the first time, but my sister Hope and my friends had been there for me. I'd worked so hard to claw myself out of it.

And in the space of the last six months, I've found a new self-esteem and taken on clients I could have only dreamed of before. I look and sound more confident than ever. I'm almost where I want to be professionally. Emotionally, that's a completely different and uphill battle.

But now, against all odds, he's back.

'Vanessa was a huge mistake,' he now assures me. 'A moment of madness. I swear I will never, ever hurt you again. If possible, I love you even more than before.'

Me too, I want to say as my voice cracks with the effort to not bawl my eyes out. The man I love still wants me. I could still have a future with him. I could go back home. But I can't let go of everything, just yet. Not like that. I'm still smarting. I'm not yet ready. And I can't let him have the upper hand this time. This time I call the shots. I've earnt the right. I've bloody *earnt it*.

'You're crying,' he whispers. 'Is that a *Yes, I love you, let's start all over again* cry, or a *Bugger off I never want to see you again* cry?'

Now, I know that all my friends and my sister would baulk at my weakness after having propped me up for months with pep talks and care packages, just being there for me so I wouldn't wilt away with loneliness. I had told myself (and them, for that matter) that I'd never, ever get back with Gabe York again.

But as it turns out, if I'm even considering it anywhere in the future, then the joke is on me, because I still love him. I always have. And now we may have another chance to make it right. Because if he's come back, it means that he's missed me, too, and if he's missed me only half as much as I've pined for him, then perhaps we'd still have a chance to rebuild our relationship from the ground up. But it wouldn't be easy. Nor would it take a short time. I would just have to make sure that I stayed strong and independent. And there's only one way to do that.

'It's a *Let's see what happens* cry,' I warn him. 'For now, I'll take on the job, but I can't promise you more than that.'

A stunned silence follows. I know he'd expected me to fall at his feet. But in these past six months, I've learnt to not be dependent on a man.

This is what I'm telling myself, but my heart is screaming, *Please don't hurt me again.* I reach over to grab some tissues from the coffee table. I couldn't bear it if he changed his mind again. I would truly come apart for good this time.

He finally exhales in relief and I can feel him smiling. He's thinking he's got me back, whatever I say. 'I can wait, Babes – it's only right.'

'Don't be too cocky. The redesign will cost you the earth.'

He laughs. 'You are worth every penny.'

'And Vanessa…?' I ask. I know only too well how she must be feeling.

'She's booking her flight to Heathrow as we speak.'

I can actually picture her, wild peroxide hair standing on end as she throws her psychedelic clothes into an equally psychedelic suitcase that no one could ever miss, hurling it around at the airport and swearing for England at everyone and anyone who happens to get in her way as she stomps off, tottering in her vertiginous stilettos. I wouldn't be surprised if she came banging on my door and threatened to gouge my eyes out with them.

'Awh, Babes,' Gabe groans. 'I wish I could drop everything and come home to you. I miss you so much it hurts, and I miss Cornwall and our home and the sea and – you know what? Screw it – I'm coming home.'

'But you can't – you've signed a *contract*,' I protest. 'It's all going to have to wait. You've got a string of concerts. This is not the way to stay credible in the music busine—' I bite my lip. I can't start mothering him all over again. Which was probably one of the reasons why I'd lost him in the first place. Being too level-headed, too stable. And to think that this fault of mine, which had been my saving grace as a child, has perhaps become my adult weakness. I'm now, as a result, a stickler for rules.

'Tell me you still love me, Faith.'

I wipe my eyes with the pads of my thumbs and, for the very first time in months, smile. 'I still love you, Faith,' I quip.

He chuckles. 'Silly. I've been a right tit, haven't I?' he says.

'And a left one, too!'

'Tell you what, Babes – I've got a few days off in a few weeks. I'm going to pop home and make it up to you.'

I warm up instantly at the thought. It has been so *long*.

'But I want you to move back into the house in the meantime.'

'Gabe—'

'I know what you're thinking – that it's too soon, but I'm not there anyway, right? Just move back in and make yourself at home.'

'I don't know…'

'Come on, Babes. It'll be easier for you, you won't have to commute or get a room anywhere.'

Well, that much was true.

'Start in the bedroom. I want no trace of Vanessa left. I want it to be exactly as it was before. I want it to *smell* like you again.'

'I'll do my best to re-source everything,' I promise, trying my best to ignore that old, familiar warmth building up inside me while I'm also wondering how I'm going to juggle all my previous commitments.

'You won't have to re-source anything,' he informs me. 'I had all of our things put into storage.'

My heart lurches. 'You did? Everything? Why?'

Another strum. 'Probably because I didn't really want to let you go, Faith. Deep inside I knew I was making a huge mistake to shack up with that whack job.'

'Be nice to someone who loved you,' I whisper, sincerely hoping that he hadn't talked about me like that too. *Who, Faith, that clingy robot who wanted all her ducks in a row?* or something like that.

'Yeah, sorry. But keeping your stuff was the only way to not completely let you go. Blimey, you wouldn't believe how lost I was. I was completely out of control, drinking and partying every night like my life depended on it.'

As if I didn't know, thanks to Twitter, Facebook and Instagram.

'But now I'm back.'

'I'm so happy for you, Gabe. Okay, then. I'll start immediately.'

'Thank you. The key to the storage unit where our things are is in my top drawer. I'll text you the address.'

'Okay.'

'You've still got the house keys, haven't you?' he asks.

'Yes.' I'm ashamed to say that I've kept them – that bundle of keys being all I had left of our home.

'Then let yourself in, Babes, and make yourself at home again,' he murmurs. 'It is still ours, no matter what it looks like.'

'I'll make it just like it was,' I promise him, and I can feel him smile on the other side of the world.

Everything will be perfect from the kitchen down to the soft furnishings. The curtains and bedding will need laundering after all that time in storage. I, too, feel drab and tired, having pretty much come out of storage myself, tucked away, forgotten and neglected before being allowed to emerge and live my life again.

He stops strumming. 'I swear to you, I'll make it up to you.'

I'm resolved to be cautious this time, but I must admit I had hoped that this would happen. No, scratch that. I'd *dreamt* it – over and over again. But never had I actually thought it could ever come true. I mean, let's be honest – when does this ever happen? Just how often do you see a return of flame? And, more importantly, how long do they usually last?

'It'll be different this time – that I promise you, Faith. And... if you think you can be with me again, we might even finally plan that nursery?'

My heart literally does a somersault in my chest. This is too much. Does he really want a baby now, too, or is it only because he knows how badly I want one?

'Let's not get ahead of ourselves, Gabe,' I caution him. I don't want him to know he literally had me at *Hello*.

'Absolutely not, Faith. We've already wasted too much time apart, but I've finally grown up. I want a family. With you.'

It's like being in an episode of *The Twilight Zone*. How is this even happening? Gabe had always been adamant about waiting. Waiting indefinitely, in fact. He'd done so much to put it off in the hope I might change my mind, and *now* he changes his?

'What has caused all this?' I ask.

'The prospect of a life without you. It's been crap so far. We've got to catch up on everything we've missed out on. So I'll leave it all in your capable hands?'

'Absolutely, I'll take care of everything.'

'Cool. I've got to run now, but we can do a video-chat tomorrow if you like?'

'Fine.'

'Great. See you tomorrow, love of my life.'

Love of my life. He's just called me the love of his life. I only hope that he won't let me down (again).

2

I Won't Let You Down (Again)

'Have you lost your bloody *mind*?' Hope screeches over the phone two minutes later. I had promised myself that I'd enjoy the moment, savour it and relish it on my own, but in the end I can't resist telling her. I need to share this with someone, and who better than my beloved, judgemental, non-identical twin sister?

'Think long and hard before you get yourself entangled with him again, Faith! And think back to what you went through.'

'In fairness, I've only accepted a job offer. It's good money.'

'Please don't kid yourself, sweetheart. You're banking on things working out this time, but they might not. He already left you once. And if he's done it once—' She sighs loudly. 'I just don't want you to end up like me.'

Meaning divorced with two kids, a hectic job as a chef and only me, Auntie Fi, as her main babysitter. Because after her husband left her, I had practically taken his place as Hope's partner, the one who picked up all the slack and took the child-minding shifts when she couldn't. I can't even begin to count the number of college exams or presentations I've prepared while bouncing Jowen or Verity – and sometimes both – on my knees. So with a failed marriage under her belt, who better than her to scare me off men for good? But this time, she's got her work cut out for her.

'He'll only break your heart all over again – and this time it'll be worse, because he'll have lulled you into that false sense of security, and when you're nice and cosy with the idea all over again, bam! He'll dump you again.'

'*Jesus*, Hope, you're supposed to be rooting for me.'

My niece Verity screams in the background. Her brother Jowen simply loves to antagonise her as if they'd been married fifty years.

'Jowen! Leave your sister alone or you'll be dealing with me!' Hope shouts, breaking my eardrum. 'Oh, Faith, sweetheart, I *am* rooting for you – you know that! But I just don't want to see you hurt again. Don't you remember how you walked around like a zombie for months? It's only recently that you've started properly functioning again, and I'm terrified—'

'But I'm okay now,' I argue. 'You even said so yourself last week – that you were happy because I finally had it together again.'

'Yes – without him! I don't doubt he loved you, Faith, and you know what, maybe in his own way he still does. But you can't deny that the two of you seem to have some sort of silent pact where your roles are well defined. He's a dick and you forgive him. Are you sure you want to live like that for the rest of your life?'

'Well, as you say, it's only until he changes his mind,' I quip darkly. 'And in any case, I didn't actually say yes to hooking up again.'

Hope snorts. 'As if we don't already know what you're going to do. I really, really wish you'd think this over.' The rest of it – *It's going to be me and your friends who peel you off the floor again* – remains unsaid. And I silently thank her for not driving her point home too much.

I know she loves me, and that she's worried I'll go under and turn to the bottle again, just like our mother had. But this time it could be different. I have recognised the pain in his voice and I know that he's finally matured. Because, unlike Hope, I believe in the ultimate good of people. People make mistakes. But that doesn't mean that there's no room for redemption. Can't a bloke change for the better in the end? I think so.

And I'm going to do my best to be a bit less uptight. Lose the British stiff upper lip and all that. I am going to try to relax. And try new things that I've never had the courage to do before.

Another scream rips through the earpiece. 'Jowen! Stop pulling your sister's hair! Faith, I've got to go before they tear each other apart. But promise me one thing?'

'What's that?'

'If you do get back with him again, do not have any children!' she shouts and hangs up.

I smile to myself. Children. By a strange twist of fate, or stroke of luck, Gabe has finally understood how important it is for me to have that parent–child love in my life. To give that unconditional love that Hope and I had never had.

With a little luck, maybe the dream of a family will, in time, come true after all.

As you can imagine, I don't waste any time in grabbing Jawsy's fishbowl and some of my essentials before driving up to the cliffs above Perrancombe. Nestled between two tiny hillocks covered in marram grass, the beach house seems to have been waiting for me all this time, and just the sight of it makes my heart sing.

I park in my favourite spot from where I used to glimpse the sea through the glass gap between the garage and the house. The architect who'd designed it, Tarquin Turner, had added that slight teaser, which was what had won me over at first glance. Gabe likes his privacy and his closed spaces and rarely leaves his recording studio which he's cornily dubbed *Tunes on the Dunes*. But everywhere else, huge windows facing south let in all the light and warmth, even on a foul day.

I stop a moment to breathe in the familiar salt air that always cleared the cobwebs from my head. Only now, I've more than cobwebs. I've got a Tube-map-like mess of scars in my heart that need forgetting. Scars that will hopefully soon be healed.

With a trembling hand, I reach for my keys and make my way to the cedar gates as my heart begins to pound. *Easy*, I tell myself. *Don't get too carried away. Remember that, for now, it's just a job.*

As I turn the key in the triple lock, I can't help but ask myself: What will I feel once I'm inside? Will there be anything left of us under all that garish stuff, or are all traces of me completely gone? Will I be able to recreate our home the way he's asked, and make it as it was before Hurricane Vanessa hit?

As it turns out, these are all questions that might not be answered after all, as my attempt to open the door is met by the screeching sound of the alarm. After a brief moment, I punch in the old code, but of course it's different now. Everything is different now. Perhaps I am expecting too much of Gabe. Hope is right in saying I should be cautious.

I cover my ears, wondering how long it will take the security team Gabe hired to get here, so I punch in his birthday. Nothing. And then, rolling my eyes, I try Vanessa's (I know it because we were in the same classes at uni), just in case, but nothing can stop this screaming harpy (the alarm, not Vanessa). But I'm determined that this won't ruin my start to the day.

I try everything from Gabe's childhood pets to his song titles, but nothing is working. In the end, I'm relieved to see Mick and Dougie pull up in the jeep bearing the logo of Perrancombe's security company.

'Mornin', Faith,' Mick greets me as if he didn't know about my moving out six months earlier. 'Gabe thought you might have some problems getting in.'

I nod. 'Yes, thank you, I—'

He punches in the code and passes me a Post-it Note. 'Here's the new code. Give us a call if you need anything. Anything at all. And welcome back!'

'Thanks, Mick. Would you boys like to come in for a cuppa?' I have missed my beloved fellow Perrancombians and am anxious to pick up the thread of my interrupted acquaintances and friendships.

'Awh gee, thanks, Faith, but we've got to get back to the paper. Maybe next time.'

'Okay,' I concede while waving the Post-it Note in thanks at him and Dougie in the Jeep who isn't missing a beat. In fact, there's not much that escapes these two. I wonder if the fact that they also run the *South Cornish Coastal Gazette* has anything to do with that.

I stuff the code into the pocket of my dress and wave them off, smiling like an idiot. When you're happy everything looks peachy pink.

I take a deep breath before plunging into the foyer and thus back into the past that had been so brutally interrupted. And then I cry out in absolute horror.

It's worse than I'd feared. Granted, I had seen pictures of the place, but nothing compares to what surrounds me now.

In the space of six months, Vanessa has turned our beloved luxury beach house into a kind of circus tent meets African safari gone absolutely ballistic.

There is not one colour left unused, nor one single style that hasn't been represented. You name it, it's there – from gamboge to tomato red, passing through a gamut of sickly greens, and from the psychedelic Seventies to burlesque baroque.

Hurricane Vanessa Chatsbury, who thinks more is more, has outdone herself once and for all.

My former home is now literally a (yellow Bakelite) horse of a different colour. Its gorgeous off-white walls and oak shelving and staircases that had once been paired with a muted palette of creams and duck egg blue is now a garish nightmare.

It's as if I've stepped through someone else's door – Alice in Wonderland's, by the looks of it, where everything is not only out of proportion, but has a nightmarish look to it. Any minute now I'll find bottles with notes saying *Eat Me* or *Drink Me*. And have I mentioned the (empty) gilt birdcages?

Warily taking in my surroundings, I struggle to find any familiar corners between the polka-dot and striped male and female mannequins just inside the living room. Not to mention the leopard-skinned bull, diamanté horns and all, crouched opposite the entrance, ready to pounce on any visitors foolish enough to come through the doors. Gabe's grand piano is covered in pictures of Vanessa and himself, which is painful enough, but to add insult to injury are the solid gold frames of every shape and size picturing them in various moments of their story.

Parking my luggage by the door, I set Jawsy down on the window ledge facing north and make my way through a maze of coloured glass accent tables that have trays on them with fake glass and ceramic food. Everything is tawdry and flamboyant and there is not one inch of furniture that is not covered in baubles or ominous objects that look like they are just waiting to pounce upon you. And nowhere, I say absolutely nowhere, is there a book in sight.

By the time I make it to the kitchen and spot the fur (yes, *fur*) carpeting, I am in a million pieces. Not only is there nothing left of my hard work, it now screams *Vanessa Chatsbury Has Taken Your Entire Life* in huge balloon letters which, incidentally, match the writing *Hi, Gorgeous!*

in the mirror hanging via a gold chain from the ceiling *above the kitchen sink*, blocking the view of the sea. You get the idea.

To make things worse, where I'd bought stuff on the cheap to stay grounded and not bankrupt Gabe, Vanessa Chatsbury – true to her lineage – lives the life of an earl's daughter by spending her rock star boyfriend's money as if it was going out of style. And speaking of style, on what planet, and I mean on what planet can you find a bathroom that is strictly made of glass walls *without* the privacy switch?

I can understand a bathtub in your bedroom for that luxurious feel, but who really wants to share their most private moment with everyone else in the house? That was the first thing on my Get Rid Of list alongside the fur carpeting in the kitchen. And what of the guest bedroom, where everything from walls to floors to ceiling, chandeliers, doors, casings and furnishings are all, I mean *all*, blood red? Or the armchair that looks like an open mouth, with teeth and all, and its tongue-shaped cushion? It's like Jack Torrance has gone haywire in here.

The need to feel Gabe's presence sends me to the master bedroom. On the threshold, I stop and gawp at yet another slaughterhouse of red animal prints.

I open the, *oh my*, red and black leopard-print wardrobe in search of one of his T-shirts and hold it to me, but it smells like *her*. She is everywhere and it's going to take me quite a while to get rid of her presence in our home.

My mobile rings again and I fish my phone out of the pocket of my dress. 'Hello?'

'Hello, Miss Hudson, owner of Hudson Home Designs?'

'Hello – yes, speaking.'

Could it possibly be the Wickfords' PA returning my many emails, letters and unanswered calls? On a Sunday? Probably not. I've been courting them for the past few years in the hope that they would feature me in their trade magazine, *Arch-Design*, or hire me as a consultant, or even simply acknowledge my existence as a designer.

'*The* Faith Hudson, the interior designer who invented those house-shaped cushions – sorry, what are they called again?'

'Home Hugs,' I answer, my heart rate picking up. Dare I believe that this is finally what I have been waiting for? My big break in the field of interior design? All I know is that I've worked long and hard enough for it, slogging year after year in other companies, always the first one to punch in and the last one to leave, killing myself every day and determined to prove myself. And now, with a little luck, I might be finally getting closer to that goal. And I'd thought that this day couldn't possibly get any better!

'Sorry, to be clear – the designer who fell legs akimbo on top of the vice president of *Arch-Design* while receiving an award for said cushion?'

Bloody hell, will that incident never be forgotten?

'Oh my God, that was hilarious!' he screeches. 'That photo of you squatting, with his head sticking out from between your thighs? It went viral in less than ten minutes. It was like a scene from *The Benny Hill Show*! Nice arse, by the way!'

I gasp and throw my mobile onto the kaleidoscopic carpet as if it was a loaded hand grenade, but I can still hear him laughing, so I dart forward and try to ring off, but my hands are now shaking so badly that I drop the phone and it takes me another few seconds to hang up on him.

Dear God, will it never be over? Years had gone by since that Young Cornish Interior Designers Awards night where I'd won first place, but completely lost my dignity, and still I get these random prank calls, probably from some old school 'friends' just looking for a laugh. Or maybe even Vanessa's friends.

Granted, I had made an absolute fool of myself by slipping on the stage and pulling the bloke handing me the Perspex house-shaped award down along with me. I happened to end up on top, straddling his shoulders. And fate had it that I'd chosen a pencil skirt which split the second I landed on him. In front of hundreds of people armed with phones to share my mishap with the rest of the world. The humiliation was centuplicated by the fact that, to avoid showing panty lines through my skirt, I'd worn a thong.

That was the night I became the laughing stock of not only my ex-course-mates, but also my future employers in the world of interior design. The mocking titles on Instagram, just to name a couple, had read: *Posterior Designer* and *Thong in Cheek*.

Of course you'd be forgiven for thinking that things couldn't go any worse from there, but you'd be wrong. Because the very next day someone had made a pillow with a screenshot of my already humiliated arse and actually launched it on the black market. Really, what kind of person would actually *go* to all that trouble just for a laugh at a complete stranger's expense? Who would be so cruel? And who has that much *time* on their hands? It's a wonder I didn't become a hermit in those days. But I had a career to launch and simply couldn't afford to hide away from the world and wallow in my shame.

At the end of the day, it had only been a small award for a small idea. The Home Hugs were born out of my habit of hugging cushions for comfort, especially when we were transitioning from one foster family to another. The cushion I had found in our very first foster home, where I had been relatively serene if not happy, had had a drawing of a row of multi-coloured beach huts. Never having been inside one, I'd always imagined there was a tiny, happy family in there that lived by the sea, and that the hut was like a castle inside.

It had been my favourite object in the entire house, and upon being removed from there, I had taken it with me, almost as if it could protect us against our next, unknown foster home.

I would give it to Hope to hold on to through the night whenever she had an argument with our host family of the month.

'You're not my parents!' she'd scream. Same words, different house. 'And you can't treat us like rubbish! We have a right to go to the common if we want! We're not your bloody prisoners!' And then a loud smack would send her back, red-faced, to our room, where she would bawl into her pillow, telling me that one day we would be free of foster parents and that we would be adopted by someone who really loved us.

It still seems like yesterday – the loneliness and the fear and anxiety of not being loved if she acted up too much, which was quite often. And I was just as bad, if not worse, quiet but needy, constantly making spaniel eyes at our foster parents of the month, following them around the house like a lost puppy in the hope of a hug. I should have known that they couldn't love us unconditionally, when not even our own parents could.

When it turned out Hope always needed that cushion, I'd pulled out my mini Singer sewing machine, dug into my stash of material, and made what was to be known as the Home Hug – a thick, triple-stitched, sturdy, house-shaped cushion you could wrap your arms around, with a chimney you could rest your chin on and even put your mobile phone in.

It was pretty and it gave us both comfort, and I wondered how many other teenagers could benefit from such a simple idea, so when the local association had invited us students from art college to enrol in a local design competition, I presented my product in the hope of comforting others as well.

But whilst I had been miserable and lonely in my day-to-day obscurity, Home Hugs had definitely put me in the sights of my schoolmates. Despite winning first place and being promised a one-year contract with a local designer company as soon as I left school, my falling on top of the company VP had been my undoing.

There went years and years of serious study down the drain in one single fall, and my butt being posted all over the media.

When I'd met Gabe and told him about it, he had laughed it off by saying, 'Well, at least they'll be talking about you forever!' It was easy for him to say. He was charming and always the centre of positive attention way before he became famous. The fame and the money had just been an added bonus to him. He was born charming and everyone seemed to gravitate around him, leaving me to wonder what he'd seen in me, the wallflower.

In truth, Gabe was, in private, the most insecure man I'd ever met. I suspect that Vanessa has drummed that out of him by now. If *she* had fallen onstage and exposed her arse to the world instead of me, she would have ridden the wave of fame to her benefit. Made lemonade with lemons and all that. She would have even made her own arse cushions and launched them on the market herself. And I'm not all that convinced that it wasn't she who made the cushions in the first place.

Not only is Vanessa my nemesis in every way, she is also the god-daughter of the ever-elusive Lord and Lady Wickford. And I'm certain that, besides my Posterior Design Fiasco, that is also why they won't answer my emails or return my calls.

Because Vanessa hates me with a passion. She has always wanted what was mine – my friends, my clients and finally my boyfriend. And what Vanessa wants, even if she has to disturb the entire county of Cornwall, she gets. Gabe included. So now she must be fuming, which means I have to watch my back at all times.

With a huge sigh, I open the triple-glazed sliding glass doors facing the sea and, kicking off my shoes, I hurry down the stone steps carved into the cliffside leading to the beach, and in less than one minute, my toes are happily sinking into the cold, clean January sand.

Down here, nothing has changed. The sea has no idea what happened to Gabe and me, and it welcomes me as if I'd never left. The waves are still beating upon the shore and the seagulls are still circling, heaving their usual cry to the four winds. I breathe in deeply and close my eyes. Better. Even if memories are flooding through me like the sea at high tide, I can only go with the flow, and accept that what is done is done. Put it all in the past and look forward instead.

I stroll down the entire length of the beach, enjoying the wet, slushy sand between my toes and the fresh, pungent odour of the sea in my lungs. It's an unnaturally warm winter's day, and there are people swimming in the sea. For a minute I consider going for a dip myself, but I'm not that hardy or even that daring. Perhaps a dip in the pool later?

I look over my shoulder, and even from this distance I can see my former home, remembering it in every shade of light, rain and shine. From the outside, it actually hasn't changed much, if you remove the purple and yellow zebra-striped awning over part of the deck, so gaudy that you could probably see it from the French coast.

Gabe hasn't said what to do with any of her stuff, so I'll look into storage in case Vanessa wants it all back. She's welcome to it. Focused on my New Life mission, I know what to do and what arrangements to make.

After a long, solitary but happy stroll, I hear my mobile ringing again as I'm making my way back to the house. Luckily, it's Gabe.

'Hey, Faith? I forgot to mention that a buddy of mine will be delivering a side table tomorrow.'

'Oh? I thought I was getting rid of everything?'

'You are, but this is something I'd commissioned for you before I— Anyway, it's oak and traditional. You'll love it.'

'I like non-traditional things, too,' I counter.

He laughs. 'You, my adorable little Miss Staid? Please. Besides, it's to help an old friend out.'

'I thought I knew all your friends.'

'Not Henry. He saved my life once, so now I owe him.'

'Saved your life? How do I not know about this?'

He chuckles. 'See? Lots to talk about in our new life together.'

New as opposed to old, of course, but who am I to retort? I'm way too chuffed to start scoring brownie points. Besides, it's not like that between us and never has been. New life, new slate. If I can overcome my wariness. Because, despite my wanting to start all over again, I'm wary of giving myself heart and soul all over again. Of needing someone who might not need me as much.

'So you'll be there to receive the table?' he asks.

'Of course. Can't wait to see it.' *And to see you.*

'Okay, then. I've got to go, but we'll talk soon.'

'Brilliant,' I reply.

'Love you, my little Miss Staid!' he calls, despite the albeit temporary professional wall I've put up between us. But he is right about one thing. I am too staid, too traditional. I need to loosen up.

Back at the house, I catch a glimpse of myself in the kitchen mirror. I look like a cardboard cut-out, and need to breathe some spontaneity into me, once and for all. Do something I'd never be caught dead doing. And the answer is right under my nose, on the back patio. I'd always been conscious of someone seeing us from the beach, even if we were way too high up to be noticed.

'To hell with it,' I say aloud to myself as, on pure instinct, and a bit of a rebellious surge, I peel off my clothes and let them fall – along with my underwear and bra – to the floor and step towards the infinity pool that seems to disappear into the sea. This ought to be a good start towards unwinding.

Completely naked, in one slow movement, I sink into the water, exhaling with a muffled shriek as it rushes over my shoulders and down my chest. It is true that we are having a freak heat wave in the middle of the winter, but January is still January. What were those bathers down there thinking? But it does feel amazing to be so natural and, if you'll pardon me the pun, *au naturel* for once.

The last time I was in this pool Gabe and I were celebrating our third anniversary. He tried to make me go starkers, but I am a prude of biblical proportions. Or I was until two minutes ago. Let the new Faith be born from these waters!

Perhaps a little too late, I now realise that I could have enjoyed this kind of luxury all along. I could have indulged in this multi-millionaire lifestyle. But, as I'm always wary that I could lose things as quickly as I obtained them, I learnt very early to not value objects so much as I value people.

My people in particular are what make me strong – my sister, her children, my crew, and my friends. I guess that's what formed my work ethic. Those things are what count in my life.

I have never won anything by pure fluke in my entire life. Every little achievement to the most important professional awards, I've earned by hard work. And it's made me who I am today – a woman who's worked very hard and played very little – and who now needs to wind down. Just a tiny bit.

So I let go of the side of the pool and float on the surface, trying to empty my mind of my plans to make this a home once again. Possibly *our* home. Without it, I had been feeling, well, orphaned all over again. But hopefully, gradually, Gabe and I might—

'What the bloody hell is *that*?' comes an almighty shriek from the front door, and for a moment I'm convinced it's Vanessa on a mission to reclaim her kingdom of horrors.

In one single move, I dart to the edge of the pool and peer back into the house and watch in sheer, unadulterated horror as four people – three men and a woman – are traversing the foyer that is in a direct line with the patio doors and pool, if not for the various wild species of beasts caught in the line of sight. If I can't see them, they can't see me – yet. But I can hear every single word.

'The designer went a bit over the top, but there's going to be a proper reno to restore it to its original beauty,' one of the younger men is saying in what I can only assume is estate agent speak. But what are they doing here?

The woman is on the elderly side, giggling at the various props strewn around the house, in particular at the red lacquered life-size wooden elephant at the bottom of the staircase.

I desperately look to the nearby life-size glass dolphin and in one mad dash, make a break for it just in time as the voices get closer. I am hanging on to my new glass Flipper friend for dear life, for once grateful that Vanessa had chosen to go as big as possible.

'Ooh, is that an *infinity* pool out there?' The woman's voice bounces against the walls and I feel my eyes widen in panic. Any second they're going to see me in my birthday suit and there's nothing I can do. This is an absolute home invasion. If only I wasn't naked, I'd have my phone on me to call Mick and Dougie. You see now why I never let my guard down?

It is at that point that one of the younger men, leading the way out to the deck all smiles, stops in his tracks at the sight of me covering my naughty bits with the sole aid of a transparent statue.

Like Cinderella caught at the stroke of midnight, I cringe, burying my nose into Flipper's blowhole. I haven't a stitch to clothe me, as I haven't even bothered with a pool towel, and I'm now stuck here.

'*My clothes!*' I mouth to him in desperation.

Who The Bloody Hell Are You And What Are You Doing Here? the bloke's face flash-reads before he doubles back to the elderly couple, steering them away. 'Actually, uhm,' he says. 'Travis, why don't you take our friends to see the upstairs while I switch the pool pump on? We'll keep the best views for last.'

At that, the other young man, who has red hair, nods. 'Sure. Let me show you the rest of the house first, and then we'll come back down to enjoy the views from here. They're one in a million.'

'Good lad,' the dark-haired man says and, after waiting a beat until the other three are off, he turns to me.

There's no way I can make it to the foyer, and I can't remember which animal I threw my clothes on. Which is a mouthful of its own. I glance around the kitchen. Vanessa is famous for not using tablecloths, and as petite as I am, there is no way a tea towel is going to do. As I'm frantically darting now from statue to statue trying to find my dress, Dark Hair throws something at me before turning around, and I make a beeline for it. It's his suit jacket.

I slip into it just as I hear the other three coming back down, and ignoring the puddles I'm making, I bolt to hide under the bottom of the – glass – stairs in the shadow of a fake fern. Thank God for Vanessa's last-minute nod to nature.

'What happened to your jacket?' the older man asks Dark Hair.

'Oh, uhm,' comes the delayed answer. 'It's so hot for January, isn't it? I think I'll go for a swim! You can both join me, if you want!'

Taking advantage of their collective laughter, I bolt to the master bedroom to wait until they've gone, but I can't get dressed as my suitcase is still somewhere downstairs.

'Just who the bloody hell are you, and what are you doing here?' The deep, harsh voice pulls me out of my reverie, making me bounce off the mattress and straight to my feet. See? I'd read his face accurately, word for word.

He is standing on the door, wide-eyed as Red Hair brings up the rear.

'Who the hell are *you*?' I counter. 'And how did you get in here?'

'I have got a *key*,' he says.

'Well, so have I,' I re-counter.

'Have you really? What's the code?'

'The code?' Damn, I've left it in my pocket. 'I don't know.'

At that, Dark Hair's eyebrows shoot up. 'You don't know?'

'I mean I don't remember it. Mick and Dougie wrote it down for me,' I say, wrapping my arms over my chest. Who cares if I wrinkle his jacket? 'Call them if you want – they've known me for years.'

His expression changes from suspicious to shocked. 'You're the girlfriend-slash-designer?'

Now that's a mouthful. It depends on whether he's up to speed or six months behind. For all he knows, I could be Vanessa. 'And you are…?'

He remembers his manners and darts forward, holding out a hand. 'Henry. I'm so sorry about that. I'm a friend of Gabe's. Well, sort of. And this is Travis.'

Unwrapping one arm from around me, the other keeping the huge jacket in place, I gingerly shake hands with them, still eyeing them suspiciously. 'Well, then you must know he's out of town.'

'Right.' Dark Hair stands there, awkwardly. And then his eyes widen in recognition. 'Hey,' he says suddenly. 'You look familiar. Aren't you, oh, uh, the one who—'

Here we go again with that damn arse video.

'Yes, it's me, the girl who fell onto a bloke's chest in front of hundreds of people! The one whose bare arse is still on Instagram, Facebook, YouTube *and* Pinterest, thank you very much! And if you want to send it to your friends in Timbuktu and have a laugh, be my bloody guest!'

He blinks. 'I was going to say the artist behind those house-shaped cushions – what are they called – Home Hugs?'

I stare at him. 'Oh. Uhm, yes, that was me.'

'Okay, guys, you've completely lost me now,' Red Hair says in an American accent.

Dark Hair turns to him. 'They're these house-shaped cushions that you hug – really anti-stress,' he explains, then turns to me. 'I thought that was a great idea.'

'Oh. Thank you.' I shrug as the heat creeps up my neck. 'It's… just a cushion.'

'No – it's *Home Hugs*. Something everyone wants and needs – a home and a hug, combined into one. With space in the chimney to stash your mobile phone, a book or your glasses. So simple, yet absolutely stonking brilliant.'

Is he really going to fall back on flattery to get out of this? 'And why are you here, Travis and Harry?' I ask as Judi Dench would as if stumbling on a handsome gardener standing around in her rose garden. The dark-haired one looks like he could easily conduct a meeting in any boardroom. And, incidentally, any bedroom, with the huge dark twinkly eyes and the laughter wrinkles. I may still be in love with Gabe but I'm not blind.

'It's Henry. I, uhm, just delivered a table for Gabe. And actually, I've got a few more things coming, so…'

'The table bloke!' I gasp. 'Weren't you due tomorrow?'

'I was, but then I got a call from Trixie and Bopper – old friends of mine, who wanted to see the house so—'

'Sorry, wait,' I say, interrupting him. 'You let just anybody in to someone else's house?'

He folds his arms in front of his chest. 'No, not just anybody. Only prospective clients.

It's my turn to freak out. 'Prospective *clients*?'

He frowns and looks out the glass doors to the sea, as if for an easy escape route. 'We may have come at a bad time. We'll get out of your hair.'

'This house is not for sale,' I inform them.

'Oh, it's for sale all right,' Red Hair assures me. 'We're going to be marketing this in the States, among other places.'

'What? Impossible!' I counter. 'You're wrong!'

Dark Hair whistles. 'Wow. Perhaps you and your boyfriend should work on your communication skills.'

'I beg your pardon?'

'I'll be back tomorrow. You can keep the jacket, by the way. Nice – or rather interesting – meeting you,' he says as he makes his exit, followed by Travis.

If first impressions are usually the most accurate, it's safe to say that the estate agents and I will never be friends.

3

Home is Where the Heart is

Prospective clients – the cheek!

I grab my mobile and not even bothering to calculate the time zones, dial Gabe's number. 'Gabe?'

'Hmph...?'

'Gabe! What's going on?'

'Wha...?'

'A couple of estate agents came to show someone around the house!'

'What? Blimey. That's got to be my manager's fault. He's adamant that I should sell the place and move to London. I'll sort him out once and for all. Don't worry, Babes.'

'Good to hear it. I've prioritised you so my team are coming in on Monday to start the renos and the last thing we need is strangers letting themselves in.'

'Sure, sure. What happened?'

'They just came in while I was swimming naked in the pool, can you believe it, and—'

'Naked…?' he says, fully awake now. 'In the pool? That's a first.'

I can feel my face turning hot. 'I – I thought to let my hair down.'

'I like you with your hair down,' he murmurs and my whole body starts doing that usual tingling thing despite my best resolutions to take it slow.

'C-can you sort them out, then?'

'Only if you tell me you were thinking of me in the pool,' he murmurs.

'Gabe—'

'Come on, no use in being coy with me, Babes. What were you thinking?'

I bite my lip. 'You know what I was thinking.'

'Tell me all the same, Babes…'

I can't do it. As much as I try, I just can't do phone sex, especially if he's on the other side of the planet. Besides, it's too soon. As much as I still love him, I need to bide my time to get back to where I was.

I think long and hard before I open my mouth, lest my frustrated libido play a prank on me. It has been six months, after all. 'I was thinking… of how to make this house a home again.'

'Oh. Good thought.'

'So I can start the renos?'

'Yeah, yeah, of course.'

'Okay, then. I have to go now,' I lie. I know me – the longer I stay within the sphere of his charm, the faster he'll crack me.

'Love you,' he says and I put the phone down, a sense of

relief washing over me. The cheek of Harry and Travis. This has been our house for more than three years. It has my blood, sweat and tears. And my mum's.

And now the next step – to recuperate part of our past that I had thought lost forever. Grabbing the storage unit keys from Gabe's desk drawer where he said they would be, along with the blank cheque (what a daft boy; darling, but daft) I rush downstairs to finally locate my suitcase from which I retrieve some clothes and then I go out front to empty my Kia of all its samples and swatches in order to make space for our stuff. It will be literally out with the new, and back in with the old. Finally, and slowly but surely, life seems to be slotting into place again.

The storage unit is just outside Porthleven, and as I make my way down row 14, I can't help but feel I'm going through a portal of some sort, back to my past, when life was much, much better.

When I open the door and step in, my heart in my mouth, the first thing I see is our duck egg settee, haphazardly thrown upside down atop a pile of furniture as an afterthought, and barely visible under a heap of throws and blankets that have been irreverently tossed there without being wrapped up or even folded. Every single object we owned had told a story of love and kindness – from the sofa cushions Gabe bought me because they depict thatched cottages with bright blue doors, to the guitars, straps and music sheets gifted to him from yours truly.

Everything else is in pretty much the same state and I can almost hear Vanessa growling, 'Get rid of all this crap.' I'm sure that if it hadn't been for Gabe, our entire life together would have found its fate at the bottom of a huge landfill.

Determined to not let that hurt me, I start trawling through our possessions, every single one bringing back memories, like the ceramic school of fish lamp we had bought in St Ives. That day we'd also been oohing and aahing at the Tate Modern, and I had felt so blessed to be in such a wonderful corner of the world with my beloved man's arm around my shoulders.

As I scrape through a pile of bath towels and tea towels thrown together, I find our very first white cotton bedspread that Elsie Lock, the owner of Lock, Stock & Barrel down in the village, had made for us a few years back.

A bit more digging produces the Christmas mugs we used to pull out on December first to pretend it was already Christmas. And the dolphin-shaped hot water bottle that Gabe gave me when we first moved in.

All these bits and bobs had made up our home, our love, our life, some even from my childhood, which I had tried to piece together through random objects. Even a tea towel was not just a tea towel, but a memory of a rare caress from a passing foster parent. A fluffy dolphin from the Garsons, a new diary with locket from the Mundleys, or a scarf from the Talbots. Nothing to each of them who have probably forgotten Hope and me completely. But to us, every single trinket meant the world, because it had meant that, even briefly, we had been part of a family.

Well, perhaps I may be on my way again to rebuilding my broken home once and for all. And, should it work out between us this time, any children we may have will be loved to pieces. They will have a warm, welcoming, happy home to live in and will grow up knowing that they belong to someone, and they won't have to ever feel lonely or sad. Because Gabe and I will cherish them.

Although my team will return to this storage unit with a lorry to take everything back home, I haul as much as I can into the boot and the empty seats of the car, trying to take back as much as I can of our old life.

Once at home, in five armfuls, I drag everything into Gabe's music room, the only place that had been untouched by Psycho-Vanessa. I would put it into my own former office but it has been transformed into Vanessa's, complete with steel desk and waterbed.

For the first few weeks I will camp down here on Gabe's sofa until I can get a bedroom decent again.

I change into my overalls and start deconstructing the slaughterhouse that is the master bedroom, not because I want to get back in there anytime soon, but because I have promised Gabe. But when he gets here we'll have that talk.

As it turns out, on my own, the task proves to be ghastly work, as Vanessa had insisted on huge, heavy props, and it takes me an entire jumbo-sized roll of bubble wrap left over from our previous job and three hours of back-breaking work just to pack away the frames and statues and odd objects hanging from the walls and ceiling, including the red and black striped pterodactyl hanging right over the bed.

It would be much easier to rent a skip and dump the wretched things, but my work ethic stops me from doing just that.

It's incredible how nothing of mine has remained, and I'm surprised how Gabe had been involved with two completely different women. He would appeal to just about anyone with those blond, boyish, half-angel, half-bad-boy rock-star looks and that Rod Stewart Circa 1978 voice that drives women all over the world crazy.

At eight p.m., unable to do anymore, I collapse onto the zebra sofa in the living room and look up at the mirror on the ceiling. And I can't help but think of the two of them together on this very sofa. So I slide down onto the carpet, only to realise with horror that it reeks of Vanessa's expensive perfume and I jump to my feet. Is there no surface in this house that she hasn't touched? I begin to wonder how long it's going to take to erase all trace of her, just like she had done to me.

The next Monday morning, bright and early, with my back hurting from all the lugging and pushing, I feed Jawsy. She seems to have adapted to her new environment quite well. This, undoubtedly, because I have moved every menacing statue of predators out of her line of vision. She forgets things every other second and I don't want the poor little soul to be scared out of her wits every time she wakes up.

In the stuffed and unattended mailbox there are several white business-looking envelopes addressed to Mr Gabriel York, and some utility bills. And a catalogue for a local furniture company. I leaf through it, studying the kitchens, living rooms, bedrooms and suddenly, there they are, just what I was hoping to resist – beautiful heart-warming nursery rooms. *No. Throw it away. Don't tempt fate. You don't need it. At least not yet.*

I make myself a cup of coffee, which I pour into Gabe's

Jimi Hendrix mug and, just like clockwork, revert back to my usual habits of when I lived here, i.e. opening the sliding glass doors to sit down and drink my coffee out on the patio facing the sea.

It's another gorgeous day, with cobalt blue skies and not one cloud in sight. Is it bad, to be this happy, when Vanessa is probably in tears right now? We had been friends during the first year in college, sharing lots of secrets. But then, in the second year, she simply gave me the cold shoulder, often making fun of my work in a very loud voice so everyone would hear. And after that, our initial friendship had rapidly gone downhill.

So maybe I shouldn't feel so bad for her after all. She was horrible to me for years. Rumour has it, she got a hold of Gabe's number and asked to see him to talk about me. I can only imagine how she would have manoeuvred herself into his bed and into his life.

But enough of that. Now it's definitely time to be happy again.

Down on the beach a woman is playing fetch with her dog, whose tongue is lolling out of its mouth in sheer, canine joy. She, too, has that relaxed, beach walk stance as she looks about her, completely content with the world. I wrench my own shoulders from under my ears as she turns and walks the other way.

I instinctively take a deep breath of cold sea, salt and my own fearful resistance to happiness. Here, where the land ends, marks the beginning of endless possibilities. The surf and the gulls sing a song of infinity and this is only the first morning of the rest of my life. Perhaps of our lives.

And now back to my task. I am so obsessed with

anything home-related, I have to stop myself from buying house-shaped candles, house-shaped soaps, comforters with cottages – the lot. Even my shower curtain in my flat has multi-coloured beach huts on it, while the wallpaper behind my headboard features rows and rows of Gustavian homes.

After I've drained my cup, I go upstairs and slowly ease my aching muscles under the jets in the wet room. I've got a meeting in precisely forty minutes with an amazing joiner, Turner & Cooke, for our new kitchen, followed by my staff to debrief them about Project Homecoming. All I've told them so far is to come to the beach house. I can't wait to see their faces! I hug myself, still unable to believe it myself. Yes, the future is looking bright.

At five to nine the doorbell rings. I straighten my navy blue business jacket and fling open the door, only to find the dark-haired estate agent from yesterday on the threshold, with two coffees and a pink box from Cornish Born and Bread, wearing a dazzling smile. Gone is the suit, replaced by a pair of jeans and a blue and grey check shirt. I had almost failed to recognise him without his suit. But as long as he's here to apologise, I can put up with him. Just about.

'Morning!' he says cheerfully. 'I thought we could start on a clean slate and a good cup of coffee.'

'Casual Friday started early this week,' I comment.

'Or not,' he murmurs as he offers me a cup and wipes his shoes on the outdoor mat. 'But please – don't look *too* happy to see me, you're embarrassing me with all that warmth.'

'I haven't got time for warmth,' I say, steering him towards the living room. 'Tell me why you're here again?'

'Work.'

I groan. Again with the house sale! 'Listen, I haven't got time to argue with you again. I've got a meeting in exactly four minutes with my joiner and you're in the way, so you can go and eat your breakfast in here – enjoy – and don't make any noise! We'll talk later.'

'No problem, I've got a few pieces to finish.'

Make that three minutes now. I go back into Gabe's office, shuffle a few stacks of receipts in an effort to calm down, but it's not working. The thought of the beach house being sold gives me hives. I wait another ten minutes, checking my mobile over and over. He's obviously not coming.

The doorbell rings again and this time it is Thea, Gothic biker chick/my PA extraordinaire. She is as smart as hell and could run a country on her own given the chance. Underneath all that make-up, she is absolutely beautiful, her Italian origins shining through her dark eyes and olive skin. She is as confident as can be, but it doesn't come from the knowledge of her beauty, which at times I think she is trying to hide.

Behind her is the rest of my full-time, core crew who are always early and never a second late, which today is a particularly good thing.

I don't know what I'd do without them all – Rudy, my PR/tech/payroll guy, eternally in love with Thea; or my muscle men Bob, Bill, Mike and Paul, respectively my plumber, my electrician, my builder and my gas guy. All of them are local, living in the surrounding villages of Little Kettering, Penworth Ford, Wyllow Cove and Starry Cove. Only Thea and Rudy live below in the village of Perrancombe. We are working on six different projects at the moment, but with them I'm always in good hands.

'Morning, folks,' I chime. 'Come in and please try not to have a heart attack.'

They follow me in, six mouths dropping in awe as they take in the place that they haven't seen since before Vanessa took over.

'Bloody 'ell,' Mike exclaims. 'It looks like a mad circus in here.'

'Blimey – I saw the pictures on her website – but it looks even worse in person,' Thea says in anguish. Believe me, when you read anguish on Thea's normally cool face, it's serious.

I lead them into Gabe's personal office, which is right next door to his music room (I've got one hell of a commute, haven't I?) and which will be our boardroom. Here, his mahogany table has been replaced with a glass table that has been covered with no less than a layer of resin in which a gazillion insects have been set. After a moment of disgust, they (my crew, not the insects) look up to the ceiling and begin to snicker at the Japanese anime-shaped chandeliers.

Thea, whose eyes bulge at the gold-plated rhinoceros in the corner by the window, sits down opposite me, now in work mode, pen poised to take notes without a further word. Good girl.

'So, uhm this is why we're here today. Gabe has asked me to renovate the house and take it back to exactly how it used to be.'

Six sets of eyes criss-cross around the table in search of help.

'Are you back together again, then?' Bill, the oldest with his shock of white hair and black moustache, asks, folding his arms.

'Not in a manner of speaking,' I reply, fully aware that he, Bob, Mike and Paul were never Gabe's most dedicated fans while Thea and Rudy thought he was the coolest of the cool. They're like bloodhounds, my peeps, always ready to pounce on anyone who wants to shaft me, from rude furnishers to unprofessional tradesmen. Thanks to them and their contacts, I now only work with the best of the best. Although I'm rather disappointed by Turner & Cooke who still have not, as of yet, either showed or even called to let me know they're running late. Not a good start. Still, Turner & Cooke is Turner & Cooke. So I decide to give them the benefit of the doubt. I always give people a second chance. And I wish my crew, whom I regard as part of my chosen family, would do the same with Gabe.

'Maybe some time in the future.'

More stunned silence follows. I roll my eyes. 'Guys – I know what you're all thinking, but I need you on my side. Okay?'

'We're just lookin' out fer ya, Faith,' Bill says with a shrug.

'And I love you all to pieces for it. Truly, I do. But I'd really appreciate your support.'

Another silent criss-crossing of eyes around the table, and then six heads nod, the downturned mouths and creased foreheads slowly shifting back into place for my sake.

'Brilliant, thank you. Now – to business. I have the keys to a storage room in Porthleven where all our stuff is, so down to the last tea towel, we're going to bring this house back to exactly as it was before—' *before Gabe dumped me* are the words that hang in the air, unsaid.

'He'd better behave this time,' Bill finally says, followed

by Mike, Bob and Paul who nod vigorously, while Rudy and Thea turn to me with apologetic smiles. I know they had been fans of Gabe and were disappointed when we broke up.

'It's going to be one hell of a job, so I'm depending on you lot completely.'

'Okay,' Mike says, listening and resting his hairy forearms on the table that reflects his kind but weather-beaten face. 'So what's the plan?'

I lean forward in my chair. 'We need to book a huge storage unit for everything here at the moment. It all has to go – every single piece.'

'Why not throw it all into one huge skip?' Rudy suggests roughly.

'Because we simply don't do things like that,' I answer. Although, deep inside, I know exactly where I would shove all of Vanessa's precious herd of animals. 'This is a business. The client is entitled to have her belongings back.'

Mike snorts. 'Client. The cheek of her.'

'Well, like it or not, we're doing things by the book. And, guys – not a scratch on anything that belongs to her, okay?'

'So I can't accidentally behead any of her jungle statues?' Paul wants to know.

'No, you cannot. Please tell the movers I want everything wrapped up and moved out carefully, as if they were our own belongings.'

'Right,' Mike sighs.

And that is why we work so well together. We are a truly tight team and we all pitch in. When Bill our electrician is in charge, we all become his workers on the bigger jobs, and Bob's when he's in charge, et cetera.

'I'm on it,' Thea says, taking notes. 'Ten large rolls of extra-strength bubble wrap to start with.'

'It'll take a couple of days to get rid of all Vanessa's – I mean – the contents of the house,' Rudy says as Thea gives him the hairy eyeball, which he returns with a *What did I say?* face.

'Okay, brilliant,' I say.

'So, Thea, we'll set up our work quarters in here for now until there's room – and breathing space – for a couple of desks to work from. I'll camp out in the music room for now. Whatever you need, you let me know. We'll order breakfasts and lunches in and set up in the dining room. And oh – the master bedroom will be the first room to go.'

I figure I can live with a couple of ebony panthers for a week or so. Or, I could actually get rid of them myself. There would be a lot of satisfaction in that for sure.

'Right, let's get started,' I say and everyone gets to their feet.

There is a knock on the pocket door that slides open and whatshisface – Harry – pokes his head in. 'Hi,' he says in my crew's direction. 'Sorry, Faith, can I have a minute when you're done or are you expecting someone else?'

'Come in,' I sigh. 'Guys, this is Harry – a, uhm, *friend* of Gabe's.' I hope he's noticed the sarcasm in my voice. If he thinks that he and his mate can sell our home, he's got another think coming.

'It's Henry, actually,' he says good-naturedly.

'Right,' I say, crossing my arms in front of my chest as Thea and Rudy smile at him while my trade mob give him the once-over. Anyone connected to Gabe does not go down well with them.

Bill dips his head, immediately reciprocated by an amused Henry. No words are wasted, which is fine by me. The less time this bloke stays, the quicker we can get on with our work without anyone in the way.

'Right, guys,' I say with a clap of my hands. 'Time to get moving. We'll all report back here for lunch. Rudy will pick it up as usual.'

Henry waits as my mob clear the room. 'Tough crowd,' he says. 'Thanks for finding time for me.'

'Only because my new kitchen guy is late. What can I do for you?'

'Actually, he's not late. He was early. He even brought you breakfast.'

I look up at him as my face suddenly goes hot. 'You…?'

'Uh-huh,' he says sheepishly.

'But… aren't you the estate agent?'

'No. I'm your joiner. Travis is the agent. And FYI, he'll be popping round at some time.'

'Okay, uhm, Henry? I'm sure you're a very nice bloke, but it's time to make things clear here. The house is not for sale.'

His mouth opens and then snaps shut, his nose evidently put out of joint.

I nod. 'I see we understand each other.'

'Oh, I certainly understand,' he assures me.

'Good. And by the way, that table that you delivered? It needs sanding down badly.'

'I'm sorry you don't like it. Shall I take it away?'

Jesus, can I be any ruder? But it's out now and I can't take it back, nor have I anywhere to hide it. 'No, that's okay, thank you.'

'In any case, it's not finished yet. I've brought my tools with me and will be working out on the back deck every day. Or have you got a problem with that as well?'

I literally feel my eyebrows disappearing into my hairline. 'Every day?'

Something akin to amusement flashes through his eyes. But there is nothing funny about this in the least.

'Every day,' he assures me.

'Why don't you just do it in your workplace? It's busy here, as you can see.'

'Because I am redoing the wainscoting as well, am I not?'

Crikey, I'd forgotten that. Where is my head? I stare him down, hoping he doesn't realise my mistake. In this business, show a moment of weakness and hunting season opens. 'Yes, of course. Fine.'

'When you're ready to discuss the kitchen, I'll be out back.'

And with that, he turns and disappears out the front door. Absolutely sodding brilliant.

As I start on my spreadsheets, I can hear everyone already packing up Vanessa's stuff amidst cackles of laughter.

I wipe the desk down, trying to ignore the dead insects staring up at me, but there's no use, I'm too freaked out, so I go and fetch an oil cloth to cover it. Better. I open the window wide to the view of the sea and adjust my chair to make calls to my contacts. It's always exciting, at the beginning of a new job. Everything is fresh and you haven't even begun to wear down the furnishers and everyone involved in the job. I've got so much to do, like sourcing out new tiling, light switch plates, and even internal doors that have been replaced with this tat. And I have to discuss the new kitchen with Harry… Henry.

But I can't concentrate. With a huff, I push my chair back and go in search of Henry who is sanding away on the deck.

There's a lot of sawdust blowing around and the noise of the sander is incredibly loud. Henry is wearing goggles and doesn't see me, so I wait patiently by the patio doors as I have learnt to never startle someone with a power tool.

When he finally looks up, he turns the sander off and removes his goggles. But the animosity I expected and deserve is not there.

I clear my throat. 'I'm, uhm, sorry about earlier. Why didn't you tell me you were the joiner?'

'You didn't give me a chance.'

'Well, again, I'm sorry. I was really out of line. And the table – it *is* truly lovely. I didn't realise it wasn't finished.' Which is another faux pas on my part, of course. He must think I'm a fool.

'That's quite all right,' he says amiably. 'I meet lots of arrogant people in my line of business.'

I stare at him, waiting for him to smile and say he was joking, but he doesn't. Apparently I've made a real arse out of myself.

'I'm kidding!' he says with a huge grin.

'Oh!' I breathe. 'Right!'

'And, for the record,' he adds, 'the reason you never came across me is because Isaac does the PR part.'

'I know Isaac Cooke. He's a good man. So you must be the Turner part?'

He smiles, like you do to idiots. 'I'm the Turner part.'

Of course he would be. Oh, shit. He really is. Turner &

Cooke. Which is *the* name in kitchens. And I've made a complete arse of myself. 'I love your company.'

He dips his head graciously. 'Thanks. We like it too.'

'I'm sorry. I had no idea. When you came in with that couple—'

'Trixie and Bopper?'

'Yes – I just assumed you were both estate agents.'

'I'm not. But they *are* very interested in buying the house.'

I flinch as the mere thought repels me. 'Well, I'll leave it with you and Travis to clear that misunderstanding up with them,' I conclude.

He blinks, probably wondering how the hell he's going to get them off his back. 'Right.' He runs a hand through his dark hair. 'So, are you going to make this house liveable again?' he asks.

'Absolutely, I am.'

'Brilliant.'

We spend the next hour or so discussing the style of kitchen I have in mind and going through the scrapbook I'd collated years ago before we'd even seen the beach house. The one I like is a normal shaker kitchen but extremely well made, with two ovens, a grill, a microwave, a pop-up socket tower, a heating drawer and many, many small, personal details that make all the difference.

'Are we on the same page?' I ask him as his fingers caress the old crinkly paper of my scrapbook of dreams.

'I'd say so. This is one of ours.'

'I'm sorry?'

'I built the original one, too.'

I sit back and look at him. 'I've been doing this for years. How is it that our paths have never crossed before?'

He shrugs. 'I told you, Isaac mainly does the PR; I do the physical labour. And besides, your original kitchen was already in when the... previous owner moved in.'

My mobile rings. It's Gabe. 'Excuse me,' I say as I go into the boardroom for some privacy to take the video call.

'Hey, Babes!' he chimes, a smile on his face so huge it barely fits the screen of my phone and my heart leaps at the sight of him.

'Hey, yourself,' I answer, my eyes hungrily taking in every detail of him – the high forehead, the piercing blue eyes and the sexy mouth. Today he's wearing a Sex Pistols T-shirt.

'How's it going?' he says, peering into the screen. 'You look tired. Are you all right?'

'Yes,' I assure him above the din of my staff throwing ideas (and Vanessa's stuff) around.

'Jesus, it sounds like a full-on war site there.'

'It is,' I agree. 'It's ghastly work already. Speaking of ghastly, I've sorted your friend out.'

'Who, Henry?'

'That's the one. He won't be bringing any more prospective buyers around here.'

He chuckles. 'Did you read him the riot act?'

'That I did.'

'Right. Well, it looks like you're on top of everything.'

I roll my eyes. 'As if. But I can assure you it'll be great.'

'I know it will be. But, Faith, all that matters is that I have a chance to win you back. Nothing else is important to me,' he assures me as his band members pass by in the background, sticking out their tongues and pulling his hair.

'Hiya, gawjus!' Stu, Gabe's drummer, calls out to me.

'Hi, guys!' I call back, but they're gone.

'Babes, some news,' Gabe says. 'Mark's broken his arm.'

'Oh, no! Is he okay?'

'Yeah, yeah. The poor sod walked off the stage during his solo last night and is lucky to be alive. But a few dates have been postponed, so I'll be coming home for a few days sooner than I thought.'

'Oh my God, really? Will you text me your flight details?'

'Not on your life! I want it to be a surprise,' he says. 'Gotta go now, luv!' he calls, blowing me kisses.

'Oh, wait, Gabe, I—'

But his image winks off, and I'm staring into black space as a feeling of emptiness invades me. No matter. A little while longer and he'll be home, even if only for a few days.

It might take a little getting used to again, with his hectic schedules, the manic, unsustainable rhythms he has to keep that drove me bonkers. And then I ask myself for the umpteenth time: Can I do it all over again, not see him for days, sometimes weeks and even months on end, only to have him back in my life as things used to be?

A knock comes at the door and Henry pokes his head in.

'Sorry, Faith? Shall we have a walk-around with the rest of the team to see exactly what we're doing?'

I look up. 'What? Sorry, yes, of course,' I say, rising to my feet to join him and my crew.

Once everything is packed up and after the master bedroom is done, one of the first things on the list will be to renovate one of the guest bathrooms, which has chequered gamboge wallpaper. If you think that's distasteful, it's because you haven't seen the vinyl border featuring unicorns. Still not enough? They are sporting punk-rock-style hairdos (or mane-dos) and tattoos.

'What the hell was she *thinking*?' Rudy groans, shaking his head as we survey the damage up close.

'Isn't it obvious?' Thea answers. 'She was planning on drowning Gabe in her psychedelic zoo – and of course, debt.'

'How the hell does she even *stay* in business?' Rudy says, voicing my own thoughts.

'There's always a sufficient amount of wealthy chavs to keep her going,' Thea answers, and I can't help but agree.

'Right,' I say, climbing atop the bidet and then the sink to reach the ceiling. 'There's nothing to salvage here, so let's get on with ripping this crap out. Somewhere under here should be the wooden cladding.'

I give it a good yank, but nothing happens, so I try again.

'Maybe we should steam it first?' Thea suggests.

'Here,' Henry says, and in one swing of his mighty legs he jumps up onto the sink next to me. 'Let me have a go.'

He pulls out a Stanley knife from his back pocket and slits the edge open, then easily pulls some off in one long draw as Thea and Rudy below collect the slack.

'It will need to be steamed indeed,' he sentences.

'Hang on,' I say, scratching at a corner, only to reveal another design of multi-coloured rows of electric guitars, but there is only one strip as if someone had changed their mind.

'Looks like Gabe lost *that* argument,' Thea says with a snicker.

I ignore her comment. Anything to do with Vanessa and Gabe's past relationship is theirs; I don't want to be reminded of it. And once Vanessa's imprint is gone from our home, it will, hopefully, be gone from our minds. It's all I can hope for in order to get a clean start.

'Get Mike and Bill to steam this up and start scraping this mess off,' I say to Thea. 'The cladding must be under all that. Let's check the master en-suite bathroom.'

Which, instead of the gorgeous white and grey-veined marble I had sourced straight from Carrara, Italy, turns out to be a palimpsest of every composite material man has ever put together, from Bakelite to satin to, believe it or not, pleather.

'Oh my God,' Henry says, stepping back to take in the entire scene, then turning to look at me in shock. 'I always thought her stuff was a bit OTT, but this... this is beyond all my wildest expectations.'

'That's nothing,' Thea says, pulling back the satin shower curtain to reveal a huge wet room with a leather swing.

I gasp involuntarily and instantly feel my face burning as everyone tries not to look at me. Yes, okay, I know it's not a normal swing, and the thought of Vanessa and Gabe having their fun in this very bathroom that had once had a claw-footed, cast-iron bathtub (where Gabe and I had started – or ended – many a happy night) is too much to bear.

It looks like what for me had been happy nights were merely a vanilla version of what makes him happy. I had no idea he'd wanted more. But he'd felt comfortable telling Vanessa. Or maybe it was all her idea. So much for knowing your partner.

Maybe I'm not the right person to do this. Maybe I should not be here for the demolition. Maybe I should leave it all to my team and just come back when all traces of Vanessa and her sex life with Gabe are gone. Because it feels much too intimate to wander around the ruins of someone else's relationship, even if it's over.

The areas of our love are still a little grey as far as I'm

concerned. But I just can't bring myself to talk to Gabe about her. I figure that the less I know, the better it is. But the sex swing is the proverbial pink elephant in the room that is very difficult to ignore.

Henry glances at me furtively, then takes my elbow. 'Actually, Faith, if you wouldn't mind, can you just walk me around the other rooms to where you want the wainscoting reinstated?'

Grateful for the rescue, I lift my head high. 'Absolutely.' There was nothing to salvage here, much less my dignity.

'You all right?' he whispers as we go down the stairs together.

I huff and square my shoulders. 'Tickety-boo, thank you.'

'If it's any consolation, you're far better than her,' Henry offers generously.

I bite my lip. 'That's very kind of you, Henry, but you don't have to cheer me up. I'm not the jealous type.' Too much information?

Once in the living room, I make a dash for the pleather stick-on panels that have covered the wainscoting. But when I peel one off, there is only bare wall. Henry eyes me, and peels back another strip, closer to the door. Still no wainscoting to be seen. We then try the dining room and a guest bedroom. Still nothing.

'It's all gone,' I moan, trying to hold it together but not doing a very good job of it. 'All that beautiful, *beautiful* workmanship...'

'Okay, don't panic,' Henry whispers, rubbing both hands over his face. As a joiner himself, he is aware of the extent of the damage that has been done to the house. 'We can still fix this.'

'How?' I almost wail. 'How can you fix what's no longer there?'

He chews on his lower lip, obviously in deep thought. 'Maybe the builders sent them to the local reclamation yard. Anyone who knows the trade would not have discarded such a valuable item, I'm sure.'

'And what if they have?' I insist.

'We'll find a way, I promise you.'

'It all has to be exactly the same...' I say, close to tears. 'I promised Gabe everything would be exactly the same as... *before*...'

'Forgive me, but if someone should be keeping promises, it's him.'

I look up at him through misty eyes. 'I beg your pardon?' He knew about the split? Of course he did, they were friends.

'Faith – I know. Sorry, maybe I should have mentioned it earlier.'

I take a deep breath to recollect myself. Why does it still hurt, even now that Gabe wants me back? Why does the humiliation feel like it will always be there, waiting in the wings? Once again, I am not like my mother. I can move on.

'It's okay,' I say, dragging an index under my eyes. 'It was all in the bloody papers. *Rock star leaves fiancée to shack up with the punk mistress of Interior Design: Vanessa Chatsbury*. I had to lie low for weeks to avoid the pity parties. Ugh, sorry.'

He smiles. 'It's okay. Break-ups are always bad. I'm divorced myself.'

'Really? I'm sorry.'

'Thanks. It's not so bad anymore. I was too busy building the business. But my son is the one who paid the price, and now I'm trying to make it up to him. No easy feat, as you can imagine.'

'Well, at least you didn't abandon him or anything. As long as you do your best, and you're there for him, he'll eventually understand.'

At least I know I would have. But all Hope and I have are a faceless father and a dead mother.

'Yes, well. Right,' he says, changing the subject and clapping his hands together in a *Let's get to it* gesture. 'Let's peel all of this off and see exactly what we're dealing with.'

'I can get someone else to help,' I say. 'It's not on your job description, and I'm sure you've got better things to do rather than peel pleather off walls.'

'I'm happy to help,' he says simply.

Which is crazy-generous. He's a very busy joiner. And a father. How does he find the time to waste? Perhaps I've been a bit too hasty in judging him? 'Okay,' I answer. 'Thank you.'

We spend the next few hours on our knees, working in silence, until he leans back on his haunches, hands on his thighs, and hastily puts the strip he's just removed back into place.

'What have you got there?' I ask, straightening my aching back and moving towards him.

'Nothing,' he says guiltily, leaning on the wall to hide whatever he's unearthed.

'Let me see,' I say, brushing past him.

It can't be any worse than the sex swing in the loo.

Or so I thought. Because there, wedged in between two strips of pleather, obviously fallen through a gap of the shoddy workmanship, is a snapshot – a selfie of Gabe and

Vanessa, taken from their bed, both with blond hair standing wildly on end. Our former bed. They are both bare-chested and she is raking her silver nails across his belly, sticking her pierced tongue out at the camera.

'It's just a silly selfie,' Henry says. 'Besides, it's all in the past.'

'Yes, of course,' I agree as the boulders begin to pile up inside my throat. I believe that before these renos I might have needed an emotional rehaul. 'No biggie.'

He clears his throat as he scrunches the picture up and throws it onto a pile of debris in the corner. 'Fancy a cuppa?' he asks.

It's a lame attempt to distract me, but I can't help but be grateful.

'I'll make it,' I volunteer and traipse with false light-heartedness across the room and to the kitchen, acutely aware of his eyes on my back as he follows me, probably wondering whether I'm going to have a bawling session or not.

I put the kettle on and open the cupboard. There, I notice a mug that says *Vanessa*. Reaching past it, I inadvertently (honestly) brush against it, and it crashes down to the counter in a million pieces as if it were thin glass. Too bad. If it had landed on the fur flooring, it might have saved itself. This is the first object to go into the skip of *Goodbye, Vanessa*.

4

Missing You

It's night-time and I'm dreaming that it is the summer. I am lying on a tropical beach somewhere in the Caribbean. There are palm trees everywhere, but my eyes are closed and I can only hear the fronds gently swishing in the wind against the sound of the surf.

Gabe is lying next to me, raining tiny kisses on my face, his hands lovingly running over my body. 'Babes,' he whispers in my ear. 'I want you.'

This is bliss. My whole life is back on track. 'I want you too, Gabe,' I murmur. To hell with taking my time.

'Then tell me you forgive me.'

'I forgive you,' I assure him, already anticipating the happier times ahead.

'Open your eyes.'

Torn between the need to sleep after all that love-making and the need for more, I groan and roll over.

'I'm too sleepy,' I confess and he laughs.

'This ought to wake you,' he says and kisses me deeply.

I wrap my arms around him.

'Faith, open your eyes.'

'They're open,' I assure him.

He laughs. 'Come on, open them.'

And that is when I wake up.

Only to find Gabe sitting on the edge of the settee, his hand on my hip.

I jump to my knees with a shriek, something between surprise and joy. 'Gabe! What are you doing here!'

He grins as he leans in to kiss me. 'I came back to see my Babes.'

I hang on to him despite myself, then remember where we're at and move away. 'You've, uhm, lost weight,' I observe.

He laughs. 'Is that all you can say?'

'How… why didn't you tell me when you were coming? How long are you staying? When did you get here?'

'Easy, easy, one question at a time, Babes. I got here five minutes ago. I wanted to let you sleep, but I just couldn't wait to see the look on your face.'

I rub my knuckles over my eyes, trying to get rid of the sleep. 'I must look like shit,' I mutter.

'Nuh-uh. You look amazing as always, and I've never loved you more.' He takes my hand and draws me back to a sitting position. 'Thank you for forgiving me, Babes. I don't know what I'd have done otherwise.'

'Look, Gabe, I'm happy you're here,' I assure him. 'But I need t-time. I can't just slip right back into a relationship like nothing happened.'

'I know, Babes. I get it – no pressure. I'm only staying a few hours anyway. I've got to catch a flight back tonight.

I get out of bed and straighten my nightie. 'You came all this way, just for me?'

He yawns. 'Sorry, jet lag. Just for you.'

I run a hand through the rat's nest that is my hair. I need a shower like I need my next breath. 'Tell you what, Gabe. You crash here – the other bedrooms are non-existent at the moment – and when you wake up I'll have breakfast ready.'

'I don't want to sleep, I want to spend every minute with you,' he insists.

'Okay, then. Just let me take a quick shower and I'll be right back.'

He lies back on the settee and gives me a thumbs-up, his eyes already closed.

Grinning to myself, I jump in and out of the shower and get dressed before I pad barefoot to the kitchen to prep a blueberry pancake batter and brew a pot of coffee.

I can't believe he's come all this way just for me! He truly does love me. There is such a thing as a happy ending after all. And maybe... I shouldn't ask for more. He's back, he wants me back. End of. *Stop questioning everything*, I tell myself. Just... sit back and enjoy the few good things in life. It's not like this happens to everybody every day, right?

'Sorry about that.' His voice comes from the threshold where he stops to take in the kitchen. His hair is sticking out in every direction and I love him more than ever. 'Man – I forgot how kitsch this place was.'

I giggle. 'You didn't take a tour of the house?'

He pulls me into his embrace, his face still wrinkled by the sheets. 'Why would I waste time looking at a horror house when I've got you to look at?'

I can feel my face burning. After all this time, he still has this effect on me. It feels so strange to be with him under the same roof again. I naturally make no mention of the sex swing in the wet room, nor the bare-chested picture Henry found behind the pleather cladding. I want to put all of that behind me now. I have to, for my own sanity, and for a fresh start.

'When was the last time you ate? You must be starved,' I say to change the subject as I turn the cooker on.

'I am,' he assures me as he comes up behind me and nuzzles my neck, his body pressing into mine, if you know what I mean. But I laugh, pretending I don't.

'Have a seat. Your favourite is coming right up.'

'Blueberry pancakes? Man, you are *da best* girlfriend a bloke could ever have.'

I glance at him as I'm about to pour and he coughs, embarrassed. 'I'm going to make it up to you in a million ways,' he promises me. 'I've even started writing a song about it. Title is, of course, "A Million Ways".'

'You don't have to do that,' I say.

'I do. I want the whole world to know what a tosser I've been.'

'I'd rather you kept our relationship private from now on, Gabe,' I whisper as I pour the batter into separate pancakes that hiss as they quickly solidify. Perhaps we are just like this batter. Perhaps we, too, can be whipped to a froth, and then make it back together again, even if it will take some time. I do believe it.

'So we still have a relationship?' he says softly, caressing my arm. 'Can I hope you will take me back?'

I flip the pancakes over, one by one. How many women have forgiven their men for cheating, and have gone on to be perfectly happy? Lots and lots. I love Gabe, and living without him has been pure hell. I dish up the pancakes and smother them in maple syrup and add a dollop of whipped cream.

'I'm willing to give it a go,' I say nonchalantly, while inside I'm literally begging him. *Please please please, don't hurt me again. I couldn't bear it.*

He exhales as if he'd been holding his breath for years and pulls me into his arms. 'Thank you, love of my life. I swear you won't regret it.'

I laugh, holding on to him with one arm, the plate of pancakes in the other. He takes it from me.

'Here, sit down, Babes,' he says, sitting opposite me and cutting off a huge bit. 'Open that lovely mouth.'

I obey and take the forkful. Not bad at all, for someone who can't cook.

He takes a bite for himself and then feeds me the next one, and we continue like this until all the pancakes are gone.

'This is how it's going to be from now on, Faith,' he promises. 'Together, forever...'

'That song already exists,' I quip, trying to hide my emotions welling up through my eyeballs.

He reaches for the whipped cream and grins naughtily. 'The only music I'll be making today is with you and this whipped cream. Think of all the babies we can make!'

'Cheesy!' I say, rolling my eyes. 'But doable.'

His eyes are studying my face. 'Yeah...? Babies and all?'

A family of my own, with the man I love? It's all I've ever wanted. But... so soon? And then that voice inside me reminds me to stop asking so many questions. Maybe, just maybe, things are finally looking up.

I smile shyly. 'Maybe. Yes.'

'Cool,' he says, lifting me off the chair and heading for the music room.

Later that afternoon, I wake to the soft sound of my name. He is sitting on the edge of the settee, his hand on my hip.

'Hey,' I murmur, propping myself up onto my elbow.

'Sorry – I wanted to let you sleep as long as possible,' he says.

'You shouldn't have. What time are you leaving?'

'My taxi is due in the next ten minutes.'

Crap, just as I was beginning to enjoy my new life. 'Oh. Okay. Do you need anything?'

'Only you,' he says, and he pulls me into his arms and kisses me at length. It feels so good to be back in those familiar, beloved arms.

'When I get back, I'm going to take some time off, Faith. We'll go off somewhere for a long vacation, just you and me. How does that sound?'

'Like heaven,' I murmur, wrapping my arms around his neck.

A horn honks in the front drive.

'That's my bloody taxi,' he groans, getting to his feet.

'That was a very short ten minutes. Right,' I say, feeling like the world is once again falling on top of me. But this time it's different. This time I have Gabe. And he'll be back after his tour. 'Let me just get up…'

'Please stay,' he whispers, kissing me on the lips. 'I'm

going to come back every time I can. Today is the beginning of the rest of our lives.'

Once again, I want to say *Cheesy*, but he's right. Today has been monumental.

He takes my face in his hands. 'Babes… I love you.'

'I love you, too, Gabe.' I can hardly believe this is reality.

'Hopefully we've started a family already,' he says and I laugh.

'Highly unlikely. But who knows?'

'Better get started on that nursery, then…' he quips and kisses me again, and then groans as the taxi driver honks his horn once more, more impatiently this time.

'I'll call you every day, Babes,' he says as he backs out of the room and through the front door.

I lie back in bed, my arms behind my head as I relive the past few hours. He really does still love me.

The sun is beginning to set. I pull on my robe, retrieve my sketch pad and sit out in one of the deckchairs. Before I know it I am mentally going through the various nursery solutions for ideas. I've done this a million times before, albeit for other couples' babies. But this time it's for our baby. A child to love. Protect. Teach. Play with. Laugh with. Comfort. He or she will never, ever doubt our love for them, not even when they're grounded. They will feel secure, warm and happy. I know it's still too soon, but I can't wait.

If at first I hadn't even dared hope for such happiness, now I'm afraid to think that something so beautiful could be an option for us. But Gabe and I will be the best parents we can be. His own parents had divorced when he was little, his mum having moved to Singapore. His parents hadn't spoken to each other for years, which was the reason why I'd never met either of them. And I had never really had any role model either. As children, all Hope and I had ever wanted was to be loved.

What is more precious than love? I have that to give in spades. I don't hope for a boy or a girl particularly. I just want them to be healthy and happy, but also kind to others, especially those less fortunate.

My longing for a home is perhaps the reason why I became an interior designer. With every home I have worked on, I have always imagined a happy family, and perhaps even my own home with Gabe and our future family.

Looking out to sea, I begin to imagine the baby's nursery. It will be seeing plenty of changes over time, so better to plan and leave room for them.

I can almost see our child – or, why not, children – playing with their toys, and then gradually looking at their picture books and then proper books and maybe writing a diary full of wonderful and witty observations on their own young life, possibly while preparing their bags for university. And then my eyes mist up. Seriously? Our baby isn't even born yet and I'm already missing it?

Perhaps they will be, like Gabe, musically talented. Or perhaps they won't be able to carry a tune to save themselves, just like me. Perhaps they'll be obsessed with homes as I am, albeit for reasons differing from mine.

I only hope that this time it's all for real. But if I'm going to trust Gabe again completely, I have to really trust him. Right?

★

Early the next Saturday morning, I head out to babysit Jowen and Verity as Hope's had to go in to work the first shift at the restaurant.

It's been a good working week both on our other jobs and at the beach house. No arguments with Henry, nor injuries, if you don't count the internal ones of my heart and pride. Henry, who will be fronting all of the joinery aspects of the house, seems to have fit in with the others in the space of a few days, especially my muscle men who have already warmed to him, probably because of his outstanding work ethic. On the days he is working at the house, Henry is always the first one there and the last one to leave. They can see the quality of his workmanship and have begrudgingly lowered their barriers. I'm more of a slow burner. We might not get along like a house on fire on a personal level, but we do work well professionally, and that's what counts.

As the kids are still sleeping upstairs, I work on sewing their costumes for their World Monument night at school. It is a special evening that will take place in the assembly hall in a few months' time. Each student is to represent a specific landmark, natural or not. Verity has chosen the statue of the Fearless Girl in New York, while Jowen has decided to not stray from the vicinity and represent the Chrysler building.

I have been working on them for a few weeks now, collating images from every angle. Jowen's is easier as all I have to do is draw and sew a foam costume for him, whereas Verity's is more of a study in image. She'll have to wear bronze spray paint and have her hair and clothes done just right. But where my sister is an excellent chef, she's useless with a needle, so I'll be taking care of that for her.

At half past eight, I get up from the table to make them

breakfast as it's time to start their day. There are not to be any lazy bones in this family.

'Verity, Jowen, rise and shine!' I call as I slide the scrambled eggs onto two plates to complete a lovely Cornish breakfast, and draw a ketchup smile on each one. Outside it is a cold but sunny morning and I can't wait to get the kids out walking on the beach for some fresh air.

'Can we have breakfast in bed?' Jowen calls from his bedroom.

'Breakfast in bed is only for birthdays!' I call back. 'If you want to eat, you have to get up and come downstairs!'

There is an audible groan, but three seconds later there is a thump-rumble-thump on the stairs and they both appear in their pyjamas, sleepy-eyed but determined not to miss out.

'There you go,' I say as they hoist themselves up onto their breakfast stools, already brandishing their forks as if ready for battle.

'Did you sleep well?' I ask as I sit down opposite them with a cup of coffee.

'Jowen was talking in his sleep again,' Verity complains as she takes a bite of her buttered toast. 'I heard him through the wall.'

'Was not,' Jowen defends, shovelling eggs into his mouth.

'You were!' Verity assures him.

'Guys – pipe down. I've got a nice picnic packed for us today and if you behave yourselves you might even get an ice cream.'

'Ooh, yay!' Verity claps her hands. 'And can I feed the gulls?'

I lean over and gently tap the tip of her nose. 'Of course

you can, love. But I wouldn't get too friendly with them. They tend to take more than you've offered.'

'Okay, Auntie Fi,' she promises.

I watch them as they finish their breakfast, the two children I love more than my own life and who have kept me sane during the past few months. If it hadn't been for their cute faces, hugs and kisses and presents of chocolate, I don't know what I'd have done.

'Can I get a pasty instead, Auntie Faith?' Jowen wants to know.

'If you promise to always be nice to your sister from now on, you can have a pasty for dinner.'

'Is Mum working at the restaurant all day again today?' Verity asks as she spears a baked bean and pops it into her mouth.

'Yes, but she made me promise to take you there after lunch to say hello.'

'Cool,' Jowen says as he downs his orange juice. But they don't fool me. They miss her terribly, and I am grateful for the time I get to spend with them because before you know it, they'll be all grown up and too cool to hang out with old Auntie Fi.

After breakfast I take them to Perrancombe for a stroll around the harbour. Truro may be beautiful, but Perrancombe is the bee's knees. Or, as the kids and I used to say when they were little, the pasty's pants.

As we amble along the harbour with the sun on our faces, I become aware of a figure waving frantically at me. As the ray of light shifts, I see it is Mrs Trengrouse, the owner of our local wool shop, The Cat's Cradle. It is a tiny hole in the wall, really, but chock-full of wool of every colour you can imagine and I used to spend hours there while decorating the beach house.

'Faith! Hello! It's so nice to see you again. How have you been?'

'It's lovely to see you, too, Mrs Trengrouse! How are you?'

'I'm grand, just grand. We've missed you around here.'

'Yes, well, Gabe and I—'

'I know, pet,' she says, putting a hand on mine. 'The whole village was worried about you. And of course everyone was on Team Faith.'

I eye the kids who are inspecting a herd of elephants made out of grey yarn. 'Awh, thank you, that's so sweet, Mrs Trengrouse, but—'

She looks at me sceptically. 'What a stunt to pull on such a sweet girl like yourself! Better off without him, luv.'

I cough. 'Oh – uhm, well, Gabe are friends again.'

Her glasses fall off her nose like in the funnies, and I struggle to keep a straight face. 'Really? Are you sure that's what you want, pet?'

I involuntarily stiffen. Mrs Trengrouse is a lovely woman, and would never say anything to hurt my feelings, or anyone else's. 'We'll see, Mrs Trengrouse. It's early days yet. But thank you for looking out for me.'

She studies me briefly before squeezing my forearm. 'You need anything, luv, anything at all, just come and see me, do you hear?'

'Thank you, I will,' I promise.

She smiles warmly. 'Must pop upstairs now. Mr Trengrouse gets cranky when I don't feed him on time. If you need anything, take it and we'll sort it later. Take care, now!'

'You too,' I reply as, smiling to myself, I shove my hands into my pockets, close the door behind me with a soft jingle and we resume our ambling amidst tourists and patrons of the various shops along the harbour, from the local bakery, Cornish Born and Bread, to the pub, The Dolphin and Barrel.

Couples and families are wandering about, just enjoying the freedom of the weekend, pure joy on their faces. That's what Cornish landscapes do to you. They nourish your soul, slow down time, lift the burden off your shoulders, fill your lungs with fresh air and beckon you into their beauty, until you forget why you were so uptight and miserable in the first place.

I sit on a bench and watch as Jowen and Verity frolic in the sand, chasing the seagulls and each other without a care in the world. It is so good to see how well they are being brought up by Hope. Even through the divorce, she has managed to give them the stability they need. Who knew that she, a former wild child, would be such a hard-working and loving mother? I am so proud of her and how far she's come.

About an hour later, the kids and I stretch out on our picnic blanket and break out the goodies, i.e. all their favourite foods in miniature. Tiny meat pies, scotch eggs, pasties, chunks of cheese and tiny rolls. There's also their daily quota of fruit and veg that I have to literally force down their throats or Hope will kill me.

Tired by their morning of running around, they lean back and, for once, eat their food in companionable silence, looking out at the tiny boats bobbing up and down in the glistening sea that is ensconced within the boundaries of the circular breakwater. These high walls have protected the village from many a storm. Everything is so peaceful here that it seems literally impossible that anything bad could happen. I wish I'd grown up here. But for the kids, things will be better. I will make sure that Hope continues to have my unconditional support even throughout the next few hectic months.

On Monday afternoon, Henry comes in with a lovely surprise.

'Faith – this is my son Orson. Orson, say hello to Faith.'

Orson is a tiny version of Henry, with the same dark moppy hair and the dark eyes that glisten with mischief. And my auntie radar tells me he is adorable.

I smile, bending so that our faces are level. 'Hello, Orson. Nice to meet you!'

'Hello,' he says cheerfully.

'Orson is going to be coming to work with me for a few afternoons, if that's okay?'

'Of course, that will be fun!' I assure him. 'Orson, would you like a doughnut and some juice? We have lots in the kitchen.'

Orson looks up at his father. 'May I, Daddy?'

'Absolutely, son. You go ahead and help yourself. I have to speak to Faith. I'll be there in a minute.'

'Thank you, Daddy. And thank you, Faith,' he says.

'You're very welcome, Orson!'

Henry watches his little boy rush off, then turns to me with a sheepish grin.

'He's so sweet. And he looks happy, if I may say so.'

Henry grins. 'Yeah. He is now. Linda had done her best to break our bond, but I guess it's too strong even for her, thank God.'

'Exes can be very mean,' I observe without thinking. But it's true. 'Did she give you a hard time with custody?'

'Oh, yeah, she tried very hard to go for sole custody, but to no avail.'

I smile. 'Good. I bet you're a great father.'

He shrugs to hide the fact that he is obviously pleased at my compliment. 'Not so much in the past. Always busy. But I'm spending more and more time with him, which is all I really want.'

'Daddy! There's chocolate sprinkles, come!'

Henry's face lights up and I laugh as I follow him into the kitchen where Orson has perched himself upon a stool, his little legs dangling, his cute face covered in chocolate.

'Is it good, son?' Henry asks as he ruffles his hair.

'Hmmmh!' he answers, nodding vigorously.

I pour him a glass of orange juice and set it in front of him along with a napkin. 'Here, wash it down with this, Orson.'

'Thank you,' he says, reaching for the glass and taking a long gulp.

'Want to help me sand down a side table later?' Henry asks him and again, the little boy nods, his face lighting up.

'Orson's my favourite helper,' he explains to me. 'He's helped me build all kinds of furniture.'

'I want to be like Daddy when I grow up!' he says and I can't help but laugh again.

'I think you already are, Orson!' I say and his eyes widen. 'Do you think so?'

'I know so!' I assure him.

He wipes his darling little face with the napkin and slides off his stool to throw it in the bin.

'Can we start now?' he asks, rolling his sleeves up in a gesture I recognise as one of Henry's.

'Absolutely, Orson. It's out on the deck – it's a table that needs a *bit* more sanding.'

Henry eyes me good-naturedly and I roll my eyes, but my face is warm with shame.

'Let's get your gloves and your goggles on and you can show Faith what you're made of, buddy boy.'

And I watch them as Henry puts the protective gear on him, explaining what he needs to do, and as Orson nods, I can't help but feel my throat constrict. What greater joy than to have a child to love and cherish? If I had had an ounce of the paternal love I am seeing here, I would be a much more secure person. I want my own child one day to be just as confident, respectful and happy as Orson is. But our children will be just as happy.

'Daddy, like this?' Orson asks as he begins to sand the top of the table.

'Exactly, Orson! You're doing a great job!'

'Right, then,' I say and Henry looks up, his eyes scrutinising me. 'I'll leave you two masters to work!'

I go back to my desk and pull out my spreadsheets and try to re-examine the costs. Not that money is a problem for Gabe, but still.

That little boy is so adorable. I hate to think that he must have suffered during his parents' split. He is only around six or so, and yet, he has a soulfulness that I've never seen before in a child. I huff. Why must some children face such traumas, already being so fragile and helpless enough as they are?

'Hey,' comes Henry's voice from the door. 'Are you all right?'

I swivel around in my chair, feeling myself turning crimson. 'Oh! Yes, thank you.'

He continues to study me as he steps into my office.

I swear I can feel my eyes pricking, so I have to turn away again and take a deep breath.

He's standing behind me, not knowing what to do.

I clear my throat. 'Funny fact – I think I'm allergic to sawdust.'

'Oh. Right. Well, I'd better get back to Orson before he sands the table down to a toothpick.'

I laugh. 'Yes.'

'Okay. I'll see you later.'

'See you later, Henry.'

And he leaves without telling me why he'd come in.

I spend the rest of the day on the phone with my suppliers as the crew occasionally pop their heads in to take a breather from all the packing up. But all day, all I can think about is children.

'You all right in here?' Thea asks as she plops herself down next to me.

'Super all right,' I assure her.

'That Orson is cute, isn't he?'

'Yes, he is.'

'And he adores Henry, who is such a loving dad.'

'Indeed,' I agree, returning to my Excel sheets. Goodness me, why can I not snap out of it? So I still want a baby. And if we're lucky, we'll have one sooner rather than later.

*

At half past five, once everyone has gone, Henry calls me from the foyer. 'We're off, Faith.'

I jump to my feet, stuff my hands into my pockets and saunter out there, feeling much better than before, but still quite unsettled.

'Thank you for having me, Faith,' Orson says.

'Thank you for coming, Orson! Can you come back tomorrow?'

Orson turns to his father. 'Oh, can I, Daddy, please?'

Henry kneels to Orson, his face awash with happiness. 'Of course you can, son.'

Orson reaches out to hug his father who covers him in loud kisses. 'Who's Daddy's pride and joy?' he asks and Orson rolls his eyes.

'That's an easy question,' he answers. 'I am! You tell me all the time, Daddy!'

'And don't you ever forget it.'

'I wo-on't,' he sing-songs and turns at the door. 'Bye, Faith, see you tomorrow!'

'See you tomorrow, Orson!' I call as Henry turns back and I have a feeling that when he came in, presumably to check on me, for a fleeting moment, he had read me through and through. I close the door behind them and now alone, I grab a cup of tea and sit out on the deck, wrapping up in a throw that I'd salvaged from the storage unit and given a thorough wash.

Tonight, the sun is a huge crimson ball. It is so close it seems I may be just about able to touch it if I reach out. And yet, it is so fleeting and precious, I wish I could hide it forever in my keepsake box just to enjoy it whenever I'm feeling down, or simply wrap it up as a gift to a friend who is having a hard day. It's true that the most beautiful moments are the fleeting ones.

I truly believe that being in magical Cornwall during this tough time has not only boosted my mood, but it has, along with my closest and dearest, kept me going. Cornwall is a reason for living.

All I have to do is go for a walk on the beach, or go for a drive in the countryside and just absorb its beauty, let it soothe all my senses and slowly, day by day, heal me. There is no place on earth like Cornwall, and I feel privileged to be here.

I shield my hand and look out to sea. Its sluggish, thick waves are lapping at the shore like generous dollops of honey poured onto a golden biscuit. I hug myself, slightly shivering against the rising breeze. It will be good to fall asleep to the sound of the waves collapsing onto the sand.

But in the middle of the night, thunder cracks the sky and lightning flashes throughout the house. I jump to my feet and, barefoot, run around the house, drawing all of the shutters closed, just in time to beat the onslaught of a pelting rainstorm. I get back onto the settee that has lost the warmth of slumber.

I wish Gabe were here.

5

Wish You Were Here

The next morning I get the strangest of calls from a woman interested in buying our home. Obviously Henry hasn't sorted Travis out yet despite my request.

'I'm sorry, but there has been a huge misunderstanding. The beach house is not for sale,' I inform her.

'Not for sale? But – I was making plans. I even called my daughter in Australia to tell her about it...' Her voice peters off, and I can only sympathise with her.

'I'm truly very, very sorry, madam. But the owners aren't selling it anymore.'

Silence. 'Oh.'

'I'm very sorry,' I repeat for the third time, only I shouldn't be the one apologising. Imagine that Travis bloke causing this poor woman such distress. I thought it had been sorted.

'Okay – thank you,' she whispers, sniffing. 'You're very kind. It's a good thing I hadn't put in a down payment.'

'I'm sure the owners would have repaid it,' I say. There is no amount of money that I would ever take for our home.

'Thank you. With whom do I have the pleasure of speaking?' she asks.

'My name is Faith Hudson. I'm the interior designer doing some work here.'

'Right. Well, thank you once again.'

'You're very welcome,' I say and ring off.

I'm going to have to have another word with Henry. And there was me thinking we'd turned a corner. He may be a great joiner, but he's hopeless at public relations.

Later that day I'm having lunch at The One That Got Away with my coastal girls, i.e. my friends Rosie, Nina and Nat. They live in neighbouring hamlets along the coast and have all had pretty much their own hell to go through before finding their happy ending.

Nina Conte, who lives in Penworth Ford, is a very talented novelist who's had her share of woes. She and her husband had moved down from London and bought an old place to renovate. Only her husband had up and left them shortly after, taking all their money as well. She says that if it hadn't been for her neighbours and friends, she would have capitulated, but I don't think so. She is the strongest woman I know. Her daughter Chloe is a handful, but Ben, her youngest is a Mummy whisperer.

Rosie from Little Kettering, on the other hand, doesn't look like she can stand up for herself, but my goodness, when she opens her mouth, you know who wears the pants in her home. But she wasn't always like this. She was a London hotel assistant manager who hated everything about her job, particularly her nasty boss who'd sent her here over the Christmas holidays to investigate a hotel. Her son Danny is the sweetest child you'll ever meet.

And Nat? She's a star. She lives in Wyllow Cove and is the oldest of us all, but you wouldn't think so as she is the bubbliest and the most fun. For years she let her husband treat her like dirt, and then one day, just as everything seemed to crash down onto her head, she just took the proverbial bull by the horns and said enough was enough. Today she is one of the happiest women I know.

'Thanks, Faith, for agreeing to help me out. I don't know what I would have done without you,' Nat says as we sit down around a table facing the sea. 'It's exactly what I wanted but I couldn't seem to put it all together by myself. I was so used to Neil dictating the décor that I was stumped.'

'Well, it wasn't that difficult, really, because you've got the sea, so I used paler hues just to soften your interiors a bit – duck egg rather than a bright blue, cream rather than white and so on, just to add a bit of warmth.'

'Yes, and it worked like a charm,' she says. 'A bit like your beach house. I suppose you've missed it as much as you did Gabe, didn't you?'

The wisdom in her eyes tells me that she knows me well. I nod. 'It was my very first real home.'

She squeezes my hand. 'I'm glad things worked out, Faith. You deserve every good thing life can offer you.'

'Thanks, Nat. So do you. And from what I can see, life is finally treating you the way you deserve, too! Your new partner seems absolutely lovely!'

'He is. I don't think I've ever had this kind of connection with anyone in my life. He understands me and appreciates me.'

'I'm so happy for you!' Rosie chirps. 'I mean, it's the

classic romance where the bloke finally realises he's made a huge mistake, bless him!'

Nina snorts. 'Bless him? He'd better toe the line or we'll send the boys in to sort him out once and for all!'

'Oh, be nice,' Nat says with a chuckle. 'Not every bloke is as confident as yours!'

'True,' Nina says as our menus arrive. 'And oh – speaking of confident, not to say arrogant – did you hear what happened in Starry Cove? Jago Moon tried to drown himself.'

The girls gasp like a Greek chorus. 'Is he all right?'

'Who's Jago Moon?' I ask and three faces turn to me in shock.

'Only the hottest, most *dis*reputable bachelor in Cornwall!' Nat informs me. 'Half the female population is in love.'

'Why would he want to kill himself?' I ask.

'He has a bit of a shady past, and quite the number of demons. God knows how many hearts he's broken. He's the typical love them and leave them kind of man.'

'Ooh, speaking of handsome men, your joiner Henry Turner is a bit of all right,' Rosie says in her London twang that she hasn't managed to shake off yet.

I almost choke on my sparkly water. 'I guess so, if you like that sort of look.'

Nat laughs. 'You mean tall, dark, handsome, sexy, charming?'

'Or the wild Celtic look?' Nina adds. 'I swear, he reminds me of my own husband.'

'Come to think of it,' Rosie says, 'our blokes all have that look, don't they? They could all be related. Even Henry.

And actually, I think he is related to Jago, in some way. Distant cousins, I think.'

I roll my eyes. 'That would explain a lot.'

'You find Henry Turner arrogant?' Nina asks.

I look around the table to my friends who are suddenly very interested in my opinion on him. My ears begin to burn at the injustice I'm doing him, but people mustn't be fooled by a man's good looks. 'Well, sometimes, he can be really nice, especially to his son. But other times, he can be a real arse.'

'Really?' Nat says. 'I hear he's a gem of a man.'

'Well, what do I know?' I reply with a shrug. 'I barely know the bloke. But I can tell you this. He and his estate agent, Travis, are obsessed with selling the beach house.'

'Your beach house? Why?' Rosie asks, her fair eyebrows furrowing.

I shrug. 'He probably thinks he'll get an offer we can't refuse – and a huge commission. Gabe's told him off. I thought he'd got it, but then I got a call from a woman who was interested and when I told her it wasn't for sale, she was heartbroken. I felt like a right heel disappointing her. And I think Henry and I are going to have to have some words. He's so arrogant he thinks he can have his own way.'

'Shame,' Rosie says. 'Henry is a catch in these parts, you know?'

'But I've already been caught, remember?' I argue.

It's just a fraction of a second, but there is a slight hesitation hanging in the air.

'Of course, and we're rooting for you, sweetie,' Nat says, putting a delicate hand over mine. 'We want you to be happy.'

'To Faith,' Rosie cheers, raising her glass.

Nina and Nat raise their glasses in suit and clink together. 'To Faith!'

'Thank you,' I say, raising my own glass and taking a sip. And I can't help but notice that they have only toasted me and not Gabe.

'Right, we're done for the day, Boss,' Rudy says to me at the end of the afternoon, eyeing Thea as he hovers.

I look up from my laptop and see that he is, as always, completely enthralled by Thea's presence. If only she had a clue. They'd be perfect for each other.

'Thanks, Rudy – great work today, as usual. See you tomorrow.'

'How about a drinky-poo at the pub?' he suggests to no one in particular, but I know he's just dying to get Thea on his own.

She hoists her bag over her shoulder, waiting for me to follow, but I'm not a drinker anymore. Besides, they need to be alone without the whole crew.

'Maybe next time,' I say. 'You go, Thea.'

'Are you sure?' she asks.

'Absolutely,' I reply as Rudy's face lightens up at the prospect of an evening on his own with her, bless him. They are perfect together, because not only do they work well, they even complete each other's sentences.

'Guys, we're going to the pub. Who's coming?' she hollers out to the boys in the foyer, much to Rudy's dismay.

'Yeah – I could just about murder a pint or two,' Bill says, and he and the others emerge, nodding in agreement.

I really feel for Rudy. I think he's loved her in silence since the day he started working for me. But so far, no joy.

'You comin', Faith?' Bill says.

I look up. 'Ah, no, thanks, I'm going to just relax here. You guys go.' Besides, I actively avoid pubs these days if I can help it.

'All right. See you in the morning.'

'Have fun,' I call and the door closes behind them and another long working day is over. I close my eyes and take a deep breath, rotating my shoulders back, just enjoying the sound of the surf. The sea seems to have calmed down again after the storm, but this is Cornwall, where nothing can be taken for granted, especially the weather.

'Long day.'

I jump to see Henry approaching the doorway. 'Oh – I thought you'd gone.'

'Without saying goodbye? Never.'

'Well, since you're here, I need to speak to you, if you have a moment?'

'Of course. What is it?' He grins. 'Am I not sanding the furniture down smooth enough?'

'Actually...' I say and gesture for him to sit down.

He takes a seat opposite me, his face completely blank. He has no idea of the damage he's done to that poor woman and her family, with his big mouth. So I tell him about her disappointment. And mine, as a matter of fact.

His eyes widen. 'I'm sorry. Travis did tell her that the house was no longer for sale.'

'Well, obviously she didn't understand because she called me here at the house. How did she even get the number, unless you gave it to her?'

He shrugs. 'I may have, but I honestly don't remember doing so.'

'Well, please sort it. I don't want any more broken-hearted people.'

He nods in mock deference, his eyes twinkling. 'Yes, milady. May I go now, or am I going to get a bollocking for anything else I may or may not have done?'

'May have done? You brought a viewer to my home, Henry.'

'Perhaps I was given the go-ahead.'

'Not by me,' I say.

He crosses his arms and raises an eyebrow at me and it dawns on me. 'Gabe...?' I whisper.

At that, Henry gets to his feet. 'I think you two need to have another chat. Goodnight.'

Dumbstruck, I watch him as he leaves, then pull out my mobile to video-call Gabe.

'Hi,' he answers on the first ring, almost as if he was waiting for me.

'Is it true?' I demand, without dallying. 'Did you agree to sell the house?'

'Er, Babes...'

'Please answer my question honestly, Gabe. Just a simple yes or no will do.'

He hesitates. 'I thought about it, yes.'

'Thought about it?' I echo in shock. 'Then why are we even killing ourselves here?'

'Because the house needs to look like a home again. No one would ever want to buy it in the state it was after Vanessa got to it. Not any sane person, anyway.'

'Gabe – I don't understand you! You fly all the way here

to tell me you want me back, and that you want us to live in our home again, and now you do this?'

'Easy, Babes. There's lots of houses out there.'

'Absolutely,' I say. 'But this is our *home.*'

And then his face falls as it finally hits him. Finally he remembers why this house is so important to me. 'I'm sorry, Faith. I hadn't thought about your mum. But I don't want to live here anymore. Vanessa has damaged my good memories of you and me in this house. I need to move on.'

'But we've been happy here, Gabe. Why would you want to leave all that behind? You say that Vanessa was a bad chapter, and I understand, but why throw the baby out with the bath water?'

'Because there are a million houses out there, Faith. We'll just buy another one.'

I look at him, trying to ignore the sensation of my blood freezing in my veins. Are we going back instead of forward? This whole New Gabe thing… was it just a ruse to get me back, while continuing to do as he pleases?

'So you're telling me that six months with Vanessa have erased three years of happy memories with me? Remember that *I* was the one who first had a past with this house. *I* had all the memories to come to terms with, not you. And I managed. Why can't you?'

'You don't know what I've been through, with that whack job.'

The words *I told you so* spring to my mouth and it is so difficult for me to push them down. But I can't keep it all in and I don't want to. 'All the same – you asked me to renovate my former home, but not so we could live in it. You took advantage of my kindness and idiocy only to make the house sellable!'

'Faith, that's so not true! I love you and want to be with you.'

'We were perfectly all right before you decided to ruin everything between us. If you truly love me as you say you do, you'll get over it and keep your promises to me.' There. That ought to shake him.

He sighs. 'Fine.'

'Thank you,' I say, trying not to huff.

The next day, I have a migraine of biblical proportions and only want to lie down for the next fortnight or so.

But I can't, so I hole up in what is my office and work like a dog all day at the end of which I sit down with my crew and we brief one another as to what's happened, what we're waiting on and our new timeframe estimates. Only I find I can't keep any piece of information in my mind whatsoever. All I can think of is that he wanted to throw our home and all our happy memories away. How could he have even fathomed the idea, after all his promises? Something tells me that this hill is going to be steeper than it looks.

'Faith...?' Thea calls me from what seems like the bottom of the ocean.

I look up from my notebook. I haven't jotted down a single thing. 'Yes?'

She closes her agenda. 'Shall I email you my notes?'

'Yes. Thanks.'

All around me is silence. Not a hostile silence, but a *Why the hell are you putting up with this rubbish?* silence.

I know. They're absolutely right. I'll have to sort this whole thing out before it's too late. Right now I need to be alone to think a way out of this.

'Right,' I say, standing. 'Let's call it a day. You've all worked so hard and once again I thank you for your dedication. I don't know what I'd do without you guys.'

They get to their feet, glancing at each other, then at me. 'I hope you sort him out, Faith,' Paul says, followed by several nods around the table.

'Thanks, guys. I will. Somehow.'

I watch as they file out, leaving me alone in the house that will not be mine for much longer if I can't pull a miracle out of my hat. But I've no time to wallow. I need to get back to work, so I turn on my laptop and get stuck in with my orders and costs, because I've initiated a process that simply can't be stopped.

With the house devoid of all of Vanessa's fantastical animals and whatnot, I finally begin to see the bones of our original home peeking through the steamed and stripped bits of animal print wallpaper. Underneath, the walls without the once gorgeous wainscoting look cold and injured, like a homeless beggar shivering in need of the warmth of a home. I am beginning to think that we've lost much more than the design features.

Without all the crazy furniture, the place looks huge, bigger than ever before. But it also looks completely forlorn and torn. I can't wait to get my crew working on the cosmetic side of it all, and I'm anxious for Henry to solve the issue of the missing wainscoting. I'm worried that Vanessa's team might have thrown the beautiful woodwork away, but I know Henry will do his best to recoup it somehow as he is a true joiner who loves his work.

A knock on my study door makes me turn.

'Have a minute for me?' he asks.

'Uhm, yes. Come on in.'

Again, I get that itchy feeling of impatience when he's talking directly to me and no one else is around. It's as if he becomes less professional and way too personal.

He sighs softly. 'I'm sorry about the misunderstanding about the house. I'm getting the feeling that it's very important to you, and that it's not just about the physical building.'

'Thank you. I feel bad for taking it out on you, Henry. You've been nothing but kind and hard-working.'

He shrugs. 'It's the only way to be.'

Still, I am ashamed.

'I'll get Travis to talk to Gabe, if that can help?'

'Why would you do that? I haven't been exactly nice to you. I'm sorry, I... have a few things going on.'

'Yes, well, who doesn't.' And he leaves it at that.

As far as the renos go, we are making good time. By next week we should be able to move into the living area where Vanessa has come full circle, treating it like a showroom of horrors rather than a place to hang around with friends. It's like someone has played years of paintball in there, leaving the victims plastered to the walls and hanging from the ceilings. There isn't an inch of free wall anywhere. No wonder it's taking weeks. I seriously can't understand why

Gabe let her run roughshod over him like this, because I know he hates this stuff as much as I do.

On the outside, he may be your rebel rock star, but on the inside, he's mush. I know that. Nor is he the loser that both Hope implies he is.

But for now, all I can do is move full steam ahead with my task. If I were smart, I'd leave it exactly as it is so as to scare off buyers. There is so much at stake here, and I'd be lying if I said that I am not disappointed in Gabe. Why doesn't he understand or appreciate my wishes? Why is he so adamant on leaving our home?

At twelve o'clock on the dot Henry returns bearing huge containers of food. 'Folks, I've got Chinese,' I hear him call from the kitchen. 'Eat it while it's hot.'

'Ooh,' Thea says, dropping her tablet atop a huge roll of bubble wrap, joined by Rudy and my muscle men.

But I'm not hungry in the least. I have decided to compose another letter to the Wickfords as the last email I sent came back as undelivered. I've tried everything, but they seem to be unreachable. Even the various phone numbers Thea has managed to find are always busy. How am I supposed to show them my work if I can never reach them? It is a well-known fact that, either as a client or an employee, you can't choose the Wickfords unless they choose you first. They work only based on personal referrals. But surely, by this time, they have forgotten the award incident from years ago?

And yet Vanessa is all chummy with them. Easy when you have your parents to pave the way for you. Hope and I had had absolutely no one, and yet, she managed to make her way up from the very bottom rung and become a multi-Michelin-starred chef, without any support from a husband.

All she had was me to keep the kids when she had to work until the wee hours.

A knock on the door makes me jump. It can only be Mr Lightfoot – startle-me-Turner.

'Faith? I brought lunch. Are you coming?'

I look up briefly. 'You go. I'll be there in a minute, I'm finishing a letter,' I say.

'Business?'

'Yes.'

'Okay, then. You certainly know how to look out for your team. They think the world of you, you know?' he says.

'They are the family I never had,' I say with a shrug.

'Yes, well. It's good to have someone to support you in times of need. Are you writing to the Wickfords?'

At the look on my face, he leans against the door. 'Thea told me.'

'Oh.'

'To be honest, I wouldn't chase them,' he says.

'I beg your pardon?'

He shrugs. 'Your name is Faith, and yet you haven't got any in yourself.'

'What's that supposed to mean?'

'That you don't need them to achieve your goals.'

'Thanks, Henry, but actually, I do. They are the be-all and end-all of British design.'

'Why are you in such a hurry, Faith? You're already doing so well. Pace yourself.'

'What do you mean?'

'The journey to complete success is half the pleasure, you know?'

NANCY BARONE

'Maybe for some. I have a lot of time to make up for.'

'But you're missing the best years of your life this way. Soon, you'll think fondly back to the days that you didn't have two pennies to rub together, believe me.'

'Maybe…'

'Don't second-guess yourself. I can see it on your face – the doubts and fears. You're worried about not being good enough. I can see that you are. And Gabe—' He breaks off, biting his lip.

'What? What were you going to say about Gabe?'

'I can see that you are wondering about your relationship with Gabe, just like I did with Linda. You're wondering how much you can really trust him now. And, quite frankly, I don't blame you.'

'I am not! And besides, how would it be any of your business anyway?'

He shrugs. 'Because I hate to see someone waste their life away on someone who just can't be counted on. Look what he did to you. What man would think of selling the home he's shared with his partner without even telling her?'

As if I was going to give him the satisfaction of acknowledging that. 'I'm not wasting my life away,' I argue. 'Gabe and I have plans all the same which, incidentally, are absolutely none of your business.'

At that, his eyes flash. 'I know my place. But what about you? Why is it that every time we're alone you immediately become belligerent?'

'I do not become belligerent,' I deny. But it's true. I've noticed the pattern. The minute we're alone, out come my claws. 'And if I did, it's probably because you've got it out for Gabe.'

102

'I'm only trying to protect you, Faith.'

'I know how to look after myself.'

He sighs. 'Okay. I know you do. I'm sorry. Peace?'

I hesitate, even if my beef is not with Henry. But I don't want to take my frustrations out on anyone but Gabe. And myself for being such a pushover. 'Peace.'

He smiles. 'I know you hate Chinese food. So I got you Indian. Will you come out into the kitchen now or am I going to have to eat all those samosas and onion bhajis by myself?'

It's amazing how quickly he drops his weapons and any possible grudge. Because Henry, from what I have gathered so far, is an up-front man. He doesn't slag people off. Gabe excepted, of course. But I have a feeling that when Gabe returns, they are definitely going to have it out. Over what, exactly, remains a mystery, but it is clear that there is some bad blood between them.

I roll my eyes and he raises his palms once again in a gesture of backing off. 'Fine, fine. Come and get your Indian before it gets cold.'

And suddenly, just like that, I'm starving.

After a quick lunch in the kitchen with my crew and Henry, I spend the rest of the day inspecting the current state of the house, making notes of our next steps. It's time to source out the white goods. Hopefully, the floorboards have been spared, because whoever laid down the carpeting and the tiling looks like they've done a right cowboy job.

When I stop for a cup of coffee, Henry is taking the last of his measurements in the kitchen.

'I'll work on this tomorrow and the weekend and be back on Monday to show you my drawings,' he promises.

I know it's going to be amazing because all his work always is. He is an incredibly talented joiner.

As I'm getting ready for bed that evening, Gabe video-calls me.

'Hey...' he says, all smiles as if everything between us was fine and dandy. 'Still angry with me?'

'What do you think? One minute you say one thing and the next...'

'I know,' he says softly. 'Forgive me, things are crazy here.'

'Same here,' I warn him.

'So – getting ready for my big return?' He was always so good at changing the subject. 'I'll be there next Saturday.'

'Please bear in mind that our home here is still an absolute wreck.'

'Never mind that. Where are you sleeping?'

'Still in the music room.'

He laughs. 'Not when I come back, you're not.'

Which, of course, remains to be seen. I'm still so angry with him about merely thinking of selling our home that I can't even contemplate that.

He sighs. A loud, pained sigh. 'Well, at least you're still calling it our home. That's a good sign for me, right?'

Is it? Every day I'm discovering things I don't like. Gabe had already broken my heart once. And now this. Luckily, I am a born optimist, despite all that has happened to me. I just keep pushing forward, not willing to be defeated, even if chances look slim. I have never ever left anything unattempted if I thought I had even the slightest ghost of a chance. Because you never know where life may take you. When it may decide to finally reward you for all the pain and hard slogging. I want to be around just in case good karma decides to suddenly dish out.

'We'll talk about it when you get back, okay?' There is no point in insisting at this distance. I'll just have to wait until we're in the same room. Once he's here and he's had time to relax, we'll talk about it seriously. I'm not like Vanessa who stomps her stilettos to get her own way. I use reason and logic. And sometimes, with Gabe, it even works. But this time, I have a feeling he's going to give me a tough time. Just how badly did she hurt him?

'I forgot to ask you, Babes – did you ever get an answer from the Wickfords?'

'As if. They are literally untouchable.'

Silence, and I can hear his thoughts. Vanessa is very close to them, and by proxy, so was he until he dumped her. And now that his name is mud in that household, there's nothing he can do to help me. 'Never mind,' he says. 'You don't need them anyway.'

Just like Henry had said. 'We'll see. So, see you on Saturday, then.'

'Can't wait. Meet you in the *bedroom*, Babes,' he says, lowering his voice to that sexy, gravelly tone he uses whenever we're alone. 'Naked.'

I laugh. 'What?'

'No nightgowns, no frills. I want to see you on the bed naked.'

6

Anticipation

On Friday morning, the day before Gabe's arrival, I decide to go for a quick stroll around the village to get my blueberry scones from my old haunt, Cornish Born and Bread.

The owner, Karen, smiles as I come in. After serving the other customers and practically shooing them out, she waves me over.

'Hi, Faith! How are you?'

'Great thanks, and you?'

'I never got a chance to tell you I'm so glad you're back. We've missed you around here!'

'Awh, Karen, thank you. It's good to be back.'

'So where is Gabe? On tour?'

'Yes, he's in Thailand at the moment.'

'When will he be back?'

'Tomorrow.'

'Must be gruelling.'

'Yes, it is, but he loves it.'

'I meant for you. To not be able to spend more time together.'

I shrug. 'Sacrifices must be made for relationships.'

'Yes, of course. But they shouldn't be only one-sided, Faith.'

'What do you mean?'

She shrugs. 'I mean, with all the difficulties that I see people overcoming in their relationships, you're the one who's had to work the hardest.'

'Do you think?' I ask, feeling my face heat up.

'Faith – I know Gabe inside and out – he was my husband's student for years. People may just see the façade of a relationship – the beautiful house, the great jobs and all. But I know exactly how hard you work to keep Gabe happy. And I'm surprised he's actually found someone to achieve this monumental feat. Because Gabe York is never happy. So I take my hat off to you, Faith. You have won him over with your kindness and solid values.'

'Thank you, Karen; that's very kind of you.'

'Just make sure he doesn't run roughshod over you again. Because he'll certainly try, sooner or later, once he knows he's got you in the palm of his hand for good this time.'

I close my mouth. Has she been speaking to Mrs Trengrouse? Is that the way the whole of the village sees us, as a relationship with an expiration date? Nobody knows what goes on behind closed doors. I barely know myself.

'Thanks, Karen. For looking out for me,' I say. 'But I'm okay.'

'The usual blueberry scones?' she says as she reaches into the glass casing between us and pulls out exactly four.

'You remember my appetite, I see,' I say with a grin as I am already salivating.

She grins back. 'I did, but if need be, Henry's reminded me how much you love them. He comes by here every morning and reserves them just for you. Of course, he thinks of the entire crew, but he always buys extra for you. I'm telling you – that one is a horse of a completely different colour. You might want to not lose sight of him.'

I laugh as I put my money on the counter. 'Seriously, Karen, you get the weirdest ideas. I'll see you next weekend.'

'I'll put some aside for Henry on Monday morning!' she calls after me.

I leave, shaking my head. Hm. He's been buying extra for me.

And finally, here we are – the day Gabe is coming back.

Which reminds me. I need to shop for tonight's dinner.

I'll plan it to death and… there I go again. Okay, no planning to death – just a few things he likes – his favourite food, his favourite wine and some San Pellegrino water for me. And then we'll finally have that chat that could either make or break us.

I've got all the ingredients for the ham roast, his favourite meal since he was a tiny boy – the pineapple, the peas and sweet potatoes. I'm going to criss-cross the ham with rashers and rashers of bacon and stud it with cloves like Hope said to do. I'm going to make his favourite dessert– apple pie – and drown it in vanilla ice cream, just the way he likes it. And I'm going to set the table with a new tablecloth that will be ours and ours only.

I've even planned breakfast for the next day – pancakes with an avalanche of whipped cream and fresh raspberries. Everything needs to be perfect. And by that evening, it is. Unable to sit still, I start pacing back and forth, talking to Jawsy.

'He's coming back, pretty girl,' I coo, wondering if she isn't lonely in that bowl all day long. I should get her a companion. It's cruel of me to expect her to live on her own, day in, day out. I'd never thought about that.

Gabe should be here in the next half hour, minute more, minute less.

An hour later, with dinner slowly sagging in the warming drawer, I pour myself a glass of sparkling water. He's late. I try his mobile, which is still switched off. He should have landed hours ago. I should've met him at Heathrow. Who cares if it's hours away. At least right now we'd be in the car together and I'd know what is to become of us and our future.

As I'm checking my lip gloss and hair in the mirror for the umpteenth time, my mobile rings.

Oh God, I hope it's not a business call – I haven't the head for it right now. All I can think of is Gabe walking through that door and I don't want it to be while I'm talking throw cushions and Berber rugs.

I know I should draw a line between business and pleasure, but how can I, when one phone call, one text might save me an hour prepping the next day? He'll never understand that. He's an artist, a free spirit, while I do the calculations and make sure that everything is exactly how it's supposed to be.

'Hello?' I answer.

'Hi, Faith.'

'Gabe? Where are you? You're late. Is everything okay?'

'I'm, uhm, delayed.'

'Oh, gosh, traffic on the motorway?' I should have booked him a room in London for the night. 'How far did you manage to get?'

He lets out a long, tired sigh. 'Faith – I'm still in Thailand.'

My stomach drops to my feet as my legs begin to feel hollow. 'What…? W-why? Why didn't you tell me? I've been waiting for—'

'I got a call from the hospital. Vanessa's there.'

A deep-freeze grips my lungs. 'Is… is she okay?'

'I'm not sure yet, but I'm going to have to postpone my trip. I'm so sorry, Faith.'

'But wait – I thought she'd already left to come back to the UK?'

'So did I. But she was staying here with a friend, and now… I'll call you back when I know more, okay? I've got to go now.'

'I'm so sorry, Gabe. Will you keep me posted? Gabe…?' I say, but the phone line is dead.

I truly hope she's okay. I never wanted anything to happen to her. But this sounds serious. Serious enough to hold Gabe back.

Maybe I should go onto the Internet and see if there's any news? I pull out my laptop and type in *Vanessa Chatsbury, designer*. Apart from the usual spiel about her business and her silver-spooned clients and her wild partying, there is nothing new there. Whatever it is, I'm going to have to wait to know more.

I consider calling Gabe back, but it seemed he couldn't

get off the phone fast enough and I don't want to stress him out any more than he already must be. I'm sure Vanessa's parents must have flown out if it's serious.

I can only continue to pace around the house, hoping and praying that she's okay. When I get back to the kitchen, the food I'd so lovingly prepared stares back at me, almost as if to ask what I'm going to do about it? For a moment I consider calling my team over for dinner, but it's the weekend and they have families and lives. I consider Hope but then remember she has taken the kids away for the weekend. I'd call my coastal girls but they are without a doubt snuggled up with their loved ones and I don't want to bother or upset them with my miserable mug.

The meal is all going to go to waste, because I can't even think of eating right now. I wonder how Gabe is coping. He's not good in any type of crisis whatsoever.

7

Un-break My Heart

After a weekend of worrying myself sick, on Monday morning, while my team is emptying the house of the last dregs of Vanessa's stuff, I am once again working like mad sourcing out more reclaimed tiles for the bathrooms, faucets and wallpaper.

Gabe has not called with any news about Vanessa, and I'm beginning to seriously worry. Has she had an accident? Is she ill? I am completely clueless.

Or... and here we go again with the doubts. Is he simply being lazy? Evasive? He knows I have anxiety and abandonment issues. Yes, I know they're only mine to solve, but you'd think that for someone who claims to love me, he'd be a bit more attentive. Why do her needs always supersede mine? Why does she always find a way to get priority over me, whether it's because he's dumped me, or because she's in hospital. Okay, I admit it. I'm downright jealous. Why do I feel like she always has the upper hand, even now that he's chosen to come back to me?

As I'm musing on that, Thea saunters into the room, barking into her mobile. 'No, Rudy, not after lunch – do it now, you lazy bugger.' Then she snaps the phone shut and beams at me. She won't admit it yet, but she's smitten with him, too. And rightfully so. Rudy is adorable, with a great sense of humour. And he's also honest – which is why he does my payroll.

'Imagine if I spoke to him like that,' I say.

She shrugs and flashes me her diamantéed smile through her dark lipstick. 'I think he loves me.'

I laugh. 'He'd have to, to put up with that kind of verbal abuse.'

'You should try it with Gabe,' she says, raising her eyebrow at me.

I frown. 'Try what?'

She rolls her eyes. 'Cracking the whip. God knows he'll need it more than ever now that he's been with that feral freak.'

As she picks up her pile of paperwork and goes into the living room, I begin to wonder – does the entire world see me as a pushover?

I have, let's say, done the guiding in our relationship. I was the one who got him an agent, and a rather good one, if I may say so myself. And every decision that Gabe made for his career, he discussed it with me first. Because he trusted my grounded common sense.

Even though he threw a strop when I cancelled the order for solid gold toilets. I mean, really. The white goods already present in the loos were very high end already.

If it weren't for me we'd have twenty Porsches in the drive. Gabe never really had any money while growing up, so he sort of lost the plot when the first six-figured royalties started coming in. Whereas I had learnt from an early age to not rely on anything at all – wealth or family. They don't last forever. Treat it all as fleeting, and when it's all gone it might just hurt a tad less. You might be overwhelmed when it's all gone, but at least you won't be surprised.

'We're bloody rich now, Faith, and it's all thanks to you! I'm going to buy you a friggin' country!' he'd sworn, spinning me around.

'Let's just settle for a house,' I'd laughed.

'I'll buy you any house you want, anywhere in the world!'

My heart had skipped a beat. Yes! A home. Finally! 'Thank you, Gabe. You choose – I don't really mind.'

'You love the sea, right? We'll buy one on the beach, then!'

'On one condition,' I'd said. 'I get to contribute.'

He'd laughed. 'Babe – that's ridiculous – what's mine is yours. You know that.'

'Gabe, thank you. But I don't want to be the rock star's kept girlfriend.'

'Bollocks to that,' he'd said. 'You are the love of my life and I owe you everything. If it weren't for you I'd still be dipping cod in batter at the chippy.'

'Don't say that, Gabe. You are immensely talented and deserve all your success. But I need to contribute. For my own dignity. Okay?'

He'd rolled his eyes. 'Fine!'

And for an entire week we went beach house hunting along the South Cornish coast.

There had been a four-bed Arts and Crafts beauty on a hill above Little Kettering, and a cosy three-bed cottage on the harbour of Starry Cove with a gorgeous back garden full of flowers, and another three-bed detached surrounded by tall trees in Penworth Ford. But Gabe had vetoed them all because they weren't expensive enough.

'This,' he'd countered, poking at a catalogue called *Prestigious Properties in Cornwall*, 'is the one for us! "Beautiful beach house high up on the cliffs, with stone steps going down to the beach."'

'Ooh, let me see? It's gorgeous, Gabe. But... it's three million pounds!'

'So? Don't we deserve it?'

As much as that was my dream home, I remember panicking. 'Why don't we buy something less expensive for now, and wait to see how your next album goes, and then maybe upgrade if we really want to?'

And then he'd suddenly slammed the catalogue down, glaring at me. 'You don't think my next album will be a hit?'

'Of course I do, Gabe. I believe in you – you know that. But this is a very fickle business. So let's not count our chicks before they've hatched, okay?'

He'd gone silent, then finally nodded, raking a beringed hand through his blond spikes. 'You're right. What would I do without your business sense, eh?'

But the very next week, at the news that his album had hit platinum, he'd called the estate agent and booked a viewing. And only when we got there, did I recognise the views and realise it was the same house my parents had vacationed in. The same house where my father had abandoned my mother.

The next afternoon, there is still no news from Gabe. God, I could throttle him sometimes. I have a mind to call him and demand information. But I'm also afraid I might not like it. I'm not one to procrastinate or hide from reality, but sometimes being with Gabe is like riding a bloody rollercoaster.

Even now, as I sit in the boardroom, i.e. Gabe's office, taking notes, my mind is seesawing between *There is a Perfectly Good Explanation* and *I Just Knew It!* Luckily I have a lovely distraction – I am responsible for Orson as Henry has just popped into town. He is humming as he works on a little project of his own. He is truly a lovely, obedient little boy. I only hope he doesn't grow up too fast and become an annoying bloke.

'Faith! Can I please—' Orson calls as he runs into the boardroom, stumbling and scraping his knee against the door hinge. 'Aaah...'

I jump to my feet as he lands on his knees. 'Orson...'

God, this is so not the place for a six-year-old to run around. I should reinspect it and cover anything that he could get snagged on. The alternative is to not allow him to come, but the thought of not seeing this little face anymore makes something inside my chest twinge.

'Are you okay, sweetheart?'

'It's nothing,' he says bravely. 'Just a little scrape.'

'Let me check it,' I say, grabbing the first aid pouch from the cupboard. 'Come, sit.'

I sit in my chair, pulling out one for him, but instead, taking me completely by surprise, he climbs into my lap, nestling himself in the crook of my arm like a tiny hatchling in his nest in the most tender of gestures. I swallow, utterly overwhelmed by this spontaneous gesture of trust.

'I wish you were my mummy, Faith.' He sighs sadly, looking up at me with spaniel eyes. His father's same dark eyes.

I freeze. 'That's very sweet of you, Orson, but I'm sure your own mummy loves you very much.'

He shrugs. 'I dunno. She's never kind to me like you are. You don't yell at me.'

I can't imagine anyone yelling at this darling little angel.

'What does… your daddy say about that? Does she yell at you in front of him?'

'Not really, only when we're alone. When I'm with Daddy, he takes care of me. But I don't think my mummy is a very good mummy. Not as good as my friends' mummies.'

I bite my lip as I apply some disinfectant to his knee, gently blow on it and put a plaster on it.

'There you go. Better?' I ask.

He nods, still gazing up at me lovingly. 'Better, thank you, Faith.'

And just like that, I'm in absolute, complete love. This little boy reminds me so much of myself, and how I needed someone's approval at his age.

When Henry later comes in laden with boxes full of cupboard handle samples, he places them carefully down as Orson rushes to meet him.

'Hey, mate,' he says, ruffling his mop of dark hair and noticing his knee. 'What happened? How did you get hurt?'

'It's nothing, Daddy. I scraped my knee when I fell.'

Henry's face instantly loses colour as he bends down to examine his son more closely. 'You fell? Where?'

'I scraped my knee on the hinge of a door. It's nothing, Daddy. Faith cleaned it up for me and even blew on it so it wouldn't burn.'

'It's fine, Henry, really,' I assured him. 'Just a tiny scrape is all. He's already up and running again, see? Although we had a little chat about the running part, didn't we, Orson?'

Orson nods. 'I promise not to run anymore and to look where I'm going, Faith.'

'Good boy,' I say.

Orson looks up at Henry who is watching us in silence. From the looks of him, I don't think he's used to anyone else helping out with stuff like this. I can tell he's used to doing everything on his own. It must be difficult, to go from a proper team to doing everything solo.

'Can I go, Daddy? I want to watch Bob put in the new piping. He said I could help if I follow his safety rules.'

Henry's face lights up with pride. 'Of course you can, mate. Don't forget to put on your safety gear and work gloves.'

'I won't!' he calls as he rushes off and I realise we are both beaming at him.

Henry turns to me. 'It's completely my fault for not covering the hinges when I took the doors off. I'm so anal about health and safety and I actually forgot to proof the place for my own boy.'

'Stop, Henry. Accidents happen all the time, but we sorted it.'

'You're very good to him,' Henry says, visibly touched. 'Thank you.'

'He's such a sweetheart. Who wouldn't love him?'

A muscle in his jaw faintly shifts. 'Yes, well.'

And there they are again, those two words. For such an articulate and intelligent man, that's all he can say when he is upset. But I've come to understand the magnitude behind those two words. I have come to understand that they are not uttered through indifference, but only when he is overwhelmed. Those two words that mean nothing per se, mean everything to him.

'Shall we have a look at those handle samples?' he says, snapping out of it.

'Ooh yes please, Henry.'

And he switches back from doting father to joiner in a split second. It's amazing how many people inhabit Henry Turner. Father, husband, joiner, boss, furniture designer, friend, adviser, cheerer-upper. I am truly beginning to see the man behind the good looks.

It has been a long day. The boys are sorting out the electrics and the plumbing, but we're still a long way off. The amount of damage that has been done to this house in the space of six months is unfathomable.

'That's great work, guys,' I say as we are wrapping up for the day. 'Thea? Before I forget – leave the second guest bedroom empty.'

'Empty for what?' she wants to know.

I wag a finger at her, unable to hide a smile.

She gasps. 'Faith! A nursery? Are you – how?'

I laugh, and it feels good, after all this time. 'Pregnant? Not yet.' If I can ever get Gabe to come back from Thailand, that is.

'Oh my God!' Thea cries, hugging me. 'I knew he'd come round, that old dog! I'm on it! Just let me know what you want and—'

'Actually, Thea, if you don't mind, I'd like to take care of this on my own.'

'Of *course*!' she hisses under her breath, beaming at

me. 'Oh, Faith, I'm so happy for you! Mummy's very first nursery!'

'Thank you. Well, I guess then we can call it a day.'

'See ya,' the boys call as they make their way out and Thea and I watch them go. My team.

'I'm out of here, see you,' Thea says and disappears as Henry sidles up into the doorway, having taken Orson home earlier that afternoon.

'Hey,' he says. 'Faith. Do you ever actually stop working?'

'Of course,' I say wearily, running a hand through my hair that feels like a rat's nest. When was the last time I washed it? Come to think of it, when was the last time I showered, even?

Henry studies me. 'This house is everything to you, isn't it?'

I huff, annoyed that Gabe doesn't get it and someone I've just met does. 'Yes. It's my first real home. My sister and I were orphaned very early. We lived mostly between foster parents.'

'I'm sorry, I didn't know. But I understand why it's so important to you. You feel safe here, don't you?'

I swallow. 'Yes.'

'I know. I'll bet that's why you came up with the Home Hugs?'

My eyes swing to his. How could he know things like that? 'That's right.'

'You see, Faith – all art is bred from emotion. You've got plenty of that in you. Use it to your benefit.'

'I guess you're right. You're so wise, Henry.'

Our eyes meet and for a moment it's suddenly like I've known him forever. Not in the sense of years, but in the sense of... depth. He sustains my gaze and I'm sure he's thinking the same, but then he rubs the back of his neck and stuffs his hands into his pockets. 'Nah. I'm just as much of a fool as your next bloke. Come on, let's grab a bite to eat, look at some other human beings for a change. I have a feeling you haven't seen a new face or eaten real food since you started this job.'

I debate with myself. It's true that I haven't had an evening out in months. And once Gabe gets back, if he ever does, I envisage lots and lots of nights in.

'I promise I'll take you wherever you want to go, we'll have a nice meal and I'll bring you back here the second you ask me to, assuming I don't bore the hell out of you sooner. What do you say, Faith?' He joins his hands in prayer. 'Please? I'm starving.'

I grin back at him. 'Oh, go on then.'

He flashes me a huge smile. 'Brilliant.'

'Just give me a minute to change,' I say, heading to Gabe's music room where all my stuff is.

I slip off my work gear and straight into my favourite blue wool dress and a pair of ankle boots and grab my bag, make sure the keys and purse are in there and skip down the stairs, realising that, actually, I'm looking forward to it.

Henry is waiting by the car out front and opens the door for me. 'Thanks, Henry. Oh, wait. I can't remember if the back door is locked.'

'I locked it. And I closed all the shutters, turned on the lights and set the alarm,' he answers. 'Always better to be safe than sorry. By the way, you look pretty.'

'Thanks. Is that *by the way* connected to the safe or the sorry?' I blurt out before I can stop myself. Gosh, now it sounds like I'm fishing for compliments. Because I am, in case you didn't know, the Queen of Putting Her Foot in her Mouth.

He slides me an amused glance. 'Neither, you silly sausage. Ready?'

I nod as I get in and put my seatbelt on. When I'm done, he nods with satisfaction and manoeuvres out of the drive and onto the main road and I relax in the comfortable seat.

'We've done well today, haven't we?' I say.

He looks at me. 'Yes, very well. I'll bet you can't wait to start your new life.'

'Yes,' I say with a grin. 'So tell me about you and Gabe. When did you meet?'

'Oh God, a gazillion years ago. We went to school together, then we went our separate ways and lost track of each other until about ten years ago.'

'It's so odd our paths have never crossed before,' I muse.

'Not really,' he says as he slows down at an intersection. 'Gabe and I were never as close again.'

'But he must still think highly of you if he asked you to help him sell the beach house. Otherwise, he wouldn't have done that. Trust me, Gabe doesn't suffer fools gladly.'

He sneaks me a terse glance. 'Yes, well.'

'Yes, well. You say that a lot,' I observe.

'I beg your pardon?'

'And that, too. You have this way of not revealing much about yourself.'

He laughs. 'Nah, I'm quiet, is all.'

'Selectively so,' I say.

He raises a questioning eyebrow at me before he looks back at the road.

'I mean, you have so much to say on the job, but on a personal level, you don't give much away. Not that I'm expecting you to,' I hastily add.

He laughs and I notice he has a beautiful profile and fine features. Up close he looks much younger, with flawless skin. And he has a nice smile. Like Orson. You can tell he's a good person. I can't imagine why he and Gabe wouldn't get along anymore.

We come to a narrow lane with hedges scratching either sides of the Jeep, and I wonder why someone doesn't take action to make the lanes wider, or even put in a proper road. But then, it wouldn't be Cornwall anymore if things changed.

Up ahead, an oncoming car appears over the hillock, and Henry slows down, pulling as far left as he can to let the other vehicle through. The driver raises a hand in thanks and disappears.

'I'm glad you're driving,' I whisper as the other man squeezes past us and Henry laughs. A hearty, good-natured laugh.

I turn to look at him. 'Are you always this nice?'

'Letting someone go first is being nice?' he replies.

I shrug. 'I think so.'

He snorts. 'I'd hate to see what you think is mean, then.'

'No, you wouldn't,' I reply before I can stop myself.

He looks over at me once again, his eyes delving into mine, but does not ask.

Before I know it, we're in Mylor Bridge, at an old eatery called Persephone's Cove. It is a huge former pilchard-salting house with a jetty into the sea. This evening the tide is out and the gulls are on the mooch in the crab pools, all the same keeping an eye out for leftovers at the tables. Judging by the amazing reputation of the food here, I wouldn't hold my breath for them.

As it turns out, it is freakishly warm for January, so the staff have brought out tables and chairs. We sit down at one at the end of the jetty and watch a group of children. They are all muddy and as happy as Larry jumping on and off into the mud pools while looking for tiny crabs. The parents are only a few tables away, confident that they are safe, and the look of pure bliss on their faces makes me smile.

Immediately a waiter comes to take our order.

'Scallops for me, please,' I say.

'Hm,' Henry says. 'I'll have the same, thank you.'

The waiter smiles and marches up the jetty and back inside.

'Fancy a pint while we wait?' Henry says.

'Water for me, please,' I answer.

He looks at me funny, but it's only a moment. I know he's guessed about my old drinking problem and I'm grateful he's not bringing it up. 'Be right back.'

I follow him with my eyes all the way up the jetty. He is taller than I thought, and his gait is relaxed but elegant, speaking of a quiet confidence. The exact opposite of Gabe's fair, delicate beauty.

I don't know Henry all that well, but one thing is for sure: he is good at what he does. And he seems to get along well with my team, so so far so good. But I still can't see him and Gabe being mates. And I still don't understand why Gabe had never mentioned him to me before.

I sit back with my eyes closed, listening to the children squealing in delight at the sighting of a crab. When Hope and

I were little, no one had ever taken us to the beach, but we used to sneak off on our own. Once we got very close to the coast before the police snapped us up and brought us back to… I can't even remember which family we were staying with, or even the name of the town. I used to remember each and every family in sequential order, along with the addresses and even the names of their pets. But now, it's all lost in the mist. Which can only be a good thing, Hope says.

We had always been starved for everything and anything a child should experience, and even today, Hope still yearns to live on the beach. Once we're sorted, I'll invite her to stay for the summer. The kids will love it. I know Gabe won't mind, although it'll be a bit uncomfortable if Hope doesn't decide to accept him back into my life.

He's not exactly too keen on her, either, and it's a shame, because the two adults I love the most should be able to spend an evening together without trying too hard while I'm cringing. I need to speak to him about it because sometimes Gabe can be a bit insensitive.

'Here we are, water for you, and for me a beer, just as cold as your ex's heart.'

I open my eyes. 'I beg your pardon?'

Henry slides into his seat opposite me, realising what he's just said. 'Sorry – that's what the sign says just outside the entrance. I figure it doesn't include exes who have reconciled.'

'Ha,' is all I can think of saying as I take a sip. 'May I ask, how well *do* you know Gabe?'

Henry swallows his mouthful. 'Fairly well, I'd say.'

'Really? So you know his parents and all?'

'Yes, absolutely.'

'What are they like?'

He swallows his sip. 'You've never met them?'

I shake my head, realising how pathetic it sounds. 'I'd hinted at it once or twice in the past, but they hate each other and live at opposite ends of the world, so...' And then it suddenly dawns on me. 'Perhaps he meant that they would hate *me*.'

Henry's brow furrows. 'What do you mean?'

I shrug. 'I don't know. Maybe they expect any girlfriend to be a gold digger.'

'But weren't you an item even before he became famous? Plus you're doing very well on your own steam, I've heard.'

'Yes,' I answer, omitting to add that I was the one who had actually sent his demo to ClapTrack Records in the first place. 'But he is the famous and rich one,' I explain. 'I'm only an interior designer – what could I possibly bring to the table compared to Gabe?'

'Awh, bless your heart, Faith. But you need to believe in yourself more.' He studies me with those dark eyes, and then finally smiles, revealing a pair of dimples I'd never noticed before.

A few minutes later our orders arrive and Henry laughs.

'What?' I say as I pick up my fork and knife.

'Your face – it literally lit up when the waiter put the plate before you.'

'I do love my food,' I answer. 'Bon appetit!'

'Bon appetit, Faith.'

And it's pure bliss. The scallops are cooked perfectly and drenched in a delicious lemon garlic sauce.

The children in the rock pools and their parents have

gone and the sun has slowly begun its descent as the fairy lights and gas heaters take over.

'Can I ask you a question, Faith?' Henry says as he wipes his mouth with his linen napkin.

'Yes?'

'You told me you and your sister were foster children. How did your parents…? I'm sorry, I'm being nosy.'

I shrug, because actually, I don't mind telling Henry. He's quite easy to relate to and I feel I don't need to impress him in any way. 'My father left my mother before she even knew she was pregnant. He… was married and my mum never knew. He left her and she died a few years after having us.'

He looks at me, his eyes mirroring his empathy. 'I'm so sorry, Faith…'

I shrug. 'It's all right, it was a long time ago.'

'So again, that's why you became an interior designer. To make homes beautiful.'

'And welcoming.'

'Faith? Seeing as we've come this far…'

'Yes…?'

He hesitates, but then looks me right in the eye. 'I don't mean to pry, but… Gabe always did have a reputation for going through money very quickly. He may well be a rock star, but I have a feeling that not all is as it seems. And you would do well to be wary of him.'

'Weren't you supposed to be friends?'

'Supposed to be, being the operative word.'

I flinch and put down my fork.

'I'm sorry,' he says. 'I only mean to look out for you.'

'You think Gabe is a big spender or a dissolute. He's not. We're very careful with money.'

'I'm sure *you* are. But Gabe takes more than he gives. He—' Henry opens his mouth but closes it again. 'Yes, well. I suppose a lot of it is my fault,' he says in the end. 'I just don't want him to take advantage of you, Faith,' he whispers as he leans over to touch my hand.

I look at his long joiner's fingers, huge and dark, covering mine. I am transfixed by the power emanating from them. He could crush me in one singe gesture, if he wanted to. He could actually even crush Gabe, too. But instead, he is gentle.

'I certainly hope not,' I confess. 'But I've been wrong before.'

'I'm sorry I even brought this up, Faith. Let's steer clear of Gabe and enjoy this amazing meal. What do you think?'

'Well, the scallops are divine…'

His dark eyes crinkle at the corners in another smile. 'Exactly. And I promise you as many desserts as you want afterwards.'

'Okay, change of subject then. How is the kitchen coming along?' I ask. 'Can I come to the joinery for a snoop?'

'Absolutely not,' he says with a laugh, removing his hand from mine.

'What about the wainscoting? What are we going to do about it?'

'Leave it to me.'

'Have you found anything?'

'Let's say you'll be very happy.'

'Thanks, Henry, I trust you completely.' Truly, I do. He knows what he's doing, and he does it well.

He chuckles. 'Thank you. How are you?'

'I'm fine, Henry, thanks for asking.'

He eyes me. 'When is Gabe coming home?'

'Oh... probably in 2099, I suppose,' I say with a laugh as my mood begins to sink at the mere mention of his delay.

'Is this life what you signed up for?'

Ouch. 'It could be. We will see if we can work things out, once he returns home.'

'For how long?'

Let it go, already, will you? I want to say, because I am having such a good time with him, despite us touching delicate topics. But I sigh and shrug. 'For as long as it takes him to write another ten songs, I guess. Plus he'll be doing national promos, TV shows, magazines. He's all the rage.'

'And you're okay with living in the limelight?' he asks.

'Better that than being remembered for going viral for falling legs akimbo on top of a man's face,' I say. But he doesn't laugh.

'That was ages ago, and you were practically a kid.'

If anything, Henry reveals himself to be a charming dinner companion. He's careful to steer clear of any more Gabe talk and instead regales me with tons of utterly ludicrous stories of the mistakes he made when he was starting out and we soon find ourselves sharing tricks of the trade, even if we work in different fields.

'It's all about making our homes more beautiful with things that don't cost the earth, and recycling older objects, isn't it?' he says. On this, for once, we absolutely agree. 'I know of this vintage place that lets you work on the product before you take it home.'

I sit up. 'Do you mean the one in Marazion? Time & Tide? I've been dying to get in there, but it's always full. I'm told you need a bloody appointment.'

He takes a sip of his wine. 'I'll take you if you like. I'm a regular. I can even get you a discount,' he offers as he puts a forkful of scallop into his mouth. He doesn't wolf down his food. On the contrary, he has proper, old-fashioned manners. In many ways, despite the low-sitting jeans and the mop of dark curls and five o'clock shadow, Henry is old-school.

He wipes his mouth. 'I'll give them a call and see when they can fit us in.'

'Seriously? Thank you.'

'Care for dessert?' he asks. 'They do an amazing tiramisu here. And cheesecakes, I think.'

'I'd love some, but I need to go to the ladies'. Would you mind ordering for me?'

'Sure, what would you like?'

I get up and smile. 'Surprise me.'

'Don't be too long or I can't guarantee there will be any left,' he says before I head for the ladies' room.

Washing my hands and checking my face in the mirror, I notice that my face is flushed and I'm jittery. I should be dining with Gabe by now, not Henry. God knows how Vanessa is doing. She might even try to convince him to stay in Thailand. I need to stay calm. Sooner or later Gabe will call me back with some info. And rather than chew him out for keeping me on tenterhooks, I'll act calm and poised.

I quickly check my teeth and reapply my lip gloss before returning to our table.

Before I sit down, I bend to the floor to retrieve the napkin of an elderly woman sitting at the next table who thanks me.

When I look up at Henry, he's beet red. He must be very excited about dessert. That, or something is very wrong.

'Uh, Faith? Please sit down. Now?'

'Why, what's wrong?'

'Nothing. Just sit down, please?'

I sit down. 'Are you okay?'

He swallows uncomfortably.

'What is it?' What could it possibly be?

'The, ah – hem of your… dress is caught in your knickers.'

I gasp as my hand goes to my butt and, sure enough, the entire hem is in my knickers, having exposed my butt completely. As there is a hushed silence, followed by some guffawing, with a furtive yank I get it out and duck behind my menu. I have just given Henry and everyone else in the restaurant a close-up shot of my derrière. Hiding behind a menu is not going to cut it.

I look around, and sure enough, all eyes are on me. Oh my God, humiliated once again in public, and in practically the same way!

And then someone says, 'It's the Home Hugs girl!'

'It is! And she hasn't lost the habit!'

'I need to get out of here – now,' I plead to Henry under my breath.

'I'll take care of it,' he says, getting to his feet and pulling my hand and I am catapulted along through the throng of tables and patrons out of the restaurant and to his Jeep.

'Phew!' I exhale as I jump into the passenger seat.

'See?' he says as he shuts the door behind me. 'I forgot to pay. I'll be right back,' he promises before he darts back into the restaurant.

I wait as he disappears back into the restaurant. I hope that no one has taken any more pictures. I couldn't stand being humiliated again on such a vast scale. The Internet can be a great tool, but in the wrong hands, it's worse than a gun.

I remember the months of laughter at my expense, at art college, at work and just around Truro where everyone suddenly seemed to know who I was for all the wrong reasons. I had longed for success and notoriety, but not in this way. I wish I could disappear tonight.

Henry truly is a gent. Such a nice bloke. I wonder why his wife left him. And then I wonder what it is that compels people who are in perfectly stable relationships to suddenly end them. Henry's wife, Gabe, Hope's husband. It just goes to show how we should never take anything for granted.

A shadow falls across the inside of the Jeep and I look up with a smile, but it isn't Henry.

One of the men has followed us out of the restaurant, cackling as he points his mobile at me, filming me up close.

And that's when Henry whirls him around and yanks it from him, holding the mobile out of the man's reach as he deletes the photos.

'Give me my phone back!' the man demands.

'When I'm good and ready,' Henry replies.

'I'll make you!' the man shakily threatens.

'You can try,' Henry says with a shrug.

'Then I'm calling the police!' he says.

'Please do, and you can also tell them how you were filming a woman without her consent.'

At that thought, the man simply raises his hands and disappears and Henry throws the phone to him and turns back to the car.

'Thank you, Henry. I'm so sorry, I didn't think people would remember me after all those years.'

'You have nothing to be sorry about,' he says hotly. 'It's not your fault that some blokes are complete arses.'

Some, but not all. Because Henry was a star to get me out of there in no time.

'I'm officially Henry's hugest fan,' Hope says when I call her to tell her about my strange evening. 'And I think he's right about Gabe. You should be careful.'

'What can you possibly mean? I am careful.'

'I know you, and certainly you know you, so please don't insult our intelligence with your faux soul-searching. You still love him and are terrified he's going to hurt you again. And well you should be.'

'Why are you whispering?' I look at my watch. 'Sorry, I had no idea it was this late. Are the kids sleeping?'

Hope sighs audibly. 'Oh, they're out for the count. Faith? You do realise that if you and Gabe stay together and, God forbid, have kids, that he'll always be on tour and that you will be the only one raising them?'

I shrug to myself. 'Better one parent than none. Besides, you're exaggerating – Gabe hinted at the fact that he wants kids now.'

'Yes, especially from a distance.'

I huff. 'Maybe calling you was not such a good idea tonight.'

'Oh, sweetie – I'm sorry, really I am. I know you wanted a home and a family, and if anyone deserves happiness, it's you. You know I'm on your side. But I love you and I want you to be careful.'

'You sound just like Henry. What is wrong with everyone?'

Silence on the other end. 'They're not in love with Gabe. And no, I don't trust him to not leave you again.'

I laugh. 'He's not going to do it again, Hope. What do you take him for?'

'Oh, I don't know – how about an egotistic wimp?'

'Ouch.'

'Tell you what, Faith. Why don't we sleep on it and talk tomorrow? I'm always here for you.'

'Likewise,' I answer.

'I love you, little sister,' she says.

'I love you more, big sister by fifteen minutes,' I assure her and ring off.

My sister Hope Hudson is one of the most loving and smartest women I know, and yet, she won't let go of this. Overprotective is an understatement where Gabe is concerned.

I pick up my phone again, walk out to the back patio and dial Gabe's number.

'Faith – hi…' he says in a low voice.

'Hi… Sorry, were you asleep?'

'No, no. I'm just outside Vanessa's hospital room.'

'So what happened to her?'

'We're not quite sure yet. She had an episode, or a panic attack or something. We thought it was a heart attack. And now she seems to have lost all her energy.'

Drugs and booze will do that, is the first thing that comes to mind, but as usual, I bite my tongue.

'Well, she's in good hands, at least,' I offer.

'Yeah, that's true. Luckily her parents had flown out the

week before. They're not very happy with me as you can imagine.'

'I understand, but Vanessa is a grown woman, and besides, the Chatsburys are never happy with anyone,' I reply.

He half-laughs. 'That's true.'

'Gabe?'

'Yeah?'

'Will you be coming back anytime soon?'

'This Saturday.'

'Are you serious?'

'Yeah. I feel like a weight has lifted off my shoulders. Finally.'

A weight. I wonder if he had spoken to her like that about me back in the day when she'd asked him if he'd dumped me yet.

'Faith? Are you still there?'

'Of course,' I reassure him.

'Are you happy?'

Am I happy? Confused is more like it.

'I've got to go now,' he says before I can answer him, which is for the best. 'But I'll text you my flight details.'

'Okay,' I whisper. 'Bye.'

I ring off, breathing in the cold evening air. The seagulls are performing a song and dance around something out to sea, their cries barely audible from where I stand, one hip on the railing, hugging myself.

There's so much to talk about, so much to forgive and forget. Can I? I know that he is truly sorry for what he's done. After all, Gabe has never been the stable one in our relationship. And so here I am again, waiting, wondering, worrying. Is it going to be like this forever?

I wander around the house alone, taking stock of not only the work progress, but also of that of my career. I have so many ideas I'd like to propose to the Wickfords – for homes, for offices, for leisure centres. The thoughts are literally bursting out of my head and jumping onto my sketch pads that are rapidly piling up on my desk. I'm like an unpublished author who's been writing for years on end in the hope of one day being validated by an expert in publishing. Or a greasy-spoon cook waiting for their Michelin-starred restaurant.

Of course, I could settle for a lesser firm, and if I can't reach them in any way, I may well have to. But it seems like such a shame to let my ideas, my labour of love of a lifetime, go to some anonymous company that does not have the resources or the inclination to do greater things.

Like this beautiful, beautiful home. In the wrong hands, it had been turned into a nightmarish jungle. But with a little love and respect, it will once again shine as it was meant to.

I continue surveying each room, noticing the quality of the work. Henry may be top-notch, but my team can match him regarding quality of workmanship and materials. Yes, with a huge amount of ghastly work and perseverance, maybe one day, if I stick to it and don't stop believing in myself and my crew, Hudson Home Designs may have a shot at becoming, in time, just as prominent as Turner & Cooke or Wickford. The Wickfords may be wealthy, but Henry Turner started out in his father's shed, and look at him now.

★

Saturday morning and I've got the entire house to myself. I'm checking my spreadsheet and narrowing down my choice for the bathrooms and waiting for Gabe to arrive once again, just like Groundhog Day. But this time, hopefully, things will be different. Especially if we're serious about each other— and starting a family. I'm not prepared to lose everything all over again, so I'm in. But this time, we'll lay down some ground rules, for starters. Clear the air between us. And if it feels right, we'll give it a shot. No more rushing into heartache. We'll start from scratch, if necessary. He'll come through that door and – as if on cue, my mobile rings. It's Gabe. He should be in the air right now, shouldn't he? An uneasy, familiar feeling grips my middle section.

'Please don't tell me your flight is delayed again,' I beg.

Silence.

Oh, bugger it. 'Are you stuck on a stopover?'

I feel him hesitate. 'I'm sorry, Faith, to do this to you again...'

I literally feel my muscles freezing. 'What...' I croak, leaning against the wall for support, '...happened now?'

'I've run into a bit of a problem.'

'With your passport? Customs? You didn't pack anything weird, did you?'

'I... never packed. Faith, I'm so sorry.'

'Never packed...?' I repeat dumbly, trying to make sense of his words.

'Faith?'

Oh-oh. Gabe never uses this tone. I swallow down the fear that something seismic is about to happen.

'I have something to tell you.'

And there it is, just as you're climbing out of the pit of despair, the universe remembers you again.

'Are you okay, Gabe? Just tell me you're not sick.'

Pause for dramatic effect. 'I'm not sick, Faith—'

'*Ohthankgod*,' I gush, relief flooding my veins. I always feared that something would intervene with our Happily Ever After. Not that it already hadn't, but once we'd got over the Vanessa hurdle, we could face anything. I suddenly know that now. 'Whatever it is, Gabe, I'm there for you.'

And then he groans. 'Jesus, I just don't deserve you, Faith…'

I can actually feel my heartbeat pounding in my neck now. 'Gabe, just tell me what it is and we'll sort it together.'

'Faith… I'm so sorry. You're the sweetest and kindest girl on the planet and—'

'Will you just tell me what's happened?' I practically scream, unable to take it anymore.

He makes a funny noise in his throat. 'I… uhm, wanted you to hear it from me first. I'm sorry to do this to you, Faith. But she's sort of… pregnant with my kid.'

8

Back to Black

*W*hen I think of my life, even before Richard had abandoned me, I can't help but notice a pattern. My father had abandoned my mother. Richard had abandoned me. And I don't know how much longer I can hold on. The girls are only toddlers, in the hands of an inept, unreliable mess of a mother. I have no job, no one to help me, no one to turn to. What other choice do I have but to give them up?

I close my mother's diary. It seems that even before our birth, fate had been leading to that inexorable end of our being abandoned, which was to become the leitmotif of our lives. Look at my mother. Look at my sister. Look at me, multiply abandoned, over and over again.

Gabe knew what I'd been through as a child. He knew how important love and family are to me. He also knew that I didn't deserve any of this. I'm not just a normal dumped girl. I'm a girl who's suffered abandonment by her father before she was even born, then by her mother because of alcohol, to continue being abandoned by foster parents.

It had gone on and on for years. I thought I had finally found the person to be still with in this crazy, sordid world. But Gabe is not the one. Or perhaps I am not the one, either. Perhaps I am unlovable. Perhaps I scare men away with my sob story. But it doesn't matter anymore, because from now on, I will be my own woman. On my own. By choice. That way no one will ever leave me again.

I had sworn to myself that I would never be like our mum, no matter what. And I'd put on a thick set of armour. I'd even done very well throughout school, although my tendencies to keep myself to myself would have made me somewhat of an oddball loner, had it not been for Hope. After all, who wanted to hear my sob story? And to be quite honest, I didn't want to tell it either. Let them think whatever they wanted about me.

'Faith! Faith! Are you all right? Open up!' a voice calls as someone bangs on my front door. It takes me a full minute to recognise Hope's voice. Dammit, now there will be no peace until I answer her.

I open an eye, just one, as my head can't take the full force of daylight. Which room am I in? I don't recognise it. I open the other eye and prop myself up, but this room is not Gabe's music room where I've been camping out. It's my entire sodding flat in Truro, and – oh crap the floor is covered in bottles! And I don't even remember buying them. I can't be doing this again!

When did I come back here? I must have drunk my heart out, because I feel sick. In one hungover glance, I make out the shop-bought chocolate cake I'd managed to polish off despite my complete loss of appetite, and an array of used tissues resting on the sea of bottles like white, puffy clouds.

What a night.

With the sheer shock of it, I don't remember much, except for turning off my mobile to stop Gabe's yammering at how sorry he was. I don't even remember bringing Jawsy here, nor do I remember the drive back. But I do remember sobbing for hours on end, with no one but my own miserable, dumped arse. No wonder my voice is hoarse and I feel completely dried up and empty. If I'd called my sister or my coastal girls – Nat, Nina and Rosie – they'd have dropped everything to come and comfort me and tell me that it would all be all right. Which wasn't what I needed last night, nor now. Because nothing is going to be all right anymore. Snow White has finally woken up and seen the dwarves for what they really are – misogynistic bastards preying on a lonely girl.

'Faith! Come *on*!' Hope insists.

I open my mouth to answer her, if only to get her to stop shouting and banging, but nothing comes out. My throat is parched with all the alcohol I've thrown down my neck and that found its way up again a few hours later.

I can't believe it's only been one night since… since… It feels like I've been lying here forever. Maybe I should stay here for another forever, or at least until the numbness subsides.

Because that's it – I don't feel any pain like the first time Gabe dumped me for Vanessa. The first time, I had gone through all the standard stages, from shock to denial, to utter madness, endless misery, asking myself over and over where I had gone wrong. Weeks of holing myself up and pretending to work from home. Days without washing or even eating. And Hope swooping in to save the day, dragging me under the shower and washing my hair while I just stood there and cried.

But none of that this time. Now I actually feel… nothing. As if I were dead. Empty. Like an old sock that someone's thrown aside. I roll over as the deafening echo of Gabe's voice comes back to me in a myriad of *I'm sorrys* and *forgive mes* and *What else can I dos* as he explained that he didn't know she was pregnant.

And then his voice had disappeared as I'd slipped into what I can only think is a state of shock. How else can you describe being completely unresponsive to any stimulation from the outside world?

'If you don't open this door right now, I swear I'll break it down myself!' Hope roars. 'And then I'm going to fly to goddam Thailand and beat the crap out of that upstart low-life who calls himself a musician! Remember I pound meat to a pulp for a living!'

And knowing her as one who does not utter idle threats, she will.

I slide off the settee and drag myself across what seems like the endless deserted wasteland of my life to let her in, almost tripping over a wheelie suitcase I don't even remember packing the night before.

Apparently, I had cleared the place of every new trace of me (as there hadn't been any old ones left). Our coverlet, our sheets and all of our most precious keepsakes, which I had brought to the beach house in a fit of absolute bliss, now lay in a pile inside the open bags. It looked like my entire life had imploded in one tiny puff of colour.

And I'm supposed to be an interior designer who makes homes better. Ha – what an impostor I am. I go into people's houses with promises of turning them into homes. How could I ever expect to make a happy home when I myself come from a broken one?

I clutch at the doorknob, open the door and there she is, my rock, carrying the contents of an entire shop with her.

'Hey…' she says as she plops down her shopping bags, eyeing me critically without telling me how crappy I look. She knows better than to say anything, let alone ask how I am, bless her. Besides, my outfit of pyjama bottoms and old wool sweater – complete with chocolate ice cream stains – are definitely a tell-tale sign.

'Who told you?' I ask as she comes in and notices the empty bottles, but says nothing, bless her.

'You left me a voicemail. I didn't find it until this morning so I drove the kids to a friend's and went to Sainsbury's. I've got absolutely all of your favourite foods.'

Ever since we were bounced around from foster home to foster home awaiting adoption, Hope was always the one to take care of me although she was only fifteen minutes older. Even now, when I'm down, who comes to my rescue but my faithful sister with a bag full of tricks and treats? Only this time, I fear, there is no remedy in her bag for a twice-broken heart. There is no pie, no chocolate or fried chicken in the world that will put it back together again.

The food, I can't even bear to look at, let alone enjoy. She lines everything up on the counter, awaiting a response.

'Thanks,' I manage from under the blanket.

As I watch her from the corner of the settee, she switches the kettle on and begins to busy herself, opening and closing cabinets, the creaking and cracking sounds reminding me that this flat is an absolute shite-hole with its cheap countertop and cabinets – nothing like the beautiful and sturdy kitchen Henry had first designed for the beach house. Or the one he's planning at the moment.

Henry, so dependable, steadfast and true. Why couldn't I have fallen for someone solid like him, rather than a rock star who was always a bit OTT?

Hope comes back to the sofa with the Home Hug I had given her when she was pregnant with Jowen. I look up at her and she shrugs.

'I didn't know if you'd found yours yet,' she says, putting it on my lap and gently pulling our mother's diary out of my reach. Instinctively my arms wrap around the cushion in a life-long gesture that is ingrained in me. Hope pulls my blanket closer around me, her warm hands lingering on my shoulders and for a fleeting moment, we're back in one of our former homes, and I have the feeling that nothing has changed. We can only depend on each other.

At the beach house, I'd been completely surrounded by Vanessa's stuff, from her mugs to her bath mats as I hadn't been able to access most of my own things yet. I'm living on borrowed items, and from the woman who stole my life, to boot.

Everything at the beach house had screamed of her after only the six months she'd been there, while of the three wonderful years Gabe and I had lived and loved there, barely a whisper. And now? Where am I, in my life?

'I've lost e-everything,' I hiccup, tears falling again.

Hope doesn't answer me, but goes back to the counter where the kettle is ready, and returns with a hot water bottle and a steaming cup of instant cocoa. Hope has never been one to fuss. She is pragmatic and straightforward – just what I need right now.

'Here,' she says, tucking the hot water bottle under my throw. 'You haven't lost anything but a bloody philanderer. Take my word for it – consider yourself lucky it happened now and not when you had kids together.'

'Is that supposed to make me feel better?'

'Not if you're a muppet, no. But if you have one ounce of vision, you'll see he did you a favour, Faith.'

'How? How is leaving me – *twice* – a favour?' I demand, torturing the chimney bit of my Home Hug between my fingers. 'And having a baby with her, when he promised to have it with me and—' I shut up, realising how pathetic I sound.

'He's gone, Faith,' she sentences as she sits down on the pouffe before me. 'Look at him. He may well be topper of the charts, loved by millions. But he doesn't love you or even that steaming psychopath Vanessa.'

'You don't think so either?' I ask, clinging to her words.

Hope snorts. 'God, no. I think her wild child image appeals to him because it simply makes him more noticeable. They're like Sid and Nancy, Kurt and Courtney. Believe me, he doesn't love anyone but himself. Because he doesn't know what love is. I already pity that poor baby.'

To be honest, so do I. Not so much because of Gabe as because of Vanessa. A baby in her hands would definitely be at risk, poor thing.

'Yuh, poor, poor baby...' I moan under my breath. It will never know what it's like to have a loving mother. Just like Hope and I, really. We have a lot in common with this baby already.

'At the end of the day, Faith, he's done it before, and you survived. Well, barely. But this time you're stronger.'

I snort as I look down at my socks, realising they don't match. Not that I care.

'Of course you are. There's nothing more he can throw at you that will hurt you. You are now completely, utterly and totally immune to him, Faith.'

'Am I?' I sniff, wiping my eyes and nose on my sleeve. Hope passes me the tissue box.

'Here. Yes, you are. You are a strong girl, even if right now you might not think so.'

'Hope, do you often think about Mum?' I venture.

She puckers her lips and tilts her head as if trying to remember her. 'I used to. Not so much anymore. I have my own life to live now thank God, and I suggest you do the same. She and our "father" are both gone, and the damage they caused is up to us to fix now.'

She's right, of course. But saying it is one thing, while executing it is a completely different story.

'So what's your next step?' she asks while cleaning up around me.

'Cash the cheque for all our losses. Charge him a bloody fortune,' I say through gritted teeth as I rake a hand through the mess that my hair is. All I know is that I'm certainly not going back to the beach house. I've earnt the right to wallow for at least one day. Tomorrow I'll have to peel myself off the floor and sort out my crew. But today, I've earnt the right to be miserable.

Hope cackles. 'Good for you, I was going to say! Why don't you come and stay with me and the kids, then? We have plenty of room and they would love to spend some time with you.'

'Oh, I dunno. I don't know what to do right now.'

'Why don't you start with a shower?' she quips, wrinkling her nose.

'Do I stink?'

'Well, let's say that you don't exactly smell like a bowl of roses.'

I take a whiff of my clothes. 'Ugh. Sorry.'

'In any case,' she says, 'not that the baby will be raised by them as a couple, with all that ceramic throwing.'

I scratch my head. 'You mean pottery throwing? What's that got to do with anything?'

'No, I mean crockery. I heard that—' Hope bites her lip.

'What?' I say, propping myself onto one elbow. 'What have you heard?'

Hope rolls her eyes. 'I was trying to spare you some more heartache, but yes, apparently they have these huge fights in front of everyone. Last week she threw a plate at him in a restaurant, and there were noodles hanging from his face.'

'How do you even know all that?'

'The miracles of the net. There's even a picture.'

I want to laugh at the idea of them being at loggerheads – truly, I do – but my head hurts too much.

'What if the baby turns out like her?' I ask Hope.

She shrugs. 'The way I see it, either way, the kid's doomed. Are you going to sit up or am I going to have to spoon-feed you?'

I reluctantly prop myself up further. 'I'm not really hungry, Hope.'

'Of course you're not. That's why I made you your favourite.'

I crane my neck towards the counter. 'You made me vegetable soup?'

'You bet I did,' she says with a smile as she stands up, ruffling my hair as she passes me by.

'But do go take that shower, Faith. By the time you get back it'll all be ready, dessert and all.'

I watch as she busies herself removing lids and heating stuff like the great mum she is. Jowen and Verity are the luckiest kids in the world.

I get to my feet, my head still slightly spinning, but manage to throw myself at her back, wrapping my arms around her waist and resting my head on her shoulder. 'You're the best of the bestest sisters ever,' I murmur.

'Get on with it, you,' she gently chides me, but I know she loves it. We'd never had any displays of affection from anyone but each other, and it was something we hadn't lost over the years. If anything, we became closer and closer with each family that returned us to the sender.

Hope blames herself because she was a wild child, but I blame myself because I was much too needy. I guess that hasn't changed. Always afraid of being abandoned until Gabe and I set up house together. And now the other shoe has finally dropped.

'Thank you, sis, for being there for me. What would I do without you?'

She turns and puts her hands on her hips, and I wonder if our mother used to do that. I can scarcely remember her.

'You'd probably starve and catch lice,' she says with a laugh. 'Shower.'

'Yes, ma'am,' I say with an American salute as I move towards the bathroom. I only hope that some of my sorrows will be washed down the drain, but I sincerely doubt it.

I throw myself under a hot shower and lather up, wondering how I'm going to break it to my team. If only I could finally catch the attention of the Wickfords with my work on the beach house. I had been banking on making it into the trade magazines and thus increasing my chances of being noticed by them. I've done my homework and know exactly what they like. But first, I have to make them know I actually exist.

After my shower, I get dressed into a pair of cleanish leggings and a long-sleeved T-shirt and wool socks. I'm always cold when I'm miserable, go figure. And then I sit on the settee again and Hope forces a bowl of soup on me. I manage to eat a few spoonfuls without hurling, but that's where I draw the line. The tiramisu will have to wait for a better day, because this day – the first where I realise that I'm definitely on my own once again – is a never-ending nightmare.

'I'm sorry, Faith, but I've got to get to work now,' Hope says, storing the food in the freezer and collecting the now empty plastic containers, which she shoves into her carrier. 'Or I can cancel, if you need me.'

And ground her here, next to a snivelling wreck, when she could be dazzling her patrons and doing what she loves best?

'Don't be silly, Hope. You go to work. And thank you. I really appreciate it.'

'Are you sure? I'm owed a few days, so—'

'No, save them for the kids. Honestly, I'm fine.'

She continues to watch me, so I pick up the remote in a gesture that looks like I'm actually taking interest in something besides my own misery.

'If you're sure…?'

'Go,' I say, turning the TV on. 'You're never alone with Netflix.'

She chuckles. 'That would be a great slogan.'

'Aren't I clever,' I drawl.

'Okay, then. But call me if you need me, Faith – even for a chat.'

As if. Once she gets to work it's going to be hell broken loose as usual in that kitchen. 'Of course. Now go.'

She turns to go, but then comes back, bending over me and kissing my cheek. 'Bye, sweetie.'

'Bye, sis – and thank you. I don't know what I'd do without you,' I say, feeling my throat getting all knotty again as she smiles and gently closes the door. *Easy, Faith. You don't want to cry yourself dry again – you've still got the whole sodding night ahead of you.*

As I'd imagined, there is nothing on TV that I'm in the mood for, and despite all the food Hope has brought me, there is nothing I want. I don't want to read anything, I don't want to do anything. I don't know what to do with myself. I'm all cried out, but I'm not sleepy – just absolutely exhausted, from head to toe.

I turn over on the settee and watch the muted scenes of a family having breakfast. Outside the sun is shining – it's got to be California – and they're all so chatty and chipper and even the family dog is wearing an ear-to-ear smile. 'Yeah,' I tell them. 'It's all a bed of roses until he gets some other girl *pregnant.*'

I flick the remote and the scene changes to a couple kissing so I immediately flick it again and there's some bloke in a space suit. He is floating off, untethered, into outer space as a woman clutching at the commands deck is silently screaming in what I can only assume is utter despair, "Come back!" And that's exactly how I feel, watching my life float off into a galaxy far, far away, and there's not a single thing I can do to stop it.

9

All Cried Out

As if someone had hit a switch, the next day is a dark and dank morning, so foggy I can barely see the flats opposite mine.

I send a collective message to my team to come over to my flat for the news. Thea, who is the smartest kid in town and also the most intuitive, has come armed with cakes of all shapes and sizes.

She plonks them down onto my kitchenette counter next to Hope's bounty, turns the kettle on and hoists herself up on the stool as the boys scatter around on the green velvet pouffes and my one bean bag.

I take a deep breath. 'First of all, I wanted to thank you guys for coming over at such short notice.'

'Why didn't we meet at the beach house?' Mike wants to know.

'Is something wrong?' Rudy asks.

I look at my crew, i.e. my second family. I've known them

for years and have always taken good care of them, and they of me. I owe them complete honesty.

'Yes, as a matter of fact, there is,' I whisper as the kettle whistles, ignored by Thea who is staring at me intently and biting on her Gothic nails, waiting for me to ring the death knell.

'Oh God, we're not fired, are we?' she gasps, and the look on her face kills me.

'No, sweetie, of course not.' I huff. 'Gabe called me. He's not coming back for a while. He and Vanessa are expecting a baby, so…'

Paul jumps to his feet straight from the bean bag as if catapulted by a set of springs. 'That little shit! I knew he was going to do something like this! I just knew it!'

Thea slips off her stool and puts her arms around me. 'Oh, Faith, are you okay?'

The boys are shaking their heads, muttering a few foul ones.

I hug Thea back. 'I will be. I just wanted to tell you that I don't know where we stand on this job right now. If we're still in, I'll simply step back from the project and you can take the reins.'

An astonished silence follows, but I can clearly hear the *Not agains* and *I knew its*. But not one *I told you so*. I love these people so much I feel like bawling all over again.

'Forget the company for now,' Mike says, clenching his fists. 'When's he coming back, so I can crown the bugger?'

I force a half-laugh so I won't cry. 'Ah, probably after the baby is born, Mike. But no worries. We've got lots of clients. We'll be fine.'

'Let's just concentrate on you,' Thea says, getting up to pour the coffees and opening the box of cakes. 'I knew this would come in handy today, one way or the other. And all those years of defending him. Jesus, what a tosser.'

She passes the cakes around and Rudy distributes the coffee mugs as we all gather, munching and sipping, each silent in their own maudlin thoughts. It's more than I can take.

'I'll try to find out what's happening with the house. I promise you.'

'It's not us we're worried about, pet,' Bill says. 'It's you.'

'I'll be fine, Bill – but thank you.'

'I still bloody don't believe it,' Paul mutters.

I sigh. 'Thanks, everyone, for your support. Can we now change the subject?'

'Wait – what about Henry's kitchen? And the rest of his work there?' Rudy asks.

'I imagine it's still on. Gabe hasn't fired anyone, as far as I know. And please – not a word to Henry.'

'But he's going to know when you don't show up,' Thea insists.

'I'll deal with it myself,' I assure them, wondering how on earth I'm going to do that.

They all eye each other and then turn to me with a silent nod. 'Only on one condition. You work from home. And you take your cut.'

'I can't,' I huff. 'I'm out.'

'Of course you can,' Thea assures me. 'You were in the process of choosing the bathroom tiles and white goods.'

I shake my head. 'I'm sorry, Thea. I need to step away from all this now.'

'So you're never coming back?' she squeaks. This is the first time I see her panicking.

'Of course I am,' I assure her. 'Only on a different job.'

'Okay. So when *are* you going to tell Henry?'

I sigh. 'Tomorrow. I'll tell him tomorrow.'

'But what if he asks us before you do?'

'Just… tell him I've got the flu or something.'

Again, they eye each other and nod.

'Go, now,' I say. 'Take the day off. Go and relax, and don't worry about tomorrow. You continue as if nothing has happened and I'll get back to you.'

'But without you…?' Rudy shakes his head.

'I'm sure you'll all do a smashing job, Ru,' I reassure him.

'I'd like to do a smashing job all right,' Paul mutters.

'Keep this one in check,' I say in an attempt to make a joke, and he turns to look at me, his eyes full of affection. Affection that I can't bear to see, right now, because I feel that I don't deserve any, especially for abandoning them.

I turn on my settee. 'Go, I'm sleepy. And don't report back.'

Rudy and Bob look at each other and shrug.

'Okay, Faith,' Thea says, kissing me on the cheek just as Hope had.

The next morning, while the rest of the world is at work, I'm at home feeling sorry for myself.

If I had once upon a time longed to have a couple of days off to myself, I'm only on day one and already at the end of my tether. I'd work on yet another email to the Wickfords, but the way I'm feeling, I'm afraid I'd actually write just to tell them to sod off, and who do they think they are for being so unapproachable?

To avoid going out of my mind, I get to my feet and blitz the entire flat – all four square feet of it – change Jawsy's water and feed her. Next I do the laundry, sort out my cupboards and even alphabetise my CDs and books. Next thing you know I'll be hitting the spice rack, I'm so desperate to have a purpose.

Maybe I could babysit Jowen and Verity? I miss them. And I miss Orson.

I wonder what Henry is up to. He'll be wondering why I'm not there. Unless Thea really does tell him I've the flu. But in that case would he call to see how I'm doing?

Are we even friends? We were certainly colleagues on the same project who shared a few meals. But friends? He might actually even remind me he had been telling me about Gabe all along, and I really don't need to hear that right now, thank you.

Although, in utter fairness, he really did warn me. Hope had warned me, and even my crew had warned me. Only my coastal girls have always supported me, but now I am starting to think that that was because they had been through pretty much the same misery and only wanted it to work for me as much as I did.

It seems that the entire world knew that this was going to happen. Except for me. Hooray for believing in the good in people. Hooray for believing in true sodding love. Well, that certainly teaches me.

But in all honesty, I think a tiny, minuscule atom of me *knew*. Perhaps the coward in me wanted to ignore it, gloss over it with a smile and an agenda full of dates and to-do lists, when all the while, deep down, I did have an inkling that something was off. And now I know.

I still haven't called Henry. I've been meaning to, of course, but I can't bring myself to hear the pity in his voice. Tomorrow. I'll do it tomorrow. Not that I'm bound to. We're just ex-colleagues. He doesn't depend on me for his commission. Let Thea deal with it all. She's certainly capable of that and much more.

At around five thirty, it's already pitch-black outside when the doorbell goes. It's Thea again.

'Hiya!' she chimes as she puts down another box from the bakery. At this rate she's going to turn me into such a blimp I won't be able to fit through the door. I'll be stuck here forever and ever, unless a troop of firefighters widen the door for me.

'Hey,' I chime. 'I'm so glad to see you. I've missed you. And the boys.'

'Not Henry?' she asks.

Did I miss Henry? Probably his blueberry muffins and scones. And the sparring. I shrug. 'I dunno. I guess I was sort of getting used to him.'

'Have you not called him, for Christ's sake? All day he's been grilling me – *is she sick? Has she got a temperature? Has she called a doctor? Have you been to see her? Can I call her?* Jesus. Can I at least tell the poor sod he can call you?'

'What?'

'Can I tell Henry it's okay to call you? He's old-school. He doesn't want to impose, bless him.'

Again, I shrug as I shift on the settee. 'I'll call him later. After I go through all the cakes.'

'Promise?'

'I promise. Just don't tell him about Gabe, okay?'

She smiles kindly. 'I won't.'

'So what's new? I ask.

'You mean, at work?'

I bite my lip. 'I mean, in your life.'

'Well, Rudy and I have finally started dating…'

'You're kidding me!' I groan. 'I've been waiting for this to happen for years and the first day I'm not around, you decide to go out? I'm so happy for you!'

'Yeah, well, nothing's changed, really. I still give him orders and he carries them out.' She smiles. 'Only, at the end of the day I get to be his *lover*…'

'Awh,' I gush. 'Finally.'

'Muscle men send their love,' she informs me.

'Please give them my love back. I'm sorry I haven't answered any of your messages on our WhatsApp group,' I apologise. I know that if I start reading them I'm going to get sucked into the project all over again, and I can't. 'What else is new? Besides work, obviously.' I'm dying for a crumb of gossip – anything from the real world.

She looks at me funny, then looks out the window.

'What? Thea?'

She hesitates. 'Uhm… it's about Vanessa.'

'Oh God, the baby's okay, isn't it?'

'Yeah, yeah, it's fine, as far as I know. So… I'm assuming you don't know that they're back? Gabe's postponed the tour. She's just had a baby shower.'

Wow, she's wasted absolutely no time, has she? A baby shower. If Gabe hadn't left me six months ago, perhaps we'd have already had a shower for *our* baby.

'No, but I imagine that's the norm.'

Thea snorts. 'With Vanessa Chatsbury, nothing is the norm. So I guess you know nothing about it?'

I groan inwardly. 'No, why?' I can't help but ask.

'She had this life-size cake made of herself. *With* bump.'

'Wow.'

Thea holds up a hand. 'I'm not finished. Inside her, let's say, stomach, there was a life-size, pink chocolate baby. And she had her midwife pull it out.'

I simply stare at her. That's so disgustingly uber-kitsch, even for Vanessa. And yet she seems to surprise me every day with her outlandish ideas. My own ideas of multi-coloured balloons and butternut icing pale into nothingness in comparison. 'Well, she is more full of surprises than a piñata.'

Thea eyes me. 'So, you're okay, then?'

Okay? I'll never in a million years be okay. 'Of course! Listen, I have to go lie down. I think I'm coming down with something for real this time.'

'Do you need me?' she offers.

'I'll be fine, thanks, Thea.' I just want to be alone. I also want to stop the world because I need to get off. And eat tons of chocolate, preferably not shaped like a baby.

'All right, then, I'll call you tomorrow,' she says.

'Thanks for the love – and the cakes,' I say reaching up as she hugs me and then grabs her bag on her way out.

I snuggle into my settee, trying to get into a comfortable position perfect for wallowing for hours on end, but due to all the lugging, everything hurts. My legs, my arms, my heart. That's a muscle too, right?

As I'm drifting off to sleep, my mobile rings. It's bloody

Gabe. Again. I don't know how many times he's called. But really, what is there left to say?

I glare at the phone and making my decision, tap on the green Answer button for the first time since the news.

'Stop calling me,' I snap into it. 'You're the last person I want to hear from. Why don't you understand?'

'Faith…' comes Gabe's broken voice. 'Please, please don't hate me…'

'No, of course not,' I say. 'I just loooove you to pieces.' Well, I got the pieces part right. The ones I'd gladly tear him into.

'I'm only doing what's best for the baby. You do understand that, don't you?'

'Of course.'

'And you know, I never wanted to hurt you—'

'Hurt me *again*, you mean?'

'Could you find it in your heart to… still love me? I can tell Vanessa that I'll help her raise the baby, of course, but that I'm still with you.'

'I beg your pardon?'

'This changes nothing between us, Faith. I still want you. I want you to finish the renovations and I—'

'That's where you're wrong, Gabe. This changes everything. Goodbye.' And I hang up, only to look at the one bottle Hope hadn't dug up during her stealthy search of my flat.

I know it's wrong, and that I'm hurting myself. But I need this right now. Tomorrow, I'll start all over again. Tomorrow I'll be stronger. But for now, I need to just wallow and feel sorry for myself. This one time.

It's only one bottle, at the end of the day…

One bottle is a lot of drinks, says that old voice inside me. A voice I hadn't heard in ages.

But I'll only have the one.

No—can't do that, remember? You can't stop at one. You never do! Remember all the pain and the trouble? Remember how difficult it was to get back on the wagon?

I groan. Yes. But that was a long time ago, when I was weak and young and—

You still are weak!

No, I'm not!

Then you don't need a drink!

I don't *need* it – not really. I just want to… t-take the edge off… And before the voice can reply, I'm twisting the cap off, telling myself that it will be the last time.

Precisely one bottle of whisky later, as I'm dozing on and off, I become aware of a tap-tapping. It's someone at the door. Who the hell is it, and why aren't they using the doorbell?

It takes me a few moments to get to my feet. Gosh, why do I feel so weak? Have I not eaten anything? This is not good.

'Faith, hi,' a rather dishy bloke says once I've pried the door open. 'I was worried about you. Thea said I could call, but I thought I'd rather see you. What's up?'

Henry! I hold my head. 'I'm sorry, I wa' going to call you…'

He takes a closer look at me. 'Have you been drinking?'

'Yesh. But nowhere near enough.'

'What happened?'

'Come an' sit down,' I urge feebly as I sway to one side but catch myself. I'm not that drunk.

'Thanks. Why are you sleeping here and not at the beach house?' he asks innocently, but even so, I stiffen. He's put two and two together, of course, clever bloke. Not that it's rocket science, but still.

'Gabe's got pershonal problems.'

Henry's eyebrows knit in confusion. 'Personal problems? I thought he lived in North Nirvana.'

'Well, not everything is as it sheems.'

'Right. Well, he'll be back soon, if he knows what's good for him. By the way, I've got something for you.'

'What ish it?'

He grins. 'Come out into the corridor.'

On unsteady legs, I follow him outside where there is a beautiful white oak cot, with ornate spindles and a carved backing. I run my fingers lightly across the top. And then my heart bursts into a million shards, leaving me breathless.

'I heard that you and Gabe are planning a nursery, so…'

'Oh my *God*,' I sob.

His face falls. 'What is it, Faith? Don't you like it?'

'Noooo, it'sh absholutely *beautiful*…'

'Then why the tears?' he asks softly, and his kindness is overwhelming.

'Becaushe… becaushe…' I wipe my eyes, the tears too many to catch in one swipe. 'I won't be needing it anymore. G-Gabe'sh ex-girlfriend ish pregnant.'

Henry's head snaps back as if he's been slapped. '*What?*'

'Yuh.' I nod, still unable to believe it myself.

'Oh, God, *Faith*…' he groans softly. 'I'm so *sorry*…'

I expect him to continue with an *I told you so*. But instead, he pulls me into his arms.

It's very warm against his chest, and I can feel the solid thump of his heart as it drowns out the sound of my sobs. This feels like a safe place – something I haven't had in a long time, and so I let it all out – the anguish, the humiliation, the sorrow – but above all, the loneliness and sense of not belonging that I stupidly thought I had overcome. But it's actually still quite a burden, even after all these years.

I had been Gabe's woman, his life partner, his significant other. But now, what was I?

Not even when we were in foster homes had I felt this sense of loss, lack of place and purpose. Every time I try and see the good in people, it turns out that I'm wrong about them. Every time I try to be optimistic and hope for something good to happen, it only *seems* like it does, but then it all dissolves. Every hope, every prayer, every pining or longing always backfires on me. It's so difficult to maintain the slightest amount of optimism. Because I know that when I do, there's some nasty surprise waiting for me in the end. So why even hope anymore?

'It's okay to cry, it's okay…' he soothes me, caressing the back of my head, a gesture of protection that completely undoes me even more, if possible, as his other arm surrounds me and I am enveloped in strong, gentle male. Solid. Dependable. And it feels like home.

'Henry…?'

'Yes, Faith?'

'I think I might be a little shloshed.'

'That's okay. Life owes you one.'

'Thank you for your kindnesh. I didn't know you were sho nishe.'

'Glad to surprise you, then. Come on, let's go back inside,' he says as he closes the door on the cot, his arm still around my shoulder.

I allow him to lead me back into the flat where I flop down onto a pouffe.

'I'm sho shorry… I don't get it,' I babble. 'In front of my team I'm all together and calm and composed, but now – in front of you…'

'You want to keep your cool around them; you're their employer, it's only natural. But you don't have to do that with me,' he soothes.

I look at him through blurry eyes. 'I don't?'

He smiles and shakes his head. 'Just let it all out. Break-ups are hard. But you'll get through it, believe me,' he says, now crouching before me, his hands taking mine from my lap. 'If anybody can do this, it's Faith Hudson.'

'Thank you, Henry. You are like a warm blanket,' I babble. 'And on top of everything elshe, you shmell delicioush. Like, shpring rain and freshly cut grash.'

A soft chuckle rumbles through his chest, and I chuckle, too. Freshly cut *grass*?

'Why are you so nishe to me? I've been nothing but horrible to you…'

'Awh, Faith, you with this strong exterior while inside you're so beaten up, you're breaking my heart, you know?' he whispers.

'I am?' I ask, pulling away enough to look up into his face, which, I have to say, is quite handsome. I know I'm absolutely sloshed, but how have I never noticed the long, long lashes, and the streaks of honey in his dark, liquid eyes?

STARTING OVER AT THE LITTLE CORNISH BEACH HOUSE

And how have I never noticed how his dark curls caress what I now see is a strong neck, and broad shoulders?

How have I never actually paid attention to any of him – the twinkle in his eye, or to the way his devilish brows knit in concentration? To the cheeky tongue that darts out whenever he says something he shouldn't, or to the dimples in his cheeks, and that magnetism that is now screaming at me? On what planet have I been living?

It's like I'm seeing him for the first time. He is a completely different person. Or, perhaps, I am.

'I like you,' I murmur. 'A lot. Do you like me?'

After a moment's silence, he whispers back. 'You know I do, Faith.'

'I haven't been very nice to you, have I? I'm truly sorry, Henry.'

'Yes, well. It was an initial misunderstanding. I've put it behind me.'

'You have? Becaushe I haven't. I don't undershtand how I could have been mean to shomeone like you. You're kind and intelligent and a great joiner. I love your kitchensh. I love everything about you. I love your eyesh and your mouth and your broad shouldersh and your huge handsh and even your tush.'

At that, he chuckles. 'You're not so bad yourself, actually.'

I sigh. 'But I guesh you're not attracted to me.'

'Don't say that, Faith. You know I am.'

'Awh, really?'

'Yes, really.'

'Then kish me,' I whisper.

He looks at me as if he's afraid to touch me. As if I

were bad luck. He's probably afraid to catch it from me. I certainly can't blame him.

'It's time for bed,' he says, scooping me up (finally!) in his arms and heading for my bedroom.

'Yesh, let'sh go,' I agree as he gently lays me down on the bed, reaching for my shoes.

We can't make love with my shoes on, I suddenly realise. Unless they're sexy stilettos. 'I'm shorry, I don't have any shexy shtilettos,' I apologise.

He snorts. 'As if you needed them.'

I spread my arms and sigh in anticipation as my shoes come off.

'Henry…?' I murmur.

'Yes, Faith?'

'I think that thish wash alwaysh meant to be.'

'Go to sleep, Faith.'

'Henry?'

'Yes, Faith?'

'Will you shtay the night?'

'Of course. I'll be here when you wake up.'

'Henry?'

'Yes, Faith?'

'Thank you.'

'You're welcome. Sleep now.'

'Henry?'

'Shhhh…'

The next day I open my eyes to a thousand Black Sabbath songs playing in my head at the same time. Wait, no, there's no music. It's only my own bloody swimming head. Why do I feel like total crap?

And then I catch sight of Henry, fast asleep, his long legs outstretched on that ridiculously tiny chair, his arms folded in front of his chest. What the hell is he even doing here?

I stare at him in panic, then look under my coverlet. I'm fully dressed, thank God.

And then I remember. Gabe is gone for good this time, what with a baby on the way. A baby that isn't mine.

'Good morning,' Henry says in a lazy, sleepy voice, getting to his feet and stretching his long, strong body.

'H-hi…' I say meekly, wishing I could hide under the bed without looking too silly. But I think I passed silly last night. I have no idea what happened but I'm feeling like absolute shite.

'You okay?' he asks, checking me out.

I nod, avoiding his gaze. 'I'm so sorry, Henry, about falling apart on you last night. I hope I didn't say anything offensive?'

Henry looks at me. I have a vague memory of doing just that, but I can't remember exactly, for the life of me.

He smiles. 'You're fine, Faith.'

'I'm sorry, I was completely sloshed. What did I say?'

His face turns slightly red and my hands fly to my face. 'Oh, my God, I said something horrible, didn't I? I'm so sorry!'

'Absolutely not,' he assures me.

'Whatever I said, please know that I never meant any of it. Please forget whatever it was. Can you do that? For my sake?'

He studies me, his eyes dark. 'I'll try.'

Thank God.

'What were your plans for today?' he asks, steadying me as I scrabble to my unsteady feet, floundering for my shoes, which are nowhere in sight.

'Uhm…' I sigh, looking around me. 'I dunno. Feel sorry for myself, I guess.'

'Not happening. Your sister called your mobile. I wouldn't have answered it of course, but I didn't want her to worry about you. She's on her way over with her kids. Her sitter is unavailable and she has to go to work, so…'

'What? Now?' I know Hope is doing it to help me, and I love her for it, but I really don't want the kids to see me like this. All I want is to be left alone to wallow a little longer. Just one more day. 'But I'm not fit to… I look like crap. I *feel* like crap.'

'You don't look like crap,' he says loyally. 'Actually, uh, you look kind of pretty…'

I stop searching for my shoes and look up at him. He is now facing me, his eyes probing into mine and I can't bear the intensity of his gaze. I just can't. I want to dig a hole and crawl into it for the next fortnight at least.

'Thank you, Henry, but you don't need to say that.'

'No, but it's true. Listen, I was on my way to pick up Orson to go to Heligan Gardens. Would you all like to join us?'

'Thanks, but maybe some other time. I have a huge headache. I don't even know how I'm going to manage with Verity and Jowen.'

'I can help you,' he offers.

'I couldn't ask you to do that.'

'Of course you can. It'll be okay, you'll see.'

I think about it a second. Knowing the kids will be happy with Orson is a no-brainer. Me, I'll just have to grin and bear the gazillion nails driving into my skull. And the thorns in my heart. 'All right. Thank you, Henry.'

He smiles. 'You're welcome. Now go get ready – they're due any minute.'

'Right. I'm just going to have a shower, then. Help yourself to breakfast. There's loads of food.'

As the hot water soaks into me, so does some common sense. What *did* I say to him last night? Did I make a pass at him? I remember being very loose-lipped. I think I even mentioned his looks. Oh God, I think I did make a pass at him! But he doesn't mention it. Handsome *and* a gent. What must he be *thinking* of me?

As much as I'd love to hide under the jets forever, I have to come out sometime, so I turn off the water, pull the bathrobe around me and towel-dry my hair while hyping myself into a state of confidence. By the time I go back into the living room, I look quite relaxed, even if on the inside I'm one huge cringe.

'Henry, you were really great last night,' I say nice and cool, only to come to a halt.

'Hi, Auntie Fi!' Verity and Jowen cheer, throwing themselves at me while Hope's mouth falls open as her eyes dart between me and Henry. And then a huge smile splits her face.

'Hi, Sis!' she chimes, suddenly speeding up like in an old movie, her every movement a flash of limbs. 'Thanks for keeping them, sorry to run, got to go, see you tonight!' and with a quick kiss to her kids, she's off like a shot.

'Hope, wait,' I call.

'Bye, Henry!' she calls over her shoulder.

'See you, Hope!' he calls back.

The impression she was under is obvious, and Henry coughs, eyeing me sheepishly, but says nothing. Which is a mouthful in itself. You'd expect him to say something like, *Oh, did she get that one wrong*, or similar. But he doesn't contest it.

'Right, guys! Have we got plans for you!' Henry says, clapping his hands together. 'We're going to pick up my son Orson and then we're taking you all to a secret garden!'

Verity's hands fly to her cheeks in amazement. 'Secret...?'

'Yes,' I assure her. 'With lots of creatures to discover!'

'Woweee' Jowen cries, punching the air. 'I love creatures!'

Henry laughs, ruffling his hair.

'Just let me get dressed and we'll be on our way!' I say and dash for my wardrobe on the way to the bathroom, where I slip on a cream-coloured wool dress. Practical but feminine.

Once we've picked up Orson from his friend's house, we make it to Heligan Gardens where the three of them are blown away by the sheer size and beauty of the place.

We spend the morning wandering around, discovering all kinds of species of plants and animals and water fountains and I breathe in deeply, trying to make my head clear of the heavy pall weighing both in my head and in my heart. The kids are ahead of us, flitting just like the beautiful, multi-coloured butterflies. Henry is smiling to himself and to us, and I breathe in deeply, the air fragrant with all the plants and flowers surrounding us. Heligan Gardens is certainly a place to return to again and again. To think that it had been rediscovered by chance after having been forgotten for so long.

By the time we make it to the garden restaurant it is gone past noon, so we sit at a table and order.

'It's lovely in here,' I observe, taking off my cardigan and we pile all of the jumpers in the empty chair at the head of the table.

The kids all order burgers and fries while Henry goes for the steak and grilled vegetables. Personally, I'm intrigued by the cheese curry, which looks delicious. Strangely, I'm absolutely ravenous now, when usually after a drink too many I can't even look at food.

'Can we have dessert, too, Auntie Fi?' Jowen asks as he digs into his burger.

I laugh and ruffle his hair. 'Let's see how you do with that first, shall we?' I compromise.

Orson nods. 'Me, too, Auntie Fi. I promise to eat up all my food!'

Henry and I exchange glances as the kids happily chomp on their food as if Orson had just said the most natural thing in the world. And it did sound natural. It feels natural. This little boy is part of me, and the thought of not seeing him after the job is done... I swallow, unable to answer him. All I can do is smile.

'Dad, tell her I can eat a horse when I want to!' Orson insists.

'Yeah, me too, Orson!' Jowen assures him, swiping his

hands across the space between us, sending my curry into my lap.

'Oh…!' Jowen gasps, scrambling to wipe it off, but it only makes it worse.

'It's okay, sweetheart,' I say as I dip my napkin into my fizzy water which they say is supposed to work miracles with stains. But this one is a huge mess – the size of a small canvas, and I can't help but laugh at the look on Jowen's face. 'It's nothing.'

Henry looks at me and grins. I'm sensing he is pleasantly surprised by my laid-back attitude. So am I, to be honest. But then, I could forgive the kids anything.

After lunch we continue our perusal, but fatigue has settled in so we soon decide to take the children home as Hope is just about finishing her shift anyway.

'Can we do something again soon?' Orson asks me.

'Of course we can, darling,' I reply. 'If your dad agrees.'

'Of course,' Henry says promptly. 'Anything you like, guys.'

'Cool!' Verity says. 'Thank you, Henry. Thank you Auntie Fi!'

Hope opens her front door and the kids make a mad dash for her. She bends to hug them as Henry and I watch from the car.

'Thanks, guys! Do you want to come in for a cuppa?' she calls out to us.

'Thanks, Hope, but I've got work to do.' Then I turn to Henry. 'Sorry, did you want to—?'

'I'm good, thanks,' he replies and waves to my family as

we wave and take off. Orson is in the back seat waving to Verity and Jowen like he'll never see them again.

'You like your new friends, don't you, Orson?' Henry asks.

'Oh, yes, Daddy!' he confirms. 'I want to spend all summer with them. Can we?'

Henry slides me a glance and chuckles. 'We'll see what we can do about that, son.'

And a sudden warmth floods me, tinged with a touch of nostalgia: plans, children, excursions.

'Right,' says Henry, and I look up to see that we've arrived.

'Oh. Thank you both for a wonderful day,' I manage, reaching in the back to kiss Orson goodbye. It almost hurts to leave him. And Henry, who has been a real gent today. And, uhm, last night.

'Bye, Auntie Fi!' Orson chimes as he wraps his little arms around me.

'Bye, sweetheart,' I say softly and turn to Henry. 'Thanks again, Henry, for a great day.'

'Sure, no problem,' he assures me. Then: 'Listen, I've got some work ideas I'd like to run past you tomorrow, if you're up for it? I have a couple of friends who need some work done.'

'Uhm...' What's wrong with me? I have to get back in the saddle as soon as possible if I'm going to eat and pay rent. 'Yes, of course, thank you. Why don't you come for breakfast? I've eaten all the cakes but I've got some excellent coffee beans.'

'Okay, then. See you tomorrow!' he calls and slowly turns the 4x4 around as I linger at the door.

★

As I lie down in bed that night, completely exhausted, memories of the day manage to cheer me up. Orson enjoyed himself immensely in Jowen and Verity's company. My niece and nephew are truly the sweetest kids. Perhaps a mite spoilt, but I understand how it happened. Hope wants to give them everything we never had. And in any case, there's still time to intervene. Henry also is very good with Orson. He's patient and creative. And caring.

And then, without any warning, the night before comes back to me in one long kaleidoscope of memories. I remember stretching out my arms, trying to kiss Henry while he is taking off my shoes. I remember him stilling my hands. God only knows what I was doing with them. If it hadn't been for his restraint, I would have made a total arse out of myself. How glad am I that nothing happened? If anything ever did in the future, I would like to remember every single moment.

The next morning I manage to drag myself out of bed. For what, I don't know exactly. Hope doesn't need me to babysit today, and I, like the song goes, just don't know what to do with myself.

It feels tremendously odd, being home and idle on a weekday. Outside, even though it's pouring with rain, from my window I can see the endless toing and froing of cars in the road and of people dashing off on foot to work at all hours.

I'm so bored I actually grab a stool and begin to

people-watch, trying to guess what kind of job they're in, or where they're going. And then I wonder if any of these people are slinking off to be with their lover under the pretence of an early-morning shift, and whose heart is going to break today. I guess that Gabe's influence is hard to erase. Well, I'm going to have to do a lot of work on myself if I'm ever going to get back in the saddle. I can't let him destroy me a second time. I am thoroughly disappointed in myself, but I am determined to never fall for the bottle again. And this time I really mean it. All I need to do is stay busy and focused on something else.

But even if I decided to do some much-needed cleaning, for instance, I haven't got it in me. And even that would take less than an hour. Perhaps I could hand-wash my sheets? That should keep me busy for a while.

Also, it feels odd – okay, terrible, actually – to be back to this flat that I hate with a passion. And as much as I love Jawsy, she can't answer me when I pour my heart out to her. I know because I tried last night and it didn't work. She kept staring at me with those vacant eyes. Or maybe she is really a he and is totally on Gabe's side. Traitor.

And then, my eye is caught by a familiar figure in the street – Henry, getting out of his Jeep. He brings his collar up and hunches under the onslaught of the pelting rain, protecting a bag under his shirt and getting drenched as he waits for the traffic light to change.

I fall back and gasp as I catch a glimpse of myself in the mirror. I look like I feel. Not that he's come to see how I look. Just, I assume, to see how I am feeling. Which is extremely kind of him.

Henry. I can't receive him looking like I do, so I make a

mad dash for the loo where I wash my face, brush my teeth and comb my hair at the same time. I pull on yesterday's dress still hanging from the bathroom door and slip it over my head just as the doorbell goes and I open it with my heart in my mouth.

'Hi…' he says, breathless, droplets of rain clinging to him. His eyelashes are so thick and long he looks like he's used a tar brush on them. So not fair. We women have to get up at least half an hour earlier than normal just to put on a decent face, and this bloke bats his baby browns at me with all the naturalness in the world. And… he smells delicious. As usual. Like freshly cut grass and rain.

I swallow. 'Hi.'

'What a total washdown, eh?' he greets me, wiping his feet on the mat. 'Good thing it didn't rain like this at the gardens yesterday; the kids would've been inconsolable!' He takes a close look at me and his face falls. 'Oh. You don't remember our appointment…'

I frown. 'Sorry, lately I'm not all that focused.'

He relaxes, handing me a bag. 'We were supposed to discuss business over breakfast. Is something wrong?' he asks.

Apart from the fact that I'm finding him utterly delicious?

I bite down on my lip and toss my hair nonchalantly as I turn to the dish rack. 'No, no. Come in. Have a seat. I'll, uh, get some plates.'

'Thanks,' he says.

When I turn around, he's taking his wet shirt off and my eyes almost pop out of their sockets. But he's got a T-shirt underneath, thank God.

'Do you want me to, uhm, put that under the hairdryer for you?' I ask as he hangs it on the back of my plastic chair.

You'd think I'd have at least one nice thing in this dump. 'I'm sorry, I don't have a dryer.'

'Nah, it'll be fine, thanks.'

I give him a plate and napkin and awkwardly sit down at the tiny bistro table he seems to dwarf with his huge body. God, I can barely look at him this morning.

Gabe in comparison looks tiny. And then I wonder what Henry must have looked like while growing up. Was he already tall and spindly, or did he just automatically turn into such a hunk of a man? How had I never noticed before? I must be lonelier than I thought.

'What are you shaking your head at?' he asks. 'I thought you liked chocolate muffins.'

'What? Oh! I do, thank you,' I say, practically tearing it from his hands and jamming half of it down my throat just to stop myself from saying something stupid as I normally do when I'm this nervous. I just hope he hasn't picked up on it, and most of all, on the why.

'So, how's it going?' he asks as he pulls another muffin from the bag and peels off the paper.

I jam another piece into my mouth just as he is asking me the question and freeze.

I nod emphatically, accompanying my gesture with an audible *Hm-hm* to say it's okay.

He laughs. 'I'm glad you haven't lost your appetite.'

No, thanks to you feeding me like a baby whale.

I swallow. 'I, uh, you know – manage to keep it down,' I say.

He laughs as his eyes twinkle. 'Good for you, Faith. Listen, if you're not in the mood for business talk today, I can always get out of your hair and—'

'I'm fine – really, I am,' I say hastily. Perhaps too hastily.

'I'm glad,' he says as he reaches into the bag and pulls out some scones and two pots.

'Ah, you were holding out on me!' I say triumphantly, striking the bistro table with a flat hand and he throws his head back and laughs.

'I was not,' he assures me as the corners of his eyes wrinkle in a smile. 'I was just waiting to see if you could handle the good stuff.'

'Handle the—? Give me that, I'll show you what I'm made of.'

I cut the scone open, twist the two pots of cream and jam open and dig my butter knife into the jam pot and slather on a thick layer, followed by a huge dollop of cream. 'Here, get your laughing gear around that,' I say, pushing the plate towards him.

'Oh, I couldn't,' he says. 'Hungry ladies first.'

I shrug and pull the plate back towards me. 'Don't say I didn't offer, though!'

He studies me, sipping his coffee as I chomp down on the scone 'Yes. I think you'll be just fine.'

'Told you.'

'So... is the beach house project still going ahead?' he asks.

I shrug. 'He said he wants it to. But my crew will be on their own.'

He stops, mid-bite. 'Oh, Faith, no. You should be there to complete it. Don't let him win. He'll think you're still smarting.' And then his eyes widen. 'Are you still smarting, then?'

'Me? For Gabe? I am angry for what he did, and... and... I'm angry that I let him.'

'Aw, Faith, it's not your fault. You trusted the bloke…'

I nod. 'I did. Because he was part of my f-family. But not anymore. I am *so* over him. I hadn't realised how much so, but I think I have been going off him for some time. He can't be relied upon anymore, and I just can't live like that.'

He grins, as if relieved.

'From now on, my goal is my company, and my loved ones. Nothing else matters.'

'I'm so glad to hear you say that, Faith,' he says.

And he lets the words hang there, in the space between us – that space of unuttered truths. He has a soulfulness that you don't expect upon seeing his confident demeanour. And yet, when he speaks, it's like he understands all there is to know about heartache and disappointment. His divorce must have affected him more than he lets on. And inside that cool, strong exterior, is a man who's been hurt, just like me, if not more. I wish I could do something to soothe it, to take his own pain away and to make him smile.

And I realise that yesterday was no drunken moment. I am well and truly attracted to this man. When did this even happen? Have I been so from the start, even when I was rude to him? I realise that it was just a way to keep him at a distance. But I don't want to do that anymore. But neither do I want to be too forthcoming after the show I'd put on. Is he not put off in the least by my new priorities? Because it sort of sounded like I had no time to date. Because I don't. I can't, not after what Gabe put me through. It would be like walking a tightrope with a blindfold – absolute folly. Not that he'd asked me anyway, right?

Henry turns around to look out the window. 'It's stopped raining. Fancy a walk through the puddles?' he offers, holding out a hand, his eyes shining with the promise of mischief. Who could possibly resist an offer like that?

I rise to my feet, letting him take my hand without even thinking. 'I'd love a walk.'

'And perhaps we could stop somewhere for lunch?'

'It seems every single one of you is determined to turn me into a blimp,' I protest.

'A beautiful blimp,' he says.

Oh wow. Is he really, really flirting with me? 'Just let me get my bag and shoes,' I say.

'Uh, Faith?'

'Hmm…?'

'Before we go out, you might want to change your clothes.'

'What? Why?' I look down and there, right on the lap area, is the huge orange plate-sized cheese curry stain from the day before. I roll my eyes and when he grins at me with that naughty expression, rather than feeling like a klutz, I instead feel like there's still hope for me.

The next day I drive to the restaurant to meet my coastal girls for lunch and fill them in on the Gabe situation.

'Oh my God, Faith – I can't believe he did this to you!' Nat moans.

'I knew he couldn't be trusted!' Nina seethes. 'Sorry. I mean…'

'No, Nina, it's okay,' I assure her. 'I should have known, too. My sister was right – a bloke who can do that once can and will do it again. What was I thinking?'

'Moreover, what is *he* thinking?' Rosie says, pink-faced.

'I hate it when blokes try to get away with things like that – the cheek!'

Nat shakes her head. 'I can't believe it.'

'Yep.' I swallow. 'I should have seen through all these postponed arrival dates and stuff. Christ, he'd even told me to build a *nursery*…'

Rosie rubs my back. 'You'll get over him, sweetie. It'll take you time, but you will get over him.'

I am over him. But this time it seems to be less about love and more about humiliation. 'What's the saying? Fool me once, his fault, but fool me twice? I'm such a muppet. I *deserve* this.'

'Oi,' says Nina, shaking my forearm gently. 'Don't you go thinking things like that – it'll only hurt you unnecessarily.'

Nat nods. 'Take it from all of us. Together we've racked up a total of five husbands, enough kids to open a nursery, and over fifty years of collective heartache. If we tell you that you can get through this, you *will*.'

'Of course, a handsome distraction is what it took us,' Rosie adds. 'Maybe you should find yourself one, too.'

'She's already got one in Henry,' Nina says.

Henry. Stomping through puddles. Laughing in the rain. And me actually daring to breathe and feel alive once again. It's too soon to even worry about jinxing it, let alone talking about it. Whatever it may be. Because he has never said or acted in a way that would make me think he's even remotely interested in me. Which is good, because I am the Bermuda Triangle of Heartbreak. Come anywhere near me and I'll ruin your life, too. No, he's better off where he is, single, without me.

'No,' I say. 'Henry and I are just friends.'

Rosie chuckles. 'Slow-burning romance – that's the best beginning, you know?'

'And besides, I'm in no mood to be thinking about a bloke.' Except for maybe Henry. 'They're all heartbreakers.' Again, except for maybe Henry.

'There are good men out there, Faith,' Nat says. 'You just have to let yourself fall in love again, so why not Henry?'

Why not Henry indeed? Good question. 'He's completely unfathomable. One day he's all prim and proper like Mark Darcy and you'd kill to know what he's thinking. But other days he's all easy-going and light-hearted and fun. I can't decide what he's really like.'

'Maybe he is both,' Nina suggests. 'Or maybe he's not willing to show his cards until you show yours.'

Nat leans in, giggling. 'Show me yours and I'll show you mine…'

'Oh, I showed him mine, all right,' I confessed as the blush heats my cheeks. 'I think I made a drunken pass at him the other night.'

Nina gasps, pointing at me. 'There you go. You like him! You have a crush on him.'

'Me?' I lie. 'Of course not. I just said I was drunk.'

There is a sudden silence. They know about my past.

'Sweetheart—' Nat begins.

'It was a one-timer. I promise. I'm done with the booze for good now. I didn't even enjoy it.'

They glance at each other, and finally at me. They believe me. They believe *in* me.

'A slip is allowed to anyone, sweetheart,' Nat says softly.

'And so is a dishy bloke,' Nina chimes in and I feel my

ears burning. 'Just look at you – it's written all over your face!'

'Yes!' Rosie claps her hands. 'Are you going to ask him out?'

'Out? We've been out. Several times.'

'Yes, but not on a date.'

'We've been to dinner, lunch, strolls in the park. What more do you want?'

'How about some romance?'

'Oh, no, no, no, no,' I hasten to say. 'We are complete opposites. And we constantly bicker.'

'Good start!' Nina exclaims. 'But it's time to bring it up a notch now. You need to have *those conversations* – you know, confessing your fears and true feelings – before the kisses and stuff.'

I put my glass of sparkling water down. 'We are not having *those conversations*.'

'Why not?'

'Because… I…' I huff.

'Sweetie,' Nina says. 'If he's been out with you all those times, it must mean something to him, too.'

I look up at my friends' faces. 'You think?'

They nod in unison.

'My sister is pushing me into this as well,' I admit. 'But I don't want to jump from one thing to another. I need more time alone—'

'Faith,' Nat says. 'Life is short – stop it with all the silly rules and fall in love again already.'

What – real love? And risk my heart once more? Go through all that again, with the possibility of getting too attached and consequently pushing him away? Isn't that a bit reckless? And above all, presumptuous? Besides, I'm an emotional train wreck right now. I don't want to make my mother's same mistakes.

'At least you could put Gabe behind you once and for all,' Rosie insists gently.

Nina raises her glass. 'To putting Gabe behind you,' she toasts and we all follow.

'To putting Gabe behind me,' I murmur.

After lunch, as I'm driving back, I stop at a zebra crossing, and who on *earth* do you think is crossing the road? You guessed it – Vanessa Chatsbury, stealer of boyfriends. I can only stare at her as a million permutations are going through my mind.

I hadn't even recognised her, as her black roots are half the length of her hair that is no longer short, but forms a neat bob. Gone is her eccentric make-up and her far-out clothes. If it weren't for the fact that I know her like the back of my own hand, I wouldn't have even recognised her.

I sit up in alarm as my mind registers the fact that something is very wrong. In fact, she is not walking, but waddling across the road because she's absolutely huge. Unless she's got an army of babies in there, she's at least seven months pregnant.

It doesn't take rocket science to realise that she was already waaaay pregnant when Gabe came to England on his flash visit, asking me to start a family with him when he had already and so obviously put a baby in Psycho.

He slept with me knowing that Vanessa was already pregnant.

What is wrong with him, and how dishonest is he? How had I never noticed what a moron he really is?

I watch in silence as she finally makes it to the other side of the road, so shocked that I fail to drive off when the lights turn green again. Only when the cars behind me start honking do I snap out of it.

I manage to keep the wheel steady as I begin to hyperventilate. To see that he had lied to me, that he had come to the house, in the middle of the night, like a thief, and deliberately made love to me, knowing that Vanessa was already pregnant... Had he truly had no respect for me whatsoever, all the years we were together? Had it all be a sham? What kind of monster does that make him? And what kind of idiot does it make me? How could I have believed in someone so blindly, for years on end? How can I ever believe in anyone again, if the love of my life, the man I wanted babies from, could do this to me? I truly am my mother's daughter.

Men are all the same – no doubt about it. I will never, ever be able to trust a man, no matter how kind and generous he seems.

Even Henry. Yes, he'd been kind and patient from the start. But in truth, what does every man want from a woman, if not to take advantage of her, own her and dominate her, just like Gabe did? Just like my so-called father did. He took all he could from my mum, and made sure he dumped her on the last day of their vacation together. Oh, men know how to take advantage and then some. But no more. I'm not ever going to fall for it again. Not with Henry, not with anyone.

By the time I get home I'm in a right state. I need a drink like I need my next breath. But I'm not giving in, throwing away years and years of sobriety. But I'm shaking so badly I can't get my key into the lock of my front door. And then my mobile rings, making me drop my bag that empties itself all over the pavement.

It is, as luck would have it, Henry. But I know he's calling from work, so I have to answer and I let out a frazzled 'Hello,' as I stoop to retrieve my day planner, make-up case, sunglasses, purse and all the stuff I've got in there.

'Hi, Faith! It's Orson!'

'Orson!' I gasp, breathless, trying to compose myself. 'Hello, darling, how are you?'

'Can I come over? Now?'

I sigh inwardly. Orson is a sweetheart, and I don't want to ruin his enthusiasm for life by seeing the state I'm in. Tomorrow seems like forever to children, and I just can't bring myself to say no. It's important to him, and he sounds so excited.

'Of course!' I chime. 'Can you tell Daddy to give me half an hour?'

'Yessss!' he exclaims and I can literally see the little darling pumping his fist in the air. 'See you in half an hour!'

I drag myself into the flat and look in the mirror by the door. Yikes. I've got my misery all over my face. I can't let the poor kid see me like this, let alone Henry, who will start going all nosy-protective on me again. But how do you erase in half an hour the disappointment of years and years of utter trust and unconditional love? How can you start afresh, if at all? Where do you find the willpower?

But when the doorbell rings, a smile escapes me. I rush

over to the door and fling it open. 'Hey youuu!' I cheer, bending on one knee to hug Orson while Henry stands quietly in the background.

'Hi, Faith! I've missed you!' he cries as he throws his little arms around my neck. He smells so good, like soap and innocence.

'I've missed you too, darling!' I can't help but confess. *Please stay like this forever, Orson. Don't grow up to be a heartbreaker!* I want to cry as I hang on to him longer than necessary, almost as if to stop his innocence from leaving his body. To stop him from turning into a lying cheat one day.

'Tough morning?' Henry mouths over Orson's shoulder.

I blow the air out of my cheeks. 'I'm all right,' I mouth back as Orson takes his coat off and puts it on the edge of the settee.

'Orson, go and see what treats I've got on the kitchen table,' I urge him and he happily skips off. It's a good thing that cakes are the main food group in my kitchen.

'So what's happened?' Henry whispers. 'I'm sorry for crowding you, but Orson wouldn't stop begging me to call you.'

What is sad is that Henry needed a push. What is even sadder is that I can't even think straight about my own feelings right now.

'It's okay. It's just that I discovered something horrible.'

His eyebrows shoot up and he leans in, putting a hand on my shoulder. 'What is it?'

I huff. 'I saw Vanessa in the street. When Gabe and I got back together, he'd forgotten to mention that Vanessa was *already* pregnant.'

He stops and his eyes flash. 'Jesus,' he mutters under his breath.

I shrug. 'Well, that's love for you.'

He spears me with his gaze. 'No, Faith. That's nowhere near what love should be like.'

I stuff my hands in my pockets, my cheeks catching fire when Orson comes bouncing back in with a doughnut covered in sprinkles.

'I'm so happy you're here, Orson!' I say, putting an arm around him. It's so natural, how we've clicked, Orson and I.

But Henry is still looking at me, unsure. And I remind myself to not fall for his kindness. Nor for his looks. Or his sex appeal. I'm done with men now. For good. In fact, I'm so done that I can't even look him in the face. We both know that there could have been something there, that something could have happened between us on several occasions. But luckily, it didn't, because I just can't do another relationship. I haven't got the strength to face all the disappointments, the lies. I'm barely holding myself together as it is.

Orson looks up at his father. 'Now, Daddy?' he asks.

Henry beams down at him. 'Now's fine, son.'

'Okay! I have something for you, Faith!'

'Do you? Thank you, Orson!'

'Here!' he says, shoving a tiny little wooden box into my hand. It is obviously hand-made, but very well made and smooth, with a tiny latch in front.

'Oh, that's so lovely, thank you – did you make it?'

He nods.

'I love it!'

Orson giggles. 'You have to open the box, silly!'

'Oh!' I laugh. 'Of course, sorry!' Inside, there is a tiny

wooden home, with carved windows and doors and even a chimney. It is absolutely delightful. The work of a little boy, but the idea of the house was definitely his father's. I feel my eyes pricking, but smile down at him as I ruffle his hair.

'It's so lovely, Orson, thank you,' I fight to not blubber, because, if I had been trying to hold it together, now I'm in tatters. Orson's show of kindness and unconditional love has come at a time when I'd needed it the most. And the fact that Henry is also behind this gesture is more than I can take. Some people will go out of their way (like Vanessa and Gabe) to destroy you, and yet others you've just met do everything they can to be kind and caring. It's just too much!

I sniff and give him my most dazzling smile and bend down to him. 'I will keep this with me always.'

His handsome little face lights up. 'Really?'

'Absolutely. And you know why? Because it's special. Because *you* gave it to me.'

And with that, Orson launches himself at me, locking his arms around my waist as he buries his head into my stomach and I hold him to me, not caring what Henry thinks. This little boy is an absolute darling and has no idea how much he has given me in sweetness and the purity of unconditional, unadulterated love, if you'll pardon the pun.

'All right, all right.' Henry chuckles. 'I think she gets it, mate. Let her be now. See you at work?' Henry asks.

'Yes, you will,' I promise him.

The next morning my phone rings as I'm still caught between slumber and waking. As my eyelids are still superglued together, I feel for the Answer button.

'Hello?' I rasp, forcing myself to wake up and possibly even sound human, if not professional.

'Babes?'

I sit up, my legs already shaking. 'What do you want?'

'Did I wake you?'

'No…' I lie.

He chuckles, but I can't join in. I have no idea why he's calling. What can he possibly want? He's already dumped me twice. And thrice is not a charm. Because it's not happening. I'd sooner become a nun and tuck myself away in a convent.

'How… are you?' he asks.

'What do you want, Gabe?'

'I, uhm, need to ask you – how far had you got with the beach house?'

Ah. The beach house. Here it comes – not only has he gone and got his ex-girlfriend pregnant, but the project is cancelled too now.

I rub my forehead where a massive headache is already collecting. It's a wonder I haven't had a conniption with all these shocks he's delivered me over the past few months. 'It's ongoing.'

'Excellent,' he says. 'So… I'd like you to baby-proof the house while you're at it. Is that okay?'

'You'll have to liaise with Thea, I'm not working on the project anymore,' I lie, when instead I'd like to scream my head off at him. But he deserves me lying to him. He'd lied to me about how far along Vanessa's pregnancy was. How much more does he bloody expect me to take?

Nor has he always been the kindest man, due to his cathedral-sized ego combined with his bouts of extreme insecurity.

He would be impossible to talk to when he was in one of his moods, which depended of course on the reviews his performances or albums received. I would have to literally hide or throw out any form of liquor available in the house because he would drink himself into a stupor. Personally, at that time, I was strong enough to not fall into that trap again. And after that it was like I didn't even exist. He could be downright cruel sometimes, snarling at me and saying things like, 'What the hell do you know about the music business?'

'The same as I know about any business, including my own,' I'd reply in defence. 'You need to stay focused and not give in to self-pity. You can't be everyone's cup of tea.'

And every time, I'd made up excuses for him, tried to help him, told myself he was more of a mess than I was and needed help. Perhaps I'd convinced myself that we were indeed two pieces of driftwood, and that together we were stronger. How wrong I'd been. Because Gabe is a life-sucker.

And now, two break-ups and a baby in, he still manages to get under my skin. Because his request is not only hurtful, it's *offensive*. But I have to think about my crew who depend on me for their income.

Look at me – an interior designer with an interior conflict. Ha ha, I'm so funny I could bawl. And actually, I think I may just be about to, so I'd better make this call short.

I huff. 'I'll let the crew know.'

'Why aren't you working on it?'

'You must be joking. I want nothing to do with you anymore, Gabe. But yes, the work will be done.'

'Thank you. I've been meaning to tell you this. It's only right that you should hear it from me.'

'Gabe – I already know she's a million months pregnant. And I will never forgive you for coming here and lying to me, promising me a family, just to sleep with me!'

'No, Faith, not just to sleep with you. I truly believed that if I came back and you forgave me for leaving you, then maybe you could forgive me this other huge mistake. Vanessa means nothing to me. She never has. All I want is you.'

It's really the end now. It serves me right to think that what we'd had together had been good while it lasted. *You've shattered my heart*, I want to scream, but am afraid of losing it completely. Wrath, yes – weakness, no.

'Faith? Are you still there?'

'I'm here,' I assure him as I use one of the swatches to wipe my trickling face. (Ew.) Whether it's my tears or my sweat, I'm still not sure. 'I'll pass your message on,' I say.

'You have great taste, Faith. With your help it'll fly off the shelf in no time.'

Is it me or has he always been this tactless?

I open my mouth to snap goodbye, if nothing else, as a loud shriek pierces my ears.

'Gotta go, Vanessa's calling me,' he says in a soft voice, almost apologetic.

'Yep.'

'Thanks, Babes.'

'Gabe?'

'Yeah?'

'Please don't call me Babes anymore. In fact, don't ever call me at all. You have Thea's number.' And with that, I hang up, my insides roiling so badly I want to heave.

*

'The bloody cheek!' Hope screeches when I tell her. 'Please tell me you told him to sod off.'

'I did on a personal level. But my team will continue the work.'

'Oh, sweetie, why?'

'Because this will be the job that I'll finally be able to impress the Wickfords with. Plus, I need to see the house as it was.'

'Oh, sweetie, I know all the reasons you love the house. But this is your chance to walk away and be free of him – and Mum's ghost. We've already discussed this, remember?'

'But I chose not to walk away. For business reasons. Because when the house is ready there will be a photoshoot – and that will be good publicity for me.'

'So… you're okay then?'

'Absolutely, Hope. It's all about work now.'

'I hope you know what you're doing, Faith.'

'Oh, this time I do,' I assure her. Because now I'm back in charge. Because I'm going to charge him a bloody fortune for the privilege.

10

Back in Black

The next Monday I text the crew on our WhatsApp group that I'm on my way to work. Wallowing Week is over. Thea is the first to text back:

Yayyy! What happened?

To which I reply:

House needs to be baby-proofed.

She sends me a pair of rolling eyes, while the men text back thumbs up without a comment. I'll be getting those in person, I suspect.

I smile to myself. It'll be good to see everyone again. Get moving again. Hopefully, I'll be able to stay out of trouble where Henry is concerned. Because, despite my sadness for what's happened to Gabe and I, I still can't get Henry's smile out of my mind.

'Morning, Faith,' Henry says casually as he comes in with a huge box of scones, a pot of cream and one of jam, and it's like I never left. But I can see the pride on his face at seeing me there at the helm of my ship once again. He's a good man, Henry.

'Mmh,' says Paul, wiping his hands clean. 'Just about time, I feel a tea break a-comin'!'

No one makes any awkward comments or asks me how I'm doing, because they know I need to not make a fuss about coming back. It's just business from now on.

Ten minutes later, Henry and I are poring over his designs and, although I'd made myself the promise to move on, my heart just isn't in it. Until only a few weeks ago, this was about my life, my man and my home. And now there is another – completely innocent human being in the picture. A baby. Vanessa and Gabe's baby.

The thought that it will be someone else humming and cooking in this very space is enough to make me want to scream until my throat is raw. But I keep quiet as a maelstrom of a migraine begins to build behind my eyeballs.

'Faith…?' comes Henry's voice through the thick fog that is my misery. 'Are you okay? You look pale. Did you not sleep well?'

Sleep? As if. The night and I have become one, lately. All of my mistakes, in love and in business, keep flashing through my mind, sometimes even stopping me from believing in myself. But that has to end now. And anyway, it's my problem and no one else's.

'Yes, I'm fine, thank you,' I say with a huge effort, sitting up even straighter than usual.

There is a break in the conversation as he studies me, and

I know what he's thinking – the unbreakable, unfathomable Faith has a chink in her armour, and it's finally about to show in public.

Not on your life, mister. I push back at a stray tendril and force a smile I'm far from feeling. 'What about that composite granite for the work surfaces?' I suggest, changing the subject. 'It's unbeatable as it doesn't stain and can take the heat,' I suggest.

He purses his lips in thought. 'It's not as strong as it looks,' he says, boring his eyes into mine meaningfully. Is he serious, comparing me to a countertop? I don't want to talk about me. We have been doing so well lately, not talking about me.

'I can assure you it can take not only the heat, but also anything you can throw at it.' There. Just to be clear.

He leans back and studies me. 'Yes, it might, but how long do you think it will last like that? Granite is what you want. Black. And it reveals nothing. No stains, no scratches.'

Unlike me. Good point, of course. I huff.

'Listen, Faith – I know how you feel.'

'Do you?'

'Of course. But you are acting like a real pro, not letting your feelings get mixed up in all this. Only remember that you are surrounded by people here to pick you up when need be. Me included.'

The simple and hopefully sincere comment defrosts me somewhat. Oh, to hell with it. Who do I think I'm fooling anyway?

'Thank you, Henry. It *is* strange, being back here again,' I finally admit. 'You go back to a place you love and yet, when circumstances change, although it's still the same house, it's no longer the same… *home*. None of it can ever be the same again.'

Henry studies me in silence, then dips his head. 'It's people that make homes, Faith. Or rather, our perception of them.'

'That's so true. When we were introduced to a new foster home, they were mostly beautiful homes. But there was no warmth, no love.'

'Thus your Home Hugs,' he says gently.

I nod. 'Yes. It felt good to embrace something, rather than having empty arms. I hate having empty arms. I don't know what to do with them.'

'Arms are meant to hold. To protect, love and nurture.'

Henry would know. I have seen the way he holds Orson. And I remember how he held me that time I fell apart.

'Come on, there's cake, I'll make us some coffee,' he says softly.

'Have we got any more scones?' I ask, straightening my shoulders.

He stops, spreads his arms in a gesture that says: *Please, you think I'd run out?* He seems to know the way to my heart, i.e. through my stomach.

And it's like I'd never left. The team fills me in on what's what, and I'm instantly back in the groove.

After a long day's work Henry comes to stand opposite me, watching me smugly from under his dark lashes.

'What? What's up?' I say.

'Guess what? We're in.'

I sit up. 'In where?'

'Time & Tide.'

I gasp. 'How did you manage?'

'I told you, I'm a regular there. Are you ready?'

'Now? We can go now?'

He chuckles. 'Ye-es.'

I drop my pen. 'Oh my God! Oh, you don't know how long I've been dying to get in there. Thank you, thank you!'

And in five minutes we're in Henry's 4x4 again, and I'm fidgeting like a schoolgirl.

'I've wanted to see this place since forever!' I tell him again as we drive down the A394.

'Yes, you've mentioned that before,' he says with a chuckle, stealing me an amused glance.

'Did you know that the Wickfords often go there and can be seen rifling through piles of stuff for a bargain, just like any common mortal?' I ask.

He laughs. 'Really? Wow.'

'Maybe I'll get lucky and bump into them today! And oh – they have this huge home in the Cotswolds and one they'll be renovating in Cornwall!'

'Strong choice.'

'I wonder who's designing it for them...' I ask myself out loud.

Henry slides me a glance as we come up to an intersection. 'That would be a great opportunity for you, wouldn't it?'

I snort. 'As if.'

'Can Gabe... not help you? Surely he knows someone who knows them, being famous and all?'

'Not on your life. I'm not asking him for anything. I'll just have to keep badgering them with emails and phone calls that are never returned. Or, I could just find out where they live and break into their home one night, hold them hostage long enough to show them my portfolio.'

Henry laughs. 'That might do it, yes.'

As Henry veers left, St Michael's Mount comes into view. Its majesty never ceases to amaze me, and today it looks so close I can almost touch it – the castle and the sea, with all its secrets and mysteries I have yet to uncover.

'Ohhh,' I gasp despite myself.

Henry turns to look at me. 'You have never been on St Michael's Mount?'

I shake my head. 'I know, I'm shameful, aren't I? It just never happened.'

'Then we'll just have to make it happen,' he says, and I let it pass. Gabe was not a fan of the cultural. Imagine his face if I had said, *Hey, let's go for a walk around an ancient castle and go back in time!* He'd have had a bloody conniption.

'But one thing at a time,' Henry says. 'First the shop, then lunch and then we'll go to the island. Can you spare the time?'

Meaning, can I tear myself away from Jawsy just a little bit longer? Or, can I do without an entire evening spent wandering alone around my flat?

'Oh, yes, please,' I answer, and a warm smile lights up his face as he turns into the parking lot opposite the shop.

'You'll love it,' he promises as he gets out.

'How is it possible that you have access to this place?' I say as we step through the main entrance.

He shrugs, stuffing his hands into his pockets as he leads the way through the door and into my idea of paradise. 'I'm a Cornishman,' he says simply. 'I know my turf. Plus, the owner's an old friend.'

'You also know your stuff – this place is beautiful,' I observe as we step through the door, and I immediately spot a beauty off to the right of the entrance. 'Oh my God, just look at this armchair! It's so primitive, and honest, and yet so skilfully designed.'

His hand runs over the smooth wooden armrests of a deep tan leather chair.

'Yes, it's made with recycled leather.'

'You really do know your stuff. How can you tell it's recycled and simply not distressed?'

'Because I stripped it off my gran's old sofa.'

I stare at him. 'You...? You made this armchair?'

He shrugs. 'With her blessing, mind you.'

I cannot believe my ears. Or my eyes. 'It's one of the most beautiful pieces I've ever seen in my life.'

He nods graciously. 'Thank you. That's very kind of you.'

And I need to say this again. 'Henry – I need to thank you for being so kind to me, and for not giving up on me since day one.'

He smiles, and I see that one of his front teeth is slightly crooked, giving him a more approachable and friendly air. How have I not noticed that before?

'No worries. You were stressed.'

I roll my eyes. 'I'm always stressed.'

'Besides, I wouldn't say we didn't click. It's the quickest a girl has ever been naked before me.'

'Silly,' I say, gently slapping his arm, and suddenly blush at the memory of myself floating completely starkers in the pool. How much had he seen, I wonder?

He chuckles. 'You've gone all red. I didn't see anything.'

I look up into his eyes. 'Promise?'

He flinches slightly. 'Well, maybe just an outline.'

I gasp and cover my face.

'I wasn't really looking,' he hastily adds. 'I was more worried about Trixie losing her rag. Bopper has a very keen eye for the pretty ladies.'

'Are you calling me pretty?' I breathe, wishing I could shut up for just one millisecond.

He looks down at me, pursing his lips in thought. 'Let's say you're just *barely* passable.'

'Gee, thanks.'

'You're welcome.'

Some nerve.

'I'm kidding!' he says with a laugh.

'You are?'

I've stopped and we're looking into each other's eyes as I wait for his answer. He takes my hand. 'Come and look at these and tell me if they're not the most exquisite Murano glasses you've ever seen.'

I follow him and look into a hutch. Inside there are blue chalices made of very thin glass. 'Beautiful,' I whisper. 'Absolutely exquisite. This entire place is amazing. Thank you for bringing me here, Henry. What a way to spend an afternoon.'

He shrugs. 'Surely you've had better afternoons in Gabe's company.'

I laugh. 'Not in a place like this, I haven't. Gabe isn't – uhm, wasn't – into this kind of thing.'

'No? I thought you and Gabe did everything together.'

'Is that the impression you were under?'

'Sort of.'

I would like to ask him more about his relationship with Gabe, but there will be time for that. Right now I'm in interior designer's paradise and we haven't got much longer before the premises close.

On the far end is a bureau that attracts our attention. Henry runs a reverent hand over it, as I begin to realise that, under that quiet easiness to him, there is a man of quality and value.

'Ready for lunch yet?' he asks, interrupting my thoughts.

'Only if it's on me,' I argue.

He looks at me in pure horror. 'Absolutely not.'

After a quick but delicious lunch at The Day's Catch just opposite St Michael's Mount, we set out to walk across the causeway as it's still low tide.

'Imagine getting trapped at high tide,' I say with a shiver.

He takes my elbow. 'I'd carry you back on my shoulders.'

I laugh, knowing that he very probably would.

I I

Somebody You Loved

The next day, Henry and I arrive at the beach house at the same moment.

'Hey...' he says as he jumps out of his Jeep.

'Hi,' I say back with a smile.

There is something new to him, something... fresh and charming. He looks as if he's in a great mood. I, too, have to admit that it's a good day, and it can only get better. After all, I don't see how it could get any worse.

We are barely through the door when a car comes into view of the long drive. A car I've never seen before. This is a private road, and we have no appointments today. Could it finally be my window casings man? God knows how long I've been waiting for him to show.

Henry glances at me and I shrug as the car finally comes to a stop and out steps... *Gabe*. Here, in the flesh, wearing his usual skinny jeans and one of his rock T-shirts. Precisely the Led Zeppelin one I'd given him on our very first month-aversary.

I can't believe I'm standing opposite him and actually keeping it together. He certainly is, by the looks of him. Only he's thinner. More gaunt, with the look of sleepless nights, I notice as he shoves his shades up over his head and plants his huge baby blues on me. And I stop mid-step as my legs turn to water and the air in my lungs wooshes out so loudly I'm sure they can hear me all around the house over the din of the power tools.

'Faith, hi,' he says. 'Henry—'

Henry glances at me uncertainly, but I can barely breathe, let alone speak. 'Hello, Gabe. What brings you here?'

'Sorry, I, er, meant to come sooner.'

Total silence. Even the work in the background seems to have stopped.

'Faith,' he reprises. 'I didn't think you'd be here, after you said that you weren't working on the job. It's good to see you. You look great. Fantastic, in fact.'

'What are you doing here?' I blurt.

Gabe stuffs his hands into his pockets, his eyes darting around as he lets out an attempt at a chuckle. 'I've got a house sale to take care of.'

'Have you, now?' Henry snorts.

'Can we... talk, for a minute, Faith? Henry, would you mind?'

I can feel Henry hesitate, and I make the decision for him. '*I* mind,' I say. 'Unless it's about business, I'm not in the least interested.'

Gabe turns to look at Henry.

'You heard her,' Henry says.

Gabe nods and sighs. 'Right. Well, then, can I at least come in and fetch my Gibson? I need her.'

It takes all the effort I have to not snort at his words. *I need her*. Once upon a time he would have said that about me. But now is now and it's no longer the truth.

I shrug, a huge knot forming in my throat. 'It's your home. Go ahead.'

'Right then,' he says, eyeing us as he brushes past me, his arm grazing mine, and I close my eyes in agony at the contact. We once loved each other. We shared everything. And now he's just a client.

'Hey,' Henry whispers, caressing my arm where Gabe had touched me, almost as if to disperse the tactile memory. 'You okay?'

I open my eyes and paste on my strongest smile, but I realise I'm trying too hard. So I square my shoulders and lift my chin. 'Not really, but thanks, Henry.'

'You're doing great,' he whispers.

A moment later Gabe reappears, lugging his darling Gibson. He stops a few feet away, staring at the floor. And I am much too angry to just gaze at him in sheer awe as I used to.

He clears his throat as if he's about to sing. 'So... I guess I'll be going,' he says.

'Goodbye,' is all I can say.

'Will you keep me updated on the progress?' Gabe asks.

'Or you could just trust Faith,' Henry suggests. 'Seeing as she's worthy of it.' *And you're not*, he seems to want to add, but thankfully he decides to leave that can of worms sealed.

It's a clear message. Gabe bites his lip. 'Okay. Uhm, then. Bye for now...'

'Goodbye, Gabe,' Henry says.

He glances at me, obviously not wanting to go. What else could he possibly want to say? *I win?*

At the door, he turns as if to say something, but changes his mind, and he walks out without looking back. Something he's extremely good at.

Henry closes the door behind him and turns to me, obviously concerned.

'He couldn't even *look* at me,' I whisper.

'Of course he couldn't,' Henry agrees. 'Who could, after the stunt he pulled on you?'

'I can't believe he'd even have the guts to show his face, knowing I was still here, working on *his* home.'

Henry coughs. 'Forgive me for the nosy question. You can tell me to mind my own business…'

'What?'

He looks at me, studying my face. 'Did Gabe actually break up with you when he told you about the baby? Did he actually tell you he was leaving you? Or did he expect you to be there for him while he sorted his problems out?'

I bite my lip. 'He wanted me to stay with him. But I couldn't. I'm not that generous a person, I'm afraid.'

'It's not about generosity, but self-preservation,' he says.

'Well, I'm not very good at that, either.'

'There *are* relationships that continue after something like that,' Henry reminds me.

'Not this relationship,' I reply. 'As far as I'm concerned, we are over, and there's absolutely no going back.'

'You won't change your mind?'

I snort. 'You mean like he did, over and over? Not a chance. I don't care if I have to be lonely for the rest of my life.'

'Right,' he says. 'Enough said. You know what you need? An afternoon off.'

'Hm? Oh, no, no, I don't think so. I've already taken enough time off. And we're already behind schedule as it is.'

'Schedule? Come on, you're your own boss.'

I smile at Henry despite myself. 'That's one way of looking at it. Are you always this optimistic?'

He rewards me with one of his brilliant smiles. 'Let's say it's a secret of the trade. Believe in yourself and everybody else will soon follow.'

'Gosh, I'll have to remember that.'

'And Faith?'

'Yes?'

'Remember to smile as well. You look so much prettier.'

I gape at him and he laughs, taking my arm. 'Let's go for a stroll around the village, and then I'll treat you to lunch. Come on.' He nudges me. 'Just you and me – what do you say?'

What do I say to the stroll part, or the just him and me part? If he's asking about the latter, I say that my judgement hasn't been that dependable lately. I've made so many mistakes, I can't afford to make any more, on any level. So I should probably say no to the stroll. It would only steer me in the wrong direction.

But it is true that once this job is over, I won't have any excuse to come back to Perrancombe and its quirky villagers. Over the last few years I have made a many good friends here, and feel much more part of the community than I ever have anywhere else. Because Perrancombe isn't exactly a metropolis where I can lose myself and go unnoticed. It's a true, veritable hug of a village.

They would have all been invited to our wedding. There would have been a short ceremony, lots of good food, and lots of music and dancing. Hope would have been my matron of honour and Thea and my coastal girls my bridesmaids. Jowen would have been my very reluctant ring boy and Verity my very lovely and proud flower girl.

And now, in a few weeks' time, I won't have an excuse to stay, or even hang out with Henry – or Orson – and just the thought makes me want to cry.

But enough of this feeling sorry for myself. It's only my problem, and mine alone. Well, and everyone else who has to bear with my miserable mug. I owe them something. And now this poor, gorgeous sod here wants to cheer me up. I can only be thankful that someone wants to spend time with me without asking for anything else in return, such as, oh, I don't know, baby-proofing his home.

'Okay,' I finally agree. 'But remember – I warned you.'

He raises his hands. 'Duly noted. Be back to pick you up in twenty minutes, I've got an errand to run first.'

'Okay,' I say. 'See you in twenty.' The poor man doesn't know what a drab afternoon it's going to be.

'What is that?' I ask, pointing at the picnic basket in the back of his Jeep.

'This beauty? Oh, it's an original vintage piece. I thought it would look good on your kitchen table.'

I glance at it, then at him. 'Er…'

He laughs, his eyes crinkling at the edges. 'Ah, your *face* – I'm kidding, Faith!'

'Oh!' I say, catching on as he shakes his head and takes my elbow.

'Let's go. I've got a great place to show you, if you've the guts.'

Oh God, what's on his mind now? I can barely keep myself together these days. I have no guts left.

Once seated, I buckle up and turn to face him. 'Where is it we're going?'

'It's a surpri-ise,' he sing-songs. I never thought that Henry could sing-song, but there it is. Unlike me, he's already proven himself in the world with a successful joinery business and can afford to sit back and chill. Good for him. I'm still trying to make myself a name in my field. And I can only do that by honing my craft, working hard and never giving up.

Thirty minutes later, he stops the Jeep and I look out the window in awe. It's a good thing I'm not afraid of heights, because where in the world has Henry dragged me but to the highest cliff in Cornwall? We're about a mile from Crackington Haven, at Cambeak Point on the north coast, and the view is absolutely unrivalled.

As we descend from the Jeep and I catch sight of the sugarloaf lookalike (well, of sorts), I wonder how on earth I'm going to traipse around the clifftops in my pencil skirt and heels. I look down the path in dismay and he chuckles.

'Come on, you think I haven't thought of that?' he says mischievously as he reaches into the boot and produces a pair of thick black leggings and sturdy walking boots, complete with thick socks and light windbreaker.

There is no way I'm going to ditch my workwear to

follow him to the most dangerous part of Cornwall, just so I can prove I'm not uptight. No way am I going to just head off into this wild nature at the drop of a hat. I've got things to do, suppliers to chase up, the bathroom tiles to confirm and those door handles are not going to choose themselves, are they?

He is still smiling down at me, the boots dangling from one hand. 'You know you want to,' he cajoles with an impish face.

I roll my eyes. What I want to do, and what I can do are two completely different things. Should I care that everyone knows I'm so uptight the strings of a harp seemed more relaxed? Because I am, I know I am, and I have to do something about it.

'Oh, go on, then,' I concede, sending him a sheepish grin as I head behind the Jeep to change. It takes me a full minute to wriggle out of my skirt and pull on the leggings and when I sit down on the edge of the open boot to pull on the socks, something akin to excitement courses through me. What's the matter with me? I've scampered up and down these cliffs a gazillion times while growing up. Why does it seem so monumental that I'm doing it now?

Why am I suddenly looking forward to this, when instead I should be on my mobile securing myself the best and most exclusive home furnishings circles of the county, or even, why not, still taking some time to wallow in my misery of newly found singledom?

Because Crackington Haven is within an AONB, Area of Outstanding Natural Beauty, that's why. Because just *being* here is a gift in its own. Because I know Henry won't let me get hurt. Because he's dependable.

To the point, he stretches his hand out to steady me as I lift my feet to get over a tiny ridge in the rock. As I stand next to him, looking out to the ultramarine horizon, he breathes in deeply and I do the same, tasting the salty sea air as it fills my lungs. It feels so foreign, having fresh air inside me while my head completely empties itself. Usually it's the exact opposite. My God, when was the last time I was aware of my own body, and breathing in this deeply, so at one with nature?

He raises an eyebrow as if to say, *This is nothing yet*, and with visible, utter contentment, he breathes in again. The breeze caresses his dark curls and he's not shielding his eyes but squinting ever so slightly as he gazes into the sun, protected by that ridiculous mass of long dark lashes that make him look like one of the Muppets. But in a handsome way.

I can tell he's an outdoorsy type who is used to hiking up and down these coastlines. Unlike me, as I am already gasping for air. God, when was the last time I actually did any exercise?

As I take in the views, he pulls out the picnic basket and a knapsack.

'This way,' he says and I follow him down a very narrow path, wide enough for only one, until we reach the bottom of a tiny hillock.

'Up you go,' he says, helping me up the next steep incline and staying behind me to make sure I don't slide back and go tits over arse. And it's a great feeling, knowing that someone's literally got your back. 'It'll be worth it, trust me.'

'It better be,' I answer him as he smiles at me over his

shoulder. Because I am already wheezing bits of lung through my nostrils while pretending I'm absolutely fit, and am thankful that he is leading so he won't see me gagging for air.

'Have you never been here before?' he asks, glancing back at me just as I am about to gulp in more air, and I stop, completely winded while pretending to have to stop and think about the answer.

'Ah...' *Breathe, breathe, breathe!* 'Uhm...' I shrug, trying to earn another deep breath. 'Dunno. Maybe... when I was little.' *And fit.*

He laughs. 'Okay, let's stop here.'

Thank you, God!

I almost fall to my knees with fatigue and gratitude as he shakes out a waterproof picnic blanket. 'Wait till you see what I've got for you to eat.'

What he *hasn't* got me to eat would be more accurate. There are my favourites: pasties, mini scotch eggs, Yarg cheese, crackers, grapes, meat pies, Cornish chutney. And, crap – apple cider, my absolute number-one drink in the world.

'This looks familiar,' I say, looking at the bottle label: *Crooked Hill Farm.*

Henry nods. 'My friend Jack makes it over in Penworth Ford. He gave me a few bottles.'

'Jack? I know him. I did his farmhouse. He's a friend of a friend.'

'You did? Of course you did – his place is gorgeous. He's a good man, Jack. You couldn't find a kinder man.'

Actually, I could, but I don't think Henry would take my compliment seriously. Not after all the times I've made such a fool of myself.

'You've gone serious again,' he says, nudging me. 'You all right?'

'Absolutely. But, I can't drink it, Henry. I'm sorry. I never told you, but as a teenager, I had a few problems with the bottle. Hope blames our abandonment, but she turned out all right. I guess I'm just the weak one.'

'Nonsense. You are amazing. I'd like to see anyone do as well with yourself as you have.'

I dart him a glance, but there is sincerity in his eyes. He truly believes I am worth his respect.

'I haven't had a drop since I was fourteen – except for the other night, when you slept over. I am truly sorry about putting you on the spot there, Henry. You were very kind to me.'

'You sound surprised.'

'I am. I mean, I was. Very few blokes have come this close without expecting something in return.'

Henry puts the cider away and pulls out a couple of bottles of water as if nothing had happened. 'Did you know that kids get caught tombstoning here?' he says.

I look up as I unwrap a pasty. 'Tombstoning? What's that? I don't like the sound of it.'

He chuckles. 'You and me both. Tombstoning is the practice of jumping off high cliffs into the sea in a standing position.'

I feel my eyes pop out of my head. 'That's crazy dangerous!'

'People looking for highs the wrong way,' he agrees. 'What do you do to let your hair down, Faith?' he asks.

I swallow a chunk of potato. 'Me? Oh, nothing really. I read.'

'Let me guess – books on interior designing?'

I can feel myself blushing despite the cool breeze. 'Yes.'

'Don't you ever do anything non-work-related? Like relaxing?'

'Oh, I relax when I sleep in on a Sunday.'

He grins. 'Define sleeping in,' he says as he takes another sip.

I shrug. 'Around seven.' *Except for when I'm miserable, and then I could sleep all day.*

He snorts, almost spluttering out his water, which he makes an effort to swallow while he laughs. 'Seven? You're not joking?'

'I'm a busy girl,' I defend. 'The minute I take my eyes off my goals I'm dead.'

Henry studies me. 'Is that the way you see your profession? Like a battle?'

'Lately, it's been a flat-out war. Plus Vanessa, Gabe's – ooff, I didn't really want to mention them today,' I apologise.

'You can mention whomever you want,' he assures me.

'She's always trying to steal my clients.'

'Does she manage?'

'Not always. Her taste is not exactly appreciated by all.'

'Well, that counts for something, doesn't it?'

'I guess so.'

'But remember – your profession is only a part of who you are. Remember the essential things in life.'

'Such as?'

He laces his fingers together over his knee as he looks out to sea again. 'Family. Love. Happiness. Without those, we've got nothing.'

Family. Love. Happiness. Funny he should mention all

those things. 'Yes, well, then I've got nothing,' I say into the breeze as he takes another sip of water. For a moment I hope he hasn't heard me. At some point I have to stop wallowing. It's been ages now.

'Nonsense,' he says. 'You've got a sister and a niece and a nephew. That's family, isn't it?'

'Yeah, well, one out of three isn't bad, I guess. It could be worse.'

'Hey,' he says. 'Things are never as bad as they seem. And when you think they can't get any worse, it's time to come back up again.'

'You are such a wise man,' I say.

He smiles and shrugs.

'And what about you?' Done with my pasty, I smack my lips and reach for a grape. 'You're so lucky to have Orson.'

'He's my reason for living,' Henry says proudly. 'My family says I'm all the better because of him.'

'Tell me more about your family.'

He smiles, and it's so wonderful to see the love on his face. 'I have two brothers and two sisters. And oodles of nieces and nephews.'

'Wow.'

'Yes. It can get pretty hectic at times, but Christmas and summer holidays are the best.'

'Where do they live?'

'They come and go, but they have a place in St Ives. My brother Evan is a lawyer and Michael is a doctor. My sister Rowena is a headmistress and my sister Becca works from home. She's a writer.'

'I always thought you were born in a vacuum or something, or had a weird childhood, kind of like Superman.'

'I never told you?' he asks innocently.

I roll my eyes. 'Henry, you never talk about yourself.'

'Of course I do – you practically know me inside out now.'

'I may know your tastes in food and furniture, but I don't know anything about you. So spill.'

He shrugs, rubbing the back of his neck as he does when he's embarrassed. 'There's nothing to say, really. Dad's a university professor and Mum is a journalist.'

'Are you close?'

'Very. We talk at least once a week.'

'Are they proud of you?'

'Dad wanted me to be a university teacher like himself and Mum wanted me in journalism, so no, I guess not really. But they pretend to be, and that's what's important.'

'I'm sure they're not pretending. You sound like a successful bunch. It's nice to know you all inherited smart genes.'

'Would you... want to meet your father someday?' he asks out of the blue.

I sit back and look out to sea, completely lost. On the horizon, there's a ship with old medieval-looking masts. Several of them, actually. Probably part of a historical regatta. History can be interesting. But other times it can be a burden. 'No,' I say finally. 'I don't think I would be able to look him in the eye. It still hurts, thinking of how he betrayed my mum's trust. She didn't even know he was married.'

'I'm so sorry... you must have all suffered greatly.'

I shrug. 'We all had our own ways of dealing with it. Hope was the rebel; I was the clingy one. Which was worse, because she was always relieved to leave every foster home when they got sick of us. The story of my life. Even Gabe—' I bit my lip. 'Even he had tired of me, just like my dad had tired of my mum. Perhaps it's fate, to be returned to the sender.'

He's silent for a moment, then squints out towards the horizon again. 'You mustn't think that, Faith.'

'It's true,' I insist, and then give him one of my best smiles. 'But it doesn't matter anymore. I'm all grown up now, and I have to move on.'

'I'm sure there are much better things in your future, Faith,' he says, patting my hand in a kind gesture and suddenly a jolt of electricity shoots up my arm, surprising me and… unsettling me as I look down at it and realise my fingers have caught his in a soft clasp.

And then again, it happens – it's like lightning coursing through me. An electric bolt of… raw desire. Attraction. Not as in, *Now, he's a bit of all right*, but rather an *What am I going to do now?* sort of thing. This… thing – roiling inside me, unsettling my nerves, making me feel hot and cold at the same time while making my breath short – is not something that I'd expected, and I instinctively know that I really am in big trouble. I don't know what's happening to me. I don't want to be the needy, clingy girlfriend anymore, especially with someone like Henry, who is larger than life, sitting like a god on a throne overlooking his lands. And yet he is still. Quiet. Serene. Regal. Monumental. He doesn't need to do anything to be as he is, but he somehow manages to infuse me with a sense of *Everything Is Right With The World*. Of course I know it isn't, nor will it be for a very long time. But for now, in this exact moment, I can't help but feel enveloped by his presence. Sucked in by a sudden yet strange sense of... happiness?

Yes. Despite my current, ongoing state of misery, in this very moment, with the breeze wreaking havoc on my hair, and a belly full of proper Cornish food and looking out onto what is probably one of the most beautiful places on earth, I am happy. I wish I could sit here forever. But I know myself. Love, happiness, a family... they are not for me. I will never be able to have all that. Because right here, right now, while I am basking in all this wondrousness and counting my blessings, I am on borrowed time. Borrowed happiness. Because Henry has brought me here today merely to cheer me up, whilst wasting precious work time.

'Henry – thank you for taking the time out to bring me here. You're so kind.'

He takes my hands in his huge ones and squeezes them gently, and suddenly, out of the blue, I know he's going to kiss me.

I can see it in the way his eyes are wandering over my face, down to my mouth and back to my eyes.

But having learnt my lesson the humiliating way, I force myself to stand still so I won't blow the whole romantic moment. Something I am officially known for. I lick my lips, hoping that there is at least a tiny trace of my lip gloss left, but I highly doubt it after the amount of food I've packed away.

He is still doing that mesmerising eye-dance thing, his gaze still concentrated on my face. I hold my breath as he moves closer to me. What do I do? Am I ready to kiss another bloke?

How long has it been since Gabe dumped me? How do

I respond to Henry if he kisses me? Do I pull away (I'd like to see *you* manage that one) or just let go to the chance that he may be an amazing kisser, and that I might actually enjoy the soft touch of another bloke's lips against mine?

But I can't seem to stop myself, and suddenly my emotions come to the fore, like a raging river beating against a weak dam, and I reach up and draw him close to me by his neck so that his face is inches from mine and in the sun I can see that his eyes are not brown at all, but the colour of dark honey, almost bordering on an uncommon shade of dark green.

Something flashes across his face and his lips part. Without a word, I close my eyes and let him take my mouth with his and for a moment, the very waves below seem to have frozen in their tracks, almost as if hushing to see what happens next.

It is the softest of kisses I have ever experienced. I never imagined his mouth could be so enticing. And gentle. Nor had I ever imagined the fragrance of his breath, or the softness of his hair. I would love Henry to hold me like a man holds his woman, to at least see how it feels. I want to know how it feels to be held in a different way from a moment ago when he was comforting me. Now I want him to hold me like he never wanted to let go. And not just because he is beautiful.

I thought that kissing anyone else one day would feel so foreign, so wrong, but as I watch Henry's beautiful face and sexy mouth near me again, I realise that they are not so foreign after all. After all this time, I now know his face by heart. I know every single feature, every blade of stubble, the exact hues and sparkles of gold in his otherwise dark irises, the length of his lashes, the boyish yet manly curve of his nose, that smell of freshly washed man. And for once, I want to let myself go to a natural sensation without worrying about what I'm going to do afterwards.

I close my eyes and let his nearness envelop me, once and for all. His lips are so, so gentle, and yet, I can feel the banked force of his body, wrapped under layers and layers of civility and kindness.

Because Henry, if anything, is a true gentleman. Most men – at least the men I've met – would have taken my clothes off and crawled into bed beside me that night when I'd had too much to drink. But not Henry. He'd stayed by my side, sleeping in a tiny chair, just to make sure I was all right.

He takes a deep breath as he pulls away. 'Faith, you drive me crazy,' he whispers, taking my head into his hands. 'I want this with you. Every day.'

I stare at him. He wants this with me, every day? But what happens when I find out I'm in love with him, and I become needy or insecure, and he tires of me? Will we start arguing, or is he going to quietly drift away from me and find someone new, just like Gabe had?

'Am I scaring you? Is it too soon?'

Too soon? How long does it take for your heart to knit itself together after years of being blown apart over and over again? How long does it take to be able to trust someone new? I don't even know if I can. Despite the fact that I want to see Henry every day, and I'm miserable when he's not around. But I am broken inside. And I don't want to break him, too.

I run a hand through my hair, wishing I could tear it out

for what I am about to say. But he needs to know. I can't lure him into another relationship that is destined to fail because of me.

'Henry, I – I can't. You're an amazing man and I truly admire you so much – for everything. You're an amazing joiner with an incredible work ethic, and you're an amazing father. If I were back in the business of love, you would be my one and only. But—' I bite my lip. 'My dad… he broke my mum's heart. I'm not… I can't t-trust anymore.' I dash a hand over my now wet cheeks. Bugger it. 'I think life – and Gabe – have broken me…'

Henry takes my shoulders. 'No. You aren't broken, Faith. Maybe just a little bruised. But you are far from broken. And I'm sorry I just came onto you like this. Normally, I wouldn't have, but you and I… I can't explain it. You make me want to be a better man. Have another shot at happiness and… you know?'

I nod. 'I'm so sorry, Henry. I'd only tire you with all my insecurities. I have abandonment issues if you hadn't noticed.' I snort and bawl at the same time. 'I'm no good for you, and you deserve someone strong.'

'I agree,' he whispers, ducking to look into my face. 'That's why I want you, and no one else.'

And then I force out a laugh. 'I want you, too, Henry. Believe me. But I can't.'

He pulls me to him, but doesn't insist. 'I understand. Let's just hang out as friends then, okay?'

In his arms, I nod, but I realise that I can't pretend we're just friends either.

★

The next day is market day and the harbour quay is a-bustle with busy stalls featuring anything and everything from knitting needles to antique furniture. I weave in and out of the stalls, aimlessly until I stumble upon Mrs Trengrouse sorting out a selection of brightly coloured yarns from her own shop, Cat's Cradle.

'Hallo, pet,' she greets me with a wink.

'Hello, Mrs Trengrouse. How've you been?'

'I'm okay. And where's that rock star of yours, then? Gone off on another concert tour, I imagine?'

I bite my lip. No one knows about the split yet. Wait until Dougie and Mick find out, then the news will be all over the sodding county. 'He's back.'

'Oh, crikey,' she mumbles.

I blink at her, unsure of what to say.

'Look, pet – you know we've loved you since the day you moved to Perrancombe. But Gabe... he's always been...'

'I know,' I say, not wanting to hear any of it.

'He'd be absolutely lost without you to steer him and keep him on the straight and narrow. It's common knowledge that you pulled him out of the drugs and drink and that if it weren't for you he'd still be singing at the Up 'N' Down pub after working at the chippy.'

'Who knows, maybe he'd have been better off,' I say before I can stop myself. But none of it matters anymore. The word will soon be out and everyone who has nothing better to do with their life will start taking sides like the first time.

'Nonsense,' she says, pulling a cotton turquoise scarf off the rack of hand-knitted items. 'Here, love. Take this – to match your lovely eyes.'

'Awh, Mrs Trengrouse, thank you so much. You don't have to—'

'I want to. You hang in there, all right?'

'Will do, Mrs Trengrouse. And thank you.'

She waves me away. 'Take care, love,' she says, her eyes kind.

As I resume my meandering through the stalls, breathing in a mixture of sea air and musty furniture, my eyes travel over the wares on offer and I reflect upon how these objects were all part of someone's life. Someone's happiness lost.

In a messy pile of textiles, I spot the corner of a nice cream and duck egg tartan table runner and pull it to me, but it's stuck. Really, they should present their wares in a much neater fashion. I glance at the other side of the pile, and there he is, pulling at the same runner – sodding Henry Turner.

'Hi,' he says breathlessly, raising his hands in defeat to release the runner. 'Sorry. We seem to like the same things. A sign?'

A sign that I probably need to stay away from him. If that kiss was anything to go by, I could very easily lose my sanity.

I look back at Mrs Trengrouse, aware that she's watching me. 'Fancy seeing you here.'

'It's in my blood,' he replies with a grin. 'There's something about the musty and threadbare that entices me. Antiques is my middle name.'

'Okay, so what have you got to say about this?' I ask, moving along to the next stall and holding up a silver teapot.

He rounds the corner until he is standing next to me. He really does smell like spring rain and freshly cut grass.

He takes the pot and turns it upside down. 'British. Victorian.'

When I make an impressed face, he grins and moves in closer, pointing at a tiny mark. 'After the American Revolution, Old Blighty needed to refurbish her coffers, so the crown levied taxes of silver. This is a duty mark with Queen Victoria's profile, which means that taxes were paid to her. Hers was a left profile, while all the other monarchs between 1784 and 1890 were right profiles. In any case, the tax on silver was abolished in 1890.'

'Wow. You sure know your history. And your silver.'

He grins. 'The passion was drummed into me when I was a kid.'

'Faith! Faith!' comes a voice from across the way. I turn and see Karen from Cornish Born and Bread who is waving, beckoning to me.

'Excuse me, I'll be right back,' I say.

'Okay, but don't complain if I've bought something totally useless when you get back,' he says with a grin.

I laugh and make my way to the cake stand, all the while grinning to myself. Gabe would have rather been shot between the eyes than spend an afternoon with what he calls rummaging through tat.

'He certainly is a bit of all right, isn't he?' Karen says as Henry is examining an end table across the way. 'Good for you. You deserve someone like that after what Gabe did to you.'

So they do know. 'Oh, no, Karen – I'm not with Henry.'

'Not yet,' she corrects me. 'Perrancombe is too tiny to keep secrets – especially a delicious one like yours.'

'I have no delicious secrets,' I say, my face heating up at the memory of his kiss.

And with that, she takes my shoulders and turns me so I am facing Henry.

Oh. Looks like the jig is up.

'Faith!' Henry calls. 'You won't believe what I've found! Hi, Karen!'

'Hallo, Henry!' she calls back.

I turn to smile at her. 'I've got to go, but I'll see you soon?'

'Absolutely, my dear.'

I buy two bottles of water and head back to Henry who is practically skipping from one foot to another like a child who has to go to the loo.

'Look!' he exclaims, shoving something under my nose. 'Look at this!'

'What is it, a vase?'

'It's a Frankoma!'

'That sounds like a disease,' I observe.

He laughs. 'No, no! This is part of the Frankoma Potteries collection, which is invaluable! And you see here? It's rubber-stamped Frankoma.'

'And?'

'Well, this particular rubber stamp was used for a very short time, so anything bearing this particular stamp is very rare. And worth, gosh, I have no idea!'

'Wow...'

'And... look at this!' he says. 'Green Art Deco glass. It's a *bonbonnière* in the rare Cameo pattern.'

I look up at him in surprise. 'No – it can't be,' I argue. 'This was last seen in an estate.'

'Well, obviously the estate had a sale!'

I re-examine it. 'I'm obviously no expert, but I have to admit that it looks pretty close to what you'd expect from an original.'

'I have an idea,' he says. 'Let's buy it and see what happens.'

'Are you always such an impulsive buyer?' I ask. 'I can't imagine what your home must look like.'

He laughs. 'Actually, my home is almost clinically aseptic and spartan.'

'Yeah, right.'

'Truly, it is. If you don't believe me, why don't you come and see for yourself?'

I swear my eyes are popping out of my head, I have to blink over and over again to keep them in their sockets. 'Me? In your home?'

He shrugs and I can tell his indifference is forced. 'Why not? It's safe to say we are just friends, isn't it?'

Friends. Nothing more.

'I promise to be the perfect gentleman, but if it makes you feel any better, you can come on a day that I have Orson, and you can bring Verity and Jowen. What do you think?'

So we are just friends after all. 'Oh.' I laugh. 'Verity and Jowen in a home full of antiques is not a good idea.'

'Nonsense. It's a perfectly childproof home. So?'

Is he defying me, I wonder? To see if we can be friends after all? I cross my arms in front of my chest. 'Fine. I agree. Thank you.'

'So you'll come?'

'Absolutely maybe,' I answer, cringing inwardly. That didn't sound as haughty as I'd intended it.

'Well then maybe I'll even cook for you,' he threatens me.

'Well then maybe I'll even bring dessert,' I counter-threaten. 'If you promise me it's not a date.'

'A date? Of course not, why would we date?' (Don't you just love him?)

'Good!'

'Good. So I'll see you at six? I want to show you a little something before we eat.'

Not in front of the children, darling. 'Okay, tomorrow night it is, then.'

And then of course, being me, I immediately go into panic mode and with a phantom appointment, leave him there amidst his antiques and speed-dial my sister.

'What's up?' she greets me as cheerfully as always.

'Hope – I need the kids tomorrow night!'

'What? Faith, I know you love them, but get yourself a date instead. I wish I could.'

'I'm serious – I need them. Henry has invited me to d-dinner.'

'So what the hell do you need the kids for?'

'Orson will be there. Henry made that very clear.'

'So then why has he invited you to his house and not just to a restaurant?'

'To show me his antiques collection.'

A loud cackle of delight almost tears my eardrum. 'Hope, I'm serious…'

'I know, and that's what's absolutely brilliant! You are in the presence of a non-dater.'

'A what?'

'Non-dating. It's my sous-chef's new thing, too. She goes out with a bloke on the pretence that it's not a date. They have drinks, talk, have dinner. And then they go home, each to their own place.'

I scratch my head. 'So what's the point of going out if there's no interest in each other?'

'Practice,' she explains. 'So when the right date happens, she'll be so au fait with it all, she won't sweat through ten outfits or make a fool of herself by drinking too much or caring too much if she drops her spoon or puts her foot in her mouth.'

'Are you serious? Is that what people are doing nowadays?'

'Absolutely serious. It's totally brilliant, and she has become uber-confident. Now she doesn't give a toss if she makes a fool out of herself. And she has the assurance she'll never see them again because the rule is to date someone not local.'

'Which becomes a huge hassle if it works out instead,' I say, making her giggle.

'Well then, let's hope you'll have the hassle.'

'Not happening. We are just friends,' I assure her. But when I ring off, I am smiling.

After having picked up Verity and Jowen (and the crème brûlée that Hope has left me), we drive for about thirty minutes during which they natter on endlessly, bless them, while my mind is in absolute turmoil.

And I finally understand why Friday is date night and not, say, Saturday or Sunday. Because, however the (non-) date goes, you'll need time to recuperate from that out-of-body experience. You need Saturday and Sunday to either peel yourself off the floor if it went biblically badly or to come down back down to earth if it went monumentally well.

I follow the squiggly lines on my screen leading to his location, but I find that we are now on a small and unmarked country lane running through the middle of the woods.

'Are we going in *there*?' Verity asks from her seat in the back.

'Ooh, it's like a mystery forest, with talking trees and whispering goblins,' Jowen says, turning in his seat.

'Stop,' Verity says, covering her ears.

'Jowen, we've had this conversation before. No scaring your sister.'

'Where does Henry live? In a haunted house?' Jowen insists.

'Jowen, seeing as you're so brave, you can get out and walk the rest of the way,' I say calmly.

He sinks into his seat. 'Sorry, Auntie Fi…'

'Good boy.' *Now, for Aunt Fi to find the frickin' front door.*

I drive a bit further down the lane until we come to a set of huge, wrought-iron gates with a sign that reads "Quiet Meadows". I think the last time someone has actually passed through these gates is probably now eternally resting peacefully in a quiet meadow himself.

I stop the car and open my door, trying to prevent my jaw from hitting the floor. 'Holy shit!' Jowen says.

'Jowen, please.'

'Ooohhh,' Verity says. 'It looks like a castle!'

More like a medieval manor, actually. Surely this is not Henry's house? I'm debating whether to ring the huge cast-iron bell, when Henry suddenly appears from around the side of the house.

'Hello, welcome, you guys!' he says. 'Come, come!'

Verity gets out of the car and makes a dash for him.

'Hello, sweetheart,' he says, bending down to her, then to me: 'Did you find the place easily?'

'Sure,' I lie, considering that I was about to reverse out and keep looking.

'Good,' he says. 'Come, come. Orson is waiting for you guys. He can't wait to see you.'

'Shall I leave the car here?' I ask. 'In case someone else has to get past?'

'No, no, you can bring it in. The kids and I will walk – it's not far.'

'Okay,' I say, getting back into the car. *Not far for you, maybe, but in these heels, I am not going through this jungle.*

So, I sigh in relief. He doesn't live in the manor. He is not filthy rich and suddenly springing this on me. I need to know who I'm dealing with at all times, and as successful as Henry's business is, I'm glad it's not enough to own a place like this one. Gabe and his money was enough to deal with as it is.

I follow Henry's gestures and pass them to park at another set of gates – finally – where there are some manicured trees, nothing like the manor vegetation where even a field mouse would have had a hard time squeezing through.

I get out of the car and follow them up the path to a huge orangery. It is the back of what looks like a coach house, completely separate from the main house on the road, thank God.

Inside, it is very bright and modern, with furniture that

is sparse but large and comfortable. The rugs are new and bright and the pictures hanging on the wall are mostly of Orson and Henry on vacation.

'Very nice,' I say, handing him the container with the crème brûlées. 'I promised you dessert, but in all honesty, Hope made it.'

'Thank you both, then.'

I shrug. 'You have good taste. Your home is beautiful.'

'Thank you,' he says, slightly reddening. 'Said by an interior designer, that's one huge compliment. Please, make yourselves at home while I get Orson.'

I exhale in relief, knowing that he's going to completely pretend nothing happened between us – not even a waggle of the eyebrows or a knowing look. Good, we're on the same page, then.

I look around as the kids flop themselves down onto one of the cream-coloured sofas.

'Please be careful,' I whisper to them.

'Wow,' Verity says. 'It's so beautiful, Auntie Fi. Almost as beautiful as yours.'

And by 'yours', she certainly doesn't mean my own dump. But yes, if this place had a sea view, it would be far superior to the beach house, as it simply reeks of excellent taste.

Another look around shows me that the far side of the house is completely made of glass to let the sunshine in all day long. I love houses that are one with nature.

'Hi, guys!' Orson calls from the door. 'Want to see my room? I've got lots of games!'

'Sure!' Jowen and Verity cry in unison, their cheeks red with excitement as they chase after him.

'I feel exactly the same way,' I confess to Henry. 'Your home is absolutely gorgeous.'

'It's actually quite small, as I said. But I decided to gut one side and take advantage of the light and views.'

'Absolutely genius,' I say.

'Thanks. Orson and I don't need much. Just a place for us to spend some time together when he's here, his own bedroom, a kitchen. And my office, of course.'

And your bedroom, I almost add, but refrain from it, as I really don't want my thoughts to take *that* turn.

'What about a bathroom,' I quip.

He grins. 'Oh, there's an outhouse of course.'

We end up in the kitchen, which is the largest part of the house. It is an eclectic mix of old and new, with an Aga and a real wood burner at the other end. The table is solid oak, and the furniture is a mixture between mid-century and modern, with clean, no-nonsense lines and I recognise Henry's touch in the simple but stunning furniture he has built himself.

'This is not how I envisaged it in the least,' I confess as we stop to look out at the verdant garden with tall trees and a hammock on the right.

'No?' he says. 'What did you envisage?'

'Well, based on the fact that you're a joiner... much more *wood*.'

He laughs. 'Yes, you're right. But I am actually building some furniture now, out in the back shed.'

'Ooh, can I see?'

'Not until it's finished,' he says. 'And properly *sanded*.'

'Oh,' I say, slightly miffed. Does this man forget nothing?

'It won't be long now,' he assures me. 'Come, take a look at my favourite spot.'

I follow him across the open space to the area on the left where there is another glass wall, and I nearly keel over.

Beyond a lovely, colourful table laid for dinner, I see that we are high on a promontory facing the sea, like the fore of a ship, and down below, is… St Ives, in all its turquoise glory.

'Oh my God,' I whisper as my breath is literally sucked out of me.

I look at him, then back at the view. 'I had no idea where we were. I thought we were in the middle of nowhere. How did you even find this hidden gem?' I ask.

He grins shyly, and I understand that Henry may have done very well for himself, but he has remained warm and genuine on the inside – a quality that many people have lost. Even with Gabe I used to have to yank on his reality chain when he got too big-headed. But Henry, I have a strong feeling, is solid and sturdy and rarely loses his cool. And that, I think, is part of what makes him a great, loving father and a dependable friend.

'Well,' he says, scratching his stubble. 'After my split from Linda I thought, right: brand-new start for Orson and me. I did the work slowly, on weekends. Fortunately most of it was done over an exceptionally warm summer and Orson likes to live simply, so he didn't suffer at all.' He grins. 'We had lots of barbecues and outdoor activities.'

Orson. Such a lovely boy. Like his father, he too, has that melancholy side of him, which only endears him to me even more. He is so sweet, so kind and so modest.

'Are you okay?' he says softly. 'You've suddenly gone… misty.'

I sniff and smile, wiping the moistness from my eyes. 'No, I'm fine. It's just so lovely to see how much you two love each other. He adores you.'

'And I him. But you have that too – Jowen and Verity cherish the ground you walk on.'

'Nah,' I quickly say.

'Of course they do,' he insists. 'And when you have your own kids one day, they too will love you to bits. You will make a fantastic mother, Faith.'

'That's so kind of you to say, Henry…'

He puts his glass down and takes my elbow gently. 'I really think so, Faith. Never doubt yourself. You are truly great. And you are an amazing designer. I love your work.'

I tear my eyes away from the view to look up at Henry's face again. It is solemn and deadly serious, but also honest and kind. His winged eyebrows that sometimes make him look so scowly are now raised in an almost plea for me to believe him. He certainly can turn on the charm.

'Tell me more about the manor,' I urge him.

'The manor? Oh, well, it belongs to an ancient family. They travel a lot.'

'I wonder what it looks like on the inside? If it's still in its original state. Do you know if it's open to the public?'

He laughs. 'Now that's an idea.'

'Have you ever been inside? What's it like?'

He grins. 'The exact opposite of this, actually. Would you like to see it?'

'Is that even possible?'

STARTING OVER AT THE LITTLE CORNISH BEACH HOUSE

'Of course. I have the keys somewhere around here. I'm their *In Case of an Emergency* person, you see.'

'Are we going to leave the kids?' I ask.

'Oh, yes, we'd better. There are lots of valuables in there and they would kill me if anything broke. But not to worry. I have my house on video camera.'

'You are one surprise after another.'

He grins as I follow him to Orson's room where the kids are putting an interactive puzzle together.

'Orson? We're going next door for a minute. Can you promise me you'll stay in here until we get back?'

'Sure, Daddy,' Orson calls over his shoulder, too absorbed by company his own age to even look at us. I smile. Happy children just make me tingly all over.

'This way,' Henry says, reaching the end of a short lane and opening a door onto the jungle, and it's like stepping into a parallel world. 'They like their privacy. I personally think it's a bit OTT but who am I to say?'

'Each to their own,' I agree. 'If I had a house like this, it would constantly be full of friends.'

He leads the way down the side path to the back door of the manor's orangery. Here, everything is the opposite of Henry's place, where white-rendered walls give way to ancient, massive stone walls and clinging vines that curl over the cast iron of the Victorian orangery that is a late addition to the medieval property. It positively reeks of history. I follow as he leads me through the rear entrance into a huge professional Georgian kitchen.

'Oh my God, Henry! It's gorgeous!'

'Is it?' he asks. 'Perhaps. A bit too stuffy for me, though.

You've seen what I like. Would you like to see the rest?' he asks.

'Yes, please!'

He leads me from room to room, stopping at the major ones. 'This is the drawing room.'

There is also an enormous library with the oldest books I've ever seen, a sitting room strewn with antique armchairs and occasional tables, and a music room with a harpsichord.

'This part is early Georgian for sure,' I observe, my eyes floating over the tell-tale signs.

'Shall we check on the kids?'

'Please.'

'Orson?' he calls into his mobile.

'Yes, Big Brother?' the child calls back and I can't help but laugh.

'We won't be long,' he says.

'Take your time, Daddy – I'm beating Jowen.'

Henry rolls his eyes. 'Cheeky little bugger.'

I follow him down the lane back to the converted coach house, babbling on enthusiastically about the architectural value of the manor.

'I guess it has its historical value,' he admits stopping in front of Orson's open door through which we can see the kids still playing. 'Come on in.'

Verity, Jowen and Orson barely acknowledge us as we enter his room.

'Okay, you guys, Orson will take you to the bathroom to wash your hands. Wait for us on the terrace, we'll be right there.'

'I'm starving!' Jowen cries as they race out of the room

as if you'd just told them there was a bouncy castle outside waiting for them.

'Come and have a look,' Henry beckons me.

'Oh, wow, it's a great bedroom—' and I stop just inside the door to stare at a large array of familiar, house-shaped cushions dominating the place. 'Those...'

Henry smiles. 'Yes, Faith. Those are your very own Home Hugs. We have the Cottage Home Hug and the Beach Hut Home Hug.'

'That's... that's...' I croak as a huge knot forms in my throat and I instantly see myself as a child again, huddled on the floor, my back against my bedroom door while Hope and our foster parents are bringing down the house once again.

'When Orson is with his mum, I take them into the living room and scatter them all over the sofas,' Henry says. 'They comfort me.'

'Thank you, that is a huge compliment. But Home Hugs aside, it is a beautiful room,' I say as my eyes fall on some pictures on the wall opposite the bed.

They are pictures of a beautiful brunette with a dazzling smile holding a baby Orson. The ex-wife Linda. Finally. I was starting to wonder what she looked like. There are other photos throughout the years as Orson is growing, but she only seems to become more and more beautiful. Some women have that innate class. I square my shoulders and look over at Henry.

'She is a stunner.'

He shrugs. 'Yes, well, I didn't want Orson to miss her while he's here, so I blew them up so he could see them from his bed.'

'You are a very loving father, Henry. Why did you split—' I bite my lip. 'Sorry, I didn't mean to pry.'

He waves his hand in a dismissive manner. 'Water under the bridge. She and I had practically nothing in common outside the physical sphere, and when I realised it a few months in, she was already pregnant. So I did the right thing.'

Like Gabe. 'But it gave you Orson.'

'Yes. You see, eventually, things fall into place. Linda is still trying to cope with the divorce. Luckily her parents are fit and able and help her out a lot when Orson is with her. It's made everything easier for me, knowing that Linda is not alone.'

'That's a good arrangement,' I agree.

'And... how are you?'

'Me? Oh.' He wants to know if I'm still smarting from my break-up. Despite our kiss I'm dying to repeat, while he seems particularly indifferent. Now isn't that ironic? 'I'm fine, thank you.'

'And you're growing... stronger?'

Meaning am I over Gabe? Good one.

'Yes,' I assure him.

'Good.'

I nod, glad that the Spanish Inquisition is over. And then my stomach growls.

He laughs. 'Hungry much?'

'Starved,' I answer.

'I'm a terrible host. Let's go.'

Outside, the enclosed patio seems stolen from a Mediterranean designer magazine, with a white linen tablecloth, silver cutlery with duck egg earthenware plates that must be at least two hundred years old. Apart from three plastic cups for the kids, there is an array of crystal glasses for us. There is also an understated but very refined centrepiece with multi-coloured flowers. Around the table there are six turquoise L'Eau chairs by Calligaris, famous for mimicking a water ripple on the seat. And all this of course is complete with a bird's eye view of St Ives and its turquoise sea in the background.

'Oh my word, Henry, this is – what's a word better than beautiful? It's so thoughtful of you. Thank you.'

'It's nothing, Faith. Just some old plates and a little love. I hope you'll like the food, because it would be embarrassing if you don't.'

'I'll love it,' I say, looking out to the bay as Henry begins to serve Verity, then Jowen and finally Orson.

He's prepared a huge cous-cous dish and at least three different kinds of colourful salads, plus a dish of mixed grilled vegetables and a selection of grilled chicken, little sausages and tiny burgers for the kids. My mouth is watering just looking at it. Great food, a great view and a home full of love. I must have booked an afternoon in Nirvana and forgotten all about it.

'Daddy's cooking is delicious!' Orson exclaims and the kids nod in agreement.

I take a forkful of cous-cous, close my eyes and swoon. 'Oh my God, Henry, this is so delicious! It's like being in Morocco…'

He chuckles. 'Here, have some meat. We need to put some real food into you.'

'Auntie Fi only eats when she comes to our house,' Verity explains to Henry. 'Our mum's been trying to teach her to cook for years now.'

My eyes swing to Henry. 'True. I just don't have the time right now.'

'Your aunt is busy with work. One day she'll have more time to do everything she wants.'

'Like going to Italy.'

Henry's eyebrows shoot up. 'Really? Where in particular?'

'Oh… Sicily, I suppose. I had a friend whose nana was from Ragusa – that's south-east – and her cooking was… I've never tasted anything like it in my life – real *focacce*, not the kind you buy in the stores, but genuine Sicilian *focacce*. They are like our own pasties, only the dough is thinner and there is a variety of fillings, from tomato sauce and cheese, onions, or parsley and ricotta cheese, aubergines, spinach – anything that grows locally. And the fish dishes! They have this special swordfish and aubergines with a mint and chocolate sauce, and the *arancini*? Have you ever tasted *arancini*? And get this – they have a *red pepper* chocolate ice cream dating back to the Mayans.'

Henry laughs, his eyes twinkling. 'You do love your food.'

'Oh, I do,' I assure him as I pop a piece of chicken into my mouth and enjoy the sensation as it literally melts on my tongue.

'And where did you learn to cook, Henry? This would even give Hope a run for her money, and she's good. But don't tell Mummy,' I turn to warn Jowen and Verity but they are now so absorbed in their food and their own conversations with Orson that I suspect I'm safe for now.

Henry shrugs. 'I don't know, I just use ingredients I like. Simple stuff.'

I put a forkful of yellow pepper and zucchini into my mouth, trying to guess the seasoning. 'Balsamic vinegar?'

'And garlic olive oil,' he replies. 'And sometimes capers. Orson loves capers. Which is really strange for a lad, isn't it?'

I laugh in agreement, take a sip of sparkling water and sit back to enjoy the view, as a sigh of contentment escapes me. 'This,' I say, 'is possibly one of the best times I've had in a long time, Henry. Thank you.'

He puts his glass down and smiles at me. 'Thank *you*. It's great to have you here. Orson's developed quite a crush on you,' he whispers.

'So have I,' I confess. *On both of you.*

We exchange a glance that lasts a little too long for comfort and Henry scratches his chin as I've seen him do when he is undecided about something. I hope he's not undecided about me.

'Right,' he suddenly says, rising. 'Orson, come and help me get dessert?'

'Yes, Daddy,' he says, jumping up and disappearing through the patio doors behind Henry into the kitchen.

'Are you all right, guys? Are you having a good time with Orson?'

'I don't want to leave,' Verity says in earnest.

Oh, how I hear her. Henry and Orson's company is so... refreshing without all the *Look at Me, I'm successful* codswallop. He's actually quite modest and I love his understated manners. Gabe should take a leaf out of his book.

'And here we have Hope's Crème Brûlée, plus our own Sticky Cornish Fudge Pudding with clotted cream ice cream,' Henry tells us as he carries out four plates, Orson behind him carrying one. 'The fudge is made with sea salt. I hope you like it.'

Oh, God, I'm already salivating as if I hadn't eaten in years. 'You made this?'

He dips his head with a grin. 'Well, Orson and I both did. He mixed the ingredients and pushed the fudge squares into the sponge. And dribbled the sauce on the top.'

I scoop up a small spoonful, still trying to be dainty, and dear me, I'm going to have to marry the man. Or at least show up on his doorstep at mealtimes.

'Do you like it, Faith?' Orson asks eagerly, his face lighting up with hope.

I don't want the poor little fellow to wait for an answer, so I cover my mouth in a semblance of dignity. 'Issgorgeous…' I swoon. 'Issreallyreallygood!'

Henry and Orson turn and high-five each other.

'Can we go play again, Auntie Faith?' Jowen wants to know after they've downed both their desserts.

'Only if Orson wants to,' I reply, and the three of them are off.

'Thank you, Henry, for this. The kids and I are enjoying your company immensely. Who knew?'

At that, he laughs and rolls his eyes. Henry is a breath of fresh air. And it's so easy to chat with someone who's never hurt you. He's a good bloke. The fact that he is devastatingly handsome and that my skin tingles whenever I set eyes on him is a completely different story.

'What are you thinking?' he asks me, and I snap out of it, just in time to catch myself staring up adoringly into his face.

I am thinking that this is not a date, but just a great evening, in a gorgeous home with a divine meal. With the best company I've had in a very long time.

After coffee, we sit and lounge around despite my many attempts to relieve him of our presence. Henry asks me to stay a little longer, at least until we can admire the lights of St Ives twinkling and shimmering down on the coast.

Up here, it feels like nothing can harm me. But I can't stay here all night as much as I'd love to. (See? That's where the niece and nephew come in handy, keeping me on the straight and narrow.) Particularly because I am scolding myself. What did I expect, for Henry to wipe everything off the table in one swoosh of his arms and make mad love to me while the kids are playing less than ten feet away? It had only been a kiss. An amazing, knee-melting kiss, granted. But it had stopped there. Perhaps he had even regretted it.

So I reluctantly get to my feet. 'It's time for us to go. Thanks once again, Henry. The kids loved it and so did I.'

He rises with me, stuffing his hands into his pockets. 'Okay. It was lovely having you. So... I guess I'll see you Monday then.'

Monday? That's the entire weekend to wait. 'Or not,' I blurt out.

'You don't want me in on Monday?'

'Oh, of course! I meant, well...'

He is looking down into my eyes. He can feel it, too. I am going to make a fool out of myself and screw up all over again, I just know it.

'What did you mean, Faith?' he asks softly, as I back up against the doorjamb, suddenly at a loss for words. Gosh, I've gone completely blank now. All I can think of is how the mere sight of him cheers me up.

'That maybe,' he says, 'we could go for lunch and possibly a stroll if you like? I promise to behave at all times.'

'I like,' I say before I can stop myself.

He grins, his eyes crinkling at the corners. 'Brilliant. I'll go fetch the kids for you, then,' he says.

But he doesn't move. Nor can I. It's like we are in a magnetic force field and there's no way out. His face is solemn, slightly heated, and his expression is one I've never seen before.

Oh God, please kiss me again. Or better, don't. Because if you do, it's all out in the open and I'll be officially screwed for good, if you'll pardon the pun.

And then, out of the blue, a clock starts chiming, scaring the bejesus out of me. I jump, and he steps away.

'Oh! I, uhm... kids...' I manage.

He runs a hand through his thick mane. 'Right. Of course. I'll go fetch the kids.'

'Thank you.' I gather their things and move to the door, as far away from the scene of attraction as possible. When he returns with them, they are all a sad lot, Henry included, and we all shuffle to the side door from where we came.

'Can't we stay a little longer, Auntie Fi?' Jowen pleads.

'I'm sorry, sweetheart, but it's really late and I have to get you home to your mum who misses you.'

He hangs his head in resignation as Orson hovers. 'Can they come back again, Daddy?' Orson asks.

'Of course, son,' Henry answers, ruffling his hair, then turns to me. 'Do you know your way back from here?'

'I've got satnav,' I say as I fetch my own bag from the *madia* against the wall.

'Goodbye, Orson. I'll see you soon!'

'Can I come and visit you again?' he asks.

'Of course you can – anytime you want! I'll have your favourite chocolate sprinkled doughnuts waiting.'

'Yay!' he cries, jumping up and down, throwing his arms around my neck.

'Easy, Orson, you're choking her,' Henry says with a soft chuckle.

But he doesn't let go. If anything, he holds me even tighter. I hug him back, feeling all of his affection as he gives me a quick peck on the cheek.

'Bye, Faith!' he chimes, waving. 'Bye, Jowen; bye, Verity!'

'Byeee!' they chime, waving as if we were on a cruise ship about to depart from the port.

In a way, this home is like a secure port in the storm. A safe haven for Orson and Henry to return to after a long day.

'Bye, Orson,' I manage as a huge knot forms in my throat and with a feeling of distinct loss, we get into the car and it takes me a huge effort to not sob.

What's the matter with me? We've had a great time, right? The kids love him, and they apparently love Henry, too. But the fact is that Orson and I have somehow created a bond.

At Hope's place, the kids rush through the front door, excited to see their mummy.

'Hey…!' Hope calls, as she jumps off the sofa to hug them. 'I've missed you lot!'

'Mum, we saw the most beautiful house in the world!' Verity cries as she throws her arms around her.

'It was full of games!' Jowen echoes.

'Really?' Hope enthuses.

'Yuh,' Verity says as she yawns and rubs eyes. 'Can we watch TV, Mummy, please?'

'Aren't you tired enough, love?' Hope asks, ruffling her daughter's hair.

'No,' she lies and Hope laughs. 'Tell you what. You go and watch some TV in my bed, just for a bit, all right?'

'Okay. Goodnight, Auntie Faith,' they chime, two sets of arms around my waist.

'Night, you two. Glad you had fun.'

'Remember we're going again soon,' Jowen reminds me.

Hope looks at me. 'Oh?'

'Yeah,' I say casually as I drop into one of her armchairs. 'They have become great friends with Orson.'

'And what about you and Henry?' Hope asks, passing me the bowl of potato chips on the coffee table. For being a chef, Hope still likes her junk food.

'No thanks, I'm still stuffed.'

'And love-struck,' she says.

'What? I am not,' I deny.

'Oh come on, Faith. He's a great guy! I can't imagine anyone else with you.'

Nor could I. But... 'We, uhm, kissed the other day.'

'What? Congratulations!' she cries, hugging me.

'No, it's not – I told him I wasn't, er, looking for a relationship.'

'Oh, Faith, you didn't!'

'I did. And now it's like he's switched off the interest, just like I asked him too, and I'm smarting but I haven't got the guts to say *Yes, let's do this*. Oh, Hope, what the hell is wrong with me? I'm such a loser.'

STARTING OVER AT THE LITTLE CORNISH BEACH HOUSE

'You're not,' she says loyally. 'Don't forget that he's recently divorced. Maybe he's just realised that he needs time, too. Don't rush yourselves.'

'I hope so. You know how important it is for me to have stability. I guess we both need our mourning time. I don't want any blurred lines.'

'Blurred lines?' Hope echoes. 'Listen, sweetie – I've been telling you for years that Gabe was not the right bloke for you. It took you longer than expected, but you're finally at the point in your life where you don't love him anymore. Correct?'

'Oh, absolutely.'

There's no denying that I have finally got over my sorrow for losing Gabe. Twice. I finally understand that my obsession with him was more about the fear of losing someone all over again – and in that very house, which represented the culmination of the journey I'd been through, from foster child to someone who had not only found love, but also a stable life and home. Of someone who had finally managed to tick all the boxes in life. But now I understand that I was the only one ticking those boxes, while Gabe had wanted more than I could ever give him or even be remotely interested in. I wasn't interested in a jet-set, out-of-the-norm fancy life. I was still craving a normal life.

There is now only anger and bitterness where he is concerned. The mere thought of seeing him makes me want to hurl.

'I know you don't want to jump into anything new. But Henry seems truly smitten with you, the way he looks at you with those spaniel eyes.'

'He does not have spaniel eyes,' I defend.

'Only for you,' Hope says. 'You could see it from the moon that he's more than keen on you.'

I bite my lip. 'I want to. I really do. But it's just too soon for the both of us. He's still smarting from his divorce, and I don't want to vent to my next boyfriend about Gabe. I want to be able to start a new relationship completely happy, and I'm just not there yet.'

'I'm not asking you to jump the poor sod's bones, but at least don't discourage him. If he is as interested as I think he is, he's not going anywhere.'

'But what would he think of me, flitting straight from Gabe to him? What kind of girl bounces from one relationship to another?'

'You mean, what kind of woman bounces back from Mr Wrong straight into the arms of Mr Right? A *clever* one.'

'But don't you think it's too soon to—?'

'To love again? Faith – look around you. Look at all the horrible things that happen out of the blue. Break-ups. Accidents. Diseases. Life is short. What the bloody hell are you waiting for – to turn ninety and suddenly realise that you've only half-lived your life because of some silly rules made up by miserable, lonely prudes?'

Well, if you put it that way. 'Then what do you think I should do?'

She takes a sip of her drink. 'Invite him over to your place for dinner, just you and him. He'll get the idea, and if he cares, you won't have to do anything. It'll all happen spontaneously.'

I bite my lip. 'I'll give it a thought,' I promise, but I already know I'll never have the courage to do something so liberating.

The next day, Saturday, sees me on the job as if I didn't have a life (you got me!). I'm debating between oak or cedar for the doors, my mobile rings. It's Gabe, his angelic face filling my screen. I am technically still working to Gabe's specifications and so cannot yet erase his number from my contact list. With a sigh, I slide the green button to the side.

'I told you to liaise with Thea.'

'Can I come over?' he asks. 'I need to talk to you.'

'About the job?' I ask defensively. There's no way I'm going to even remotely entertain the idea of speaking to him about anything else.

'Yes,' he says. 'I won't be long.'

'Right.'

'See you in a mo.'

'You mean now?' My insides do a triple back somersault.

'If you don't mind.'

I glance at the samples sitting next to my laptop, trying to decide.

'Fine. But you can't stay long. I've got stuff to do,' I warn him.

'Be there in a flash,' he says, and rings off.

But here in a flash, he is not. As a matter of fact, he's thirty-five minutes late and I've a mind to go out just to teach him a lesson. And just as I am debating on what to do, my doorbell rings.

I huff and buzz him in, thinking of a way to keep his stay very short.

'Hey,' he says as he climbs the stairs. 'I went to the beach house and Thea told me you had moved out.'

I move aside to let him by and then follow him inside and close the door.

'Why would I stay there?' I ask, already resenting him. 'It's not my home anymore.'

He takes a look around and sits down on the settee. 'Nice digs.'

'Why are you here, Gabe?'

He looks at me as if I'd slapped him. 'Faith, come on, when are you going to forgive me? You know I'd never do anything to hurt you deliberately.'

I snort. 'As if that was enough.'

'Please don't look at me like that,' he says, sitting up. 'I can't stand the thought of you hating me. I hate myself enough for two.'

'Good.' I was always the mature one in our relationship: the one to hold the reins, to apologise first, et cetera, simply because Gabe has always been an extremist in everything he does. There were never any half measures with him. Either he was all in or all out. Either elated or depressed. Optimistic or pessimistic.

To the point, it was always me to pick him up whenever he was down. Or yank him back down to reality when he got too big-headed. I guess I was a bit like the string attached to a kite, anchoring him to earth, while Gabe soared on his various thermals of optimism, ambition and grandeur. And on his bad days I would have to hide the second bottle of wine because he would actually start complaining to me about everything and anything, me included, and then – finally – fall into a drunken sleep.

And I'd have to wait a full twenty-four hours for him not only to sober up, but to get back to functioning fully.

That had always bothered me about him, but because I loved him, I accepted the bad with the good. Like you do with family. Not that I'd really know. But Gabe wasn't my family, and because of him, I'd never have one now.

'So what did you want to talk to me about?'

He runs a hand through his hair. 'Have you got a beer?'

'No, I don't drink,' I remind him. That's another thing – his forgetting even such monumental things about me, when instead I remembered all his likes and dislikes. I once heard someone say that when in a couple one person loves more, that love can't last. I wish I'd heeded it at the time, but I'd been so infatuated with Gabe's endearing youthful attitude. Now, it only reminds me of how gullible and naïve I have been. 'There's water, if you're thirsty.' The last thing I need is a drunk, bawling Gabe in my home.

He sighs. 'No thanks. Water doesn't wash away my sorrows.'

'For Christ's sake, Gabe—'

'Yes, sorry, I'll get to the point. Is it okay if I move back into the beach house? I'll stay out of your way.'

'Why?' I say, but then I realise I've broken my own rule. This is supposed to be a strictly business meeting.

'We've split up.' He looks up at me with those huge, imploring baby blue eyes. 'I'll sleep in my studio. You won't even know I'm there.'

'I'm sorry, Gabe, but due to insurance, health and safety, we can't have you there.'

'I understand. But Jesus, Faith, how else am I to see you?'

I blink. I'm certain I haven't heard that properly, what with all the banging and drilling and sawing on-site, I must have lost a few decibels of my hearing somewhere along the way.

'If only you could find it in your heart to forgive me. It would make everything so much less complicated,' he whispers.

No, I still don't think I've heard that properly. 'I beg your pardon?'

He comes to stand right before me. 'It hurts to think how much you hate me, when all I did was leave her for you, because I love you.'

You have to admit, there is method in his madness. 'You mean after you left me for her, Gabe.'

'But then I left her for you because I realised what a huge mistake I'd made. It's not my fault if she got pregnant.'

'Ah, that's really rich!' I snort, turning away, but he catches my hand.

'Please, Faith. I didn't mean it that way. I wanted to start all over again with you. And then Vanessa told me she was pregnant. What was I supposed to do, abandon her because she was up the duff?'

The opposite of what he did to me, i.e. leave me because I simply wanted a baby. Although he'll never admit it. Kids wouldn't exactly look good on his bio.

'I'm hurt too, you know?' he whines.

'Oh, are you really?'

'Of course. When I told you about the baby, you could have accepted it. We had just got back together again, but you refused to stay with me. Lots of women choose to stay with their partners even if their ex-girlfriends are pregnant. Won't you reconsider, Babes? I miss you. Life is just absolute shite without you.'

I tear away from him, and his hand drops to his side. 'You were supposed to be honest, Gabe! You flew back to

England, in the middle of the night, and crawled into my bed. Sofa. Whatever. And you knew Vanessa was already pregnant. You *lied* to me and cheated on me again and again! You took advantage of my idiocy and the fact that I still loved you!'

'Babes—'

'I'm not your Babes!'

'But you still love me, I can see it in your eyes…'

'No, Gabe. What you see is horror of the person you have become. Or perhaps always were, and the horror you see is for how I let you get away with it for so long. You, you—' I clench my fists as my ears begin to burn. Just one swing. One swing is all I need and I'd feel better. 'You'd expect me to just slot myself into your new life, while you traipse around the globe, sleep with both of us, coming in and going out of my life while I help you raise your child on your days and become Vanessa's best buddy? Well I'm sick and tired of you jerking me around as if I was your rag doll! You've made your bed, so now you can sleep in it. You make me sick!'

His eyes drop to the floor, and for a moment I can almost swear they are shiny. He always did that, just to see how far he could push me into doing something I didn't want to. I watch him in silence. Back then, I'd always crack and he would have his way. But not this time. I didn't almost go over the edge and become an alcoholic for nothing. I step to the front door and hold it wide open for him.

He can't believe I'm doing this, and frankly, I never thought I would have had to, but *yay me!*

I'm not taking it anymore, and he's just got it.

In the end, he nods and whispers a broken goodbye as he

slowly walks past me and out of my flat – once and for all. I close the door behind him and sink onto the settee, swiping at a stupid, stray tear.

On Monday morning I drive up to the beach house, park alongside the cars of my crew, my body limp with the emotional stress, and my brain a mess. As I'm closing the front door, Henry's Jeep pulls up.

I linger on the threshold, relieved it isn't Gabe again. But then, Gabe was never an early bird. He's probably still in bed, snoring for England.

'Hey,' Henry says as he makes his way towards me with a huge smile and an equally huge paper bag in his arms. He's brought breakfast again. He doesn't have to, of course, but just to know that he is thinking of everyone warms my cockles – and gets my stomach grumbling.

'Hey back,' I say, and I can't help smiling. His good mood is so contagious I'm already feeling better. Perhaps today won't be a crappy day after all.

'Newsflash – Gabe and Vanessa have split up,' I inform him as I move aside to let him in.

At that, Henry halts, his eyes checking mine. 'Are you serious?'

'Absolutely.'

He puts his bag down on a bale of bubble wrap, clearing his throat. 'Does that mean that you and he... uhm...?'

'God, no,' I hasten to answer him.

'And he called you to tell you that? The cheek. The bloody *cheek*,' he mutters, and for a moment I let myself go to the belief that he is jealous. But he is only being protective of me, like the rest of my crew. Still, it's a nice, warm feeling.

'He actually came over to my flat.'

At that, he rests his hands on his hips, shaking his head. 'I hope he didn't upset you too much?'

'Oh, I know how to handle him by now,' I reassure him. 'But I'll be happy to finish this job and put all this behind me,' I confess. 'Coffee?'

'Sure, thanks,' he says, closing the door behind him and picking up his bag of cakes again.

'I'll give you an extra huge cup of coffee if there's a blueberry scone for me in there,' I offer over my shoulder as we head for the kitchen.

He grins. 'Yeah? What makes you think that there is?'

'Because you always get me one.'

'How would you know that?'

'A little birdie told me.'

'Maybe the little birdie was wrong,' he suggests.

Wrong? Oh, crap. The fact hadn't even occurred to me.

'Your face!' he says with a laugh. 'Of course it's for you – who else could it possibly be for?'

I look up into his eyes. I like the way they crinkle at the corners when he smiles, which is a lot more, lately, I've noticed.

'Oh! Thank you, Henry. I – er, if you're sure…?'

'Silly,' he says, reaching into the bag. 'I'm just teasing you. Here it is. For you. And only you.'

We stand in silence in the kitchen for a few moments as I'm desperately scrabbling for an idea for small talk. Luckily, Henry saves the moment.

'By the way, Orson sends his love,' he says. 'It's official – he's absolutely smitten with you.'

'Really? I think he's adorable, too!'

He pauses again, and the silence is calling for an *And I think you are adorable, too, Henry*. But that would only lead me deeper into the maze that are my feelings at the moment.

'So,' I finally say, clapping my hands. 'Would you like to take a look around after breakfast? I could use your advice on a couple of things, if that's okay?'

His eyes widen in surprise. 'You want my opinion?'

I blush. 'Well, you are a joiner, after all. The best. And after seeing what good taste you have, I'd be grateful for your opinion.'

'Sure, if you like,' he says, and he looks around the kitchen. 'I'm going to put an extra rush on this so you can move on to a different job.'

'That would be great, Henry, thank you.' But how am I going to manage to see him – and Orson – after that? I only hope that my next clients will need a kitchen.

'So, Faith? Why do you think Vanessa and Gabe have split up? Do you think he wants you back?'

I snort. 'He might think so, but I think that he just needs some time away from Vanessa.'

'And more time close to you?' he says softly.

'Oh, that's not happening,' I hasten to reassure him.

'I hope not,' Henry whispers, his eyes sweeping over my face, down to my mouth, then back to look deep into my eyes in that caressing way he has. 'It would be a travesty.'

'A travesty…' I echo, a second away from melting into his arms. I can already feel my knees buckling, for goodness' sake.

'Faith! Henry! Come upstairs! We're ready to tackle this bitch!' Thea's voice rings loud throughout the house, jolting me – and him, I think – out of la-la land.

'That's, uhm, us,' I manage, licking my lips that have gone desert dry all of a sudden. 'I think they're in the master bedroom.'

Henry's eyes widen and he takes a step back, running a hand through his hair. 'Bedroom – right.'

He follows me upstairs, and for a moment I can't help but imagine that we are alone and moving into a bedroom to be together and—

'Where the hell have you two been? We've been looking all over for you,' Thea says, looking over her shoulder as we make our way into the blood-red slaughterhouse full of members of my crew armed with crowbars and hammers.

'We need all the hands we can get to move this monster,' Mike says. The monster being the huge mirror clinging to the ceiling like a cloud of bats.

I shudder at the thought of its purpose and Henry, who is standing shoulder to shoulder with me in the crowded room, turns to look at me, touching my fingers with his. It is a gesture that goes unnoticed by all but me.

'Right, let's give this bastard all we've got!' Henry says, and I can't help thinking he means Gabe.

'Are you actually telling me that the two of you were practically nose to nose again and you didn't *kiss?*' Hope hisses when I tell her. 'What the hell is wrong with you, Faith? Have I taught you absolutely nothing? Honestly, I don't understand you sometimes.'

NANCY BARONE

'Join the club,' I quip.

'So what are you going to do now?'

What can I do? Make a fool out of myself by jumping from one long-term relationship into a new one with a man I work with, and who, incidentally, I'm professionally in awe of? 'Aaaabsolutely *nothing*.'

'Faith...'

'Let it go, Hope,' I warn her. 'I'm not ruining his renewed opinion of me by falling at his feet. Plus, I've been kicked around enough lately. It's time to stand up for myself.'

'*Now* you find your backbone?' she wails.

'Now I find my backbone. And you know what? It feels *great*. I'm my own woman now.'

'Great, just great,' she groans. 'At this rate you'll be on your own forever.'

'Being on your own isn't so bad. Look at you.'

'Sweetie – I'm on my own because my husband dumped me. And now I'm glad he did. But you? You deserve to be with someone like Henry. I'm sick and tired of seeing you so lonely.'

'I'm not lonely. I have you and Verity and Jowen and the girls down the coast. And my team.'

Hope groans. 'Don't pretend you don't know what I mean. You need to *belong*, Faith.'

My eyes are suddenly burning. 'I belong to you, don't I? Aren't we a family?'

'Of course we are, you silly sausage. You are my and Jowen and Verity's world – you know that. But you need a man of your own with whom—'

'To have my own kids,' I say hotly. 'Got it.'

'Oh come on, Faith – don't be like that. You know I want only what's best for you.'

'But maybe I'm not ready for what is best for me,' I argue. 'Maybe I need to be alone until I am no longer angry with Gabe.'

'Good luck with that,' Hope shoots back. 'You will always be angry with Gabe, and you know what? You have the right to be. But you can't let your past with him keep you from a future with Henry.'

She's right about the past bit, I know she is. But regarding my future, Henry might be attracted to me and even enjoy my company, but is he, with the state his own life is in, even ready for a mess like me?

12

Unfaithful

'Faith?' Henry calls from the threshold the next morning. I turn and look at him, unable to ignore the fact that he looks positively delicious in a pair of tatty Levi's, construction boots and an old check shirt with his sleeves rolled up. His arms are the perfect amount of hairy and—

'The team has just offered to help me take the old kitchen out. Is that okay with you…?'

Just don't look at him. Even if his voice alone is enough to fry your knickers, just ignore it all.

'Faith?'

'Uhm… yes, yes, of course, I'll come and give a hand too.'

'Thanks,' he says with a smile. 'We need all the help we can get today.'

So do I. If I can make it through today without embarrassing myself any more than I already have, I'm ahead of the game. Because Henry is a bloke just like any other. No better, no worse. Just average. At least that's what I keep telling myself, but he constantly proves me wrong.

'Here,' he says, adjusting a pair of goggles on me. 'We don't want those gorgeous eyes of yours to be without protection.'

You see? One day he's cold, and the next day he's hot. Where do I stand with him? I don't know, and I can't ask. I'd simply die. Defeated, I look up at him and that beautiful mouth of his that curves into a sensual smile as his dark eyes caress my face the way no one else's ever have. He is so close I can smell his deliciousness, and I actually have to look down because he is truly too beautiful to behold without making a right fool of myself in front of my staff.

'There you are,' he whispers and for a moment it's like we're completely alone in the room.

Never mind protecting my eyes, who the hell is going to protect my heart? Because that's it – I think it's too late for that now. I am undone. Completely, absolutely, crappily undone.

But I can't afford to be hurt again. So this time, I'm being very wary. I don't want to go back to the darkness of those moments, when I felt that I was sitting at the bottom of a well with no hope to ever surface again. Besides, it's not like I'm going to act upon my desire, am I? Yes, I know what you're thinking – that I already have. I look up at him, seriously wondering how I'm going to not get my heart broken again.

'Don't forget your gloves,' he says as he holds them open for me and as my cheeks catch fire, I slip my hands into them like a child being dressed by her father before going out into the cold. His touch is delicate, yet incredibly sexy. If I feel this way while he's slipping a pair of grubby working gloves onto my hands, just imagine what it would be like to have him slip my clothes off. But I can't think of that now or I'll burst into flames in front of my crew, which would be rather embarrassing and tricky to explain to the Health and Safety board.

'You ready?' he murmurs, uncaring of everyone else who seems too busy with the task at hand to notice our tender exchange.

I nod, still unable to maintain his gaze.

He claps his hands shut and turns back into the Turner part of Turner & Cooke, which is fine with me. I can deal with Turner & Cooke. I love Turner & Cooke. It's the Turner part alone that I can't deal with. Unless there's a desk between us.

'Let's get the bugger out, then,' he says and we turn to face the job.

In silence, we all marvel at the ugliness of it, like a horrid painting that no one comprehends.

'That sure was a bloody red kitchen,' Mike says, causing the others to laugh.

'Yeah, it would absolutely put me off my dinner,' Rudy agrees.

Henry's eyes meet mine. 'Soon it'll be just how it was,' he says. 'You'll never even know this dreadful thing was here.'

'Amen,' I say.

'Yes,' Henry agrees. 'Carefully, though.'

Bill snorts. 'What, we're salvaging this piece of rubbish, too?'

I nod. 'I told you, I don't want anything of hers damaged.'

Henry eyes me, and I sense that he is glad I haven't gone psycho-bitch on Vanessa's possessions. I could never do that to anyone. Even if nothing is to my taste, it's not mine to throw away.

Henry, of course, is leading the team, and after we've removed the cooker and sink, down come the cupboards, and up comes the counter and the blood-red tiles and splashback. Normally at this point in a reno, it feels good to throw out the ugly for the beautiful. But the fact that this was once my home makes it even more difficult.

'Let's take a break,' I call after a couple of hours of this ghastly work and the tools are gratefully put down.

I take off my gloves and goggles and go sit out on the back patio. After a moment Henry appears with a couple of mugs containing coffee.

'Thanks, just what I needed. How's Orson?' I ask and he turns to me with a smile.

'He's doing well, thank you. He's with his mum today.'

'Oh, that's good,' I say.

'I'll bring him back here to see you when it's safer.'

'Of course. Let me know when you do so I can bring mine in too – I mean, Jowen and Verity. Who are not my kids, obviously.'

Henry laughs. 'Obviously.'

And then he looks at me, doing a double take.

'What?' I say. 'Have I got something on my face?'

But he doesn't answer, his eyes widening. Oh dear, it must be very bad? Spinach in my teeth? Only I haven't eaten any. Raspberry seeds from the jam?

But he's not looking at just my mouth. His gaze is travelling all over my face. He's going to kiss me again. Unless there's a spot where I've exaggerated with my foundation, or perhaps even missed a spot. Except that I'm not wearing any and – oh! I catch my breath as he leans in, closer and closer until I can see the gold specks in his dark eyes. He *is* going to kiss me.

But look at me. I'm an absolute mess with my hair tied up in a tight bun, in my work overalls and a tatty T-shirt. No make-up, none of the usual accoutrements that might make a female more attractive. All this time I'd fantasised about our second kiss, the seal-the-deal one, hopefully; and it's going to happen now that I look like *this?* I can barely breathe at the thought of him kissing me again and I watch, transfixed, as he slowly leans in and gently – *gently* – touches his mouth to mine.

The patio suddenly starts spinning, but I don't care, because all I want is to continue feeling those soft lips on mine for as long as possible.

This is what I've always needed. Tenderness, yet eagerness. Passion. Strength. And a man who makes me lose my mind like never before.

There are entire worlds in his kisses, and the look on his flushed face is new to me. I have never seen Henry like this before.

'I'm sorry...' he whispers against my lips.

'Don't be,' I softly moan as we wrap our arms around each other and I'm instantly surrounded by fresh, hot male. The stubbly face as he nuzzles my neck is just a bonus, awakening in me something I had thought gone for good. I don't know how, but the rest of the world has entirely disappeared from what is now a bubble of Henry and me. The perfect world.

'Wow,' I breathe as the kiss ends and he looks down at me, studying my face for a reaction.

'Wow indeed,' he echoes, kissing me again. 'You are amazing, Faith,' he murmurs.

'So are you,' I manage, drawing in a gulp of air.

'I know what you think about dating, but I would really like to see more of you,' he says softly.

I look around the deserted patio. The beach is teeming with people. I know that no one can see us. And suddenly, against all my fears and worries, desire flares up in me like a rocket. I want Henry. I want to make love with him. Right now, no matter what the consequences. But the crew is scattered all over the house and I can't risk it. Besides, if this is going to happen between us, I want it to be special. I want us to take our time.

'So would I,' I whisper back. 'But anyone could come out here at any moment.'

At that, he chuckles. 'I meant that I wanted to see you alone, off the job. But that idea works for me too!'

Gong! Faith Hudson makes an own goal, and it's a biggie!

'Oh. I'm sorry. I hadn't—'

But he takes my mouth again, and the kiss is suddenly less tender. Deeper. Needier. And it's a wonder I don't melt into his arms.

'Never be sorry, Faith,' he whispers between our kisses.

'I won't,' I promise.

It is, despite my best attempts to forget, Valentine's Day. But has he asked me out, or made plans to see me? No. And there was me thinking it was the perfect day to meet up with someone you want to kiss. Perhaps he's simply busy with Orson. Or perhaps I've misread this whole thing, and that whatever this *thing* between us is (or isn't) it's nothing but a passing, animal attraction. Maybe not even he knows what he wants. And, lo and behold, once more, if I'm not careful, I'll end up with a broken heart.

So rather than stay in and wait for a call that might never come, assuming I even want it to, I ditch my phone and get in my car to go for a country drive. To cheer myself up, I buy a bouquet of flowers. Would it be too pushy if I showed up on his doorstep with them? Absolutely, yes. If he wanted to see me, he'd have asked. So I'm staying away.

As it's too cold to get out of the car, I simply drive to Helston and take the A394 and then the A30 through the countryside in the direction of St Ives. The countryside, even in the grey light, is absolutely breath-taking. The trouble is that, at this hour, I was expecting there to be more cars around. But as the minutes pass, and the sky becomes darker, I meet fewer and fewer people on my way.

This is ridiculous. I shouldn't feel edgy, just because everyone else is already ensconced in restaurants or nice and warm inside their own homes. I'll simply pick up lunch at the first place I find and then go back home. The last thing I want is to sit in a place full of love-sick couples. Ugh.

The skies are cloudy, but they are all different shades, ranging from white to grey to black, as if it didn't know its own intentions. A bit like Henry, really.

Okay, yes, I'm not happy today, but what single girl is happy on Valentine's Day? Even a self-professed loner like me feels... well, lonely.

I stop at a café and order a nice bowl of hot beef stew to warm me up. I'm the only one around and the owners are staring at me as if I'm nuts. The waitress comes to my side as I'm finishing up.

'Do be careful on the roads,' she says as I give her my bank card and climb back into my coat. I follow her gaze to the window to see that the clouds are now scurrying across the sky like children pouring into a schoolyard at the sound of the bell.

'Thank you, I will,' I assure her before she closes and locks the door behind me.

By the time I get into my car, the sky has turned ominously dark, the swirling clouds now finally having decided they are going to unleash one almighty storm after all.

Before I know it, it starts to come down heavily and my wipers begin to swish and sway to keep the windshield clear. But as I go, mile after mile, my spirits, which hadn't been at dizzying heights to start with, begin to drop, and I wish that I hadn't left my flat as there is now a river of water now coming at me in the road, slowly collecting mud and pebbles as it goes.

I swallow and wipe my eyes as if to see better. After a few pained miles and still not one car in sight, I begin to wonder what I'd do if I ran into car trouble. Having left my mobile at home so I wouldn't be tempted to check it every minute for a message from Henry, I am now, in effect, completely isolated in my travels. If something happens, I'm dead.

I clench my jaw and shoulders as the muddy water turns to mud that is now splashing over what is no longer pebbles on the road, but actual rocks. It's getting worse and worse and soon I won't be able to proceed. I'll be stuck here, in the middle of nowhere, possibly all night if my car doesn't get swept away by the flood. I could end up in the river. And I don't have a soul to give me the courage I need to reach my destination. At this point I'd even be grateful for Jawsy to talk to.

I think of Hope who for once on Valentine's Day is snuggled up at home with the kids. I think of Henry and Orson who have no doubt drawn the curtains and are settling down in front of the log burner. And here I am, on my own, because I couldn't face being on my own on such an annoying day. I fleetingly wonder whether my mum had had a day like this, when loneliness overwhelmed her and before I know it, I'm swiping at a tear.

But then, it gets worse, as who is coming at me from the other direction, but Gabe? I recognise his SUV immediately, huge and secure in the midst of this hell. As we are slowly moving through the mud, I can see quite clearly that he is not alone, and that there is a woman in the seat next to him.

She looks relaxed and safe, stretched out in the comfy seat that I used to occupy. And actually, I can see them bobbing their heads simultaneously. What album are they listening to? Probably one I bought him.

And then I put my foot down. All I want is to get home safe, without resenting the fact that he's still quite happy with someone else, while I'm so broken I can't even enjoy the attention of a nice bloke like Henry. It's my fault if I'm in this situation, just like it's my fault I'm here alone on this damn road, still far from home, on my own and shivering inside my coat despite the heat being on full blast.

I should have invited Henry over to my flat. I should have given him the chance to continue our conversations there. But I had made it clear to him that I wanted to be with him after all, hadn't I? I imagine all the couples in the world today, kissing and having dinner and making love, and here I am on a dark, isolated, almost impassable road in the middle of nowhere.

I'm glad that Gabe hadn't even turned to look at my car. Sometimes it is better to go unnoticed, rather than be totally humiliated by his smugness, or worse, his pity. I chose not to be with him. But I didn't choose to not be with Henry, especially today, day of all lovers. It serves me right to be here all alone, when I don't even know what I want.

Who am I kidding? I want Henry. I want his arms around me and his baritone murmurs in my ear. I want to laugh with him and eat scones and muffins and ruffle Orson's hair as he works his magic with his wooden toys. I want to be a part of them. But I guess I won't be after all. It's going to be another year before the next Valentine's Day and – I know I'm being silly – it's just another day like any other, but it was important for me to start afresh, and on such a symbolic day for love. But it didn't happen.

By the time I manage to get back to Truro, I'm a wreck in every way. I pull myself up the stairs, completely soaked down to my knickers and socks. Inside, the heat is not on. There is something wrong with the thermostat, but as it's a Sunday, there's no one I can call. My landlord doesn't even pick up at the best of times. Resigned and exhausted by my misadventures, I drag myself under the shower to try and wash the misery off me, but it clings to me like a second skin. St Valentine's Day my arse.

*

The next morning my crew trickle in in dribs and drabs, and the din begins. I'm still in a foul mood and have a headache of biblical proportions.

'Good morning, Faith!' comes a joyous voice from the door. I turn and look at Orson who is wearing cute little jeans and a *Kiss the Carpenter* T-shirt. Now here is a sight that cheers me up.

'Good morning, you look just like a professional carpenter!' I say, getting to my feet to admire him closely, just as Henry is coming through the door with a tool box and a huge pink box from Cornish Born and Bread. And I already feel better.

'It's half-term!' Orson cries happily. 'I get to stay the whole time with Daddy!'

'Good for you, sweetie!' I chime, ruffling his hair.

'Yes, we spent the entire day building a bookshelf for his room,' Henry explains sheepishly. 'I wanted to call you, but it didn't seem fair.' The words *to have to share my son with anyone* are not said, but are pretty obvious.

'Ri-ight,' I say for Orson's benefit. What am I even on about? The bloke's got a son. And he'll be spending as much time as possible with him. Orson is a very lucky boy, to have a father who is trying as hard as he can to keep a semblance of a family. He is a good man, Henry, and I don't blame him if he has no time for other things. Like trying to see if a relationship could work. I'll save him the soul-searching. It won't, at least not with me. Because, after what I saw last night and the way I felt, I know once and for all that I am well and truly beyond hope.

Orson hands me a familiar-coloured box. 'Blueberry

scones, your favourite. Daddy says it's only right to return the kindness.'

'Did he?' I say with a grin. 'Thank you, that's very kind of you, Orson, and much appreciated.'

Orson seems to swell with pride as I take the huge box from his little hands.

'I have a little surprise for you, Orson. Verity and Jowen are coming in today, too. Are you happy?'

'Cool!' he calls. 'Daddy, did you hear?'

'I heard,' Henry answers him, his eyes swinging to mine in a silent message of thanks. And perhaps even of *Thanks for being patient*. But perhaps I'm only imagining things.

'Maybe you could teach them how to make something, Orson?' I ask, tearing my gaze away from Henry's.

'Sure!' he says, flushing with pleasure, and yes, shyness – his father's exact same trait, which is so endearing. In Orson, I mean.

'Hey, little helper,' Mike says, high-fiving Orson as he joins us. Orson just loves the chatter and the noise.

Henry observes the scene with benevolent eyes and as I'm watching him watch Orson, his eyes suddenly swing to mine again with a smile. He's so happy when Orson's here.

The doorbell goes, and by the insistent ring it can only be Jowen who's been trying to play songs on the doorbell, particularly one of Gabe's hits, 'Ain't nothing wrong with me' (and that, ladies and gents, is a mouthful).

I fling open the door and in a second, Hope delivers me two munchkins climbing all over me, smothering me with kisses. They are such fantastic, affectionate children.

'Auntie Fi!' they cry in unison as if they haven't seen me for years, and it certainly feels so.

'Hi, guys! Orson's here!' I say as I straighten their clothes. 'Are you coming, Hope?'

Frazzled and breathless, she closes the car door and joins her hands in an apology. 'I can't, I'm already late. Some other time.'

'Bye, Mum!'

'Goodbye, darlings!' she calls wistfully, but takes to the road as if our drive was on fire. The drama (and dilemma) of working mums.

In the kitchen, Orson is watching Henry taking measurements.

Henry is very observant of his son's interactions, and every now and then he flashes me a smile as Orson teaches the kids a few basics about wood. Stuff that I'd learnt only after years in design school, go figure.

I have a feeling that their presence is doing him some good as well. Goodness knows how difficult the divorce must have been for Orson, and I can only imagine the pains Henry must have gone through to keep Orson from the ugliness of it all.

Later that evening, with the crew gone home, Henry is trying to figure out a way to peel the kids apart for the evening.

'Henry?' I call, moving to the kitchen where he and the kids are all busy measuring something under the kitchen counter.

He looks up. 'Yeah?'

'I wonder if I could have a word?'

'Sure,' he says, jumping to his feet and following me into the main hall.

I know I should be more au fait with him, but I don't want to make any more assumptions or mistakes.

'My, uhm, sister is coming over with some food and I was wondering if you and Orson would like to stay? I've got some Pixar DVDs for the kids, too, if that's okay?'

Henry's face lights up. 'I'd love to. But, if it's okay, would you mind asking him yourself?'

I smile. 'Okay, let me go fetch him, then.'

I go back to the kitchen where the three of them are howling with laughter at God knows what joke, but it must be a good one.

'Okay, you two, go wash up for dinner. I want you in clean clothes before Mum gets here.'

'Awh, are we already going home?'

'No,' I say with a smile. 'Mum is bringing some dinner and we're eating here.'

'Can Orson stay?' Jowen asks hopefully.

'Absolutely yes.'

'I can?' Orson asks, his eyes wide.

'Yes, dinner and a movie, would you like that? Daddy says it's okay.'

'I'd love to!' he cries. 'Can we have popcorn, too? Daddy always buys me popcorn when he takes me to the movies.'

'Of course! You can have anything you want, darling.' And I bite my lip. Too intimate? I can't explain it, but perhaps the fact that his mother is not a very good one endears him to me.

When Hope arrives the skies are just about to unleash an

almighty storm so Henry and I come out to help her unload the car.

'Hi!' she calls as we rush over to her and take some trays as the first drops begin to fall. 'I hope it's good.'

'It will be,' I assure her as Henry lights some tea lights and places them in glasses full of water and Hope dishes up the food.

The three children are peeking through the curtains at the coming storm.

'Look at that black sky!' Jowen enthuses. 'It'll belt down in a minute!'

Orson, slightly younger, turns to look at his father for comfort.

'Storms are safe if you're indoors, kids. Come away from the windows and you'll be fine,' he assures them.

And they are not safe when you've been caught out in driving on your own and the mud is splashing over boulders blocking the road.

Verity bounces joyfully to the table, followed by Orson. Reluctantly, Jowen joins us and plonks himself opposite me, his eyes widening when he sees the amount of food his mum's prepared.

I have never seen three kids so happy to eat. There's just about all of our favourites – lasagne, roast beef, risotto, potatoes à la Julienne, mixed grilled vegetables and, get this, three kinds of dessert.

'I think I've just gone to heaven,' Henry murmurs. 'Thank you, Hope.'

'Do you cook?' she asks.

'That's a big word for me.'

'Well, for someone who makes kitchens for a living…'

'You'd think, right?' he says with a laugh.

'Dad's an excellent cook,' Orson informs her in between bites. 'And he makes the best cakes!'

Hope makes an impressed expression and nods at me as if to give me the go-ahead, bless her.

Later that night, Henry sends me a text:

Thinking of you. I've got something planned for you to make up for a missed Valentine's Day. Hx

Oh? I text back. *Tell me more?*

Nuh-uh.

Please?

Never.

Well then maybe I'm busy, I text back.

☹ ☹ ☹ he types in and I laugh.

Goodnight, Faith. H xxx

Goodnight, Henry. F xxx

The next day I try to glean from him any info about my surprise, but he's not having any of it.

'Can you at least tell me what to wear?' I ask as a last attempt.

'Something warm and comfortable.'

'Okay, so my PJs should do, then!'

He laughs, his eyes twinkling. 'That's very much in the neighbourhood of what I was thinking.'

Pyjamas? As in the neighbourhood of... bed? Is that what he has in mind?

What do I do now? I'm nowhere near ready for such a monumental turn of events. Not that I don't want to, mind you. Kudos and brownie points galore to him, of course. But I have to be prepared beforehand. Work my way to it. I know I'm always saying that I want to be more spontaneous, but shouldn't I be starting with something slightly less seismic, something more in the neighbourhood of open-heart surgery?

So when that evening he hands me a black blindfold, instead of saying something in the neighbourhood of 'Ooh, kinky,' all I can do is swallow.

'Your face!' he cries with a laugh, his hands on his lean cheeks. 'I promise I won't do anything you won't want me to.

Oh, goody. I'd better start thinking about our safe word. As in *I don't do kinky*.

'Come on, don't you trust me?' he says and I find myself looking into his dark, dark eyes. Eyes that are deep and unfathomable. Gabe's were a serene, angelic blue, and yet look where that got me.

To say that I'm not intrigued would be a lie. 'Oh, go on then.' So I follow him to his Jeep and let him blindfold me, as trusting as a baby.

As we travel down to the main road, I try to glean from the slant of the car, but he is driving smoothly and I have no idea which way we're going. At one point he puts his hand on my hand resting in my lap, grazing my thigh and I sit back and relax. Who am I kidding? It's all I can do from containing my excitement.

'What about Orson? Don't you have him for half-term?'

'I do, but my parents were dying to have him for just one night.'

I swallow. So am I, if you know what I mean.

'So I thought I'd spend my one night off with you.'

Now that's a statement of intent if I'd ever heard one.

'I don't get many nights off,' he explains. 'Family is very important to me...'

'Of course...'

'I'm doing everything I can to make sure that Orson doesn't suffer...'

'Yes, I understand.'

After about thirty minutes, Henry cuts the engine as I become aware of a clinking sound. It sounds like glasses, only in the distance. He removes my blindfold and I look around me to see that we are in a marina.

'Surprise,' he murmurs.

'A boat ride? At this hour?'

'It's a full moon, the best time. When it poured own the other night I was worried it would ruin my surprise, but we were lucky in the end.'

I haven't been on a boat in ages. I take a deep breath as we stroll down the jetty to where a few boats are bobbing on the gentle waves.

It's a balmy, quiet evening, as all the merrymakers of the evening have staggered home, and even the gulls seem to have disappeared with them, leaving the gentle lapping of the sea behind.

Henry speaks to a man and helps me board what is, in effect, not a boat at all, but a sizeable yacht. 'N-nice,' I say.

He laughs. 'Do you like boats?'

'Only ones that float,' I confess.

'Well, this one looks pretty sturdy, so I wouldn't worry. Come, let's have a seat on deck. It's a beautiful night, isn't it?'

'It is,' I agree, breathing in the salty air.

The man, who I assume will be our skipper, brings a platter with hors d'oeuvres.

Dinner?

'You like my surprise?' he asks.

'I like. Next time, I'll take you to a great place I know.' And then I stop, my face going hot. 'Sorry, I didn't mean – just because we kissed – twice. Doesn't mean that—'

Henry passes me a glass of sparkly water and throws his head back in a hearty laugh, his eyes crinkling under the incredibly long lashes. 'Faith Hudson, you say the damnedest things sometimes.'

'Right,' I say, feeling like an idiot as the yacht slowly leaves the marina.

'But I wouldn't say no to another great restaurant,' he says as he takes a sip of his own drink. 'So, where is this place?'

'It's the L'étoile. Hope is head chef there.'

'Ah, yes, she mentioned it. I'll be delighted to sample her food again. You were right, she is amazing. You two did well for yourselves.' The phrase, *Your parents would be proud of you* hangs in the air, but I pretend I don't feel its far reaches.

'Thank you. She did. I'm still trying to get the attention of the Lord and Lady Wickford.'

'Is there no one at all who knows them and could set you up?'

'Only colleagues. But why would they help me access the Wickfords rather than nab them themselves?'

'So you don't have any interior designer friends, then.'

'No. I have other amazing friends, such as my coastal girls.'

His eyebrows go up. 'Coastal girls?'

'They're my friends: Rosie, Nat and Nina. They started out as my clients, but then the business lunches turned into friendly lunches and the rest is history.'

'It's nice to have that,' he says wistfully.

'Don't you have a best friend?'

'I used to, many years ago, but not anymore. I'm surrounded by colleagues and clients. I guess my brother Evan is my best friend.'

There's a lull in the conversation, but it's not an embarrassing one as we are both enjoying the sea breeze on our faces. 'Where exactly are we going with this thing, Henry?' I ask before I can stop myself. Now that sounded like a relationship status request if I'd ever heard one!

His eyes swing to mine furtively, but then he looks out to the dark sea studded with the lamps of nearby fishing boats. 'Just for a short coast hug. An hour or so, is that okay?'

I nod. It's more than okay. I'd stay here forever with him, if I could – sail across the world over and over, just to be with him.

'So,' he says. 'Whenever you're free, can we go? To your sister's restaurant?'

'It's not hers, but yes, of course. I'll book for next week, if you like.'

'Okay, then. Next week it is.'

'I'll give you a call to let you know when.'

He grins. 'Or, you can tell me when you see me at work.'

I feel myself blushing. 'Yes. Silly me.'

We are both silent again, simply enjoying the sight of the now distant houses of the coastline, twinkling like fairy lights.

'This is so relaxing,' I say. 'Thank you. For not leaving me alone tonight.' As opposed to Valentine's Day. 'Sorry, that came out rather different than I'd intended. I meant—'

'I know what you meant, Faith,' he reassures me in a deep, low voice. I turn my head towards him, and even in the dark, I can see his eyes flashing as he slowly turns me around to face him completely.

And then, the world once again turns completely upside down as Henry gently cups my chin, the burning emotions on his face visible even in the moonlight, and before I can take my next breath, his mouth descends onto mine in a new kind of kiss. It starts slowly, delicately, softly and on his lips, the whisper of my name, spoken like I've never heard it before, and I know that the time has come for us to have more.

But not here, as lovely as this is, sailing off into the moonlight, with a skipper around.

'Shall we head back…?' he murmurs against my neck and my head falls back like a puppet's whose strings have been cut.

'Uh-huh…' I softly moan, the yearning in me so sudden and intense I don't know what's come over me. I haven't felt like this in years, not even with Gabe, and as Henry's mouth works me up to new levels of want, I'm praying that we can get back to my flat before I burst into flames.

But we do, and all the worries concerning 'it' happening between us, fade into nothing when he opens and ushers me gently through my front door, while all I can do is gape at him in sheer, unadulterated lust.

I don't need to worry about a thing, because Henry picks me up and carries me into my bedroom, his mouth still doing all those magical things he's been doing in the Jeep all the way home in stretches of clear road. His eyes had promised me so much more, and here we are now. Alone.

He gently lays me down on the bed, removing every item of clothing until I am as naked as the day I was born.

He looks down on me as he pulls off his own shirt, the look in his eyes so naughty that I know I'm already deeper in trouble than I'd thought.

'Let's finish what you tried to start in this very room weeks ago,' he murmurs, lying next to me, raking his hands through my hair as he takes my mouth in what is no longer a gentleman's kiss, but a proper branding of my mouth, and my entire body knows what it wants, once and for all.

The next morning Henry and I wake up literally entwined. Our clothes are strewn all over the place and the bed is an absolute battlefield.

I smile, remembering last night's naughty shenanigans. Henry is truly a generous lover. Very, *very* naughty, but in a gentlemanly way that I never thought existed.

'Good morning. What's that smile on your face?' he drawls lazily as he pulls me closer into his arms.

'Good morning,' I murmur as I snuggle back into him.

'How are you feeling?' he asks, rubbing his stubbly face against my neck and already I'm feeling the heat, despite the fact that I've only just woken up.

'Exhausted. So you can have the first shower. I need to catch up on my sleep!'

He laughs, and I can feel his abdomen contract and expand against my side. He has the body of a god. And the manners of a lord wrapped up in the lust of the devil. How is he not too good to be true? How is he here with me?

Henry's phone rings a childish tune. 'Oh, Geez, I'm sorry, that's Orson,' he says. 'Do you mind if I—?'

'Of course not,' I assure him as I pull away enough to give him some privacy. My own niece and nephew have the knack for calling at the wrong time, too, so I might as well get used to it.

'Hey, buddy boy!' he says and then stops to listen to his son enthusiastically relaying a story. 'Really? Yes… yes… oh? Of course, just a moment.'

Henry grins at me. 'He wants to say hello.'

'Awh, that's so sweet,' I gush reaching for his mobile. 'Hi, Orson!'

'Hi, Faith…'

'How are you?'

'I'm okay. Sort of.'

'Why? What's wrong?'

Henry's eyes narrow and he straightens.

'It's just that I miss you…'

A wave of tenderness sweeps over me. 'Oh, Orson, sweetie, I miss you too!'

Henry visibly relaxes and, kissing me, mouths the word *shower* and I nod, watching him go in all his naked hotness before turning all of my attention to this darling little boy.

'You have to help me,' Orson whispers. 'I overheard my grandparents talking about Mum and Dad. They're going to try and get back together again. And last week Mum kissed him. They never used to do that, but now…' He audibly gulps. 'She's always there and I'm afraid she'll come back to live with us. I don't want her in our home. I'll go to her when I have to, but I want to stay alone with Daddy.'

'Hang on, Orson,' I whisper back. 'Did you say that your mum kissed your dad?'

'Yes! On the lips! And then he took her by the hand to his bedroom.'

My heart almost stops. 'T-to his bedroom?'

'They were in there for four entire episodes of *Creeped Out*!'

Creeped out is exactly what I am. Linda and Henry, in his bedroom? I hadn't managed to make it there yet myself because of my sense of respect for Orson. But I guess Linda being his mum trumps everything. The time we've just spent together, Henry and I, skin against skin, has no bearing against the importance of a family. But then why string me along?

And then I understand. It was all a pity thing after all. Of course, the poor girl dumped by her boyfriend twice, kicked out of her own home – twice – what bloke with a modicum of decency would deal her a third similar blow? Well, I have absolutely no need whatsoever for his pity.

Orson is still waiting for my reaction. I clear my throat, trying to remove the boulder that's lodged itself in there. 'And... you don't want her to?'

'No. But they've been doing that a lot lately and I'm afraid she'll come back. What should I do?'

What should he do, indeed? 'Talk to him, Orson. He's your daddy and would do anything for you. If you tell him how you feel, he'll be able to help you.'

'I don't need any help. I just want him to stop kissing her.'

Oh my God in heaven.

'Can you tell him to stop?'

How can I not let this darling boy down without betraying him?

'I'll see what I can do, Orson. But you have to talk to him, too, okay?'

'Okay. Bye, Faith…' he says, slightly despondent.

I can't bear to hear him like this. 'It'll be okay, sweetheart.'

At that precise moment, Henry saunters back into the bedroom with a towel wound around his lean hips. I swallow and turn away. It's all I can do to not look at him. Or scream at him. But if I start, I will never stop. How could I have been such an idiot?

'Hang on, Orson, I'll pass you back to your daddy.'

'Oh-kay…'

I take a huge breath and fight to internally mop up the pieces of my heart that have melted inside me as, without looking at Henry, I pass him his mobile back.

'Hey, buddy boy,' he says and, as much as I want to scream at him, I make a desperate dash to hide in the loo. He's left it in complete order. No damp towels on the floor, no misty glass. If anything, it looks even cleaner than before he had his shower. Apparently he's good at covering his tracks.

Henry and his ex-wife. Who knew? So much for the broken-hearted man who's all spaniel eyes with me. *Fake* spaniel eyes, I now know. How long has this been going on? And what do I make of the other day at his home, when I couldn't remember being that happy in a long time? God, will I never learn? When Gabe left me I was desperately miserable, but at least I was miserable on my own, without anyone else to worry about. I'll have to make a hasty retreat from Henry's life, but how can I un-hear what Orson has told me?

I turn on the hot water as high as it will go and sob as softly as I can under the jets, trying to wash off all of Henry's kisses and the stamp of everything we did to each other only last night. This is definitely the shortest story I've ever had. And definitely the last. I am done with men. All of them!

'Hey, Faith?' Henry's voice at the door makes me jump. I thought he'd gone, anxious as he must be to get home.

'Yes?'

'Are you coming out anytime soon?'

'Uhm, no,' I call.

'Are you all right?' he asks.

'Yep.'

'Oh. Okay, I just wanted to tell you that I'm not coming in today. Is that all right?'

Of course you're not. You've got to see Linda.

He stalls, presumably as he's unsure of just how much I know. Why else would I be giving him the cold shoulder?

'Yes. Well. I'll see you tomorrow, then. But I'll give you a call later on, okay? Call me sooner if you need me.'

Need him? What makes him think I need him? I've been doing splendidly on my own, thank you very much. Faith Hudson does not need a man in her life to get out of bed in the morning.

'It'll be fine, Henry. I'll see you whenever.'

An astonished silence. He must be wondering what's got into me. Well, he should be able to put two and two together. But he doesn't. 'Oh. Okay, then. I'm going.'

'Yes, bye bye,' I chime as my heart literally falls apart.

There is a moment of hesitation – I can feel it through the door – before the front door opens and gently closes. *Exit Heartbreaker Number Two.*

13

Lyin' Eyes

The rest of the day goes by in a daze and at five o'clock, I need to sit down alone with my thoughts and a sobering gallon of coffee. Orson obviously has problems with accepting his own mum, so naturally Henry had to go back there immediately. I understand he wants to break their reuniting gently rather than come right out and tell him. I do. But he could have at least told *me*. The woman he slept with *the very next day*. This looks just like a Gabe rerun, and I'm not having it.

And above all, I'm not having the *You broke my heart just as it was mending* conversation with Henry. There are no misunderstandings of any sort and no explanatory conversation is going to lead anywhere. He was inside me practically all night after weeks of playing the chasing game with me. And yet all that time, he was on the road to getting back with his wife. Even if for the sole sake of Orson he could have at least admitted it, rather than sleep with me.

Simply hinting how important family is, is not an admission of getting back together with your wife.

How could I have been so idiotic to think that I could come out of an extremely painful relationship and swan right into a new one, with little more than a few sleepless, sobby nights?

It just doesn't work like that in real life. Mr Darcy is never silently waiting in the wings for a girl to sort herself out and pop up when she's ready. Relationships always happen at the most inconvenient times. And this is an inconvenient time. Not to speak of the sheer effort to start all over again, investing yourself heart and soul, almost blindly, into something new. So better to cut my losses and once again concentrate on my career and let Henry get back with his ex-wife.

And once again, it's my fault. I've allowed yet another man to completely enchant me. I believed in all his words. I believed we had had something special. Well, it had been special only for me, because here we are again – the needy Faith Hudson is once again dumped by a bloke.

Only this time there will be no more crying, or drinking, or wallowing. He is a closed parenthesis of my life. As much as it hurts, I am going to have to move on. For my own sanity. I cannot and will not go back to the depths of fear and depression all over again. This time I've learnt my lesson.

About an hour later, just as I'm coming into my flat, my mobile rings. Of course it's Henry, wondering why I was so cold with him.

I watch as my phone finally falls silent, only to restart. The last thing I want to do is answer him and bawl my eyes out. Not happening. I've cried enough in the past. And yet, despite my three years with Gabe and our two break-ups, this one hurts even more. Probably because I'd thought I'd become too clever to ever fall for another bloke again. Well, the joke's on me.

My phone beeps. A message from Henry:

Are you all right? You seemed rather cold this morning.

I could just ignore it, but knowing him, he'd actually come all the way here just to see if I'm okay and I just can't risk that right now. So I type in:

I'm okay. See you tomorrow at work.

Assuming I'm going back to work there. It seems to be my destiny. What was my home, the beach house, is now a place I'd avoid like the plague if I could. My phone beeps again:

I don't understand. Did I do something wrong?

I almost laugh at that one. Wrong. No. His lovemaking was absolutely perfect and much, much more. It was hot and tender, respectful, yet naughty. It felt like an open door leading to a real relationship, and not a one-night thing. Little did he know I'd be on to him. But after Gabe, I'm not yet ready for full-on confrontation, and I don't think I ever will be. I type in one last message:

No, it's all good.

Maybe some other day I'll be able to look him in the eye and read him the riot act. But tonight, all I want is to be left alone and forget about everything. Concentrate on a future without Henry, or any other man.

The next morning, while I'm still alone at the beach house and trying to pull myself together, the doorbell rings. Irrationally hoping it's Henry and yet dreading it, I decide I'd settle for my splashback deliverers (who are already two days late). I fling the door open, only to find Travis, the estate agent. Not a great start to the day.

'Hiya,' he says.

'Oh. Hello. Henry's not here.'

'Awh, damn. I was hoping to catch him here.' He leans in with an apologetic grin. 'His missus and I don't really see eye to eye.'

Ah. So he knows Linda.

'Hey, can I bum a cup of coffee off you?'

Can he instead go to hell and never darken my door? 'Uhm…'

'You're a lifesaver,' he says and gives me a thousand-watt smile as he saunters past me. But I am in no mood for pleasantries of any sort, neither today nor ever. As a matter of fact, I'm on steam mode.

He follows me into the makeshift kitchen where I put the kettle on and he pulls out his mobile. 'Let's see if I can catch him on his cell,' he says.

He waits a few moments, but nothing happens. 'Oh, man. It's still off. I really needed to talk to him.'

'I don't know what to suggest,' I say. 'He should be

coming in. He's got a lot of work to do and we're already behind schedule.' Which isn't true, of course, but I need to mask my sense of loss behind a semblance of purpose.

'Listen,' he says. 'I'm really sorry we upset you about the sale and all. I'm just doing my job.'

'So am I,' I counter. 'And we won't be much longer. You'll be able to sell it and get your commission and move on to the next victim.'

'Oh, come on, Faith. You know it's nothing personal against you, at least not on my behalf. Gabe just wants to sell and move on.'

Move on. But moving out doesn't necessarily mean moving on.

If only I could gather the funds, I could buy my home back. But I'd need the professional break of my life to secure a mortgage that huge. So I make a mental note to go straight to the Wickfords' offices in London (yet again) and ask for an appointment in person. That would mean a few days in London, but it would be worth it. It will also be worth getting away from here for a bit. Okay, not away from here, but away from... *him.*

I need the distance to maintain a sense of self-control. Whenever he's near, I get jittery and become frazzled and confused. I need to get my bearings, and I need to not see him if I'm going to clear my head. Because I am not in love with him. I am not. I'm just... momentarily lost. And that's normal, after what Gabe did to me, right?

As it turns out, Henry is actually the next one to arrive, and he finds us chatting over a cup of coffee.

'Travis, what are you doing here?'

'Charming your girlfriend here. Or trying to.'

Henry's head swivels and our eyes meet. There is actually confusion on his face, bless him. Better to make things clear.

'I'm not his girlfriend,' I correct him.

I eye Henry who stares at him, then at me, as if to say: *What the hell is going on here?*

Well, what did you expect, when you've been away kissing your ex-wife? I glare back.

'Great!' Travis exclaims. 'The coast is clear, then!'

Henry looks completely frazzled as he is trying to put the pieces together. He'd probably thought I'd never find out. But actually, it's not up to me to do any explaining, but him. I'm not the one who slept with my ex-wife only the night before jumping into the sack with someone new who has just had her heart broken. You'd think he'd be a bit more responsible or respectful.

'Travis has been trying to contact you,' I explain.

'Yes, well. I've been a little busy...'

I'll say. Only I don't. Which is a good thing. Learning to be diplomatic at all times is still on my to-do list. Maybe next year.

Travis turns to me. 'Well, Henry's here now, are you happy?'

'Oh, I'm absolutely cock-a-hoop about it,' I drawl.

'Cock a what?' Travis laughs.

'She's absolutely thrilled,' Henry snorts, crossing his arms, his face now all dark and scowly. Too bad for him. He can't have everything.

'We're behind schedule,' I say, reaching for higher, safer ground again. 'I need that kitchen ASAP.'

Henry glances at Travis again, then turns to me. 'Faith, may I have a word with you?'

Huh. He wants a word with me. He's the one who's been sleeping with his ex-wife and he wants a word with me? For what, drinking coffee with his mate?

'Uhm, I can't. I have to go. My family is waiting for me.'

Henry's eyes fall to the floor. 'Right.'

14

Don't Speak

The next day I make a point of getting to work late and being constantly surrounded by people so as not to give myself any time alone with Henry. I just can't speak to him right now. I haven't got the strength to face him.

But apparently he's not satisfied with that, as he knocks on my office door just as his mobile is ringing. 'Excuse me, it's Orson,' he says. 'Hello, buddy boy! Yes, I'll be home early tonight... Yes, she's here...'

He holds out his phone. 'He wants to say hi.'

'Thank you,' I say, getting to my feet to move away from Henry, past the threshold and into the foyer.

'How's it going, Orson?'

'I miss you, Faith!' he cries.

'Awh, sweetie,' I coo. 'I miss you, too!'

'Can I come and see you at the beach house? With Daddy?'

'Ah, Orson... I really don't know—'

'Please?'

Good luck, with that one. 'Maybe you could ask your daddy to take you to work when this house is clear of all the rubbish and it's safer for you?'

'Just as long as it's not here. Mummy's *always* here now.'

And Orson is not happy about it. The poor, poor boy.

'Can you please talk to him? Tell him I'm sad?'

Can I? Butt my nose into Henry's and Linda's business? Hardly.

'I'll tell you what, Orson. You first have a chat with your daddy and then I'll tell him, too, okay?'

A long silence. He is hurting, because he expects more from me. I can put a plaster on his scrapes, but healing his family is something beyond me. *I'm so sorry I can't do more, Orson. But I wouldn't let anyone hurt you. Please believe that.*

'Okay. Thank you, Faith…'

'You're welcome, sweetheart.'

'The kid hates his mum? Oh my God, it's like bloody *Corrie*!' Hope exclaims as I fill her in. 'How are you?'

'Me? Never mind me – it's Orson I'm worried about.'

'You love that little boy, don't you?'

I find myself nodding vigorously. 'I truly do. There's something about him. He's so defenceless, so trusting, you know?'

'Like you,' Hope says. 'He reminds me of you when we were little. So hopeful, so desperate to be loved by someone.'

'Yeah, well, I'm all grown up now,' I assure her. But still desperate to be loved, apparently. After all these years, I still haven't learnt my lesson. 'So what do I do? I have to tell

Henry how Orson feels, but I have absolutely no right to do so. He'll think I'm doing it for… other reasons.'

'No, he won't. You have to do it. Get him alone and tell him.'

'In person? I can't. I can't face him. I'll do it over the phone. Because I can't just drop in on him and say, *Hi, Henry! By the way, did you know that your son is actually afraid of his mother getting back in your life, and that he's begged me to tell you to not take her back?* No, it's easier like that.'

'You're forgetting something, Faith.'

'And what's that?'

'Orson asked you for help.'

'You're absolutely right,' I agree. 'At the cost of getting chucked out, I'm going to have to do it in person.'

'Good girl. You're doing the right thing.'

'I hope so…'

'Do it now.'

'Now?'

'Now.'

'Right. Talk to you later, then.'

'Good luck, Faith.'

'Thanks. Something tells me I'm going to need it.'

So I muster all my courage and send Henry a message:

Need to talk to you. Can I come and see you at home?

To which he immediately answers:

Yes.

It takes me longer than usual to drive up there as my heart is in my mouth and I can only think of Orson. I'm so distracted I keep forgetting to look at the satnav and the voice is so irritating I finally snap the volume off.

And then the massive gates of the manor finally appear and with a gasp of relief, I park there and continue down the side path on foot to his hidden home as the kids and I had done the first time, with not only my heart in my mouth, but pretty much all my other organs. My legs, too, feel hollow and I'm surprised I manage to make it to his personal back gate. There, I ring the doorbell and wait, taking deep gulps of air to calm myself down.

The gates buzz and I pull them open just enough to slip through, wondering how on earth I am going to do this.

'Faith!' Orson cries, running down the path to meet me, his adorable face aglow as he throws his little arms around my midriff. 'I missed you so much!'

'Me, too, Orson,' I squeak, clinging to him more for my own benefit than his. He smells like his home – clean and citrusy. I get down for a better look. His face is still red from excitement, and his eyes are serene. There is absolutely no trace of sadness in him whatsoever. Could I have misconstrued it all? Made a mountain out of a molehill? Had he exaggerated a little bit, had a bad day? Or maybe he's just getting used to having her around again?

'How are you?' I manage, gently pushing his hair off his face, when instead I would have loved to scoop him up and cover him with raspberries.

'I'm okay,' he says, taking my hand. 'Come – there's cake!'

'Oh wow,' I enthuse, letting him lead me to the back door

that is ajar. Just how am I going to justify my visit without putting Orson on the spot?

We glide through the orangery and with every step that takes me closer to Henry, my resolve begins to crumble. But once I'm over the kitchen threshold, it becomes a moot point.

Standing beside him, giggling, is Linda in the flesh. I recognise her from all of Orson's pictures in his bedroom. Even though she is wearing an apron, she looks like an exotic movie star with her long black hair and huge dark eyes.

She is playfully dotting Henry's face with chocolate icing and he is looking down at her with eyes full of love. There is no mistake that this is a portrait of domestic bliss. Have I got the wrong end of the stick, in every way? He will never believe that Orson doesn't like his mother.

'Hello, Faith,' he greets me with a barely sufficient amount of amity. 'This is Linda.'

I cough. 'Uh, hullo. Nice to meet you.'

'Hello, Faith. Henry and I have just had a baking contest. Of course, he won. You're just in time for a slice. Coffee, tea?'

'Uhm… whatever is easier, thank you,' I say as I sit on the stool Henry has gestured to somewhat indifferently. It's hard to believe that only a few hours ago he was making crazy love to me, and now here he is, all prim and proper, the perfect husband. God, if she only knew!

I glance at Orson as he hoists himself up on the stool next to me, his little face flushed with happiness. If I had ever wondered what Henry's home life was like, here it is, all over the kitchen island. Love, giggles and chocolate cake.

Everything looks perfect. And yet, he's asked me to talk to his daddy, so here I am trapped in the midst of it without any idea of what to say and how to say it.

I have no reason to be here, especially when Henry has his own life, which, it is now more than obvious, he does. I want to make my excuses and leave. But Orson's words are still haunting me.

Why did Orson say that to me, and how do I get out of this now?

'Did you, uhm, bring that memory stick?' Henry asks, turning the kettle on and reaching into a cupboard to avoid looking at me.

It takes me a split second to catch on and when he does look down at me, I can see that his eyes are devoid of that usual sparkle. He is obviously put out by being caught out and doesn't want Linda to think that there is anything between us besides a professional relationship.

'Uhm, yes,' I answer, right on the beat, digging into my bag. It only contains my life's work, but I have several copies. I'll get it back from him later.

'Good, good, thank you,' he says as he shoves it into his pocket before pulling out a sharp knife and starts cutting the cake into slices, which he puts onto small dessert plates. 'Our first cake is ready. Linda, if you'll do the honours.'

'Love to,' she says with a smile. 'We call it Lemon Sunshine with vanilla frosting,' she explains as she gives Orson a generous slice and an even bigger one to me. 'But maybe we should call it Orson Sunshine – look at how he loves it. Don't you, darling?'

'Hm-hm,' Orson agrees as he dives into it with his entire face and Henry laughs, ruffling his hair. Then he begins to pour his chocolate cake mixture into a new cake tin, completely intent on his task, careful not to spill a drop – nor to look at me.

I watch him closely, my mind racing. Exactly what part have I misunderstood? How could Orson sit here, all happy, with what he's told me? I am becoming more and more uncomfortable by the minute.

I watch his son and his ex-wife, who is daintily picking at her own slice of cake, and I realise that somehow, somewhere along the line, I have made a huge mistake. Orson's plea is the only reason why I'm here. But to the outsider, as I am, they seem perfectly happy. They have probably ironed things out. And are doing very well, indeed.

'Linda, why don't you go get yourself cleaned up?' Henry suggests while wiping his hands on a tea towel. 'Faith and I have business to discuss anyway.'

Linda looks back and forth between us with a smile. 'Faith, can you stay for lunch?' she offers and I stiffen.

'Oh – thanks, but I can't.'

'All right. Maybe next time, then?'

'Maybe. Thank you.'

And with that, she puts her plate in the sink and leaves us.

Henry looks down at his son. 'Orson, you can go and eat your cake in the living room if you like.'

With a huge smile, Orson slides off his stool and grabs the cake. 'Thanks, Daddy! Faith, are you coming?'

'In a moment, darling,' I promise.

'Okay,' he says, jumping off like a grasshopper.

I push my plate away and rest my elbows on the breakfast bar, piercing him with my stare.

'Why have you finally decided to contact me?' he asks,

still avoiding my gaze. His lashes are the longest things I've ever seen and they hide his eyes all too well.

'Because Orson asked me to. But don't worry, I won't be long.'

His face freezes. 'Right.'

I take a deep breath. 'Look, Henry, what you do in your private life is no business of mine. I couldn't care less.'

He puts his own fork down and looks up at me, straight into my eyes. 'Then if you don't care, why are you here, Faith?'

'Because I know just how important family is, and how not having one as a young child can be soul-destroying. It leaves a scar that never, ever heals.'

Look at me. Years on and I'm still not okay. I will never be okay, and I certainly don't want Orson to have to suffer all the pain that I went through, the fear and humiliation of not having a family like everybody else. I don't want that sweet little boy to suffer just because I still haven't found what I'm looking for.

'What are you talking about?' he says.

'Orson told me that he's not happy.'

His head snaps up, his eyes narrow. 'He told you that?'

'Yes.'

'I see. And of course you catapulted yourself all the way up here to come and gloat about it?'

'I'm not gloating about anything. I'm merely answering your question – and answering the distress call of an unhappy child.'

'Don't you worry about my child. *I'll* take care of him. I don't need you – of all people – to tell me how to raise him.'

The message is clear – bugger off, Faith. I don't want you in our lives. What else do I need to get it through my head? They are a self-sufficient family, thank you very much, and don't need me in any way whatsoever. Why on earth would I even think so, just because a little boy has become fond of me?

What else do I need to hear? Henry is just another mistake on my behalf. I had seen the affection in his eyes and had taken it for something else. Maybe there had been something else. I can't imagine all those moments we have spent together bore no importance to him at all. But as a father, Henry has a duty to his son, first and foremost. Everything else comes, as it most definitely should, last.

'I – I have to go,' I whisper, grabbing my bag, and dashing through the back door and down the cobbled path all in one breath.

Once on the grassy side lane, I break into a proper run until I reach my car where I jump in and turn on the radio nice and loud to drown my thoughts.

I don't even remember how I got home, but when I get in through the door, my mobile rings. It's a number I don't recognise. It could be about my request for a mortgage, so I have to answer it.

'Hello?'

'Hello, Faith? It's Linda. It's a shame you left so soon. I wanted to thank you for being so good to Orson. He loves coming round there and spending time with you.'

I swallow. 'It's my pleasure. He's a delight.'

'He is, and I'm truly blessed,' she says softly. 'We both are, Henry and I.'

'Yes, of course.'

'If I may be blunt, Faith?'

Oh God, she doesn't faff around, does she? 'Yes?'

'You must understand what a terrible time our little boy has been through.'

'Of course.'

'So I don't want him to be confused. Whilst I appreciate your kindness, I'd like you to keep in mind that Orson is just a little boy. He thinks that you and Henry have something going on. And I understand that Henry is charming and all, but please do bear in mind that Henry and I are back together again.'

At my lack of a response, she sighs patiently. 'Look – I know you must be surprised. Henry has always been that soulful, unsuspecting ladies' man. I don't blame you. But he may have forgotten to mention that we have been working on our relationship again recently, and we have agreed that it's what's best for Orson.'

So Orson was right. They are getting back together again. And, if this is indeed what's happening in the Turner household, how can I have put my nose where it doesn't belong? Who am I to presume he would tolerate my butting into his private business with his son?

There have been no binding promises between Henry and I. No agreements. Just sex. Mind-blowing sex, in fact, and all the while he's getting back with his ex-wife. It doesn't matter if it's solely for Orson's sake. He should have been honest with me. It's like Gabe and Vanessa all over again.

Perhaps Orson had been exaggerating when he said he didn't like his mother. And I'd believed him. Probably because I wanted it to be true. I wanted Orson and Henry to need me. But they don't. No one does, and I have never felt so out of place in my life.

15

Too Good at Goodbyes

'And then what did you do?' Hope wants to know.
'What could I do?'

'Did he not call you? To explain?'

'Explain what? The bleeding obvious? He's back with his wife. That's where I bow out. I don't want to do to someone what was done to me. He still cares for her. She was baking in his home. Their home.'

'Faith, sweetie – caring for and being in love with are two completely different things,' Hope points out.

I shake my head. 'No, you weren't there; you didn't see it. Even Orson was happy, which is the one good thing about today.'

'I don't understand it,' Hope confesses. 'From what you've told me, and from what I've seen, judging the way he is with you… he's definitely interested.'

I shrug and contemplate something even more obvious. 'Maybe he was just interested on a physical level, just for fun while waiting for his wife to come round.'

'I don't know, Faith – he just doesn't seem the type.'

'God, have I learnt nothing about men all these years?'

'Don't be so hard on yourself, Faith. Just let it go. Find someone new.'

'Oh, no thanks. From now on, I'm completely off men.'

The next work day with Henry is, to say the least, cringeworthy. He avoids me and I avoid him, spending the entire day getting someone else to deliver a message to the other, and of course, it's all work-related. I don't even partake in the usual *breakfeast* he's brought, and today of all days, he seems to have outdone himself with a mountain of blueberry scones. The cheek. And to make matters worse, he's brought Travis along, presumably to talk about the purchase of the beach house. He couldn't be layering it on any thicker.

'You know, Faith, you're wasted here in Cornwall,' Travis says as I am supervising my muscle men from the door as they lay tile in the bathroom. I've come up with an original pattern, completely different from the suggested ones and it works brilliantly if I may say so myself.

'Tell that to Cornwall,' I throw over my shoulder.

'Seriously, you should be working in New York.'

'New York,' I sigh. 'As if.' Anything to get away from here would be a dream.

'Have you ever been there before?'

I shake my head.

'Never been to New... Are you serious?'

'I only wish,' I say wistfully. 'And yet, it's my professional dream – all those beautiful homes and penthouses dying to be furnished.'

'Well, then you should definitely come.'

Down on his knees filling in the grouting, Bill looks up at me and rolls his eyes and it's all I can do to not laugh out loud.

'*Me?* And do what, exactly?'

Travis points a finger at me. 'You'd do very well there, with your work ethic.'

'Thanks, but I'd be like Jawsy in the Atlantic Ocean.'

He frowns. 'Jawsy?'

'Oh – that's my goldfish.'

'Ha – you are cute, you know that?'

I make a face. 'Coming from you, I'm not sure that's a compliment.'

'Of course it is. Just because I've dated some of the hottest women on the scene doesn't mean I can't appreciate a true English rose when I see one.'

'Uh, okay, Travis. Do you ever not flirt?'

'Sure, with a girl I don't like. You, I like. A lot, actually.'

'You barely know me.'

'But I like what I see. Although I feel that there is much more beneath the surface. What is under there, English Rose?'

'Travis – we're done for the day. Are you coming or not?' Henry wants to know as he marches towards us. My, this loo is certainly getting crowded all of a sudden.

'You go on ahead, Henry. I'll see you tomorrow,' Travis says, not taking his eyes off me.

Henry's mouth opens wide, then shuts with a snap. 'Right.'

Bob gets up, dusts off his knees and straightens his back. 'Okay, so no one goes in there until tomorrow evening.'

I nod. 'Thanks, Bob, you've done an amazing job as always.'

He removes his gloves. 'Faith, there's a list of things on your desk. We'll go over it tomorrow.'

'Oh. Okay. Have a nice evening, Bob, and say hi to Eve for me, will you?'

'Consider it done,' he says, picking up his toolbox and heading for the front door. 'See you tomorrow, Faith. Travis, I'm sure you've got somewhere to be?'

I suppress a gasp at Bob's rudeness and check Travis' face. But he's completely unfazed. 'Me? Nah. I'll probably just escort Faith home.'

Oh, God. 'Oh – I don't need escorting,' I inform him. 'But thanks anyway.'

'I'm off,' Bill sighs before he pulls the door shut.

'Bye, Bob,' I call as I head for the boardroom to sit and read his notes. He's itemised all the pieces to be delivered. As I go through the complete list, I become aware of the fact that Travis has followed me.

'And now I know why my American charm isn't working on you in the least,' he says.

I look up. 'I'm sorry?'

'You *do* have the hots for my buddy Henry.'

I baulk. 'I have *not*.'

'Come on. I can see it in your eyes. The minute he walks into the room you light up.'

'Nonsense. Henry is just a work colleague. He means absolutely nothing to me. I'd sooner hook up with Gabe again.' But even as I say it, my heart hurts. We will never be friends again, and come the end of this job, I will never see him again, either.

'Well, if you're not interested in Henry, that's definitely good news for me!' Travis says and turns to look behind him. 'Uh-oh.'

I turn too, only to see that Henry has just walked in, and by the look on his face it's obvious he's heard every word. On the one hand I'm sorry, on the other, it serves him right. He's no better than Gabe, playing with two decks of cards, and if I want to go out with Travis, it's none of his business.

Without another word, Henry leaves.

'Ouch – he's no happy camper, that one.'

'Too bad for him,' is all I can say.

'So… I don't need his permission to date you?'

'Of course not. But I'm not dating anyone right now, Travis.'

'Is that a promise? I don't have to worry about any competition, which I'm sure I have in spades.'

'No competition anywhere.' As if. I'm done with bloody romance. From now it's all work, work, work.

'In that case, will you have dinner with me?'

'I'd rather not complicate things any further, Travis.'

He laughs. 'Come on, have a heart – I'm a stranger in a strange land! But don't worry, I'm not as bad as my reputation has me. I'm actually a really nice guy, you know?'

Despite myself, I smile. 'I'm certain you are.'

'We can talk shop. I have a business proposition for you.'

'Oh?'

'Yeah, I just got a great idea you're gonna love. So, what's your answer?'

Henry is with Linda. Whatever happened in the past, they've patched things up. They will deal with Orson when the issues arise. What else can I do? They are happy together now. And there is absolutely no room in his life for me. If anything, Henry tolerates me and probably won't even come back tomorrow, or ever. I saw him loading his tools – every single one of them. He's moved on. I should do the same. Even if the mere thought kills me.

Travis is waiting for an answer. He's nice. Easy-going. I can literally hear my sister telling me to get on with my life and stop pining after unavailable men. My coastal girls would say the same.

Oh, what the hell. 'Okay. Thank you, Travis.'

He claps his hands together. 'Cool! Pick you up at seven?'

'Seven it is.'

He spins around a couple of times and pumps his fist with a loud 'Yes!'

Travis is perfectly on time, wearing a suit, nonetheless, and I'm glad of my own choice, i.e. a turquoise dress with a hint of a sleeve, and high heels. The last time I dressed up had been for dinner with Henry a million years ago, it now seems. *Stop thinking about Henry*, I scold myself. *You did what you had to do. You took a risk, and you ultimately lost. You've chastised yourself endlessly. Enough is enough.* If only I could believe me. Because Henry—

'Hi,' Travis says, producing a bouquet of flowers. 'To say thank you for saying yes,' he explains.

I take the flowers from him and put them into a vase. 'That's very kind of you, Travis. Thank you.'

'You're very welcome.'

'Let's go, I'm starving.'

He laughs. 'I love a woman with an appetite.'

'That's promising,' I reply as I lead the way out the door.

'*Mademoiselle*,' he drawls as he opens his car door for me. I wonder what Henry is doing tonight. Is he cooking the family dinner and maybe watching some TV with them, or are they all out on the town, too?

It soon becomes apparent that Travis, despite all his bravado, is a little nervous. He talks endlessly, which is a good thing as it keeps me from thinking about Henry overhearing what I'd said about my sooner choosing Gabe, which is a mouthful in itself.

I never meant for him to hear that, even if it does serve him right. I am sick and tired of being jerked around by men who think that I should be grateful for the slightest interest shown in me.

When we get to the restaurant, we are swiftly seated at a table by the window and Travis leans in. 'Like it? I know how much you love your seascapes.'

'It's absolutely gorgeous, Travis, what a kind thought. Thank you.'

'So, what's a gorgeous gal like you doing in a smudge of a village like Perrancombe?' Travis asks.

'Oh, I guess it's all Gabe's fault.' And I've already stumbled on Hurdle Number One. The ex. 'He... he is from Perrancombe, and seeing as I didn't have any ties myself...'

'No family?'

'Uhm, just my sister and her kids. They don't live far. And you?'

He takes a sip of his wine. 'My parents are in New Jersey, living in the same house since they got married forty years ago.'

'Wow. Do you miss it?'

'The house? Nah. It's too small. Luckily I'm an only child so I didn't have to share a room with anyone. And I got all the attention.' He grins.

'What's it like, to live in the United States?'

'It depends on who's president at the time of the question,' he says with a contagious laugh and I can't help but giggle. 'No, seriously, it's much better now. Plus, I spend most of my time in New York, selling real estate to high-flying hot-shots.'

'Wow, sounds exciting.'

He shrugs. 'I thought Henry had told you.'

And there's Hurdle Number Two – the Henry topic. I take a sip of water to moisten my dry mouth and suddenly I am weary of doing the same thing over and over again: break up, reconcile, repeat. Gabe and I have done it twice, and with Henry I've managed to break up without actually even being with him. I'm getting better and better at going straight to the bad bits. And now I just want it all to end. To think of something else rather than have my heart broken over and over again like in a bad Groundhog Day film.

'Politicians, magnates, religious leaders. Everyone wants the best parts of the Big Apple. I was serious earlier. You should come with me when I go back.'

I snort inwardly.

Travis puts his glass down. 'I know – we'll get you a working visa. I could get you a gig or two to start with. Good ones. One of my best friends – she's a pop star – has just bought in Park Avenue. Amazing pad – you'd go nuts.'

I shake my head. 'That's really kind of you, Travis, but I couldn't possibly—'

'Why not?'

'Because I don't even know if I'd be good enough.'

He laughs. 'Please. I've seen your work, you have excellent taste. And besides, do you know how many designers are really crappy and get the best jobs? Look at whatshername – Vanessa Chatsbury. Geez, talk about kitsch. And yet, she's got commissions up the wazoo, and you know why?'

I look up and shrug, resigned. 'Because it's who you know…'

'Exactly, Faith. If she can do well with her lack of taste, why the hell wouldn't you with your elegant style?'

I bite my lip.

'Come on, kid,' he insists. 'Where's your sense of adventure? What have you got to lose?'

Nothing. I have got absolutely nothing to lose. I'm practically done with Rosie and Nat's cottages. And it's better if I don't go back to the beach house, what with the ghosts of Relationship Past and Could Have Been Relationship Conditional still lingering there.

And despite my best efforts, the Wickfords still don't even know I exist while, conversely, Vanessa is the best thing since peroxide dye, so it's not like I'd be missing out on any amazing opportunities here. And a chance to finally succeed at what I do – what idiot would not grab the opportunity?

It wouldn't be for long, anyway. It's not like I'm going to take New York by storm. But if by some crazy fluke I managed to find something worthwhile there, I could always pop back to see Hope and the kids – or perhaps they could even come and visit me?

I'd get a flat with an extra bedroom and the kids could sleep with Hope. Besides them, I realise as my throat constricts – no one else would really miss me. My coastal girls could come out, too, although I can't see them wanting to leave their new loves anytime soon. Nor can I blame them.

If I had a man like theirs, I wouldn't lose sight of him either. But it's plain that I don't know how to keep a man. And besides, Perrancombe has existed hundreds of years without me and will hardly even notice my departure. And Henry – that ship has sailed. He certainly won't miss me, will he? If anything, he'll be glad I left.

'I, uhm, that's a tremendously generous opportunity, Travis. I'll think about it.'

'Great! I'll take you to see my complete portfolio and how the other half live. It will leave you speechless.'

'I can't believe it – my sister is going to New York!'

'Calm down, Hope. I haven't even said yes yet.'

'But you're going to, right?'

'Possibly, if I can get a working visa.'

'Faith, you have to, if only for us to come and visit! Seriously – it's a great opportunity, handed to you on a plate. And Travis seems to fancy you. Why wouldn't you go?'

'Because...' I huff. 'I think you're right about Travis fancying me and I don't want to lead him on. I don't want to take advantage of his kindness. I don't want him to expect anything in return but friendship.'

'But by the way you describe him, he sounds like a nice bloke, under all that brash. He's funny, successful, and he's offering you a change. And, best of all, he's not Henry.'

Well, she's certainly spot-on about that. But that can only be a good thing, right?

'My advice?' Hope says. 'Apply for the visa, and see how you feel when you get it. Because when is something like this ever going to happen to you again?'

'You've got a point,' I answer. Besides, if Gabe is determined to sell the beach house, it'll be good to get away for a bit. I only need to remember to cancel my request for a mortgage.

'Good girl. Think about it, and think hard. And Faith? Avoid Henry as best you can. For your own good.'

'Aren't you full of advice today,' I groan.

'I love you, sis,' is all she says.

I rub my forehead. 'I know, I love you too. And I'd miss you guys if I went.'

'But it would only be for a short while. Maybe I could move to New York too. Get a job and work my way up.'

'What, and start all over again? You've too much to lose, Hope!'

'Maybe. But some things are worth risking, aren't they?'

I suppress another groan. 'I have to go, but I'll call you later in the week,' I promise. 'Give my love to Verity and Jowen.'

'Will do, and Faith?'

'Yes?'

'*Start spreading the news…!*'

'Ha,' I snort before I ring off. There is no doubt what her opinion is. Nor how fickle she is. But I have a feeling that despite having spent three years of my life with Gabe, Henry is going to be a lot more difficult to forget.

16

New York, New York

That night, I lie in my bed with only Jawsy to keep me company. I have put her on my night table because that's the only time I'm home to spend any time with the poor little soul. Besides her, I have been sleeping alone since Gabe left, bar that one night when Henry slept in the armchair next to me and that one, unforgettable night spent together.

For now, I have to think about the immediate future, because, in a few months, if I apply for a working visa, I might be waking up in New York. New York, with entirely different opportunities. Getting out of my own rut. Starting new projects, meeting new people, having a refreshing take on things. Looking at the world with new eyes and all that. Of course I'd miss my people here, and I'm sure the minute we lift off and I see the last of my coast, I'll start bawling like a baby. But I have to do something, anything, because at the moment I have reached a situation of complete stalemate.

I'd only stay for a short while in any case. Consider it a

break, if not my *professional* break. A change would do me good, because I can't see things getting any worse than they already are.

So when Travis calls the next day, I jump on the phone, relieved for any kind of distraction.

'Hiya, pretty lady,' he drawls. 'You busy?'

I look around my flat. It's taken me precisely forty minutes to do a completely thorough clean. It's good to take a day off every now and then, but now I'm bored to the marrow. 'Yes.'

He laughs. 'You still gotta eat. How about lunch somewhere?'

'Uhm, no thank you, Travis.'

'I want to talk business with you.'

At that, my ears perk up. 'Oh?'

'And good business at that,' he says. 'Pick you up in twenty?'

Now I am intrigued, but I don't want Henry to know. 'Well… all right. Thank you,' I answer, and I can't help but notice the irony in the fact that only a few weeks ago I was dining with Henry. But Henry has chosen not to continue with me. He's made his life choices and they obviously don't include me.

Believe it or not, Travis is right on time.

We drive out to a tiny restaurant in Sennen Cove. There is a deck jutting out into the sea, and we are lucky enough to get the table at the very end.

'I'm in the mood for fish,' he says. 'What about you?'

'The scallops look great,' I answer, recalling the last time I'd had scallops. Henry had brought me a beer with a wry comment he'd read on a sign at the bar, *Beers as cold as your ex's heart!* And they're not wrong about that.

'Cool! Two scallops it is. What vegetables are you going to order?' he asks, flipping through his menu.

'I'll just have a salad, thanks, Henry.'

'Travis.'

I look up. 'Sorry?'

'You just called me Henry.'

'Oh! I'm sorry. I'm just used to working with Henry every day and—'

Travis puts down his menu, studying me. 'Is he really that hard to forget, Faith?'

Apparently, he is. I'm never going to be able to erase him from my mind. 'There's nothing to forget, Travis. I already told you, there's nothing between Henry and me.'

'Good, because if there is, I can't take you to New York with me, because the last thing I wanna see is you pining for a guy you can't have.'

'I'm not pining for anyone, Travis. In any case, we agreed that you and I are just friends, and if my coming to New York is going to be a problem—'

'Of course not, Faith. Who do you think I am, a filthy Hollywood producer?'

'No, of course not. I'm sorry.'

'You wanna be just friends? Fine. But you will change your mind because I'm a charmer and you just won't be able to help yourself. And don't say I didn't tell you.'

Ha. 'So, I'm putting my visa application together.'

'Good. At first you'll come out as a tourist, see if you like it, visit my offices, et cetera.'

'I'll love it,' I reassure him. Anything to get away from Henry.

'You will, and New York will love you. Because I have a business proposal. It's a small thing to start with, but if you play your cards right...

'I'm listening.'

'I need someone to stage some new lofts I'm selling in New York. The paint isn't even dry yet. You'd be perfect.'

I bite my lip. 'You think so?'

He shrugs. 'How can you not? Look at you, the typical delicate English rose. You reek of quaint Englishness.'

'And people want that in a New York loft? I highly doubt it.'

'Maybe not in the city, but once you're done with that, there's more property in the Hamptons, Martha's Vineyard, Cape Cod. It will be your playground for as long as you like.'

I think about it. A chance to start all over again, away from all my mistakes. 'That sounds lovely, Travis. Thank you.'

'So you're definitely in?' he asks.

I nod. 'I'm definitely in.'

Travis takes my hand, and I look up. He is confident, smiling, optimistic. 'You and me, kid, are gonna do great things together.'

The next morning, with great trepidation, I fill in my crew about Travis' offer.

'Oh my God, you're going *international*!' Thea cries, jumping up and down.

'Well, technically, I'm not going anywhere yet until I've made a decision. And in any case, I'd only be going for a holiday first. If they grant me a working visa, we'll see from there. Obviously we'll keep things going here as well,' I reassure them.

Mike turns to me. 'Are you sure this is what you want? Running away isn't always the best solution, Faith.'

'I'm not running away. I just want to see what else is out there.'

'He who abandons the old for the new...'

'Mike, leave her alone,' Bob says. 'She has the right to start all over again if she's not happy here.'

'But that's not the case, I *am* happy here,' I assure them. 'I just want to – I just want to see what's on the other side of the world, is all.'

Bill shakes his head. 'Faith, Henry is almost done. After this job, you won't need to see him at all.'

'This has nothing to do with Henry! I just want a change of scenery. For a while, at least.'

'Oh, you'll do very well in New York!' Thea assures me, but my muscle men don't seem to think it's a good idea.

'Thank you, Thea. I'm leaving next month.'

Silence as gazes swing around in a circle. 'How long will you be gone?' Mike wants to know.

'I don't know. As a Brit I can't stay without a visa more than ninety days, so...'

Thea nods. 'Enough time to get the lay of the land.'

'Exactly. Now, if you'll all excuse me, I have work to do.'

I spend the rest of the day lying low, as bumping into

Henry is the last thing I want to do now. But I can't just leave without telling him. Even if I know he has no interest in me, how can I put an ocean between us without even saying goodbye?

'Faith, I need to talk to you if you have a moment?'

I jump at the sound of Henry's voice and turn to see him standing on the threshold. He's back! 'Henry! You scared me!'

'Yes, well. Busy week?'

'Absolutely.'

'With Travis?'

I flinch. 'He took me out to dinner, yes.'

His mouth snaps shut and he clams up again. When he finally speaks, his face is unreadable. 'Well, I'm not here to discuss your social life. I simply need your approval for the kitchen accessories,' he hastens to tell me.

Of course not. My social life is none of his concern, seeing that his own days and nights are all pretty much booked, having a son and a wife. What would he need me for?

'Oh. Yes, of course,' I say, following him into the kitchen where several boxes lie open. I take out some cupboard door handles and inspect them as he waits in silence. 'Beautiful,' I comment.

He nods. 'No one questioned your taste.'

So what is it, then, that you questioned? I want to ask. *How long you could get away with having me on the side as you got back with your wife?*

'I trust you had a good time with Travis?' he asks.

I grind down onto my teeth so violently I'm sure I've cracked one.

'No matter,' he says when I fail to answer. 'I assume you and Travis have a lot in common.'

'Perhaps,' I defend. 'He's a lot of fun and he makes me laugh.'

His eyes flash. 'Good for you. I'm glad someone makes you laugh. Every other man seems to make you cry.'

The cheeky sod! How dare he! 'Only the ones who are no good for me,' I point out. 'But Travis is good to me. He believes in me and, most importantly, has time for me.'

'Time for what?'

I shrug. 'Anything I need. And he's invited me to New York. He's going to introduce me to some of his clients.' Seeing as none of Henry's have materialised. There. Two can play at his game.

'Travis?' he repeats, incredulous.

'Travis,' I assure him. 'I've applied for a visa, but in the meantime I'm going back with him.'

'That's very sudden.'

'Yes, well, take the bull by the horns and all that.'

'You don't really know him well enough to take off with him into the sunset, do you?'

'Firstly, I'm not taking off into the sunset with anyone. And secondly, I've known him for as long as I've known you. Besides, even people you know extremely well can hurt you. Look at Gabe. Look at...' *you*, I almost say. 'In any case, Travis and I have been spending a lot of time together lately and we have a lot in common.'

Silence. A long silence. 'Then I wish you every happiness.'

'Thank you. I'm sure I will be very happy.' Better than now, in any case.

17

Situationships

The next day, Henry and his crew put together the most beautiful kitchen I've ever seen. It is in the same style and spirit of the house. I'm glad that he has understood exactly what I wanted, and the feeling I wanted to create. A feeling of beauty and happiness, just like the life I've lived here.

But I mustn't dwell – I've got lots of work to do before I go. As far as the Wickford Dream is concerned, my emails and phones calls remain unanswered, and barring disguising myself as one of their cleaning people or dog walkers, I've run out of options. If I can't even get their attention, how am I supposed to impress them with my work? They call themselves the patrons of interior design, and yet they are completely unapproachable. I've tried absolutely everything, bar parachuting myself into their back garden. I probably would if I knew their home address, but their offices alone are like a bloody fortress.

My eye falls on the table that Henry delivered the day we

met. It's a beautiful piece of oak wood, honed with expertise, patience and love. The lines are simple with subtle details that don't scream out *I'm better than the rest*, even though it is much more beautiful than any table I've ever seen before. It has lines that speak of hours and hours of dedication. When he made it, he wasn't looking for industrial perfection, but rather a uniqueness that holds all the expertise dictated by pure attention to detail and... otherness. Anyone who is capable of making something so beautiful deserves some serious respect. But that still doesn't change the fact that he's played with my feelings.

You know when you're on a bad roll and everything's going awry, and it can't get any worse? Well, think again, because it can. Proof? A feature article on none other than Vanessa Chatsbury herself. She has just won an award for Designer of the Year, presented to her by guess who? Exactly, the *Wickfords*.

I stare at the two-paged slap in the face that pictures her at some ceremony venue that I have completely missed.

Another picture shows Vanessa baking a cake with her mum in a huge Victorian kitchen, her long arms around the Maggie Smith lookalike who is bursting with pride for her daughter. Not only does Vanessa have a home of her own, she has parents who still put up with all of her shenanigans. I swallow the lump in my throat. I'd do anything to have a photo with a mother who loves me and is proud of me. Vanessa truly has everything.

But I wouldn't trade with her. Because I have Hope and Verity and Jowen. Let Vanessa win all the engineered awards. I'll meet and impress the Wickfords someday. Maybe not today, or tomorrow. Maybe I'll be able to do some good work in New York, because I am obviously done here. Maybe this town really isn't big enough for the both of us after all.

For years I had put Gabe at the fore of my life, while all the hopes and dreams I've clung on to all that time have brought me nothing but upset, disappointment and heartache. I guess that, in order to move on, I had to move out first. Now, if only I could move out emotionally. I have to do this if I don't want to go insane. So New York it is. A brand-new start. Start spreading the news indeed!

The next day I get to the beach house uber-early. Now that I know what my goal is, I want to put this job, the house and Gabe all behind me.

And Henry. Not my biggest error of judgement ever, granted. But possibly the most painful one, which is a mystery of its own. You'd think I'd be much more hurt by Gabe's two-fold betrayal than the so-called misunderstanding with Henry. But I'm not. Because just thinking about Henry makes my heart ba-boom without any control, and all the could-have-beens make me want to cry until I suddenly burst into fits of laughter. But, as they say, onward and upward; the sky is the limit and all that codswallop.

As I'm the first one in, I go into the new kitchen to brew a pot of coffee. As I'm preparing all the mugs for everyone on a tray, I catch a slight keening sound. Is it a seagull? No, it's not acute enough. I stop to listen carefully, and there it is again. It's coming from Gabe's office.

I put my cup down quietly and tiptoe to the closed door and slowly open it a crack, only to find Gabe slumped at his desk, his head on his forearms. He is shaking visibly and loud hiccups escape him. I know that sound. He is trying to suffocate his sobs, like when his cousin Charlie died.

I open the door all the way and take a step towards him. It is so rare to see him cry, especially like this, so it must be something dreadfully serious.

'Gabe?' I whisper. 'Are you all right?'

Gabe bolts to a sitting position, swiping at his eyes.

'What's happened? Is everything okay?' To see him cry so desperately, for one horrible second, I fear the worst has happened and that the baby's life is in danger.

'Nothing's okay, Faith, and it never will be...' he bawls, pushing his fists into his eyes again.

I pull myself up onto the desk. I hate to see him like this. 'Tell me,' I say gently. 'Don't keep it all bottled up. Dr Banks said it's not good for you.'

'Sod Dr Banks. What does he know about heartbreak?'

'I'm sorry...' I say, and this time I mean it. People breaking up and families falling apart is my worst fear, even if it has nothing to do with me.

'Don't be,' he hiccups. 'It isn't your fault, really...'

I nod in sympathy, then stop as his words sink in. 'Wait, what do you mean it's not my fault *really*?'

He heaves a huge sigh, wiping his eyes that have become like two huge red traffic lights as he looks up at me pleadingly and takes my hand.

'I know I've hurt you, Faith, and I'm really, really sorry...'

I look down at him and his blond spikes that are less spiky than usual, and the downturned mouth that I've kissed so many times no longer holds any appeal to me. Even the iconic tongue and lip design on his Rolling Stones

T-shirt seems to be sulking, and I can find in my heart no tolerance for this man who has already hurt me so badly in so many ways.

'Vanessa is furious with me. That's why we split up and despite the fact I've seen other girls, there's not a day that goes by that she doesn't accuse me of still being in love with you.'

I make an effort not to snort. 'Well then, talk to her. Reassure her.'

'Reassure her, of what? She's absolutely right.' He sits further back, his eyes on mine, beseeching, his hands holding both of mine in his. 'I am still in love with you, Faith – more than ever.'

Oh my God, Please don't, I want to say, a sudden knot in my throat. *It's taken me forever to come to terms with it all. I can't go through all those ups and downs again.*

Gabe runs a hand though his hair. 'I can't believe I'm saying this – I promised myself I'd behave and not say anything. But I *miss* you, Faith.'

I stare at him, feeling my eyes actually pop in shock. 'You what…?'

'Yes, Faith, I really, really do. We've tried to patch things up for the baby's sake, but it's an absolute bloody nightmare. Vanessa screams all the time and I can't take it anymore. Our flat is an absolute tip despite having a housekeeper, and she is always miserable for some reason or other.'

'I'm sorry to hear that, Gabe.' Truly, I am. Once you've loved someone as much as I loved Gabe, all you want is for them to be happy, and often to your own detriment.

He looks around the room. 'This place, Faith, without

you? It's nothing but a shell. I miss our happy home. Please come back to me...'

And before I know it, he's reached out and pulled me towards him by my shoulders, our faces inches apart. We are so close I can see his eyes are bloodshot from all the crying. Wait, no. I can smell liquor on his breath. Fresh liquor. He's been drinking again. And it's not even noon.

I instinctively pull away, but his hands are firm on my shoulders, dragging me back to where he wants me. I push him away and jump back.

'I am not a doll you can throw around as you like, Gabe!' I cry. 'You *left* me! And then you wanted me back. And you got her pregnant. You've done me enough damage, and you've made your bed. Now sleep in it!'

'I know – don't say it,' he says, holding his head as if to keep it together. 'But, Babes – this is *us* here. *Historical Us.* Just like the new song I'm writing. It's about you.'

'Oh, *Gawd*...' I groan.

'Are you really willing to let me go – forever?'

'Why not? You bloody well were.'

'But I've realised the error of my ways.'

'Gabe – for years I was your adoring number-one supporter. I did everything for you. I liaised with your agent, I gave you advice on your career and even your songs. I cooked and cleaned. I made a home for us. We were everything to each other.'

He lurches forward again for my arms, but I move back.

'Gabe, you broke my heart. And now you do this to me? Just how lowly do you think of me if you expect me to come running as if I was extremely grateful to you for taking me back – twice?'

He opens and closes his mouth but nothing comes out.

'No, Gabe. Not happening this time.'

'But I love you,' he finally whines.

'I loved you, too. But now? It's much too little, much too late,' I snap and march out of the room, my head about to explode.

As I slip into the loo to wash my face, I hear a car pull up in the drive. I can't wait to get the hell out of this place. It used to be my home, but now, just like Gabe, it has brought me nothing but misery.

When I go back into the kitchen, I step into a whirlwind of arms and legs. It's Gabe and Travis, wrestling each other like two completely clueless schoolboys.

'Stop!' I scream. 'What is the matter with you two? Gabe! Travis! Stop right now!'

They haven't even seen, much less heard me, but a flying fist catches me right under my left eye. I buckle under the pain, swaying back until I reach the wall. Only it's not the wall. It's – you guessed it – Henry, followed by the rest of my crew who tear the two apart.

'What the hell—?' Henry demands.

I try to answer him, but my entire world is spinning and fading to black. The last thing I remember is being scooped up into his arms.

I am lying on a soft surface with half my face missing. At least I think so, because I can't feel it.

'There you are...' says a low voice, almost a growl. I open my eyes to a bright ceiling and then I close them again.

'This way, Faith,' the voice says, a little gentler,

accompanied by a hand on my chin. I'd recognise that touch anywhere. *Henry.* 'Open your eyes.'

'It hurts too much,' I croak.

'You'll be better by and by,' he assures me. 'It's just a black eye.'

And then I remember. 'Travis… and Gabe.'

'Yes.'

'I tried to stop them, but—'

'It's okay,' he whispers, taking my hand. 'They've been sorted out.'

'Where is everybody?'

'On strict orders to not bother you. Now that you're awake, I'm taking you home.'

'No, uhm, it's okay…' I say. 'I can stay. I've got work to do.'

'I insist,' he says, wrapping me up in a quilt and bundling me into his car like a sausage roll in the space of a minute.

My crew is now at the front door, waving sympathetically. I roll my window down. 'I'm so sorry, guys, I'll be back tomorrow…'

'Bye, luv.' Thea blows me kisses while all the men are scowling, but there is no sign of either Gabe or Travis.

'Are you warm enough?' Henry asks as he drives off slowly.

'Yes,' I murmur. 'Thank you. You didn't have to drive me. I could have gone by myself.'

He snorts. 'With one eye closed? Not happening. At least not on my watch.'

'Oh. Well, thank you.'

He doesn't answer. Nor does he say anything for the rest

of the drive home, which is nice as it allows me to nurse my headache in peace.

Upon arrival, he helps me out of the car and into the lift where he stands opposite me, his eyes fixed ahead but I am under the impression that, should my knees buckle, he will be there to catch me.

Henry. Honourable, lovely Henry. I love everything about him; the way he is always so well-mannered and gentlemanly. The way he lowers his eyes and his lean cheeks redden in utter shyness. How can he not know how gorgeous he is? He was certainly raised properly to respect people and be honourable, even to his own detriment.

I can't believe Henry is here in my flat. I thought I'd never see him here again. And now that he's here, I have so many things to say to him.

Once inside the door, he leads me to the settee and helps me onto it. Then he reaches inside my tiny freezer and pulls out a bag of peas which he places onto my eye.

'Oh, ouch. Thank you. I—'

'Thea has texted your sister. She's going to be here in a few minutes.'

'Oh, but you needn't have worried. I'm perfectly okay.' If you don't count my heart that is in smithereens, that is.

'It's done, now. I've got to go.'

'Okay. Thank you once again.'

'It's nothing,' he murmurs and without looking at me, he gets up and leaves.

'He *what?*' Hope cries as she's adjusting my cushion. 'How could he leave you on your own like this?'

'He didn't leave me. He knew you were coming. Plus, it's only a black eye, I'm not dying.'

'But still. What's wrong with this bloke?'

'Nothing, apart from the fact that he's finally realised he's still involved with his wife.'

'So, moral of the story?'

I shrug. 'I guess I should be grateful he came to my rescue at all.'

'Some knight in shining armour,' she snaps.

'Hope, really, what did you expect, for him to confess his undying love to me?'

'Something along those lines, yes.'

I huff. 'Okay, impending and very necessary reality check: he's back with his wife, remember?'

'Then he should dump her.'

'Why, just to make you happy?'

'And Orson. And you. What good can come out of his being married to someone he doesn't love?'

'How can you say that?'

'I don't know. Listen, I need a huge favour, but if you're not up to it—?'

'I'm perfectly fine, it's just a black eye.'

'Okay, then, good, because I'm at my wits' end.'

'Of course, shoot.'

'That geography project at school?'

'The World Monuments night? I'm done with the costumes, they're ready to go.'

'Great, thanks. Because I can't. Turns out I have to do an extra shift. We've got a dinner for members of the G8, can you bloody believe it? I've tried to get out of it but—'

'I'll go,' I offer. 'When is it again?'

'Oh, God bless you, thank you! It's Friday evening at five.'

'Sure.'

'Okay, then, I'll text you the details. I owe you one!'

I'm more than happy for the chance to spend some time with Verity and Jowen, probably the closest thing I'll ever have to kids of my own. Plus, they'll look really cute in those monument outfits I sewed for them.

'It's nothing, Hope. Now please go home.'

'Are you sure?'

I roll my eyes. 'Go.'

'All right, then. Call me if you need me.'

'Don't worry, I'll be fine,' I say, shooing her away. 'Give my love to the kiddies.'

'I will,' she says, kissing my cheek. 'You're an absolute star!'

Alone again. Actually, I don't mind. I need the time to think. What the hell had happened back there? Why were Gabe and Travis fighting?

And speak of the devil, my mobile rings. It's Travis. 'Oh. Hi.'

'How's the eye?'

'It's better, thank you,' I answer.

'I'm really sorry about that.'

'What happened, Travis? Why were you and Gabe fighting?'

Travis sighs. 'Let's just say that Gabe is not exactly a man of his word. But that's okay because I have a couple of interested buyers.'

Oh my God. 'Oh?'

'Yes, one's a friend of a friend back in the States. And one's a local. Had his eye on it for years now.'

Let it go, Faith. It's not your home anymore. Just accept it and move on. 'Right.'

I spend the rest of the next day running errands and on the phone with Thea who reassures me every time she picks up that yes, everything is under control. Both Gabe and Travis are off site. But the amazing news is that Henry has actually found the *original* wainscoting that has been unceremoniously dumped at a reclamation yard, and he is working hard to restore it.

He's been true to his word. All that time I'd worried about it being gone forever, and once again, he's come through. I can't ignore his enormous effort and very considerate gesture. Granted, he did it before we fell out, but still. I'll have to at least send him a message to thank him, because in a few days he'll be done and gone. I'll bet he can't wait to get out of that madhouse.

A sudden string of pings from my mobile alerts me to an entire series of missed calls. They are all from Henry. What can he possibly want from me? I know it's not about Orson or work, because Thea would have told me. I swipe at my eyes. I can't be doing this. I can't be suddenly tearing up every time at the mere thought of him.

I'm almost home, so I press the off button on my phone and in that split second I've taken my eye off the road, someone, out of absolutely nowhere, materialises right in front of me. I hit the brakes, but it's too late.

18

Jolene

I slam the brakes and jump out of the car and onto my poor victim who is on her knees.

'Oh my God, I'm so so sorry, are you all right? Lie still, let me call an ambulance!' I cry, feeling her for broken bones. And then she looks up and I gasp and jump back as if I'd seen the Antichrist. It's Vanessa Chatsbury in the flesh. 'Are... you okay? The baby...?'

With my help, she picks herself up and dusts herself off. 'No, it's okay, Faith. You didn't hit me, I just panicked and tripped. I'm okay...'

She takes my hand and cackles. '*God*, am I unfit with this fat arse! I was just popping in to see you, funnily enough. I'm sorry I didn't call, but I didn't have your number. You must be wondering what I'm doing here.'

I stare at her, my mouth opening and closing like my little Jawsy. 'Yes. What *are* you doing here?'

'Long story. Can I come up?'

I study her briefly. Apart from the fact that I have

envisaged running her over, back and forth, a million times, I am grateful that in reality I have inflicted no harm on her. Granted, she is pale and blotchy at the same time and it looks like she's literally cried her make-up off. Break-ups are painful. I've done the legwork.

I move to one side to let her in through the main entrance, wondering what the hell she could possibly want from me, seeing as she has everything that I have always aimed for in life, professional recognition included.

I am especially aware of the state I'm in. And I'm also aware of the fact that my place is so tiny, but really, living on my own and working practically eighteen hours of the day and coming here only to sleep and shower, who do I need more space for?

'I come in peace,' she huffs as we stop at my front door.

Peace, between her and me? This I need to see.

I guide her inside and to the settee onto which she eases herself slowly.

'Thanks,' she wheezes. 'Sorry again for popping round without notice, but I have a feeling you wouldn't have wanted to speak to me. Not that I can blame you.' And then she takes a good look at me. 'Oh my God, Faith, what happened to your face?'

My face? She looks absolutely awful, with peroxide-tipped dark roots shooting out of her head and a sweaty face. 'It's nothing. Would... you like a glass of water?' I offer. 'A cushion?'

'Yes, please, to both,' she huffs, adjusting herself as I dash forward to shove one of my Home Hugs behind her back.

'Ah, perfect, thank you,' she says and I go to the sink and pour her a glass of water, all the while still wondering what the hell she wants. Is she, as is her custom, going to lull me into a false sense of security, only to go completely psycho-bitch on me? Although, to be honest, she looks too exhausted.

'Here, put your feet up,' I say despite myself as I pass her the glass, wondering what the hell is wrong with me, letting the enemy into my home.

She fans herself, shaking her head. 'Ah... great. I don't know why you're being so kind to me, but thank you.'

I shrug. 'You're expecting a baby.'

'But that's the very reason why you should hate me, Faith,' she says softly.

'I know. I did. But not anymore.'

'I know. We're done, too.'

I'd say I'm sorry, but in truth, I'm not.

'I know what you're thinking. That Gabe and I slept together long before he left you. Which we did. I know – he's awful, I'm awful. We're both awful, and now, at my weakest, karma's come back to bite me on the ass.'

'Why, is the baby okay?' I blurt out.

'Yeah, she's okay.'

'Awh, it's a she?'

She stops. 'You realise that you're acting way too nicely? If it had been you, I'd have kicked your arse all the way to Timbuktu.'

'I did kick your arse,' I confess. 'Plus I almost just ran you over.'

She grins. 'That's okay, I deserve it.'

Which still doesn't answer my erstwhile question. 'Vanessa? Why are you here?'

'To tell you that I'm sorry. You and Gabe were happy when I came along.'

I shrug. 'I was, or thought I was. Gabe obviously wasn't.'

'He never is.'

How true.

She half-laughs. 'You'd think so. It's his specialty, isn't it? Playing with girls' hearts like that. But as far as I know, he isn't with anyone. For all I care.'

I don't care either. I'm done with crying and wondering where I went wrong. I now know it's not my fault. I did what I could for Gabe. I have absolutely nothing to blame myself for. I was a good girlfriend, and if he didn't appreciate me, that's just too bad for him.

'My sources tell me he's going back to Thailand tomorrow. He has to finish his tour. Good riddance. He's ruined my life completely. I can't sleep, eat or think about anything except how he's humiliated me.'

Well, luckily I'm over it, while Vanessa is only at the beginning of her personal hell.

'What about the baby?' I enquire. 'Will he be back in time for the birth?'

She stares at me. 'Okay, let me be clear. I don't want him anywhere near me or the baby. Ever.'

'Okay,' I say carefully. If I know her at all, she'll change her mind in a few days. She'll want him back. But again, it has nothing to do with me anymore.

'So how are things with you?' she asks.

'Me?'

'Yeah. I hear the house renos are coming along well. I'm relieved. I hate that horrid theme.'

'But… you… designed it,' I stammer.

'I did,' she agrees. 'But my tastes have now changed. I guess it has to do with being constantly sober since I found out I was pregnant.'

I still can't believe we are having a conversation, let alone this one.

'Look,' she says, pulling out a tissue, and for a moment I think she's about to cry. But she only blows her nose, thank God. 'You need to know that I have always envied you.'

'Well, many women want Gabe.'

She looks up at me with those bloodshot eyes. 'No, not because of him, but because you are the self-made It girl.'

My eyes almost pop out of my head. 'You're joking, right?'

She looks up. 'Why would I be? You've worked extremely hard to be where you are now. You clients rave about you. I want to be more like you. I never wanted to hurt you, you know.'

'Then why have you always been trying to ruin me?' I ask softly.

She sniffs and bunches her tissue up in her fist. 'I have been, haven't I? I have always looked down on you as the middle-class upstart from nowhere, and I couldn't understand why my aristocratic connections weren't enough to erase you once and for all. I was afraid of you professionally.'

'So you thought to hurt me by taking my boyfriend…'

She looks up at me with big dark eyes. 'Yes. I'm sorry.'

It's so bloody funny I can't help but grin. 'Don't be. You've done me a favour.'

'So you forgive me, then?'

'Not unless this is one of your usual ploys to get something else out of me? Because I have absolutely nothing that you would want.' Except for maybe Jawsy. He's one hell of a conversationalist.

'No, I promise, no games. I just want us to stop feuding.'

I shrug. 'As long as you behave yourself and stop trying to steal my clients.'

She lowers her head. Apparently she has just discovered a thing called shame.

'All right. I promise.'

'Good. Thank you.'

'And maybe we could be friends…?' she suggests, blowing her nose again.

'Er… I don't know about that, Vanessa…'

'No, you're right! I'm a disaster!' she wails.

'Don't say that,' I plead. As much as I dislike Vanessa, I never wanted her to be miserable. I only didn't want her to be happy with my boyfriend.

'Can we… be at least professional friends? Recommend suppliers to each other and all that sort of stuff?'

I hesitate. None of this is really Vanessa's fault, at the end of the day. It's Gabe's fault. He's the one I have an issue with.

'And maybe hang out? I don't have many friends left, you know, after…'

'Well,' I debate, wondering what I'm getting myself into. Vanessa is anything but friend material.

She runs a tired hand through her new bob. It kind of looks nice on her. She looks almost normal without the bizarre hair. 'God, what I'd do to never have met him.'

Her and me both.

Her hand slides down to her belly. 'Do you think it's

better to have loved and lost, or to have never loved, Faith?' she asks me as if I was the bloody oracle. But on second thought, she's right to ask my opinion as I'm the expert on losing a bloke. I've done it three times in the past three years, and two of those in the last few months.

'I... guess it is better to have loved and lost. You would never have had a baby – your *daughter* – to look forward to,' I answer, thinking of Henry. Would I have preferred to have never met him? I know he and I could never hit it off. For a million reasons, plus the obvious one that he lies next to at night. And yet, I wish I'd had the chance.

'It was always you,' she breathes as if exhausted. 'Every time, all he talked about was you. Even when we were in bed—'

'Yes, well, that's a little too much information, Vanessa.'

'Again, Faith. I truly am sorry, for doing that to you.'

I shrug. 'You were in love. I guess that's kind of a synonym for blindness.'

She wipes her eyes and giggles. 'Yeah! I can't believe that you and I are having this conversation. It shows that, at the end of the day, it's all about female solidarity, isn't it?'

I nod in agreement. 'I think that there should be more of it.'

'So, how's working with Henry?'

'You know Henry?'

'Of course – everyone knows Henry. He's an absolute gem, and so so talented. And of course, a knicker-melter.'

I snort.

'You don't think so?' she asks. 'Oh my God, you're turning red! No!'

'No, what?' I ask, trying to play it cool as the heat rushes up from my stomach, blasting its way up my face and to the tips of my hair.

'You've fallen for Henry Turner, haven't you?'

I look up at her, my former nemesis, and find in her eyes an understanding that I never thought I'd see. So I'm probably just imagining it.

'No.'

'Liar. I can see it all over your face. I don't blame you. He'd be perfect for you.'

'Fat lot of good it does me,' I mutter as I swipe at a tear straying down my own cheek this time. What is wrong with me? I haven't cried in months, and I have to go and do it in front of bloody Vanessa?

Her face softens. 'Hey... why don't you just tell him your feelings?'

'Because he's gone back to his wife,' I blurt out in a squeak. 'Among other things.' These two definitely have something in common. Maybe they should hook up.

'Oh. Well, that does it. He has always been remarkably loyal.'

'Hurray for loyalty,' I say with fake cheer.

'I'll bet he fancied you, too,' Vanessa says.

'Yes, well,' I say, using one of his expressions. Like it or not, Henry has left a visible mark on me, and I don't mean the black eye. That was either Gabe or Travis playing silly buggers.

Vanessa downs the rest of her water and struggles to her feet. 'I really have to run to my gyno appointment. But it was good talking to you.'

'Do you need a ride or something?' I ask before I can help myself.

She stops and looks up at me. 'Thank you – my parents are taking me. They're being really supportive and have promised to help me raise the baby.'

I swallow a lump in my throat. I have no idea how it got there. 'That's... family for you...'

'Yeah. My mum especially is over the moon.'

'Oh. Okay. Good luck then.'

'And you, Faith. I wish you all the best. Talk soon?'

I nod.

'Good. See you!'

'Uhm, Vanessa?'

She looks at me, her face serene.

'What... made you change like this?' I ask.

She smiles and rubs her bump. 'Motherhood. I want to be the best I can for my little girl. Nothing else matters now, you know?'

I swallow the rock in my throat and nod again. 'I know,' I whisper.

And with one last smile, she squeezes my hand and waddles out the door, obviously much happier and at peace with herself. Lucky her. Because the mere thought that I could have had Gabe's baby, as much as I wanted it, now makes me shiver in horror.

I understand now that mine has been a teenage obsession for my boyfriend who became a rock star and grew out of me. I was not in love with Gabe, but the idea of an amazing life next to someone I'd dreamt of for so long.

But now, that dream is over, thank God. If only I could talk to Henry. But to what end? He's happy with his ex-wife. I can't question his actions. I have absolutely no right to. Family comes first.

*

It is finally World Monuments night. Jowen has got his Chrysler building suit on, which is just a zipper job dividing the dome part from the rest of the body, while Verity looks formidable as the Fearless Girl, with her bronze-painted hands on her bronze hips and chin raised in defiance.

'You guys are perfect!' I exclaim as I spray some more coloured hair spray to secure Verity's stiff ponytail. 'You'll be great!'

She nods. 'I know, I know. Auntie Fi?'

'Yes?'

'Thank you for being here.'

I wink at her. 'I wouldn't have missed it for... the *world*!'

'Corny!' Verity says with a giggle.

But it's true – how many of us go through life never actually enjoying its tiny, insignificant moments? Even here, backstage, we are all moving under the directions of one of Verity's teachers who is waving a clipboard to shoo us around like cattle while not enjoying a single moment of it.

'Hi,' I say as I near her.

She whirls around. 'Ah! North America,' she tells me, as if I didn't know.

'I just wanted to say that everything looks great.'

Her face lights up. 'Really?'

'Yes, really. You've done an amazing job, and from here it's all pretty much a no-brainer. I'd hate for you to miss the real enjoyment.'

'The enjoyment?' she echoes, wondering what the hell I'm on about.

'Look at all the children's faces – look at the parents. See what a great time they're having, and how excited they are? If you enjoy it, too, you'll remember more of it.'

She finally nods, if only to get rid of me, but I can't help but spread this feeling of living life to its full because you never know when things will go pear-shaped. 'I suppose you're right. Thank you.'

I beam at her. Where has this come from? 'You're very welcome.'

'Right,' she says, turning away from me. 'We're doing Asia first, then Europe, then the Americas, and finally Africa, so please assemble with your continent promptly. Now, please, *Tempus Fugit!*'

I watch her go, still highly strung, and shrug to myself. I tried. She'll learn in her own time.

I catch sight of the Eiffel Tower and the Colosseum, scanning the rest of the monuments for La Sagrada Familia that I'd spotted earlier, but there's no sight of it anywhere.

'There you are, I've been looking all over the place for you!' says one of the assistants as he comes to a stop right before me. 'Sorry I'm late – it took us forever to find it, jammed as it was between the leaning tower of Pisa and Big Ben. Oh, well. You have exactly ten minutes to get ready!'

'Get ready for what?' I ask.

'For your exhibition,' he says, shoving a garment bag at me. 'The parents wear a costume as well. Sorry, we had a whole bunch, but you didn't show for the selection, and now you're stuck with the leftovers. Did you bring the green paint? No matter, we have some in the back. Go, go, go!'

I stand there, dumb-struck. Green paint? 'There must be some mistake. Their mother can't be here so I'm filling in, but—'

'Hurry, Auntie Fi,' Verity pleads, pulling my hand.

I look down at their anxious faces and want to murder my sister for leaving out this tiny detail. She knows I hate being on a stage in front of everybody. She knows and still— Oh, *crap*...

I let them drag me to a dressing table under a naked light bulb and open the bag, only to reveal a pale green suit. What the hell is this, an alien costume? This is not bloody Comic Con! And then I see the spiked crown. Oh God, I'm going to be the Statue of bloody Liberty. *Well, thank you very much for this one, Hope!*

Sighing inwardly, I slip the tunic over my head, pull my hair into a bun and proceed to vigorously apply the green paint, which, funnily enough, doesn't manage to hide my now purple and yellow eye.

As I'm doing so, my phone rings. It's Travis.

'Hi, doll!'

'Hi, what's up?'

'Have you got an answer for me regarding New York?'

'Funny you should ask that right now,' I quip. 'I'm dressed as the bloody Statue of Liberty as we speak.'

He sniggers. 'What?'

'Indeed. It's my niece and nephew's geography night at school.'

'Sounds like fun. I'm sure you look great in green.'

'Not as good as I'd hoped,' I answer as I apply the finishing touches of green to my chin. The things you do for love of your blood.

'I've been meaning to ask you, Travis – what news on the beach house?'

Silence.

'Travis?'

'The uhm, house has already sold, Faith. I'm sorry…'

I drop my green face paint, my frozen image reflected in the mirror. 'What? When?'

He hesitates. 'A while ago.'

'A while ago?' Gabe has been lying to me about this as well, for all this time?

'Faith? You okay there?'

'I'm s-sorry, I can't t-talk right now,' I blubber and hang up, dashing for the ladies' which, thankfully, is deserted.

I sit in one of the stalls, my arms wrapped around my knees, and silently sob into the folds of my costume. Why, why, why? Not only had he been cheating on me, but he'd sold our home from under my nose. How could I have not known any of this? Granted, the deeds were in his name, but… *God*, when am I going to remember that he didn't care about me enough to include me in his life decisions? Why has he treated me like I had meant absolutely nothing to him?

And then a thought occurs to me. How had he sold it without any viewings? I'd worked from home the entire time, even receiving clients from there, so I was never out for too long. How had Gabe managed to sneak in viewers behind my back? Unless…

I dig out my mobile from the pocket of my jeans underneath my robe and dial Travis.

'Hey…'

'Sorry, Travis. I just need to ask you something.'

'Shoot.'

'Did you sell the beach house on Gabe's behalf?'

'No. I represented the new buyers. I had just taken it on after the new buyers bought it.'

And then it dawns on me. 'Sorry – do you mean that you are working to sell the house for the *new* buyers? They're *reselling*? Oh my God, maybe I still have a chance! I need to speak to them!'

'Faith...'

'Travis, please, you don't understand how important this is to me! To you, it may just be another listing, but this was m-my home.' *And the last place my mother had been happy. Until she wasn't anymore. All because of a man breaking her heart.*

'Faith, I understand, really I do. But you'd have to be rolling in it to afford to buy it.'

'Which means I can get a mortgage.'

'I know you're doing well, but we're talking millions here. You *know* that.'

I bite my lip. Of course I know. Unless I can get into the Wickfords' graces and earn that kind of money, it'll be quite impossible.

'It's time to let go, Faith. Come with me to New York. Get a fresh start.'

'Just tell me who bought the house off Gabe, Travis.'

'Come on. I can't give you that information.'

'Travis – I have a right to know who I've been killing myself here for. Please. Who am I working for?'

A loud groan, and then: 'Henry.'

19

If I Can't Have You

I can't believe it. My heart is pounding its way out of my chest and into my brain. Henry? Apparently so caring. Apparently so lovely. I had actually hoped – no, *believed* – that there might be something between us. All those kindnesses, those silent looks, the things that remained just under the surface, the words he never said during the day, the naughty ones whispered into my ear, the love that never made it to the surface. But instead, he is The Enemy, the gift that just keeps on giving! First he lies to me about Linda, sleeps with me and then he sells my home without even telling me. Can anyone else see a pattern here?

'Faith? Are you still there? Look—'

'I have to go, it's almost my turn,' I lie as I jab my index against the red icon on my screen and shove my mobile back into my pocket under my costume. I want to hide in here forever, but the kids will be looking for me, so I wipe my eyes and nose and find my way back to the auditorium and our seats, but a massive thing steps in my way.

'Oi – you there!' it says. I look up to see the Kremlin, in all its glory, sneering at me through the turquoise green and white striped dome. Someone's father, unfortunately for them.

Okay, with my green drapery, tablet and torch, not to mention the twenty-five windows in my crown, I may not be as beautiful as him, but at least I don't look down at other monuments. And try to embarrass them on an international level.

'You Gabe York's girlfriend?'

I groan inwardly. 'No, I'm the Statue of Liberty,' I reply cheekily.

He takes a closer look at me, becoming more and more brazen. 'Yeah, it is you. I recognise you. I heard that your house is for sale. What's the least you'll take for it?'

I stop. 'I beg your pardon?'

'I wanna buy the beach house, but I ain't payin' full price, yeah?'

'Well, you don't have to buy that one, then.' Imagine my poor home in the hands of this chav. In comparison, Vanessa's treatment of it would resemble a relaxing session of chromotherapy.

'Listen. I'm buyin' it, and that's the end of it.'

The finality in his words makes my insides lurch. Oh, the arrogance of someone who, God knows how, has managed to accumulate so much wealth and arrogance that he thinks he's entitled to everything under the sun, and that the rules of polite society don't apply to him. How I'd love to take him and people like him a peg or two down, on behalf of people like me.

'Oh, you don't want *that* house,' I say instinctively.

'And why not?' he insists.

'Well, it has its issues,' I say, only *partially* hating myself, because most of me hates Henry.

'What kind of issues?' he asks, his eyebrow shooting up.

'Oh, well, nothing that can't be fixed with a few concrete injections here and there.'

He scratches his head under the dome, arrogance replaced by doubt. 'Are we talking subsidence?'

God, I am awful. But he deserves it for being an absolute swine. 'Oh, I wouldn't go that far. I'm sure it's something any old Larry can fix. Besides the mundic block and Japanese knotweed, I mean.'

His face falls. '*Mundic block?*'

'Yes,' I say gravely. 'You know what that is, don't you? It's basically blocks of concrete mixed with mine waste. Over time, the chemicals cause the concrete to degrade.'

'Well, I'm not buying a house built in mundic block and repatched by any old Larry.' And with that, he and his other colourful foam domes march off.

Yes! Crisis averted for now. I haven't a clue of how I'm going to do it, but I need to get my home back. Because I can't go to New York anymore now. For several reasons. I look at Jowen and Verity, the children that Hope and I brought up together so lovingly all these years without a father, and I know I can't leave them.

We raised them together, and I can't just stop now. I'd be leaving them behind who knows for how many years if New York worked out. And Hope – we've been each other's support system since we were little girls. What am I going to do without her?

And Thea and Rudy and Mike and Paul and Bob and

Bill and... I suddenly realise that I can't bring myself to leave what has become my home, with all the people I love. How can I possibly leave them? We're in this life together. *They*'re my family.

And, well, then there's that other reason that I can't confess to anyone but myself. And Orson was also a beautiful part of it. But all this was before Henry got back with Linda. I know I haven't got a cat's chance in hell to be a part of Henry and Orson's life anymore, of course. And the thought of never seeing them ever again... I swallow.

I don't want to be the odd one out like in my relationship with Gabe. I always seem to be the one who, just like as a child, gets the boot. As if there were no room for me anywhere, and I know that I have no place in Henry's life, but the thought of never seeing him and Orson ever again – I don't know how I'm going to do it.

I have to tell Travis I'm not going to New York. He'll understand. Perhaps, in the future, I may reconsider if the offer still stands. But for now, I can't. So, no, I won't be going to New York anytime soon. Not until I can sew my heart back together again. And Travis needs to know.

The vibrating of my mobile interrupts my thoughts. Speak of the devil. It's Travis again. Maybe I should tell him now that no, I will not make a brand-new start of it, nor be a part of it, New York, New York.

'Just checking on you – you okay?'

'It's going very well, thank you – the kids have stonking costumes and are having a whale of a time.'

'That's good! Look, I know you're upset. Can I swing by, later on?'

'I'm sorry, Travis, but I've got the kids for the night

because Hope is pulling a double shift and won't be home until late.'

He laughs. 'You sure got saddled down there, kid.'

Saddled down? I understand that he's an only child, but they are like my own children.

'Maybe. But I'm their aunt, Travis. It's what families do.'

'Not all the way from New York, you won't.'

Ah. Just the ticket. 'Listen, Travis…'

'What?'

'I'm so sorry, but… I don't think I'll be able to come to New York after all.'

'Listen, I know you're upset about the house. But New York is a great opportunity.'

'I know it is, and again, I'm ever so grateful…'

'But…?'

'It's just that… I don't want to leave Cornwall at the moment,' I mumble.

'You don't want to leave Cornwall?'

'This is my home, and I belong here. Perhaps in the future…'

A long silence, and then: 'This is still about Henry, isn't it?'

'What? No.'

'I get it now,' Travis finally says. 'You were holding out for The Big Guy.'

'What do you mean? Why did you call him The Big Guy?'

'*Hello?* Don't you know who he is? Doesn't his name ring a huge, clanging bell? Tarquin Henry Turner? What kind of an interior designer are you anyway, if you don't even recognise the name of a top architect?'

I gasp as it finally dawns on me. Henry is… *Tarquin*

Turner? The internationally *acclaimed* Tarquin Turner? How am I supposed to have recognised him? The bloke is a mystery as much as he is a national treasure. How was I supposed to know what he looked like? I've never seen a picture of him, what with this mania of secrecy. I had always admired his work, but thought he was some old geezer, a recluse, seeing as he never gives interviews or makes any public appearances either. And, truth be said, it's not like Henry Turner is a particularly unique name, is it? He could, in effect, have been any Tom, Dick or Harry. But the joke's on me.

'I had no idea, but that makes no difference,' I defend. Because, whatever I feel for Henry, my own *private* Henry, I'll just have to keep it away in my heart. 'Look, I'm sorry, I have to go – it's almost our turn. We'll talk tomorrow, okay?'

'Right,' he drawls and hangs up.

On stage, one of Verity's teachers taps the microphone, introducing the Taj Mahal, the Chinese Wall, and finally the Hanging Gardens of Babylon. The overall cheer is so loud we have to cover our ears.

When it's North America's turn, the kids and I cue up behind the Canadian National Tower and, believe it or not, Niagara Falls, with layers and layers of white, blue and green foam jumping off a ledge. You'd think someone would have to be crazy to attempt anything that difficult, but it's rather quite good. I only hope I won't trip or do something to embarrass the kids. The stage and I are not very fond of each other.

'And finally, New York!'

'There's our cue,' I whisper, moving to nudge Verity and Jowen forward, but they're already centre stage, whirling and twirling, especially Jowen who was initially contrary to even wearing a costume. They are absolute naturals and the crowd loves them, strutting their stuff, beaming brighter than the Trevose Head Lighthouse. And then the assistant pops out of the blue, nudging me forward.

Despite my reserve, I saunter out on stage like the most confident model and strut my stuff for the kids, showing the audience the details of all of my pleats, the torch and tablet. Verity and Jowen are ecstatic, jumping up and down as the crowd cheers them on. New York is definitely one of the favourites so far, and why wouldn't it be? It's a great city, or so I hear.

And then we take our final bow and move off the stage, hugging and revelling in the audience's cheers. I swear I have never seen them so happy.

'They loved us!' Verity cries, jumping up and down, hugging us.

'How can they not?' I reply, holding them to me. 'You guys are fantastic!'

'Thanks so much, Auntie Fi! Let's send Mum some selfies!' Jowen suggests, and we strike all sorts of silly poses. See? I can't renounce this. This is love. Family. *Life*.

The Kremlin waddles past, glaring at me, the turquoise stripes on his face closer to purple. Maybe that will teach him to be an arse!

After an evening of soaking up fruit juice and praises for the quality of our costumes, as we are getting ready to leave, my mobile rings again. I should have left it at home, but Hope might need to speak to the kids. I glance at the screen. It's Travis again. I hope he isn't offended by my decision to stay in Cornwall.

'Where the hell are you and what are you doing?' he booms. Obviously, he is.

I stare at my mobile. His face is almost as purple as the Kremlin bloke's. 'I told you, I'm with my niece and nephew. Why?'

'Because my client just rang me to tell me that he will never buy anything from me again, that's why!'

'What? Why?'

'Because you told him that the beach house was slipping into the goddam sea!'

'What...?' Oh crikey. So that chav was Travis's interested party? I bite my lip. 'I didn't exactly say that...'

'You certainly said enough to scare him away! And mundic block, Faith? I'd never even *heard* of it before you mentioned it!'

'I'm sorry, but there will be more buyers. Why is he so important anyway?'

'Only because he's the hugest financial investor in the south-west of England!'

The *Kremlin?* How is that even possible? My throat is suddenly dry. 'I'm sorry, Travis, I truly am. I was just trying to stall the sale until I could somehow find the money to get my home back.'

'As if you were ever going to have three million pounds!' he booms.

Ouch. But who am I kidding? He's absolutely right.

'Henry was banking on that sale, Faith.'

'Henry. And why would bloody Tarquin Henry Turner need the commission from the sale of my home?' Henry is perhaps many things, but greedy, no. If anything, he is generous. This just doesn't tally up.

Travis laughs bitterly. 'Well, I hate to break it to you, Faith, but it was never your home in the first place.'

'What are you talking about? Of course it was. Gabe and I bought it three years ago.'

'Bought it yes. Kept up the mortgage payments, no.'

I know I've misunderstood, because it can't possibly be true. It's utterly ridiculous. 'Wh-what?'

'The guy's in debt, Faith.'

'You're wrong, Travis. Gabe has loads of money.'

'And you believe that just because Gabe told you so? The bloke who's lied to you since the day you met him?'

'What?' I whisper as my knees become rubbery.

'Henry designed and built the beach house,' Travis says with an exasperated sigh. 'And then he sold it to Gabe. Who started going broke, only Henry didn't know. At first Henry chipped in to help pay the mortgage so Gabe – and you – wouldn't lose the house. But after Gabe left you, Henry decided not to help him anymore. So he bought it back from the bank. And now he wants to sell the place off forever. You must be real proud of yourself, Faith! For years you've been squatting in that house unlawfully, and when Henry finally comes to claim what he's due, you have the gall to ruin his reputation with one of the most important investors in the area? What has he ever done to you?'

I simply stare at my phone, his words making no sense. Gabe didn't pay the entire sum? He lied to me? We owe Henry? Henry, who *designed and built* the beach house?

'That's impossible – Henry can't have designed that house – my parents holidayed in it when Henry was still in primary school!'

'No, Faith. Henry built the beach house after tearing

down the old one standing on the same plot, which, funnily enough, actually *was* falling off the cliff.'

The house where my mum was abandoned is not the beach house…? It no longer exists? And for years, I thought I'd vindicated her by living there, and it turned out that the only place I've ever felt at home, my safe place, and I was nothing but a squatter?

'But… but…' is all I can manage as a million things race through my mind. But, most important of them all, I have offended Henry. Not only have I alienated him, but I have also ruined his reputation with an investor, and potentially, his career and perhaps even Orson's wellbeing? Oh, my God!

'But… why didn't he tell me any of this?'

'He didn't have the heart to tell you,' Travis explains curtly. 'If Henry had been a lesser man, he'd have sued you and Gabe for it. But he didn't want you to suffer any more than you already had. He gave up a lot of money, just for you, Faith.'

Henry… did this? For me? No, no, no…

He has been absolutely selfless, and what have I done? I've lost him three million pounds – twice. I've caused him so much damage without even trying!

'I've got to talk to him,' I cry, looking desperately around me. 'Verity! Jowen, we have to go!'

'Well, he's in a late meeting right now and frankly I don't think he wants to speak to you,' Travis informs me.

'But I have to speak to him!' I plead. 'If only to apologise,' I cry and hang up while he's still ranting at how inconsiderate I have been. Well, he's bloody right. Never, ever have I wanted to hurt Henry in any way, despite what happened – or didn't happen – between us. But evidently, I've lost him money and done his career an unimaginable amount of damage with one single lie.

My lip begins to tremble as the enormity of Henry's sacrifices for me and for his former friend Gabe sink in. We owe him our livelihood, to say the least. And Gabe? He'd lied to me from the start, making Henry look like a shark having a hand in selling the beach house, when all he had wanted was to recuperate his three-million-pound loss. He'd been out of pocket for years on end, just to help out a friend who actually ignored and denied his debts.

'What is it, Auntie Fi?' Verity asks as Jowen unzips the top of the Chrysler building from his head. 'Are you okay?'

'We have to go, we have to go!' I urge them and dash for the door.

'Okay!' Jowen agrees, all too happy to have an excuse to keep his costume on and they both follow me out into the parking lot to my car where they pile in without further ado.

'Auntie Fi, where are we going?' Jowen asks from the back seat where he is sprawled horizontally and will remain so until I can get him out of his costume, which is going to be a feat of its own as he seems to want to go to bed wearing it.

'To make amends to someone I have hurt badly,' I answer, wiping my eyes with one hand while with the other I grind the gearstick, tunnel-visioning the road. Will he ever forgive me for any of it all?

'Who did you hurt, Auntie Fi?'

'Only the kindest, most selfless man in the world,' I mumble.

'You mean Henry?' Verity asks me.

'Uh, yes...'

I look at her costume of the Fearless Girl and hope that she will always be so, even once the costume is off for good. I wonder if it would fit me at all, because right now I need all the courage I can muster to talk to him. Even if he's married and just about as emotionally screwed up as I am, that doesn't mean I shouldn't be grateful for everything else he's done for me.

'You must never be afraid to go after what you want, Verity,' I inform her through a tight throat. 'Because you should never be ashamed. Of anything.'

'I'm not, Auntie Fi,' she reassures me.

'Good girl!'

I want her to never be afraid to go after what she wants, as opposed to me. All my life I've lived in fear of stepping on other people's toes, afraid of the sound of my own voice. Even the bloody Wickfords – I was never confident enough to actually go and find them, march right in there and tell them what I could do.

And Henry – if I'd told him about my growing feelings without being afraid, maybe he and I would actually be together. But a bolder woman beat me to it. Granted, Linda had dibs on him being Orson's mother, but still I should have had the courage to go up to him and tell him while he was single. But it's too late for all that now. I'll be lucky if he ever forgives me.

'What did you do?' Verity insists.

'It's not what I did, it's what I didn't do.'

'Can't you just say you forgot?'

'Oh, sweetie, if only it were that simple,' I whisper as I

finally get to the main road. His office is a good ride away, but I have to give it everything I've got if I have half a chance to apologise. I don't want to lose his friendship. I have come to care for him much too much.

I speed-dial Thea. 'Yellow,' she greets me.

'Thea! I need you to babysit Verity and Jowen, can you?'

'Of course! Are you okay?'

'I'm in a pickle. Can you meet me at Henry's office in Truro? I'll look up the address...'

'I know where it is. See you in twenty.'

'Thank you, you're an absolute star!' I call before I ring off. 'I promise I will make it up to you, guys,' I repeat, feeling horrible for dragging them away from their night. Apparently I've got a lot of making up to do.

'Are you kidding me?' Verity chimes. 'This is like in a real romcom!'

'What do you know about romcoms?'

'I watch them all the time, Auntie Fi! This is where you rush to tell him you love him!'

Clever girl! If only I could. But life has its own course.

And in a moment, it all becomes instantly clear to me who the complete, voluntary villain was here. Gabe was not, as he'd claimed, a victim of circumstances, but of his own stupidity and flightiness. He'd bought a house he couldn't afford. I had no idea whatsoever that we had been in trouble. The one thing I leave in Gabe's trust, and he manages to screw it up royally.

To think that all these years I'd revered him for his musical talent, his engaging smile and catchy way with words and music, when instead I'd completely overlooked his immense ability to weave tall tales, his selfishness, his temper tantrums and his instinct for survival at any cost, including those of his friends. And my own.

How could I have not seen what he was doing to me? How could I have been so blind to it all, defending him in the eyes of Henry, who had instead been the victim for years on end?

Henry's kindness and generosity have no end. And I have made an absolute fool of myself in his eyes.

My phone rings loud on the Bluetooth system and without taking my eyes off the road, I push the answer button, hoping it's Henry. Even if I don't deserve him to call me, unless it's to cover me with insults. That's what I deserve.

'Hey, Babes…' comes the dreamy voice of the man who has ruined my life.

'Kids – put your headphones on and listen to your music.'

'Yay!' they agree, and in one second they have zoned out, allowing me to deliver one of my special masterpieces. And do I owe it him.

'Don't you Babes me,' I start on him like an old, disgruntled wife. Thank God we had never married. 'When the hell were you going to tell me that our home was never ours? That you lied to me and never actually paid Henry for the house? I can't believe you kept it from me all this time!'

'But I did it for you…'

'Me? You did what for me exactly, Gabe?'

'You wanted that house.'

'Yes, for my own reasons, which you never understood. But you know what, Gabe? You're right – I should have never trusted you with it. Knowing your financial skills.'

'But, I did it for you – I'd have been happy even in a hut with you,' he moans.

'Oh, don't even try that on, you miserable, lying, cheating...' My eyes swing to the rear-view mirror as I clamp my mouth shut, but whether it's to stop yelling or to stifle a sob, I'm still not sure.

'I'm hanging up,' I warn him and ring off.

All I know is that, together and in different ways, we've wronged Henry terribly. Gabe has tried to put him off, and instead of making it better for Henry, what do I do? I lose him the very buyer who will put Henry back in the black. And all for a house? Bricks and mortar? What the hell is wrong with me, if I can value an object more than a person?

He must think very lowly of us – *I* think very lowly of us, and although I feel my faults very keenly and am deeply ashamed, there is nothing I can do to put it right but grovel for his forgiveness. And then, he'll never have to see me ever again.

As I make a wide turn, my mobile rings again.

'Hi, Faith. It's Vanessa.'

What a coincidence. 'I have just found out what a—' I sneak a peek at the kids in the back and readjust my verbal register. 'I've just discovered a thing or two about our golden boy – not.'

'What do you mean?'

I don't know why I'm even telling my nemesis something so personal – perhaps to ward off any future probability of her making the huge mistake of giving that tosser another chance. A chance he simply doesn't deserve. After all, we ladies have to stick together.

'That Gabe had never fully paid for the house. Did you know that?'

'No!' she gasps.

'Yes!' I assure her.

'Unbelievable! But what do you care now anyway? We're both free of him, and that can only be a good thing.'

'Of course,' I agree. 'I can only pity his next victim. But more than that, I'm angry with myself for—'

'For what? Why are you mad at yourself?'

I huff. What the heck, I might as well. 'Well... I've sort of scored an own goal.' I roll my eyes at my own idiocy, because even I can't believe what I've done.

'What do you mean?'

'I bit the hand that fed me. Henry Turner designed and built the beach house. But Gabe never paid for it.'

'Why not? Money's never been a problem for him.'

'Well, apparently he couldn't pay for the house. By that time we were already living in it, and he asked Henry for some more time. Henry agreed, being his friend. But things just got worse and worse for Gabe who, however, never owned up to it. He never told me we were living off someone else's charity. Henry brought a couple around a few months ago to look at it, but I didn't know the house was his.'

'Of course not, how could you?' she sympathises and for the first time ever I feel that she understands where I'm coming from.

'So how did you score your own goal?' she asks.

'Well, in order to keep my home, which I thought was rightfully mine, I... told a prospective buyer that the house was sinking into the sea.'

Vanessa gasps. 'You didn't!'

'I did. I've ruined Henry's reputation. And there's nothing I can do to help him get it back. I'm on my way to his office.'

'What are you going to do?'

'I'm not quite sure yet. He'll most likely have me kicked out the minute he sees my face,' I moan.

'Not if I'm with you.'

'What? Oh. Thanks, Vanessa, but I don't think—'

'Relax, his family and my family are very old friends.'

'Really?'

'He'll listen to me. I'll meet you at his offices!'

'Where are they?'

'Breakwater Street in Truro. You really had no idea of who he is, did you?'

'No, of course not.' But it doesn't change a thing. And considering what I've done to him, his security will probably throw me out the minute they see me. But with Vanessa, I might have half a chance. What an ironic turn my life has taken, if I need my nemesis to help me talk to the man I had been slowly building a special friendship with. But Henry is worth the humiliation. Anything to undo the damage I've caused him.

'Okay, thank you, Vanessa!' I call into my mobile. 'See you there!'

Checking traffic, I merge onto a wider road as my satnav goes completely barmy on me, giving directions to turn left, right, to go straight and finally go straight at a T-junction by ramming into a low stone wall. I pull over onto the kerb to check my whereabouts, and, yes, gather my wits. I reprogramme it for Breakwater Street in Truro. That should be straightforward enough. Only it isn't, and it takes me longer than I'd anticipated, and when we finally pull up, Vanessa is waiting for me at the entrance alongside Thea.

'Okay, guys, off you go with Thea! She'll take you to her home and order you a pizza, is that okay?'

I'm a horrible, horrible aunt. But they don't seem to think so.

'Good luck, Auntie Fi!' Verity shouts as they pile into Thea's car.

'Go get him, girl!' she calls as she drives off.

I make a mad dash for Vanessa.

'You're takin' the piss, right?' she demands, wide-eyed, as I rush to the doors, forgetting all about my costume.

I look down at my forgotten bronze and green pleated garment. 'Oh, crap!'

But to think that Vanessa has the gall to criticise one of my outfits is truly rich.

'Never mind.' She hastens me towards the door. 'Let's go, go, gooooohmy*gawwwwwwd*!'

'What? What is it?' I cry as she doubles over, grabbing my wrist.

'Pain! The baby!'

'What?' I gasp.

'The baby, the baby – I can't lose my baby, I can't lose my baby,' she cries and I feel her fear in her grip, see it in her lost eyes. 'It happened to my mother, but I can't – I couldn't stand to lose my baby!'

The motherly love she is feeling shakes me to my very core, snapping me out of my own plight. Vanessa is carrying a baby. A real person inside her. And she's afraid of losing it.

'You won't,' I promise her. 'Don't be afraid.' Which is exactly how I'm feeling as I steer her to my car. 'We'll get you to the A&E in a jiffy!'

Without further ado, I bundle her into the back seat.

'Hurryyyy!' Vanessa pleads, beginning to cry again.

'Hang on just a little longer!' I say in an even voice.

'To whaaaat?' she screeches.

Trying to keep it together, I reverse out of my parking spot and shift into first gear, heading off like we're being chased by the devil himself. With any luck the coppers will be on our trail and we can get them to escort us to the A&E like you see in the movies.

By the time we get to the hospital Vanessa and I are pretty much in the same perspiratory state and I wouldn't mind having a little screaming session myself.

'Please don't leave me, please don't leave,' she wails as she bends over at the waist, huffing and puffing.

'Of course I won't leave you, Vanessa,' I promise.

'And please don't tell Gabe!'

'Of cour— What?'

'I don't want him anywhere near me! I'll kill him if I see him!' she hollers, and something tells me it's not just the cramps speaking.

Thankfully, bless the NHS, just as we pass the threshold, a nurse with a wheelchair comes rushing to our assistance, and Vanessa is whisked away into very capable hands.

I pull out Vanessa's phone from her bag and call her parents who promise they're on their way, thankfully.

Gabe. Vanessa has specifically asked me to not call him. What right have I to go against someone's wishes? Gabe has, in my biased opinion, forgone any rights to anything, but luckily I can't be blamed for Vanessa's decision.

I pull out my phone and send Hope a voice message to explain that the kids are with Thea and that as soon as I'm done I'll fetch them and bring them back home. When she texts back a thumbs up, her faith in me warms me from the inside out. I know she trusts me completely because I've co-raised them, but it feels so good to be appreciated and trusted with something so precious as her children.

And then I begin to think of Vanessa's baby and pray with everything I've got that they'll both be okay. She doesn't need Gabe, and the good thing is that her parents will be there for her. She's lucky in that. And I know that, despite her craziness, Vanessa is going to be fine. She has a support system behind her.

I look up as Vanessa's parents, breathless and worried, burst through the main entrance.

I point to the left and, nodding blindly, they race in that direction.

Henry. Should I try and call him? To what end? He'll only kick me out. But I have to make good what I did wrong. Surely Verity and Jowen know the Kremlin's kids? Perhaps I could get his name off them and speak to him directly?

Mr Chatsbury is signalling to me from across the corridor and I jump to my feet and rush to his side.

'She's okay – they're both okay. She's still pregnant,' he croaks, breaking down from the sheer relief. Poor, poor man. It's so wonderful to see the love he has for his daughter despite all the trouble she has put them through all those years. Most parents do love their children, no matter what, and it's so beautiful to see a huge, iron-hard man like him succumb to love.

Before I can help myself, I throw my arms around him. 'I knew it. Oh, thank God!'

'Thank you, Faith,' he sniffs. 'For what you did. I know that you and Vanessa—'

'Forget it – it's all water under the bridge,' I assure him. And, strangely, something I thought I'd never in a million years think, I realise it is. In the face of something like this, old grudges don't matter anymore. Life is not about keeping score.

'Go on in, she wants to see you,' he says, wiping his eyes.

I smile at him and head off for room twenty-two and stop at the door. There she is, haggard but all smiles. 'Hey…' she chimes softly. 'Looks like we made it.'

I nod. 'I'm so relieved you're okay. You're both okay.'

'Thanks to you and your quick response. They should have you on their emergency team here.'

I bite my lip. 'Vanessa, anything you need—'

'I know,' she says, smiling up at me. 'Who knew, you and me, actual… friends?'

I nod and swipe at a tear. I don't know why I'm crying. All I know is that I can't I stop.

'You need to go, now, Faith. Go talk to Henry.'

I bite my lip. 'Are you sure?'

'Faith – you saved our lives. Now go and talk to him.'

'Okay.' I roll my eyes. 'If he'll even listen.'

'Of course he will. I know Henry – he's a reasonable man. If you explain it to him—'

'There's nothing that can excuse me, Vanessa. I acted badly.' Apparently she wasn't the only monster around. 'I have ruined his business. How can I ever fix that?'

'By going to him – now.'

'Okay, then.'

I pat her arm awkwardly. We'll get there, eventually, I think. 'Get some rest.'

'Keep me posted!' Vanessa calls after me and I wave back at her. Friends. Indeed, whoever saw that one coming?

I go back to my car and head to what is hopefully the last leg of my *Making Amends Journey*.

About thirty minutes later, only a few minutes away from Henry's offices, my mobile rings.

'Faith?'

'Travis…'

'So you haven't seen Henry yet?'

'Not yet. I'm going to his office right now.'

'It's no use. He's left.'

'Left for where?'

'The airport. That's all I know.'

'Oh for Christ's *sake*,' I groan, preparing for a U-turn. 'Okay. Thanks. I only hope I'll get there in time before he…' I swallow, unable to speak. I have to speak to him before he leaves. I can't bear the weight of this any longer. So what if he hates my guts now. I still need to explain. To say I'm sorry. To tell him that I never meant him any harm. And that I forgive him for leading me on, when instead he was getting back with his wife. Technically, we're even. But I still need closure.

'So you really do love him, then,' Travis says softly.

'Travis—'

'I guess I wasn't good enough for you.'

'That has nothing to do with Henry. Please don't be upset, Travis. Ours was always a friendship – you know that.'

'Well, I was kinda hoping it would evolve into something better.'

'Yes, well. I'm sorry.'

He sighs. 'No hard feelings, Faith. I tried. And good luck. I'll put in a good word for you in New York anyway – just say when.'

'Thank you, Travis. You're a great friend.'

'Yeah, yeah, whatever.'

'Bye!' I chime as I ring off.

I know I'm still dressed as the Statue of Liberty, but at this point, what does it even matter anymore? I've already ruined my chances of work in this corner of the world anyway, so I might as well go the whole hog and try to save someone else's career. And I've got a very narrow margin of a window to do it.

20

If I Could Turn Back Time

At the airport, I screech into a semi-parking spot between two dark, shiny, expensive-looking cars that look like Transatlantic liners, but my car is small and I easily slip out through the crack in my door.

Oh God, I hope I'm not late.

Still wearing my headpiece as it is weaved into my own hair and all the accessories – i.e. the torch and the tablet which are attached to the costume, all I can say is I'm here, I'm green and I need to come clean.

So once inside, I scan the flight boards, realising that I don't even know where he's bound.

I could call Travis but by the time I catch a hold of him it might be too late. He's probably already taxiing down the runway this very second. I run to the desk and ask someone from the staff to tannoy him. Behind the desk, the young man's eyes pop out of his head, but he's too polite to say anything as he does my bidding. If he's still in the building I might be able to catch him before he whisks off.

Too nervous to sit, I wait by the desk. Several minutes pass, but nothing happens. 'Can you repeat the announcement, please?' I ask.

The young chap nods, hiding a smile. He thinks I'm trying to impress someone with a romantic Hollywood gesture. If he only knew how unimpressed Henry will be.

I wait a few minutes more, and he looks up at me with a kind but resigned shrug. 'I'm sorry, miss, but there doesn't seem to be a Henry Turner in the building.'

'What about the flights? Can we check the passenger lists?'

'I'm sorry, but that information is—'

'Confidential,' I conclude sadly. He's gone God knows where, and it'll probably be weeks before I see him again. I nod my thanks to the young man and turn away. It might be too late now, but I whip out my phone. Travis will at least know where he's gone. Not that it makes a difference now.

'Miss? Are you sure he's a passenger?' the chap asks me.

I whirl around to stare at him. 'What do you mean?'

'Are you aware that we have conference rooms?'

I clutch at the edge of the desk. 'Conference rooms…?'

'For business meetings. Would you like me to check if he's booked one? That I can do.'

'Please!' I breathe, watching him type away on a keyboard.

His face lights up. 'Ah. Right down the first corridor, last door to your left.'

'Oh, thank you, thank you!' I whisper, unable to manage anything more. I'd vault over the counter and kiss him if I could, but I really don't want to leave any traces of my green paint on him.

So I race down the first corridor and make for the last door to my left, skid to a halt at another sodding reception desk where a wide-eyed woman in a neat updo and a proper business jacket jumps at the sight of me, as you do when a green woman appears before you out of nowhere. She blinks at me repeatedly, as if I'm a dust particle in her fake lashes that will disappear if she bats them hard enough. Unfortunately for her, I'm still here.

'Faith Hudson to see Mr Henry Turner,' I gasp, barely able to breathe now. Boy, am I unfit, if only ten yards have left me wheezing. But it's not the physical exertion – my heart is jackhammering its way up my throat for a very different reason.

'Mr Turner is unavailable at the moment,' she answers, trying to mask the horror spreading across her face as she takes in every detail of my appearance.

'It's pretty urgent,' I rasp. 'A matter of life and death, actually…'

'I'm sorry, but Mr Turner is in the middle of a meeting. A very important one, in fact.'

'That's exactly why I'm here!' I cry with a bit of poetic licence. 'To save his butt!'

'But…' she counters, uncertainty on her face.

'Please! Where is he?' I beg.

She picks up the phone on her desk. 'I'll announce you. Your name again?'

'Not necessary,' I inform her as I round the desk and open a door leading to a flight of stairs. I catapult myself up them, snagging my costume on the banister finial, and I'm aware of a blast of cold air, but push it to the back of my mind as I'm running like the wind now, taking the steps two at a time to what I now realise is the third floor and wheezing like a chainsaw.

When I get to the top, there's a young man standing by the door, but by God, I'm ready to take him down too.

'Hey! Stop!' he cries as I whizz past him without altering my pace. I'm getting good at this.

There is a short corridor flanked by doors on each side, but instinct tells me to head for the set of double doors at the end.

'I said *stop*!' cries the bloke from behind me, and as he is the only thing (metaphorically) standing between me and doing the right thing, I make a break for it by sprinting towards the double doors and slam into them with all my weight, only they swing open too easily and I am hurled through the air and land flat on my face.

All around me is darkness and silence, until a familiar voice reaches me. A full, baritone voice that I can't quite place.

'Faith...? You're here...'

Where the bloomin' hell is *here*?

'Ow, ow, ow,' I hear myself say, rolling over onto my back, which hurts like hell, and, on top of everything else, I sound like Donald Duck.

'I'm sorry, Mr Turner,' apologises someone else from above me. 'But she just came out of nowhere and—'

'Just fetch me a cloth and some ice,' comes that deep, caressing voice again. Is it...? Dare I hope... Henry? What's he doing in my home? I open my eyes to see I am surrounded by a group of curious faces staring down at me. Faces I've never seen before. And I'm not at home. Something is definitely wrong here.

And then he comes into view, kneeling down to me. 'Heddry…?' I whisper, my voice cracking, and I can taste something coppery in my mouth. My nose is bleeding, but I don't care. 'Is it really you…?'

'Jesus, Faith, are you all right?' he demands, but his voice isn't angry, but more pleading as he helps me sit up, and I realise that my entire front is covered in blood.

'I'b sorry,' I say. 'I cabe to speak to you, Heddry – to beg you to forgive be…'

At that, he looks over at the gobsmacked group of people. 'Uh, ladies and gentlemen, if you'll please excuse us. Let's get you cleaned up. You sound like you may have broken your nose.'

'Doh!' I suddenly sob. If you can imagine me begging in a nasal voice, it basically went like this:

'I came here to tell them, especially Mr Kremlin!'

Henry's eyebrows shoot up. 'Mr Kremlin?'

'Kremlin!' I repeat. 'As in Moscow! He was wearing a foam costume at school!'

'Faith, you need to stay still now while we call for a medic…'

'Henry – it's important! They have a right to know what I did to you!'

He looks at me uncertainly, and then at his small audience. 'Faith, I hardly think—'

'Please,' I beg, struggling to my feet and turning to the wide-eyed people at the conference table. And there he is, the Kremlin bloke. 'I need to tell you the entire Truth, Mr Kremlin!'

'Oh God,' Henry groans and runs his hand through his dark hair. 'You've done enough, Faith, trust me.'

'Mr Kremlin,' I say, hobbling towards him as Henry's hand steadies me and applies a handkerchief full of ice cubes to my nose.

'Later, Henry,' I say, pushing it away. I know that, with blood spattered all over my green face and costume, I look like nothing they've ever seen before, but I have to get this out now or I'll never forgive myself.

'Please, I have to apologise to you especially. I lied to you when I said that the beach house was slipping into the sea. I only said that because I thought you were a buyer.'

At that, his eyebrows rise even higher. 'I *was* a buyer, young lady, but after your stories of mundic block and Japanese knotweed—'

'I know, and I'm so, so sorry! It was all a lie so that you wouldn't buy the house! I was being selfish because I wanted it for myself! But I can assure you that it's solid and sturdy and as safe as a mother's arms. And because Henry designed it. Anything he designs comes from the heart. And he has a huge heart! He is a true gentleman. Did you know that he helped us pay the mortgage several times? I've only just found out myself.'

'Faith—' comes Henry's voice from behind me. I look back at him, biting my lip. He is more beautiful than I even remember him. Because it seems that I haven't seen him for years and years, during which I've yearned for him like craving for water through the drought of a desert.

I turn back to Henry's investor. 'If you don't buy the beach house, someone else will, and you'll be regretting it for a long, long time, sir.'

'And why is that?' he wants to know.

'Because you'd be buying a piece of Henry's heart. He put his entire self in that home. That house is founded on the man's integrity.'

'Faith...' Henry calls me.

I turn to him in earnest. 'Please let me finish Henry – you deserve more than that. Did you know, sir, that instead of kicking me out of his home, he even made me some truly exquisite furniture – as a gift?'

Henry groans under his breath. 'Faith, thank you, but my guests aren't here to hear about my private life and those close to me.'

'Am I, then? Still close to you?' I ask hopefully.

All heads turn to him.

'As a friend,' I assure them. 'He's got a wife. And an adorable little boy – his name is Orson – whom I love with all my heart, but I would never go near a married man. I've had that done to me, and believe me, it's the last thing I would do to anyone else, and I'm—'

'Faith – enough, now.'

'Oh, Henry, I'm really, really sorry for everything that I've done to you. I never meant to hurt you or let alone damage your company! You are an honest man with solid principles and if anyone doubts that, well then I say they don't know their arse from their elbow!'

'No one is doubting his value, nor his honour,' one of the women seated at the table reassures me. 'As a matter of fact, we are here to listen to his recommendations.'

'Oh? Good! Well then, in that case,' I turn to give him a heavy pat on the chest, 'Good luck. I'll leave you to it. I'm sorry for barging in on you like that.'

And, having done what I'd come for, and having no other excuse to stay and just gaze at him adoringly, with a heavy heart, I turn to go.

'One moment, young lady,' the woman says.

'Oh God,' Henry groans under his breath, wiping his brow.

'It's okay, Henry – I've got you covered,' I whisper to him.

She gets up and comes to stand opposite me, her eyes narrowing. 'Aren't you Faith Hudson, the interior designer who did Gabe York's home?'

'Yes, it's precisely her,' Henry assures her. 'But please don't—'

I blink. Oh my God, if she takes one single dig about my viral arse, I'm going to give *her* a nosebleed. 'Yes, as a matter of fact I am.' I wipe my eyes, ready for it. I'll face the humiliation. Anything to restore Henry's reputation.

She holds out her hand. 'Pleased to meet you. Patricia Wickford.'

A huge, eerie sensation is mushrooming in my mind. 'Sorry? Did you just say Patricia Wickford?' *The elusive Lady Patricia Wickford?*

'Yes. And this is my husband Robert.'

As in Lord Robert Wickford? 'Oh my dear *God*, so you really do exist!' is all I can say. 'I was beginning to wonder.'

At that, Lady Wickford throws her head back and laughs. 'You see, Bopper?' she says, turning to her husband. 'I told you we were too reclusive!'

'So this is the young lady you were telling us about, Henry? The prodigy?' the older man wants to know.

At that, Henry coughs. 'Yes, Bopper – the up-and-coming designer who years ago won the award for her Home Hugs.'

Lady Wickford's face lights up. 'Yes, yes, of course! I love them!'

'My dear, I also seem to remember you had quite a spill that evening, didn't you?' Lord Wickford says.

'Bopper, you old sod, don't embarrass the girl,' she murmurs affectionately, then turns to me again. 'Please forgive him. He's not very good at holding his drink. I'm going to have to bribe the hostess to let us onto our flight. But he does have a good memory. So, Faith Hudson, we finally meet.'

'Yes.' *And you two*, I suddenly realise, *are the couple who came to see the house the day I met Henry.*

'I absolutely hate Gabe York's music,' Lord Wickford sentences. 'It's too loud and in your face.'

'Oh.' *Shitty, shit shit.*

'But I absolutely loved his house before Vanessa got to it.'

'Oh!' My breath escapes me so loudly it almost comes out as a scream. 'You do?' I brave a look around the table as people nod in agreement.

'Absolutely,' he says. 'It's the work of someone with excellent taste. Not that you'd know by looking at you now. I can only assume that you weren't exactly planning to be here at our business meeting.'

'That's right, Bopper,' Henry intervenes. 'Miss Hudson had no idea of our meeting. A word, Faith?' he says, turning to me.

'Uhm, okay.'

With a hand to my elbow, he guides me to the next room and closes the door. 'Just where the hell have you been?' he demands. 'I've been calling you for days! Why didn't you answer me?'

'I only just got all your missed calls. In any case, I thought you wanted to sleep with me!'

His head snaps back as if I'd slapped him. 'You've made it very clear that that's not happening,' he says in his deep, deep voice.

'No, it isn't. So why did you call me?'

'Because I remembered that I had your memory stick from when you last came to my home. And Trixie and Bopper were in between flights so I arranged to meet them here – with you. In proper clothes, not looking like... what is it you're wearing anyway?'

'I was at my niece's and nephew's World Monuments night at school. I was the Statue of Liberty.'

'How very apt. Right, let's get back in there. Jesus, you look horrible.'

And you look absolutely gorgeous as always, I almost say, but catch myself just in time.

'We hear that you're going to New York with Travis?' Patricia says when we go back into the conference room.

I refrain from rolling my eyes. Does Henry tell them everything? 'No, not anymore.'

'You're not?' Henry asks, doing a double-take.

I shake my head.

'But why? Travis has offered you a tremendous opportunity to work in the United States.'

'I don't want to work in the United States. I want to stay right here.' *With you. Only you are still in love with your ex-wife.*

Henry's eyes almost pop out of his head and then he checks himself.

'Well, that's excellent news,' Lord Wickford says. 'We

wouldn't want to lose you before we even got the chance to work with you, now would we?'

I turn to him. 'I beg your pardon?'

Lady Wickford laughs. 'Henry, you devil! Have you not told Miss Hudson about our plans?'

I stare at them, one by one. *Plans?*

He clears his throat. 'Actually, I tried leaving her a message, but it must have got lost, what with her trip to Italy and all…'

'Italy?' I ape, my eyes swinging to Henry's.

'Sicily, wasn't it?' he says.

I'm only a nanosecond behind. 'Oh! Yes, Sicily – an absolute paradise!'

Lord and Lady Wickford exchange smiles and nod in agreement. 'We did Taormina, but thought it was too elitist, you know, with all the rock stars like Bono and Mick Hucknall and Sting milling around. We like the simple life, small villages, you know?'

I swallow. 'Well, then, I can certainly give you some pointers on where to go for peace and quiet.'

'Brilliant, brilliant!' she enthuses. 'Now, we need someone to do our new offices in Truro, Faith. May we call you Faith?'

I nod in total stupor. This must be *The Twilight Zone* or somewhere abouts.

'Excellent. And you must call us Trixie and Bopper. Any dear friend of Henry's is also ours.'

I nod again, my mind still racing. Offices in Truro?

'Bopper and I are off to France, but it seemed important to Henry that we see your work and oh am I glad that we did!' she says, taking my hands as if I were her very best friend and confidante. 'We absolutely love what we've seen of your work, Faith.'

'I, uhm, thank you…'

'So please pitch away,' she says, sitting down at the table again.

'Pitch…?' I squeak, my knees turning to water. Years and years of killing myself to get their attention, and now that they are actually waiting for me to say something totally brilliant that will knock their socks off. I've got nothing but a torn shift (so that's why my back was freezing) and a bleeding nose?

And all these years I have strived to look the part, to never leave anything unplanned, and now, at the most important moment of my career, instead of looking professional in the outfit that I had actually bought especially for this one day in the future, I have green paint on my face and arms and I'm wearing something akin to a sack of potatoes and a spiky crown with its twenty-five bloody windows.

'Er, Trixie?' Henry says. 'Faith had no idea we were expecting a pitch. Perhaps another time, when you return?'

The gurus of interior design turn to look at me. 'Oh? The fact is that we don't rightly know when we'll be back. Shame.'

'I can do it now,' I assure them.

Henry's eyebrows shoot into his hairline in shock. 'Now?'

'Of course. Is that okay?'

His gaze swings to Lady Wickford who eyes Lord Wickford. 'Why not? It'll be in the most peculiar circumstances, with you dressed as the Statue of Liberty, of all things, but perhaps that's a good omen?'

'Okay, then, Lady and Lord Wickford, get ready for some original ideas.'

And I don't know what's happened to me, but suddenly I'm in Wonder Woman mode. I start telling them what they lack and I see Henry's face going pale, but I ignore him. Enough of this deference. They need to know what's missing in their exemplary style. An injection of spontaneity. And I am giving them just that, not with my ideas, but with whom I have finally let myself go to finally be.

I'm so lost in my project that idea after idea comes to me and I can tell by the look on Henry's face that I'm totally smashing it. The couple are nodding at me and my confidence is growing by the second.

A month ago, if you'd told me that I would be doing a pitch to the ever-elusive Wickfords, I'd have laughed at you. But I would have been harbouring that hope in my heart. But if you'd told me that I'd be covered in green paint, I'd have said you were delirious. But now *I'm* delirious. I can't even believe myself as all of my most personal and intimate ideas are flying out of my mouth. And what's even more crazy is that they are nodding at me and smiling. It might all be politeness in the name of their friendship with Henry, but nothing can stop me now. For almost twenty minutes I dazzle them, checking Henry's face every now and then. He, too, has sat down next to them, his eyes fixed on me, his face mirroring his pride.

When I'm done, Lady Wickford rises, followed by her husband and Henry. 'My dear, you are a force of nature! I love your style and ideas – Bopper, what do you think?' she says, turning to Lord Wickford who raises his hands almost in defeat.

'Absolutely smitten,' he says. 'Simple ideas, and yet... genius.'

Lady Wickford nods. 'Yes, yes!'

Henry exhales, and some colour returns to his face. 'Brilliant,' he breathes. 'Thank you for your time, Trixie – Bopper. I know you have a flight to catch.'

She looks at her watch. 'Yes, we do have to go now. Would you both like to join us for dinner and to discuss the details of our offer next Friday?'

Dinner? *Offer?* 'Oh, absolutely, thank you,' I manage to say.

'Brilliant, Henry will bring you,' she sing-songs, reaching up on her tiptoes to kiss his cheek.

'Good fun, Henry!' Bopper calls as they head off.

We both watch as, arm in arm, Lady and Lord Wickford float out of the conference room.

I am still in shock. What can I possibly say?

'Thank you, Henry, for organising this,' I whisper, looking up at him. I had had no idea that he had planned this. He'd believed in me enough to contact them and ask them to give me a chance. Well, at least he believed in me? Or had he done it just to ease his conscience about what he did to me? Nothing can erase that, and if we'll never be lovers, I can at least express my gratitude to him for changing my life with one single phone call.

'And thank you for waiting all those years for Gabe. He never – I had no idea, Henry.'

He looks down at me, his face set as stone, his blazing eyes the only mobile part of him.

'You've cost me quite a lot, Faith,' he says, so angry that his voice is barely audible.

'I know,' I say, clearing my suddenly dry throat.

'I had absolutely no idea Gabe had never actually paid for

the house and he never said anything to me about the debt. Once the record deals came pouring in, I assumed we were doing okay. I know I've caused you nothing but trouble lately, but if you can find it in your heart to forgive me…? I'll work for you for free, in order to pay our debt.' God knows how I'm going to eat, but there are more important things than food. There's dignity, and reputation, and not hurting or taking from others.

'It's not your debt to pay, Faith,' he replies, his eyes slowly sweeping across my face, down to my lips and then back to my eyes and it's all I can do to not throw my arms around him and pick up where we'd left off the last time we were alone together. But I can't. He has a wife and a son, and even if I have no children of my own—

'*Shit!*' I suddenly cry, gathering my costume from around my ankles and making a mad dash for the doors.

'What? What is it?' Henry calls after me.

'I forgot to pick up the Chrysler building and the Fearless Girl!'

21

Bridge Over Troubled Water

'I can't believe it!' Hope says on speakerphone as I am getting dressed for my Friday night dinner with the Wickfords just returned from France – oh, *pardon*, my new *amis* Trixie and Bopper – and Henry.

'Believe it. Henry is going to be here to pick me up in a few minutes.'

'Henry, huh?' she sing-songs.

'Please don't,' I beg, huffing as I climb into my new dress. It's not green, luckily, but it should leave a lasting impression on them as I've chosen well – a proper turquoise cocktail dress. No slits, no plunging cleavages that will embarrass me in any way. 'It's hard enough as it is, seeing Henry and – well.'

'But why do you have to go with him, then? And he was happy to, after what you did to him?'

'What about what he did to me? In any case, he couldn't refuse, after all that, could he?'

'No, I suppose not. Rich people are so complicated.'

'Yes, but they do seem nice.'

'So what are you and Henry going to talk about on the way there?' Hope wants to know.

'Terrific question. I don't know. It'll be pretty quiet in that car, I suspect. I've apologised, so what else is there to say?'

'Well, good luck, keep me posted.'

'I will,' I promise as the buzzer goes. 'That's him! Got to go.'

'Good luck!' she calls. 'Love you!'

'Me, too!' I call just before I hang up and answer the door.

If on one hand I'm shaking myself to pieces about discussing the Wickfords' response to my pitch, on the other hand, sitting next to Henry in his 4x4, desiring him so much and knowing that I can't have him isn't much of a picnic either.

There are a million things roiling around in my mind, but at the top of the list is how I've lost him. I truly wanted him in my life, and Orson. But I screwed up and he's gone back to his wife and now it's much too late. Whatever he felt for me in that brief spell, is definitely, permanently over.

I turn to the impassive face next to me, wishing I could just reach up and kiss his lips, and that his indifference would melt into an astonished face and then, finally, a searing kiss, hopefully without swerving into the wrong lane or crashing, which would serve our sinner arses just right.

But we are past that. I'd had a sliver of an opportunity to tell him my feelings for him, and find out if he, too, felt the same way. But, seeing as he and Linda have patched things up, it is probably better this way.

I wonder if he's told her he has a business meeting tonight, and if she believes him?

'Right, here we are,' he says finally, parking on a narrow lane. I have not paid any attention whatsoever to my surroundings, and now turn to baulk at him.

'What are we doing here at your place? I thought it was at the Wickfords' house.'

He slides me a sexy grin. I wish he'd stop doing that. I'm already unsettled and frazzled enough as it is. I truly hope that this dinner goes well because I am going to have to throw myself into work from now on just to get Henry off my mind. How I'm going to manage that, I don't quite know yet.

'This *is* the Wickfords' house.'

I gasp as it dawns on me. 'You and the Wickfords are *neighbours*?'

'That we are.'

'Aren't you just *full* of surprises. Why didn't you tell me?'

He dips his head. 'I promised to respect their privacy.'

'Oh. Of course. Sorry.' I turn and look at the manor. 'Such an old family must have a million stories to tell.'

'Oh, there are plenty of those in this house,' he promises me as he gets out and opens my door for me, textbook English gentleman. 'Come on. I bet they've got quite a few to share tonight.'

'Wait,' I beg, holding on to his arm as he rings the bell.

He turns back to me. 'What's up?'

Suddenly I'm not so sure I'm ready for this.

'Relax, Faith. You'll be fine. They already love you,' he assures me. 'Come, now.'

If the first time I'd seen this house by day, by night I am dazzled by the number of lights of every kind – LED, candles, silk shades, paper shades visible through the windows.

My eyes swing to his again, and that delicious, naughty mouth curves into a smile as he leads the way and the door is thrown open by... *Orson?* My heart gives a sharp tug as he calls my name and throws himself at me with utter joy. Henry and the Wickfords are much closer than I'd actually thought.

'I've missed you, Faith!' he cries, digging his face into my waist.

'I've missed you, too, Orson!' I assure him, holding him close until Trixie appears.

'Hello, Faith! So happy to see you! Orson, love, will you take Faith's clutch please?'

'Okay,' he replies and I wink at him.

'You look stunning, Faith!' she says as she embraces me. 'Doesn't she, Henry?'

Henry turns to me and something familiar flashes in his eyes. Desire. Desire I can't help but reciprocate as our time alone replays itself in my mind like in a dream I can't seem to wake up from.

'Yes, truly stunning,' he agrees, his eyes lingering. This is all so wrong. And I realise that being in the same room with him is going to kill me. It can't possibly get any worse.

'Hello, love! You're looking very beautiful and much less green, if I may say so!' Bopper says as I turn to greet him.

'Hello,' I say like an automaton. 'Your house is beautiful, and very festive.'

Lord Wickford grins. 'Yes, we have a lot to celebrate tonight.'

'Yes.'

'Has Henry told you about the feature yet?'

'Feature?' I ask, looking up at him, but he avoids my gaze as his lean cheeks begin to turn a dark shade of red.

Lady Wickford – I still can't bring myself to think of her as Trixie – laughs. 'I know, he's always just too modest! It's taken me years, but he finally conceded to let us do a feature on him – and you!'

I blink. 'I'm sorry?'

She laughs. 'My darling, he's not told you! Henry is the only architect in the entire world that Bopper would actually get off his arse for. You more than deserve that feature in our magazine.'

'*Me?*'

Just like that? I've been chasing these people for years and now, with a single word from Henry, everything magically falls into place? I scratch my head. 'I'm sorry, I'm not quite sure I've underst—'

'Come on, Faith,' Lady Wickford says. 'Don't you think it's time you got your break?'

'Oh, I certainly do,' I vow.

'We saw your work. We love your style and we've listened to your pitch. You're in.'

'I – thank you. Thank you kindly. And Henry. Thank you.'

I'm so happy I may even blubber. But all that elation doesn't last long. Because, when I turn to the sound of a new voice, there she is. Linda Turner, Henry's wife on Lord Wickford's arm.

'Faith, come! You've met our daughter Linda, is that not right?'

Their daughter? Linda is their *daughter*?

'Oh, yes, of course, nice to see you again, Linda,' I murmur, looking for a gaping hole in the old oak floorboards that will swallow me forever.

Linda reaches out to hug me as if we were the best of friends. 'I hope you don't mind me crashing your dinner, but I wanted to see you again. Orson thinks the world of you. Huge congratulations, by the way. I hear you're very talented.'

'Oh, th-thank you,' I whisper. What else can I possibly say? As much as I have dreamt of being here – dinner at the Wickfords' home – I just can't do it. I can't sit through a dinner knowing that the man I am in love with (yes, I'm absolutely up crap's creek, I know) is married. This is just not my idea of happiness and honesty. And the fact that she has completely forgotten she'd told me to piss off and leave Henry be is very worrying.

'Now, Faith,' Trixie says, 'come and sit down. Why on earth have you never reached out to us?'

I've never reached out to them? Are they taking the mick?

'And you, Henry, why have you waited so long to introduce us?'

'Yes, well—'

'We're so grateful to our son-in-law for bringing your work to our attention', she continues, waving him away. 'I've so many questions to ask the woman who captured our Henry's heart!'

My eyes swing to Henry who is becoming visibly crimson. There is something very wrong here. Captured Henry's heart? What are they even talking about? And even if that were true, his in-laws are actually *happy* about it? What kind of madhouse have I been invited to? I knew the rich were peculiar, but really? Oh, shitty, shit shit.

As it is, the rest of the evening goes by in a blur during which Trixie regales us with some horror stories of jobs they'd royally screwed up in their youth, including Vanessa's grandparents' home.

'They turned a million colours,' Trixie recalls as Robert (I just can't address him as Bopper) guffaws, slapping his knee in delight.

A few moments later, Henry turns to me and whispers, 'Can I have a private word with you?'

I blink. Henry wants a private word with me? 'Of course...'

He turns to Trixie and Bopper. 'I almost forgot I have a little dessert for you, Trixie,' he says. 'But I left it at home. Do you mind if Faith and I pop back and get it?'

'Henry, is it by any chance your almond parfait dessert? You know I can't afford to gain an ounce at my age!'

'Just the ticket. But you are beautiful just the way you are, Trixie!'

She laughs. 'Oh, you devil, you! Go on, then!'

Henry chuckles and turns to Orson. 'I'll be exactly five minutes, okay mate?'

'Okay, Daddy!' Orson chimes.

I follow him out of the house and down the path to his own home that is in such stark contrast. Once inside, he closes the door. 'Have a seat.'

'Thank you,' I say. 'But I prefer to stand.'

'That bad, eh?' He sighs as he reaches into the fridge to retrieve a cake dish. 'Let's have it.'

I swallow. 'Well, first of all, I wanted to thank you, Henry. I truly appreciate you thinking of me, and I'm honoured to think that someone like you would even consider me.'

At that, he lowers his eyes and I wonder if maybe he hasn't done it all just to soften the blow Gabe dealt me.

'I won't disappoint you, Henry. I can't thank you enough.'

'Don't thank me, Faith. You deserve it.'

When I think back to all the difficult years of slogging over my course books while everyone else was out partying, I have to agree. I think I actually do deserve it. I'd always, always gone the extra mile, gone into work an hour early, stayed an hour late, worked on weekends to pay my way, never knowing whether I'd eventually make it or not, but it wasn't going to be for the want of trying.

And all this time, despite the naysayers – and Vanessa who was in most of my classes basking in everyone's attention – despite them all, I charged on, and not without momentary doubts in my darkest moments. But I did believe in myself, knowing it was just a matter of time, and not giving up.

Has my definitive moment finally, truly arrived, then? I can only hope so. This job, working for the Wickfords, is the dream of a lifetime.

'I can't believe I have a chance with them, so thank you. Henry?'

'Yes, Faith?'

'Why didn't you tell me you'd designed and built the beach house?' I ask him.

He shrugs. 'Would it have made a difference?'

'I would have told you how much I admire your work…'

'You can tell me now. And I can tell you how much I admire yours. And you, by the way.'

'You…? Admire me? What for?'

'Of course. I admire your strength, your talent, your resilience, your intelligence. Shall I go on to tell you how I feel about you?'

'But… you're working things out with Linda. Are you not?'

'Yes. We are. But as Orson's parents – not as a couple, Faith…' His eyebrows shoot up. 'Jesus, is that what you've been thinking all this time?'

'Well, why wouldn't I? Orson said that you and Linda are spending more and more time together, and that you hold her, and… and—'

'Faith – it's part of her therapy.'

'And – her what?'

'After the divorce, Linda was having emotional issues. She was in total denial. Her psychiatrist suggested making the break more gentle, less traumatic for us all. So that's what I've been doing the past few years.'

'Years?'

'Well, she's the mother of my child. I wouldn't want Orson to grow up traumatised or feeling abandoned. I want him to know that I'll always be there for him, no matter what happens between his mum and me. And now, she finally seems to have accepted it all.'

Oh, if only my own father had been as caring! Orson is so blessed!

'And as far as you and I are concerned, we simply didn't get off on the right foot, that's all. But believe me, I'm far from hating you. As a matter of fact, I've grown quite fond of you.'

'I'm glad, Henry. I'm sorry if I've not been at my best with you. It's just been a rollercoaster ride with Gabe and—'

'It's all right,' he says softly, taking my hands.

'Thank you, then. For putting up with me.'

He smiles, and it's like a light at the end of a long, twisting, dark tunnel. 'You're very welcome, Faith. When you came to see us, the day you gave me your memory stick, you were very hostile. Why?'

My face catches fire. 'Well, while you were in the shower – the m-morning after, Orson asked me for help because he didn't want you to get back with Linda. He was upset about you and her. He said that you were in the bedroom with her for quite a while.'

'Yeah, we were – there's not much privacy there with Orson in the living room.'

Exactly as I'd thought. Linda is the mother of his son. She's stunningly beautiful, rich, high-placed in society. And I'm not any of those things. Why would Henry prefer me, when he can have her instead?

He shakes his head and takes my arms. 'Linda kissed me – not the other way around. And the only reason I dragged her into the bedroom was because I wanted to give her a piece of my mind without my little boy hearing any of it. Faith,' he breathes, his eyes wide. 'Honey, are you serious? Did you really think I could do that to you? I told you I wanted you.'

Oh my *God*. Does this mean that all my efforts to stay away from a married man – a man I'm wildly attracted to – were for nothing?

And I suddenly realise I've a lot to make up for. This lovely man has been nothing but damaged by his acquaintance with me. 'Oh, Henry,' I moan.

'Now listen up,' he says gruffly. 'You've cost me my serenity ever since I met you. Knowing you were in love with my former best mate, and that you were hoping to rebuild your relationship with him. Start a family that I knew was destined to fall apart. Watching you work so hard in order to build that family, all the while he was planning his life with someone else. Someone much wealthier than you. But only financially. Because you, Faith, have every quality that a man dreams of in a woman. You're smart, generous, fun, and you care about others. You have vision and imagination.'

Would you interrupt him at this point? I didn't think so either. So I listen in silence as he continues.

'I didn't have the heart to tell you that what you thought was the last place your mum was happy was a completely different house. I wanted you to have that link with her. It was a home for me too, once upon a time. But now, I really, really hate that house, Faith. I had to watch you from afar while you stripped your life of its bare bones, trying to eke out a life while you deserved so much more.'

'What are you saying, Henry?'

His eyes flash with renewed vitality. 'I'm saying that you're dangerous. So I'm not letting you out of my sight ever again. If you'll still have me.'

In response, I throw my arms around him. 'I'll still have you,' I assure him. 'And you forgive me, too?'

He kisses me. 'Sweetheart, there's nothing to forgive. You did what you thought was best. Everything else is water under the bridge. But I feel I need to explain, so you don't doubt me in any way.'

I can feel my eyebrows shooting up into my hairline. 'What do you mean?'

'When you first told me about pursuing the Wickfords, I wanted to help you. Truly, I did. But Linda and I were still dealing with all sorts of ugly things, and even if Trixie and Bopper were on my side regarding practically everything, I didn't want them to think that I was recommending you because I fancied you or anything.'

'Why would they think that?' I ask.

He blushes. 'Because you are the most beautiful woman I've ever seen in my entire life, Faith.'

I giggle. Oh, the things a bloke will say.

'I'm serious, Faith,' he says, slightly hurt. 'Just look at you. What bloke wouldn't be wildly attracted to you, for Christ's sake? And it's not because the world thinks you have an amazing arse.'

'Oh. So you don't like my arse, then?'

'Oh, I do,' he assures me.

'So you're attracted to me now?' I tease. This flirting and sense of playful power is something completely new to me and I'm liking it.

'Now? You must be joking. I was attracted from the first time I saw you. I thought to myself, Henry, whoever this girl is, do *not* let her out of your sight.'

'I seem to remember I was buck naked at the time.' I chuckle.

'Oh, that had nothing to do with it,' he says, waving the thought away.

'You lying hound.'

He grins. 'Well, I must admit that ever since, all that time, the thought of you, in my arms, completely naked, kept me going.'

I swallow. 'It has kept me going, too.'

'Really?' he asks hopefully.

'Really.'

'You don't know what that means to me, Faith. I was so terrified that you would capitulate when Gabe came back. I thought to myself that there was no use in competing with a return of flame.'

'You thought wrong, Henry. Gabe is part of my past, and I'm so, so grateful that I met you. And not because you're related to the Wickfords, or because, as Travis said, you're friggin'... bloomin'... Tarquin Turner. I hadn't even made the connection. How dumb am I? I just thought you were my joiner.'

He throws back his head and laughs that joyous, hearty laugh. 'To be fair, Henry is my middle name, which I took on quite early. You would not believe the hard time I had in school with Tarquin. So I thought I'd keep them separate.'

'I can imagine.'

'And no one ever recognises me because I never appear in public or have my picture taken. First, because I want to protect Orson from the limelight, and second, because I wouldn't want people to think that my success was due to being the son-in-law of the Wickfords.'

'I can understand that,' I assure him. 'And I can't believe that I'm finally getting my break! I've dreamed this forever, and now...'

He winks at me. 'Play your cards right and they'll

recommend you to plenty of their clients. You'll be so busy you won't have time for anything or anyone else.'

At that, I take a step closer to him. 'Oh, I'll always have time for you, Henry! I don't know where I'd be without you!'

His jaw muscles move under his lean face. 'Nonsense. You're here on your own steam. The Wickfords love what you did to the beach house.'

'But it was you who showed them my work.'

He dips his head. 'Well, you gave me your memory stick. I didn't want your trip to my home to be a total loss.'

'Hmm...' I murmur, snuggling up to him.

'Remember when you made a pass at me?'

'How noble of you to remind me of a drunk moment,' I quip.

He chuckles, caressing my cheek with his thumb. 'I wanted you so badly, but I could tell that it wasn't the same for you. At least, not really. You were still in love with Gabe.'

'I'm not, of course. I just want to forget everything that had anything to do with him now.'

'But the beach house? You won't miss it? I know how much you love it...'

I shrug. 'When Gabe and I went to view it, I recognised the angle and the view of the breakwater and assumed it was the same house. I didn't know *someone* had built where the holiday house had stood.'

He chuckles. 'Silly. So... you're okay with losing it?'

'Part of the reason I loved it so much was because it was one of my last connections to my mum – she wrote about that week in her diary. But now that I know that's not the case, the beach house is only where Gabe dumped me. And I don't need that memory. I will always love the beach house, in a way. But not at the cost of my heart, and above all, my dignity. It's not my home anymore. It never really was. I understand that now. And I have resolved to pack up all my sadder memories in a box – and leave that box at the beach house.'

'I'm so glad to hear that, Faith. Truly I am. In that case, can I run something by you?' he asks.

'Of course.'

'With you now in my life, I want a new start for us all and to not be living right next to Linda.'

'I think that's a very healthy idea.'

'Good. Because I want you to come and live with Orson and me... Faith? Did you hear what I said?'

My eyes have never left his face since. 'You want me to come and live with you?'

'Yes, Faith. I love you. With all my heart. I can't even think of not seeing you and kissing you and holding you.'

And then, he takes my hand and pulls me to sit on his lap. I am so lost in his eyes, in the face that I have come to know and love completely.

'I love you, too, Henry. I think I fell in love with you long before I can admit. Yes, I'll come and live with you and Orson. Have you asked him?'

'Actually...' he whispers as Orson suddenly runs in, tittering and bearing a small box, which he puts in my lap. Another present. I wonder if it's another one of his artefacts? They are so beautiful. He has inherited his father's talent.

'Thank you, sweetie,' I say, but he covers his mouth, giggling, and darts out of the room again.

'Open it,' Henry urges me softly.

I delicately lift the cover, and inside is a small pale green box. Only this is not the same green as my New York costume. This is Tiffany green.

I look up at him in shock.

'Go on,' he whispers, his beautiful dark eyes moist.

With trembling hands, I lift the jewellery box out of its case and slowly open it.

'Faith Hudson, will you marry me and make me the happiest man on the planet?' he asks, caressing my face.

I can't speak a single word, but I throw my arms around him and hold him close to me, nodding.

He laughs, kissing my shoulder. 'Right. We'd better go house-hunting, then!'

Epilogue

Ihave finally come to terms with the loss of my previous life. I now understand that Gabe and the beach house were nothing but a raft to hold on to while waiting for my real life to start, and not one lived vicariously through a famous fiancé.

I am my own person, finally, free of all the anger and pain that up and until now have influenced my every decision. Luckily my snarkiness has saved me from many a tumble.

It had taken me quite some time, but now I also understand that a house is not just about feeling warm and secure in myself. A house will never be a home until it is filled with real life, problems, tribulations, but also laughter, plans, but most of all, it must be the hearth of selfless, unconditional love on behalf of both partners. With Gabe, I had been the only one making sacrifices. But Henry is the complete opposite. Henry is selfless. And any home that Henry and I choose for ourselves and Orson will be just that.

Smiling, I sit and join my friends and family who form our wedding party gathered around the wedding table in our back garden. We wanted something simple, in our new home in Starry Cove, a tiny village further down the coast.

There's Hope, my matron of honour along with Jowen and Orson as our ring boys and Verity as our flower girl. My beloved coastal girls and Thea are my bridesmaids. All the people who count for us are there, from Henry's huge family to my muscle men – Bill, Bob, Mike and Paul – and their respective wives, to Vanessa with baby Grace.

They are, mother and daughter, in absolute awe of each other. The baby's eyes are wide open and she's staring at Vanessa as if she had a set of lime green horns on her head (which, in the past, wouldn't have seemed so strange for her).

'Hey,' I coo as I take a step towards Vanessa and the pink bundle in her arms.

'Hi…' she says, angling the baby so I can see better.

'She's grown,' I marvel, caressing her small head.

'Say hello to Auntie Fi, Grace…' Vanessa whispers.

I swallow and look at the tiny human being swathed in a delicate lace blanket. Vanessa and Gabe's baby. I used to think I'd feel bitterness. But, go figure, looking down at this beautiful little girl, love is suddenly pouring out of me in waves, and not only that, it's coming out of my eyeballs, too. Because Grace is a very lucky little girl. She has only arrived a few months ago but is already loved by many, me included.

I am so blessed to be here with all the people who have held me up during this amazing journey of self-discovery and finding love. My sister, Hope, my coastal girls and my loyal crew. And Trixie and Bopper. Who knew that the elusive duo of design would become very good friends of ours? Even Travis. I didn't move to New York, as you can imagine. Because this is my home, and these are my people, in what I know will be our forever home.

All we have to do now is renovate it.

About the Author

NANCY BARONE grew up in Canada, but at the age of twelve her family moved to Italy. Catapulted into a world where her only contact with the English language was her old Judy Blume books, Nancy became an avid reader and a die-hard romantic.

Nancy stayed in Italy and, despite being surrounded by handsome Italian men, she married an even more handsome Brit. They now live in Sicily where she teaches English.

Nancy is a member of the Romantic Novelists' Association and a keen supporter of the Women's Fiction Festival at Matera where she meets up with writing friends from all over the globe.

Acknowledgements

Hello Dearest Readers!

Thank you for choosing to read my book! There are truly some lovely stories out there and your choice makes me all the more appreciative! This is my fourth book with Aria and there are many more in the making!

Like my heroine, interior designer Faith Hudson, I am obsessed with houses.

When I was six years old and visiting my extended family in Italy one summer, I remember peering through the wrought-iron gates of the house next door, utterly fascinated.

Perhaps it was the archway of purple bougainvillea. Or perhaps it was the beautiful front garden, or the fact that through the open front door I could see all the way to the back of the house where there were another two gardens, but I remember thinking how lucky those people were to live in such a large house with so much greenery in the centre of the village. I also remember thinking that I would never be able to have a house like that.

This week, my DH and I will be exchanging contracts on that very house. Who could have ever imagined that after having lived and worked in three different countries, I'd end up right back next door to my Nana's old home?

Despite it being the house of our dreams, it took us three years to get there. And just like for Faith Hudson, moving was an ordeal, especially if you think that the DH and I went from living for two years among stacks of boxes (he did most of the packing, bless him) to rattling around once the house had been completely emptied, as we still couldn't move due to a glitch in the paperwork.

I am thankful to all the friends and family who have morally supported us throughout this nightmare. Very soon we will be moving in and making more happy memories with them.

This is also the year I met my brilliant editor, Martina Arzu, who has the patience and kindness of an angel. Many thanks to you, Martina, for understanding me and supporting me!

This year also sees the release of my books agented by the uber-brilliant Lorella Belli, owner of the LBLA. Lorella, what would your authors do without you? Thank you for being on board!

This year I also managed to write a movie script with the consultation of a new friend. It is now in the works!

But most importantly, someone very dear to me has given me some great personal news and I feel that with this year we have finally turned the corner in many ways.

I hope that you also feel you have accomplished more than you'd hoped for and that this year is your best yet.

Thank you for spending your free time with me!
Sincerely,
Nancy Barone